LOVE IN
New York City

**COMPLETE 5
BOOK
COLLECTION**

KACI BELL

Copyright © 2023 by Kaci Bell

All rights reserved.

No part of this book may be reproduced in any form or by any electronic or mechanical means, including information storage and retrieval systems, without written permission from the author, except for the use of brief quotations in a book review.

Contents

Crushing On the Boss
Kaci Bell

Chapter 1	3
Chapter 2	8
Chapter 3	13
Chapter 4	20
Chapter 5	26
Chapter 6	30
Chapter 7	34
Chapter 8	38
Chapter 9	43
Chapter 10	48
Chapter 11	51
Chapter 12	55
Chapter 13	60
Chapter 14	65
Chapter 15	69
Chapter 16	73
Chapter 17	77
Chapter 18	83
Chapter 19	88
Chapter 20	92
Chapter 21	96
Chapter 22	101
Chapter 23	106
Chapter 24	111
Chapter 25	115
Epilogue	118

Perfect For Him
Kaci Bell

Chapter 1	123
Chapter 2	129
Chapter 3	136
Chapter 4	140
Chapter 5	146
Chapter 6	150
Chapter 7	153
Chapter 8	158
Chapter 9	166
Chapter 10	175
Chapter 11	182
Chapter 12	185
Chapter 13	192
Chapter 14	197
Chapter 15	201
Chapter 16	204
Chapter 17	209
Chapter 18	217
Chapter 19	221
Epilogue	225

Taming the Big Shot
Kaci Bell

Chapter 1	231
Chapter 2	239
Chapter 3	244
Chapter 4	254
Chapter 5	258
Chapter 6	262
Chapter 7	268
Chapter 8	272
Chapter 9	276
Chapter 10	281

Chapter 11	284
Chapter 12	291
Epilogue	294

Saved by the Boss
Kaci Bell

Chapter 1	299
Chapter 2	305
Chapter 3	312
Chapter 4	319
Chapter 5	325
Chapter 6	331
Chapter 7	335
Chapter 8	338
Chapter 9	340
Chapter 10	345
Chapter 11	350
Chapter 12	354
Chapter 13	360
Chapter 14	366
Chapter 15	369
Chapter 16	373
Chapter 17	377

Sunshine for the Boss
Kaci Bell

Chapter 1	383
Chapter 2	387
Chapter 3	393
Chapter 4	399
Chapter 5	405
Chapter 6	410
Chapter 7	413
Chapter 8	420
Chapter 9	424

Chapter 10	429
Chapter 11	433
Chapter 12	438
Chapter 13	442
Chapter 14	445
Chapter 15	449
Chapter 16	453
Chapter 17	456
Chapter 18	460
Chapter 19	463
Chapter 20	468
About the Author	471

Crushing On the Boss

Kaci Bell

1
Jennifer

The sun's glare was turning down as I finished my final touches while getting ready for my date with Peyton. Laura was so kind to me and let me borrow her green dress, as I didn't have the chance to purchase a dress after work. It paired perfectly with some black chunky heels to complete the look. She was a lifesaver. My small New York City apartment wasn't anything spectacular, especially with my minuscule salary, but it allowed me to live in the city and close to work. I put my hair in an uncomplicated but stylish twist and my jewelry shone brightly against my neck.

As I grabbed my small clutch and purse, my doorbell rang. I checked the clock, noting how punctual Peyton was, and opened the door. Outside, Peyton stood tall, looking dapper in a gray sweater, black chinos, and a white dress shirt underneath, holding a bouquet of freshly picked daisies, which he shyly offered to me.

"Happy anniversary," he said, pulling me in for a quick kiss. "You look gorgeous. Is that a new dress?"

One thing that I truly appreciated about him was that he was always giving me compliments, something I wasn't able to experience with my previous partner.

I smiled, taking the daisies from him and grabbing a vase to put them in before we head out. "You didn't have to get me flowers, babe." I nudged myself into his chest and his chin rested on the top of my head. "So, where are you taking me?"

"It's a surprise," he said as I shut the apartment door behind me and grabbed his hand.

It had been six months since I first walked into the restaurant and met Peyton. He walked toward my table, smiling wide, and the sun lit up his blond hair while he took my order. My best friend Laura gave me crap about it all night, because every time he came out of the back, my eyes would wander over to him. By the end of our dinner, he came over and asked if I would be interested in getting together when he got off, and even though Laura told me he could be a serial killer, I said yes. I hadn't expected to meet someone and have an instant connection, but that's what happened. We talked all night, and by the end, he was the missing piece of the puzzle to my life here in New York City. He was the first semiserious relationship I'd been in since arriving in the city ten years ago, and I was almost afraid to say it out loud, but the two of us were perfect for each other.

"Can you believe it's only been six months? I swear it's like we've been together for ages," I said as he opened the door for me and I slid in.

He was acting strange, like something was bothering him. With no words exchanged, we drove until we reached our destination, the restaurant. A place of such grandeur was something I had never encountered before, making me uneasy, yet I forced a grin on my face as we settled in at the small table. From the moment we left my apartment, he had not even glanced my way. He seemed to avoid making eye contact.

"Is there something bothering you?" I asked as the waiter approached, and we each ordered a glass of wine. "You just seem tense. Did something happen at work?"

Peyton had been having a dispute with the proprietor of the restaurant he worked in, and he'd been discussing it for quite a while.

Two weeks ago, he thought about walking out, but like everyone else in this city, bills had to be paid and finding a job wasn't as easy as one would think, even in New York City.

"It's been a crap day. Honestly, I just want to chug a couple of glasses of wine and forget about it."

Our anniversary ended up being ruined by work problems. Our first fight was over him taking out his problems on me, not in a physical sense, but it would dampen his mood, which caused him to snap at me. So, the fact I had to deal with this tonight was insulting.

"I need to talk to you," he mumbled.

My mouth moved, not knowing what would come from his lips.

"I don't know how to say this, but I think it's time we go our separate ways."

Wait, what? He was breaking up with me on our anniversary? What kind of man does that? I tried to subdue my temper, but it just kept increasing.

"It's not you, it's me. I just... feel like maybe we want two different things right now. You deserve the husband, house, and kids... and I'm just not ready to commit to that."

Why couldn't he have told me this before we left for dinner? There I was, all dressed up, and he knew he was going to break up with me before we even left my home.

"What do you mean? What happened? You couldn't have done this before we came here? Are you freaking kidding me?"

He brushed his hands along the back of his head as his eyes glowered at the table. "Jennifer, listen... no need to cause a scene, okay? Things happen. People grow apart. It's a fact of life. I could've just strung you along another two years and wasted your time. Would you rather me do that?"

Oh, Peyton was testing me, and I had been careful not to share my anger yet, but that glass of wine sitting in front of him deserved to be plastered all over his face. "So, what you are saying is... for the last six months, you have known you had no intention of getting serious, yet never once mentioned it to me?"

As I was getting older, the ticking of my biological clock was getting louder and louder, and when I met Peyton, I thought I had found the one; however, now it had been a complete waste of my time.

"It's not you. It's me. This relationship isn't right for me. I love you, but I'm not in love with you. That spark I need in a relationship to commit to marriage isn't here. Isn't that what you want? The whole shebang: husband, kids, dog, and a white picket fence?"

I had to avert my eyes, the tears stinging my vision. He knew how to crush a girl's heart.

"I'm so sorry," he said, reaching out to touch my arm.

With a swift movement, I brushed away his hand. "Save your apologies for someone else." The wineglass was taunting me, telling me to throw it in his face, but causing a scene wouldn't be for my benefit. I took my last sip, pushed the chair back, and stepped out the door, feeling the sun's warmth on my skin. Peyton didn't even try to come after me.

Tears streamed down my cheeks, and my shaking hands fumbled with my phone as I tried to text my best friend.

Me: 911. Meet me at my apartment.

My arm was flailing around like crazy in the sky to get a taxi, and I left the restaurant without looking back. My best friend was the glue that helped me put the broken parts of my heart back together many times before.

Laura had been my friend for years, and I was thankful to have her. When the taxi pulled up to my apartment building, she was standing outside with two bottles of wine. She acted as if she already knew.

Taking an unhurried stroll up to my apartment, we took our place on the cozy couch. She opened the bottle of wine and the rich aroma of the grapes filled the air as she poured two glasses. "So, spill. What the heck happened? You interrupted my weekly dose of *Grey's Anatomy*. I wasn't sure whether I needed to grab bail money. Who are we getting rid of today?"

She handed me the glass. "Peyton broke up with me."

"Oh, that little... He wasn't worth a crap. You deserve so much better than him, Jen."

"Yes, you've told me many times, but I loved him. He said he wasn't ready for commitment."

"Typical guy. When the stakes become too high, they usually decide to take a step back and run away from it. You're going to get through this."

In the past two weeks, Peyton and I had discussed our plans for the future, including traveling, marriage, and even starting a family. Until this evening, everything had been going as expected, but now something had changed.

When our eyes met, Laura gave me a clear sign of disapproval by shaking her head. "I told you he wasn't the right one for you from the start. He never showed full commitment to you."

Despite being aware of the signs, I had brushed them off, convincing myself that I was being overly cautious.

"How could he do this to me?" I asked, angry and betrayed. "He just threw away everything we had built together. How could he be so heartless?" Laura tried to comfort me, but it was of no use.

Over many hours, I have spoken aloud my fury and distress. She listened patiently and attentively, as any good best friend would do.

"Just remember to be resilient. Your life may feel like it's crumbling, but you'll find the man of your dreams."

The more we talked, the more I realized it was for the best. I wanted a future with him, but it became clear he wasn't ready for that. He refused to commit, and I ended up heartbroken. Despite the anger and hurt I felt, I was also grateful to have the situation end. I'm too old for someone with commitment issues.

Is my ideal man even out there?

2
Matt

Tucked in between a real estate and car insurance office, the small firm was on a busy street which brought in a lot of traffic. My office desk had various case files piled high. With a sigh of exhaustion, I carefully set my briefcase down. Despite it being only eight thirty in the morning, they gave me a huge backlog of work that I had to complete.

I fired up my computer, the hum of the processor filling the room, and took a sip of my freshly brewed coffee before beginning my day. I typed away, working on the current case. As I typed, the stress on my shoulders dissipated.

The hours I put in as a lawyer were extensive, and the pressure was intense, but it rewarded me with the satisfaction of helping people. I rummaged through my desk, which was organized chaos, searching for McNaugh case files. Ten years at this firm, and my office had never been fuller.

At twelve thirty, I had made considerable progress, so I took a quick break and hustled to the diner to get some food before my one thirty call with a client. We got fresh cases almost every week, so I had to make sure that I understood everything and typed up notes for myself.

The afternoon was dragging on, but I could see the progress I had made in clearing the stacks of paperwork on my desk, but now it was time to go home. I clicked off my computer, the hum of its fan slowly dissipating, and then locked the filing cabinet with a satisfying click. As I walked down the hallway, my boss called me into his office. Mr. Stephens, an older gentleman with silver hair and kind blue eyes, clasped his hands on his desk and furrowed his brow. "I need to talk to you about something, son."

The endearment hit, knowing my father wouldn't be calling me that anymore. "Yeah, I was just headed out. What's going on? New case?"

"No, this is a personal matter. Are you still interested in a partner position?" he asked, his eyes on mine.

"Yes, sir. Have you reconsidered bringing on a partner?" This was confusing because when I started here, Mr. Stephens said he wasn't bringing in any partners. Had he changed his mind? The firm was growing, and we needed to at least bring in another lawyer. We were drowning in our cases right now as it was. Too many clients could mean no sleep.

"The firm isn't ready to bring in a new partner yet, but I found you a great opportunity." he drawled.

My eyes roved around the room, taking in the soft light that filled the space. "I'm not understanding, sir. What are you saying?"

"I have spoken with Mr. Curren and he would like to offer you a partnership in New York City. He wants to bring on someone who isn't afraid to put in the work to get things done. Apparently, they have been having issues with the younger kids burning out. When I told him about you, he was eager to bring you on."

Wait, did he say New York City? Being a couple hundred miles from my mother was one thing, but thousands of miles? With her health, it wouldn't work. Mr. Stephens doesn't know about my personal life, and I liked to keep it that way. So, I couldn't fault him for trying to seize this partnership for me.

"Listen, they are open to doing a year trial run and will even lease an apartment for you so you don't have to spend a dime. You should at least consider it, Matt. You're going places and I can't be the stumbling block. If it's not to your liking, you are still welcome here."

Mr. Stephens handed me an envelope, the weight of which felt heavy in my hands. "This is the official offer. Consider it over the weekend, but they need an answer by Monday. They want you to be in New York City by then because the person you are replacing is retiring. Think about it."

"Thanks, see you on Monday."

"No offense, but I hope you're on a plane instead. Have a good weekend."

A top-notch law firm offered me a partnership position in New York City. Even though I had achieved this success through hard work, a sense of guilt and hesitation surged through me when I pondered its effects on my mother. When my father passed, her health declined, and I was the only person she could turn to.

As I held the offer letter in my hands, it flooded my mind with emotions and doubts. I wanted to seize this opportunity, but now was not the time to be selfish. My mother made so many sacrifices for me growing up, and I owed her the same. She was my biggest supporter, and if I moved away, I could only visit her twice a year.

If I moved to New York and an emergency happened, it wasn't just a three-hour drive to be there for her, but a couple of plane rides. Things weren't that simple all the way from New York City.

Turning it down was the right decision right now. My mother needed to be my priority, and her happiness and well-being were more important than any offer. Experience had taught me that sometimes the greatest things in life were not the things achieved or gained, but the people we could love and care for. There was no definitive time frame for my mother's Parkinson's. The symptoms would continue to get worse over time, and every weekend I could, I made the drive out to Sikita to visit.

After leaving the firm, I placed my briefcase in the car and drove to Sikita to spend the weekend with my mom.

On the road trip over to her, I listened to a playlist my dad sent me before he passed. It was all his favorite songs on Spotify and the easiest way to honor his memory with every trip. The two-hour drive went by in a flash and I pulled into the Home Away from Home center. If my mother was coherent today, she would wait by the door for me. The first couple of times, the night care nurses made a big deal since it was late, but when they heard about my situation, they apologized.

When I arrived at the center, my mother was waiting by the entrance. She was a tall, imposing figure and her face was full of warmth and love. My heart swelled at the sight of her and she enveloped me into a hug that was so tight I could feel her heartbeat against mine. She held me for a moment and then pushed me back to get a good look.

"Let's go to your room. It's late," I said, grabbing one of her hands and leading her toward the bedroom so we wouldn't wake anyone.

As soon as the door closed, she started in. My mother always wanted to know how the job was going, if I had met anyone yet, typical mother fashion. "No, I'm still single. Who has time to find someone? I spend most of my days in the office and then sleep when I can."

"Oh honey, you need to remember that your life is going to go by, and you will wake up one morning, old and gray, and regret all the things you wish you had done."

"I'll have more time to focus on my personal life soon. Speaking of, I got an offer to become a partner. Don't worry, Mama. I'm not taking it." I opened a bag of chips from the gas station as my stomach growled.

The excitement faded, and she looked at me. "Why would you do that? You have been working yourself to death."

"It's a wonderful offer, but you mean more to me than any partnership ever will. New York City is too far away. I'm not leaving you behind."

The effects of her Parkinson's had worsened, and she sometimes could not leave her bed. I would love to scoop her up and take her with me, but it wasn't an option.

She held my gaze for a few moments before a faint sigh escaped her lips and she shook her head. "Son, don't hinder your life because of me. You will have a whole life after I'm gone and you shouldn't be sidestepping opportunities like this because of your sick mother. Go chase your dreams, just like your daddy taught you."

I gripped her hands in mine. "Daddy wouldn't have wanted to leave you alone here. I already hate living hours away, and if I take it, I couldn't just come visit every weekend like now. It's thousands of miles away."

"I can handle knowing you are living your dream, son. Your poor mom was stuck in that small town all her life and you have the chance to go to one of the best cities... please take it. If not for you, then for me." She wrapped her arms around me. "I'm so proud of you, son. Even as a young boy, you had the dream of becoming an excellent lawyer and making partner one day. Your daddy would be so proud of you. Go pack your bags and book your ticket. I'll see you again soon."

She shoved me out of her room, and a dutiful son never argued with his mother. With purpose in my step, I walked out to my car and dialed the number on the offer, leaving a message that I was ready to accept and book my flight the next day.

New York City, here I come.

3

Jennifer

The clock on my desk read 8:02 a.m. and Mr. Longford usually arrived by eight on the dot. After ten years as his assistant, it took something serious for him to miss work. With a sigh of resignation, I looked at the towering pile of reports that needed to be sent out and the emails clamoring for my attention. A loud racket at the door alerted me to my boss's presence. He stepped through the doorway wearing his usual well-pressed navy suit, white shirt, and matching tie; his salt-and-pepper hair was combed back. The other lawyers in this office were renowned for their short tempers and quick tongues, but not Mr. Longford; he was a gem.

I sprang from my chair, yellow Post-it notes rustling in my hands, the edges digging into my palms. I attempted to smile, but my lips felt like sandpaper. "Good morning, sir. I'll leave your messages for you on your desk." My boss stood with a younger man in a navy suit and spoke without taking his eyes off him. "Jennifer, this is Mr. Kneeland, who will replace me. I'm ready to hang up my hat." His words were heavy, like a hand on my shoulder, and the ground shifted beneath me.

My stomach tightened, and I fought to keep my fear from

showing on my face. *Why is he just now telling me?* I put on a polite smile and offered him my hand. "Nice to meet you, sir."

The man's dark-brown eyes scanned over my body as if he were undressing me with his gaze. His rough hand grasped mine, and a smirk tugged at the corner of his lips as he said, "Pleasure is all mine." I saw something pass between him and my boss before he handed me a white paper cup that exuded the warm aroma of brewed coffee, and a kind smile lifted the corner of his lips. "I know how hard assistants work, so I brought this for you." My gaze flicked over to Mr. Longford, and I tilted my head.

He stood up a little straighter as I took it from his hand. Coffee was a way into this girl's good graces. Most of the workers here had their coffee delivered, but it was so expensive. "Thanks. I'll leave you guys to work. Don't forget your meeting at noon, sir. I'll have the conference room set up by eleven thirty."

Mr. Longford smiled, revealing a set of straight white teeth. "See, Matt, you won't have anything to worry about, because Jennifer has things covered. I've never had to write her up. She's a keeper." He winked at me, and Matt's eyes followed my every move as I walked behind my desk. My cheeks burned and my heart raced as I sat down in my chair.

A wave of sadness washed over me as I thought of Mr. Longford's impending departure. Every Friday morning, he would have breakfast delivered to the office, and we'd settle in for an hour and go over the schedule for the upcoming week, and sometimes even share stories about our weekend plans. He listened to my ideas, and he had become like a father figure. The firm was lucky because he had a knack for calming down even the most difficult clients, and he knew which cases to refer to the newer partners who were looking to impress. I hoped Matt could carry on that same tradition.

Confusion and uncertainty bubbled in my chest as I tried to make sense of what this meant. He had mentioned retiring before but hadn't been specific about when. Whoever held the answers needed to provide them soon, so I could begin planning a retirement celebration worthy of his thirty-five-year legacy. An accolade he more than deserved.

The steam from the creamy latte warmed my hands as I slowly sipped it. I had a flutter of surprise in my stomach as I saw my name written on one side of the cup. I couldn't be the only one who thought it was weird Matt brought me coffee. And he didn't just get any coffee; this cup was from the best café around—Coffee Chaos—the best coffee within a five-mile radius. His taste in coffee was almost as good as his taste in suits.

Everyone loved to fuss over Starbucks, but they weren't even close to being as good as Coffee Chaos. The small family-run café with its inviting ambience was a preferred spot by many of the locals. Most women who patronized the store order their drinks drowning in sweetness, but not me. I liked mine bold and robust. The barista was always willing to accommodate my desire for extra shots of espresso, something that must have baffled her as she watched me leave the counter each time. I tapped away at my computer, attempting to get through my never-ending email inbox. Despite my best efforts, the task seemed insurmountable.

My eyes darted over to Laura, my best friend who had been stuck with Mr. Curran since day one. He was notorious for losing his temper, especially when the job wasn't going perfectly, and he loved to yell right outside his office door in front of the entire staff. His office door slammed open almost every day as he bellowed criticisms of her work, regardless if she'd done anything wrong or not. He stomped around, face red with anger and spit flying from his lips. Everyone else averted their gaze to avoid becoming a target themselves. He was a complete menace.

Mr. Curran perched behind his desk since dawn, wearing a pair of glasses on the edge of his nose and a deep scowl that never seemed to fade. Laura stayed until late in the evening to keep up with him, her eyes heavy and back aching from hours of sitting at her desk. My boss strutted in a bit before eight in the morning and left by six every day, never staying past seven. If only Mr. Curran retired soon and freed Laura from her misery.

My gaze shifted from one end of the inbox to the other, watching as the number of emails dwindles from over a hundred to thirty-four. I knew what was coming—Mr. Longford was going to announce his retirement to the clients. His replacement would need to be briefed to take over all his ongoing cases. I could just imagine competing firms biding their time and waiting for this news so they could swoop in and try snatching up our corporate clients with lucrative offers once they got wind of his retirement. It was such an underhanded move, but part of the game.

The clickety-clack of keyboards punctuated the hum of the office. I read two more emails marked urgent, archiving them in a folder before standing up and walking over to Laura's cubicle. We were like sisters, but right now her focus was on her computer—her fingers typing away as she bit down on her plump lower lip. "Did you know Mr. Longford is retiring?" She looked up, pausing from her work with a small shrug of her shoulders. "Yes, didn't you?"

I waved my hands in frustration as she was still typing. "I'm his assistant! You would think I would be the first to know. Can you figure out when his last day is? It looks like he will be busy with his replacement."

Laura's slender fingers stilled on the keyboard, and she grinned. Her eyes sparkled, as if it was a secret shared only between us. "Can you believe our luck? A guy that looks like that graces us with his presence. You are so lucky!" She wiggled her eyebrows before turning back to her computer.

Her sharp wit and quick tongue made me chuckle every time. She made me laugh even in the darkest of days at work, which was no small feat, considering most of the men had a permanent scowl on their face. Some of the newer partners were good-looking, but their attitude was less than desirable. It was all about how much money they were bringing in and they rejected any other topics of conversation in favor of self-aggrandizing stories about their achievements. They overestimated their worth compared to their salary.

I rolled my eyes and took a drink of my lukewarm coffee. "He's just like all the rest," I muttered under my breath. "I've got enough work to keep me busy for a year, and now I'll have even more. But what choice do I have? Gotta pay the bills somehow, right?"

She leaned back in her chair. "Look, I don't want to be negative Nancy, but Mr. Longford's replacement is going to have it rough. The last three new guys flamed out within a month, and I'm stuck picking up their slack every time, because you know how my boss loves to work eighteen-hour days." She glanced toward her boss's office behind her. "It's exhausting. If I didn't have to worry about bills, I'd be out of here faster than you can say 'overworked and underpaid.'"

Her computer chimed, the familiar sound of receiving a new email. Laura shook her head and continued typing. "Mr. Curran is on a warpath today. I swear he has emailed me twenty times already, and I haven't even had time to finish my first cup of coffee. Why can't he be the one retiring? He's like five years older than your boss." She patted her leg and leaned back in her chair. "Oh wait, there is always a chance I would get stuck with someone even worse."

Mr. Curran strolled out of his office and his eyes landed on me, looming over his assistant's desk. His pinstriped suit was immaculate, his expression scary. The disapproval was radiating off him as I sat on the edge of her desk. Laura peered up as his eyes shifted between the two of us. I chose my words and met his gaze without flinching. "Anyway, I'll get out your hair," I said and stepped away from her desk. His stern gaze followed me until I was back in my chair.

I spun the tape dispenser around in my hands, and a chill ran down my spine as I contemplated all the changes that would come with his departure. Laura had been working longer days and I would soon be in her shoes.

As his assistant—oh, wait... Stupid me, I just assumed I was staying on as his assistant, yet I hadn't even thought to confirm that with them. *Surely they wouldn't be letting me go?* My fingers tugged at the hem of my shirt as I thought about my future with this company. What if he already had his own assistant? There would be no room for me. The bills wouldn't pay themselves. I needed this job to survive.

I took a deep breath and tried to swallow the anxiety bubbling up in my throat. Years of experience had taught me to expect the needs of my boss. As Mr. Longford's assistant, I was his scheduler, excuse maker, even wedding gift sender when necessary. I knew everything about his personal life, including what groceries he ordered. *Pathetic, right?* I started thinking about Mr. Kneeland. He was in his late thirties, had brown hair, a bit of scruff, and big brown eyes. Judging by his looks, he had no problems getting attention anywhere he went, and that worried me. Dealing with crazy ex-lovers or clingy one-night stands was not my thing. That was where I drew the line.

I stared at my computer, clicking away as emails and phone calls flew in from every direction. Suddenly, Mr. Longford and Mr. Kneeland emerged from the conference room, laughing uproariously. As I listened to their jocular tones, I couldn't help but think that one of two things must be going on. Either my boss was telling some of his unfunny jokes or Mr. Kneeland was trying to butter him up. They walked right past my desk without stopping and went into his office. I took it the meeting went well.

My mouse pointer drifted over the home icon on my desktop before I double-clicked and brought up the shutdown option. I detached my phone from its charger, slipping it into my purse as I grabbed my keys. My work day was done, unless Mr. Longford had a last-minute request. I was looking forward to a long soak in the tub for some much-needed relaxation. The chair squeaked as I rolled it beneath the desk.

Knock. Knock. Knock.

He called out to come in.

I stepped in, my eyes shifting around the room. He was sitting at his desk with a pile of paperwork in front of him, his glasses perched on his nose. He waved me forward until I was standing next to Mr. Kneeland, who was sitting in a chair in front of his desk.

"Things going well today, sir? You seem more chipper than usual," I asked.

He removed his glasses. "It's all because of this guy. You're going to like him. He has an old soul despite his young appearance."

Well, there went my worries. "So, you are keeping me on as your assistant, then?" My eyes landed on his.

"I wouldn't dream of anything else. Taking over his spot are some big shoes to fill, but hopefully you can keep me grounded. The master scheduler, he calls you."

Before I started here, Mr. Longford had an assistant who couldn't for the life of her keep his schedule straight. She kept overbooking him for meetings, and when they let her go, he found my application. "I'm great at making sure you don't have to be in two places at once."

Flashing my eyes around the room, I surveyed the area. Mr. Kneeland was staring at me, and I didn't dare meet his eyes. "Well, it was nice to meet you."

"I'll see you in the morning with another cup of coffee. I stop on my way to work, so I can save you a trip. Mr. Longford said your favorite is a venti mocha with extra whipped cream and two extra shots of espresso?"

A grin crept onto my face. "Precisely, sir."

"Oh, and don't call me *sir*. No offense to my partner here, but I'm not a sir. You can just call me Matt."

He wanted us to be on a first-name basis after one day?

"Understood. See you tomorrow, Mr. Longford and Matt," I said, shutting the door behind me before grabbing my purse off the floor and racing for the elevator.

Tomorrow should be interesting...

4

Matt

Moving around in the oversized bed, I extended my arms above my head and saw the sunrise pour into the penthouse. The rays turned everything yellow, casting strange shadows across the plush carpet and modern furniture. The air was cool and crisp, and my skin prickled with goosebumps beneath the blanket. In the distance, the city roared to life—sirens wailed and horns blared. I grew up in Amesbury, a quaint, sleepy town where even streetlights dimmed after a certain hour. But here in New York City, the world was always open. That's why I loved it. Even at three in the morning, I could get a hot coffee or fresh pastry on practically every corner. The city never slept, and neither did I.

Initially, I was uncertain if it was the ideal match for me, but trying it out for one year was beneficial for both of us. I needed to take the risk of trying something new.

Taking my time, I slowly rose, my feet sinking into the exquisitely soft and deep carpet beneath me. In the past, I could only just about make do with my average salary, so this was definitely not something I could normally afford. To ensure I had enough to cover the must-haves, I allocated a sufficient amount and the rest I put away in my savings accounts. My gaze swept across the room, taking in every detail—modern furniture with sleek lines and a few tasteful decorations giving it warmth and personality. The apartment came fully furnished as a package deal which was one less thing for me to worry about.

The bathroom had heated flooring, but I could learn to live with it. I twisted the golden knob on the shower. I stepped into the bathroom and twisted the golden knob of the shower. The hot spray washed away all my thoughts as I closed my eyes, enjoying a moment of solace before the chaos of New York began again. I tilted my head up toward the stream of water, humming softly. The marble walls glistened in the light, reminding me how lucky I was to have such luxurious amenities during my year here. A heavy sigh escaped my lips. No way could I find something this nice on my budget. The shower tiles were cool against my feet, but the steam embraced me like a comforting hug. As I lathered the shampoo in my hair, the smile on my mother's face came to the forefront. Without her pushing me to accept, this wouldn't even be happening.

Exhaling deeply, I emerged from the shower, my hands pressing against the wall for support. Wisps of steam curled around me like a comforting embrace, allowing me to collect my thoughts before I dived into the day's events. With a sense of purpose and energy, I reached for the towel rack and dried myself off. Once done, I stepped out refreshed and re-energized for the day.

I threw on my suit and heard the clink of my laptop bag and briefcase as I picked them up. Mr. Longford had so many clients. If I wanted to be up to speed before he left, I would have to study the files right away and take advantage of the quiet moments between clients and conversations. Already I could feel the next few hours slipping away as I headed out into the hallway.

The city was bustling with people and cars, adding to the wild symphony. Every corner boasts brightly lit establishments with unique aromas escaping from their doors. My mother had always been a small-town woman, never daring far from Amesbury. I walked down the cement path, my long gray jacket billowing behind me as I navigated through the crowds. The chill in the air pinched at my nose, but my matching suit kept me warm.

As I reached the two-block distance to Coffee Chaos, my excitement bubbled up. The sweet smell of freshly brewed coffee filled the air as I stepped in, and I noticed someone had placed a vase of sunflowers on each table. I joined the line of eager customers, musing over what I would choose. The café was an inviting blend of modern and rustic with a long counter with chrome espresso and frothing machines, bottles of coffee flavorings and toppings, and towers of paper cups and lids. A glass case held a selection of breakfast muffins and scones, but I was not a breakfast person. They spread bistro tables with trendy wrought-iron chairs throughout the café.

When it was finally my turn, I ordered my go-to flat white espresso with micro-foamed milk and a mocha topped with extra shots of espresso and a generous dollop of whipped cream.

The woman behind the counter lifted her eyebrow. "It comes with two shots, so you want an additional two? It wouldn't be for Jennifer Jenkins, would it?"

I curved my lips into a satisfied smile and gave a slight nod. "Yes, that's right. She's my new assistant."

After paying, I stepped back and waited for my coffee. People occupied all the tables, typing away on laptops and cocooned in their own bubble of music or podcasts. A few had notebooks open and were scribbling away at the pages with fervor. Toward the other end where orders were picked up, there were a few comfy leather chairs around a small coffee table with stray newspapers and magazines. How could they possibly stay so focused with the chaotic bustle of the café all around?

The room was overwhelming to me, but that was most likely because I hadn't adjusted to the big city yet. The coffee grinder was going, employees calling out names, the ding of the cash register. All together, it practically made my head throb. As she called my name, I stepped to the counter, the scent of freshly roasted beans filling my nose. The barista was wearing a bright smile as she passed me two steaming cups. I took them and thanked her, feeling the warmth on my fingers. Stepping back out onto the street, I inhaled a deep breath, let it out, then took a sip from my cup. The taste of the coffee sent a warm feeling through my body, and I was ready to continue on to the firm.

I stepped into the Weston, Crawford and Curran firm and was instantly taken aback by the grandeur of the building. The architect must have had a field day creating this masterpiece. Someone meticulously crafted every detail to create an atmosphere of luxury and sophistication. The walls were a deep navy blue, and golden accents adorned the baseboards and doorframes. The floors were a gleaming marble that seemed to sparkle in the light, and the furniture was a mix of modern and traditional pieces, all of which were of the highest quality.

The elevator dinged, and I stepped inside, expecting to be alone, but I heard someone coming toward me. It was Mr. Longford, the senior partner. He stepped in and asked me how my morning was going, and the smile that lit up his face when he saw the second cup of coffee in my hand was one I would remember for a long time.

"You know, if you bring her coffee every morning, you are gonna move mountains. That girl is obsessed with it. Sometimes she has five cups."

Mr. Longford told me about her love for coffee from that local café, but since it was so expensive, she only had one cup a week. The rest of the time, she was forced to limit herself to drinking the breakroom's disgusting filth. I agreed, it's nothing compared to the brews at Coffee Chaos.

Mr. Longford and I got off the elevator on the eighth floor and he went straight to his office, offering me a smile over his shoulder as I stopped right in front of Jennifer's desk. My eyes took in the royal-blue pencil skirt and the black blouse she was wearing, and the way the bob haircut hit right under her chin. She didn't even notice me for a moment, too busy looking through some paperwork on her desk, but when her eyes met mine, she had the sweetest smile.

"You didn't have to do this," she said as I handed her the cup.

"I was serious about bringing you a cup. Even braved the barista for the two extra shots of espresso and she knew who you were by the order." This was more than just a cup of coffee. This was a gesture of appreciation, a token of connection with a colleague. After everything we would go through for the next year together, it was the least I can do.

She laughed, took a sip, and her eyes rolled to the back of her head. "It's so good."

I smiled as my hand slid over my chin before walking into my future office. "I'll talk to you later."

Mr. Longford's office was a sleek and stylish workspace. It was soon to be mine. The walls were a crisp white, and the furniture was a mix of modern and retro, from the mid-century credenza to the oversized tufted leather chair. The room filled with light from the floor-to-ceiling windows, making the sleek chrome accents and the black and blue accents around the room pop. They arranged his desk in the center of the room, covered in papers, folders, and manila envelopes. There were a few books on the shelves, some framed photos of his family, and a large monitor sitting atop a tower of electronics.

Directly across from his desk was a corner of the room that held two armchairs and a coffee table. The chairs were a deep blue and the table a chrome, and the perfect place for us to talk. I took a seat in the armchair and he took the other, the two of us facing each other.

"So, I'd like to know a little more about the guy who is taking over for me. My clients aren't needy, and I have been working with most of them for years. Some of them are older than me. Taking over for me, you will be in a good place. Most of the new partners get stuck taking the cases no one else wants, but you'll be busy with my workload, so I doubt they will assign you many extra ones."

Hard work wasn't anything new to me, so if they needed to give me more cases, I'd handle it. I was in a new city where I didn't know anyone and that meant I'd have no life. There was no reason to make friends if I might move back to Texas in a year. Although, even in these two days, New York City was growing on me already.

He nodded. "Next time, you can pick me up a cup, too." He laughed. "I'm just kidding. You don't have three hands and I'll be out of your hair in no time."

His eyes moved around the room, and he gestured to the windows, commenting on the view of the skyline. He asked me some questions about the firm I came from and my ambitions. I explained I had agreed to this position for one year but would give plenty of notice if I decided not to stay. He understood, knowing this city wasn't for everyone, especially someone from a small town. The warmth of his smile was comforting, knowing that he just wanted me to succeed.

"Alright, let's get to work now, shall we?" He flipped open a folder that was sitting on the desk and pulled out some paperwork. He explained the project to me and asked me if I had questions. I asked a few, and he answered them all, giving me more information than I asked for. His responses were thorough.

"Well, if you can do me a favor, and even if you get caught up in the next few days, give this old man until the end of next week before you boot me out of my office."

My jaw tightened as I cringed. "Sir, I would never do that. When you are ready, I'll take over. In the meantime, it's an honor to work with you."

5
Jennifer

I took the last sip of the steamy coffee Matt brought me, then tossed it into my trash can with a satisfied sigh. The hot liquid felt good as it rolled down my throat, and I welcomed the small boost of energy it provided. Glancing up, I saw Laura in the doorway, looking anxious.

"We need to talk," she said. I could see her trying to peer around the corner, making sure her boss was still out of his office. Mr. Curran despised gossip and would punish anyone caught.

Laura gestured for me to follow her, and I obliged, following her down the hall. We hid in an old storage closet.

"So, did Matt get you that coffee?"

I gave a quick jerk of my head.

"He's got a thing for you, you know," she blurted out before I could stop her.

I rolled my eyes, not believing her for a second. "What are you talking about? That's ridiculous," I protested.

She shook her head in amused disbelief. "Come on now, don't be so naïve. You've been here long enough to know how these things work. He's into you."

I let out a cackle that made my sides ache. Who wanted to date someone they worked with? That was just asking for trouble... especially when your bosses were as strict as Mr. Curran!

I had no desire to stay and listen to her any longer, so I hurried out of the closet, my heart racing when Matt emerged from the office, and I made my way back to my desk. The way he carried himself with an air of confidence and poise and the gray suit he was wearing which seemed tailored to his body gave him a certain appeal.

Laura nudged me in the ribs and raised her eyebrows. "Can you feel it? I think he's giving you the 'I want you' vibe," she said.

My cheeks burned as I glanced away, not wanting to give away my excitement.

He stepped closer, and my heart raced. His gaze was intense, and he seemed to size me up. I was afraid he could sense my nervousness, but I refused to turn away.

Finally, he spoke, his voice quiet, yet gripping. "Hey," he said. "I'm sure you are already on the ball, but have you arranged a party for Mr. Longford yet?"

I leaned on my left side. "He's been so busy with you, I haven't really sat down with him yet."

"It's next Friday. If you need any help, let me know," he said. His eyes raked over me again, and I was glad I wore my four-inch pumps today because it gave me a bit more height, making us almost at the same level.

"Sure will. Thanks."

When Matt walked away, Laura nudged my shoulder again. "I told you—total 'I want you' vibes. Please tell me you picked up on it too?"

Okay, so maybe she wasn't crazy because I caught him checking me out at least three times since he arrived yesterday, but I didn't want to call attention to it. Laura had no shame. After everything that happened with Peyton, I wasn't ready to jump back into a relationship, anyway. Men weren't anything like in the movies. They weren't romantic and definitely didn't sweep us off our feet. Instead, they thought paying for my dinner meant they got dibs at the end of the night. *Sorry, not sorry.*

My past relationships had only brought me bad luck and heartache. A relationship wasn't what the new boss was looking for, and I wasn't the one-night stand type. Nope, I had to remain guarded and protect myself from any further pain. That was my only option.

So, I stayed silent and tried to keep my feelings under wraps.

I stared into the half-empty office. Many of the assistants and partners left early. The corridor was eerily quiet. There was still some time before I could go home.

Laura came back over with a stack of papers in her hands. "Can you believe he is making me work late again tonight? It's like he knows I don't have a life. I still have *Sex in the City* episodes to binge." She glanced toward her boss's door as if she were saying it straight to his face.

"Well, if it makes you feel any better, it'll be me and you both after Mr. Longford leaves."

She sat on the edge of my desk. "Get a move on with party planning."

"Thank you," I said. "I'll start planning tonight after a glass of wine. I'd invite you over, but you will be here. Bummer."

She nodded, her face softening in response, leaving as he walked out of the office behind me.

I kept my eyes glued to Matt's every movement. Every time he came near me, it was like a jolt of electricity shot through me. Yet he was always professional and polite.

"You guys headed out?" I asked, hoping they said yes so I could leave early too.

"Well, Mr. Longford said we have a long day tomorrow, so we are busting out a tad bit early today." His eyes scanned the floor. "Where is everyone? It's like a ghost town here."

A smile crossed my face. "Most of the assistants left hours ago. It's just you two and Mr. Curran here."

He shifted his stance and scratched the back of his neck. "Well, what are you still doing here?" He popped his head back into the office. "Hey, everyone else is gone. I'm sending Jennifer home early."

I flashed a tight smile. "Well, that's sweet of you. Thanks." He watched me as I shut down my computer, unplugged my phone, and grabbed my purse. A flush ran through my body, knowing he might be staring at my backside right now. I couldn't blame him. This skirt was one of the best ones for that. I glanced over at Laura, who was mouthing 'go for it.' "Oh, I still need you to add me to your Google calendar. If I'm going to be working for you, I'll need access so I can get it situated with my style of work."

"You have a style? Like isn't a calendar just that? You input text, date, and time? I'm confused."

Oh gosh, don't embarrass yourself in front of him. Get yourself together, girl. "I'll get it all switched over and set up, and then I'll explain it to you."

He bit his lip, leaving a tinge of red. "Sounds perfect. Well, good night, Jennifer. See you in the morning."

When he walked out of the vicinity to the elevators, my chest heaved. It was unprofessional to get hot and bothered by my boss.

6
Matt

After leaving Coffee Chaos with two cups of coffee, I felt the winter air bite into my skin. The streets were bustling with people of all ages, their cacophony of accents making up the soundtrack of the city. The smell of freshly baked pastries and the sound of honking horns filled the air, and the amber hues headed up into the sky.

Adorned in my dark-gray suit and navy tie, I walked with purpose. I had a mission ahead of me: to get through thirty case files today. Jennifer awaited me at the office and she was going to be a wonderful asset. I could focus on the job itself, rather than the administrative side of matters. It elated me to have someone of Jennifer's caliber on my side. Mr. Longford made it clear she was the best assistant he ever had, and I was the lucky one to have her working for me.

She was a stunning woman with a short brown bob and bright-blue eyes. With a job such as hers and mine, a social life was tough to maintain. Too many people tried and failed, ending up with unhappy spouses and multiple divorces under their belt. When I meet my future wife, I would make sure I could give her the world—the house, the kids, the white picket fence. I had no time for such a pursuit right now.

I cleared my mind of my worrisome thoughts and advanced unwaveringly toward my destination. The possibilities seemed limitless, and it filled me with an energy I thought had gone forever.

As I rounded the corner, I spotted the building where my life was going to be for the next year: The Weston, Crawford and Curran firm.

With a determined push, I opened the bulky glass doors and then proceeded to the elevator. The door dinged as it shut and I pressed the number eight. I walked into the office and stopped in front of Jennifer's desk. She gave me a polite greeting and thanked me for the coffee, but something was off. She wouldn't make much eye contact and seemed distracted. *Did I do something wrong?*

"Did you get to do anything enjoyable after you got off?" I asked cautiously, trying not to make her uncomfortable.

Jennifer didn't answer immediately. Instead, she stared at her computer and tapped on the keyboard. "I had a glass of wine. I also redid your calendar," she said after a few moments.

She wasn't being her usual self, but I shrugged it off. "Oh, what does HAFH stand for? I need to color code it."

Honestly, I didn't even think about her having access to that. "It's an acronym," I said. "But I'd rather explain it to you in private. Do you want to come into Mr. Longford's office?"

Jennifer hesitated before getting up and slowly walking in. I took a deep breath and told her HAFH stands for "Home Away From Home" and explained that my mother had Parkinson's. Her eyes softened a bit, and she was finally making eye contact with me again. I didn't want anyone's pity, and neither did she. My mother might have it, but she wanted to live life until it was her time to pass. "After my father passed, when it got to the point she couldn't take care of herself, I almost moved back, but she refused. Instead, she found HAFH and asked if I could get her in."

Jennifer crossed her arms and looked at me skeptically. "So, why did you move to New York City?"

I couldn't help but smile, remembering how my mother encouraged me to never give up on my dream. "My mother told me to. She's a big part of my life, even though she can be quite particular about what she wants."

"Aren't all mothers? My mom thinks what I do is a joke, yet I work more hours than most. Heck, Laura spends almost twice as much time here as me. This job is no small feat."

My mother's symptoms, the tremors and the rigidity, were getting worse. The amnesia had just started rearing its ugly head.

"So, the fifteenth is when you pay them? I can put it under financial, then. I apologize if it seems like I was being intrusive."

"No, it's okay. Don't be sorry."

Her hands pulled to her sides, and I stepped closer. "That's the one weekend a month I tried to visit her before I moved out here. Now, I'll be lucky to see her at Christmas."

"We'll make sure you get out there, don't worry. The firm usually closes down for the week between Christmas and New Year's. It's the only week everyone is off."

That's good to know. With having Parkinson's, she was more prone to falls and pneumonia. Keeping her healthy was my top priority.

"So, I got it under financial for now, but if you want me to change it, let me know," Jennifer said, tapping the iPad screen. "Do you want to see what I've done? I can explain it to you really quick if you have time."

I stepped closer. Her lavender perfume hit my nostrils, causing me to roll my eyes back in my head. When she tapped the stylus on my chest, I smiled and paid attention to the screen. She had completely transformed my previous calendar. She arranged the series of appointments and tasks neatly and added colored tabs.

"So red is for urgent matters, yellow is cases, blue is for personal, and green is for financial." She flipped through my calendar and now

I could see firsthand what Mr. Longford meant. She took her job seriously and was very particular. *Who am I to step on her toes?*

I thanked her as she closed the iPad.

"I'll be taking some time today to finalize the plans for his retirement party next Friday. Will he be in today?" She looked around the office, noticing we were alone.

"He wasn't feeling great this morning and was going to get an extra hour of sleep. I'll just be using his office and going through case files if you need anything."

She nodded and her heels clacked as she walked out of the office and shut the door. This was soon going to be all mine. All of my hard work, eighty-hour workweeks, and sleepless nights were catching up to me, and my dream was coming true. New York City might not have been my first choice of places to live, but getting the offer from this firm spoke wonders about my reputation.

Jennifer's mother might think her job was a joke, but all the things she did for her boss, Mr. Longford, made his life easier. His exact words were, "She's a lifesaver and once she gets to know you, your whole life will be organized."

Assistants didn't get enough compliments, but not under my watch. She would know just how much I appreciated her every day, but besides coffee, how could I show my appreciation?

7
Jennifer

As I filled our wineglasses, I could smell the sweet aroma that filled the air. This was the first night Laura had been off before eight in weeks. New York City might seem like since it was full of people, it was easy to find friends, but it was quite the opposite.

"So stop thinking and spit it out. What's going on?" Laura asked.

"Why did you have to say anything at all? Every time we are around each other, I feel like he's taking me in. He's my boss, and as much as it makes me feel sexy, it's wrong on so many levels."

Laura raised her eyebrows. "You think? Sometimes those are the best relationships. The risk... the adrenaline coursing through your veins every time you sneak away into a coat closet to get a quick kiss."

"Dear God, come on. You act like we are in some rom-com. This is real life." I took a sip of my wine. "There's not anything wrong with me, but if he hasn't settled down already, it's obvious he has no intention to."

Laura put her glass on the table. "Wait. Think about what you are saying... You are only at max seven years younger than him. It's difficult to find your person, and using that logic against him will not benefit you."

She was right. Age shouldn't matter. *I'm thirty-three and still undoubtedly single.* "It's just this feeling I get when he looks at me. Like... like he's interested."

Laura's cheeks flushed. "Oh, believe me, do you forget I sit across from you? I see every interaction and he might not act on it outright, but he finds you attractive. But heck, what man wouldn't? Look at you."

I ran my fingers through my hair before throwing it over my shoulder with a bright laugh. "The wall Pilates is doing wonders. My butt has never looked so good."

My mind thought back to that royal-blue pencil skirt, Matt's eyes wandering down me. There wasn't much that made me shy, but his gaze did. I had always been confident, but a man like him gave me a thrill. He took care of his sick mother, and from my perspective, had the shape of a perfect man, but he was my boss. I drew the line there. As much as his gaze intrigued me, it could be nothing more.

"Girl, listen. Every woman in the office wants him. He's hot with a capital *H*, and fresh meat in this office is scarce."

I flexed my fingers around my wineglass. "He's so charming, and he has that amazing smile. Why couldn't I have met him outside of the firm? It's like life wants to show me who's in control... and it's not me."

"Mm-hmm," Laura replied. "I give it a month before they will remove the company policy. It's a total double standard. Men get praised for messing around with their assistants, but the women... they get reprimanded. Leave it to the lawyers saving their own hides."

I felt the cold, wet surface of the glass as my fingers traced circles in the condensation. "Listen, he's hot, we both agree, but I'm not the type of girl to do anything more than have a harmless crush." My gaze shifted to the window, where the sun was setting in the distance. The sky was afire with shades of pink and orange, a beautiful contrast to the darkness of the night.

There was a knock at the door, signaling the takeout had arrived. I got up to answer it, and the delicious smell of Chinese food filled the room. After handing the guy cash, I shut the door and set the bag down on the coffee table. "I am so hungry!" I picked up a container of fried rice and dished it onto a plate.

Laura followed suit, eating as she gave me the scoop on her life. "Mr. Curran might be retiring too." The level of excitement in her voice was hilarious. "I overheard his wife telling him she wants to travel, and he promised her he would retire by seventy."

I didn't understand why he was still working. Unless he was a lavish spender, he should have money tucked away to last him the rest of his life. "I mean, I don't blame his wife. He's always at the office."

"That's not even the best part! Surely the world won't screw me twice. I'm so ready to have a boss that gets off at a decent time. My looks are taking a real hit from the lack of sleep."

Laura wasn't the model type, but she was hardly ugly. Her bright-red hair and green eyes gave her an allure. She was as feisty as her locks, and everyone knew. Whoever ended up being her new boss was in for a treat. She was an extremely dedicated assistant—even Mr. Curran knows that—but sometimes she didn't quite know when to think before she spoke.

"We will reinstate Happy Hour nights. Remember when we used to go to that bar on sixth? What was it called? The Boardroom... that's right. Girl's night and do karaoke. God, it was a blast. I miss that."

Laura took her last sip of wine and refilled the glass without missing a beat. "Going out and enjoying myself is going to be the first thing on my list. Hopefully, he doesn't wait too long because I'm ready."

Laura got paid more than I did, but she also worked a lot more hours. She deserved it, and even though Mr. Curran was as evil as they come, he gave her a decent raise every year.

"Why don't we do that tomorrow? Maybe Mr. Curran will leave early so we can enjoy ourselves." I wiggled my eyebrows.

"If it happens, I am totally down!"

It was nice to hang out with my best friend again. My mom warned me as I got older, friends drift apart. Over the last three years, our schedules conflicted. When we got the chance to have a girls' night, we took it.

As the night went on, Laura had a little too much wine, going all out for her first early night, and passed out on my couch. I didn't have the gall to wake her, so I threw a blanket over her on the couch and headed to my bedroom.

Matt might be good-looking, but it didn't have to go anywhere. Our reputation would be dragged through the mud, but that didn't mean he couldn't visit me in my dreams.

8
Jennifer

This morning was weird. A bunch of clients caught wind of Mr. Longford's retirement before he reached out to everyone, and showed up at the office, less than impressed. The phones kept ringing.

"Alright, that's the last call you had to return. Looks like we are all caught up." I plopped down in the chair in front of his desk. Matt was using one of the side tables as a workstation. They acted as if the world was ending.

Mr. Longford took his glasses off and wiped his forehead as if sweat covered it. "At least my week has been busy. I'm gonna miss this place."

Many of his clients were sad to see him go, but they got to meet Mr. Kneeland today, and he won them over. Seeing him in his element was nice; he was confident, charismatic, and very personable. He maintained one of the main things people loved about my current boss: personality.

"Looks like I have my hands full with all of your clients. You accrued so many over your time here. How do you keep up with all of them?"

He was on retainer, but that didn't mean he worked for them

every month; he was just on standby if needed. Sometimes I wondered if I should have gone to law school so I could get paid like them.

"Listen, let's all go to lunch today. The next few days are going to be a blur, and I'd like to have lunch with you two before I leave. Are you free?"

"Sure," Matt and I said in unison.

Mr. Longford nodded his head. "I'll have a car come pick us up at one."

I walked back to my desk to get some more work done before we left. Laura was typing away on her computer. Earlier, she came over to tell me that Mr. Curran just took on three more clients and that she asked for tonight off. He wasn't happy, but since she was never able to take all her vacation time every year, he didn't decline. When she caught my glance, I mouthed 'girls' night' and she smiled. We both needed it after a day like this one.

By one, I had answered thirty emails, got four case files put away, and was ready to go when they stepped out of his office. "Let's hit the road."

I grabbed my purse and followed them into the elevator. Mr. Longford continued the conversation they previously had from the elevator all the way until we pulled up to the restaurant.

"Sounds like you are getting everything together," I said to Matt, and he looked down at me. "I don't know how you do it. Not in this short amount of time."

"Just imagine doing all this without an assistant. That was me before this firm."

I was his first assistant? Now I understood why his calendar was so out of whack.

They quickly escorted Matt, Mr. Longford, and me to our seats.

Mr. Longford beamed at us. "I'm so glad you both could make it," he said with a twinkle in his eye.

I smiled, feeling the weight of their eyes on me. I had never been in a situation like this before—being invited to lunch with two influential and successful men. As long as I had worked for Mr. Longford, we had never been out to lunch together. We always had it delivered to the office.

The server brought out a menu and Mr. Longford talked about his plans for the following week while we looked it over. He occasionally glanced at me, a look of admiration and appreciation in his eyes.

"You seem to be quite knowledgeable about everything, Jennifer," Matt said. "Mr. Longford here has been lucky to have you as his assistant."

Mr. Longford chuckled at the comment and glanced at me. "She's been a godsend," he said with a grin. "It's good to have someone competent around to make life easier. God knows I have had my fair share of horrible assistants, but Jennifer here deserves another raise or two."

Matt nodded. "I'm sure you've noticed, Jennifer, but it's important to make sure the people who make our lives easier feel appreciated. It keeps them happy."

My face flushed. *Is there something hidden behind those words? Is he trying to tell me something?* He seemed to keep his eyes on me most of the time during lunch, and my heart was fluttering in my chest.

Just as I was about to ask myself if I was reading too much into things, Mr. Longford cleared his throat and changed the topic.

"This lunch is to get one last pleasant meal in with you guys before I go," he said with a sad sigh. "My wife and I have been planning a trip to England, and I figured it was time to do it before I get too old."

My heart sunk, and I asked if he was all right. "I don't want everyone talking about it," Mr. Longford said with a wave of his hand. "But my health has taken a turn for the worse, and I'm afraid this is the best choice."

Matt nodded and patted the older man's arm. "We'll definitely miss you."

"There are some things that I would like to see continue after my absence. Jennifer and I always get breakfast and coffee delivered on Friday mornings. We go over the agenda for the following week. Could you continue that?"

Matt smiled. "Of course. It's a tradition, after all."

My mind raced thinking of spending every Friday morning alone in his office. Laura was going to have a field day with this information.

Mr. Longford and Matt made the lunch more friendly than work related once they brought the food out. They were going back and forth, telling their best jokes. By far, Matt won, but I didn't tell him that. Instead, I sided with Mr. Longford because I only had him in my life for such a short time.

"What about you, Jennifer? You have any funny jokes?" Matt asked, taking a sip of water while the server brought the check. "Let's hear it. Everyone has at least one."

He's wrong! I didn't have one. The only joke I knew... "Why did the bicycle fall over?"

Matt and Mr. Longford looked at each other and then shook their heads.

"Because it was two tired."

They both chuckled, and I was sure it was just to make me feel better about having one of the lamest jokes ever. It looked like I would need to do some research for some funny jokes to have on standby. Apparently, they both thought they were comedians. Go figure.

"Alright, gentlemen. It was nice, but I need to get back to work. I'm behind schedule and can't stay late today," I said, getting up from the table and grabbing my purse.

"That reminds me. Can you send me that list of places you recommend around here? I'll be venturing out of my apartment soon and would love some recommendations," he said to Longford.

"Yeah, I'll send that email when we get back."

They stood with me and followed me out, hailing a cab, and riding back to the office with me. I ended up in the middle of the back seat, and it forced my leg to rub against Matt's. Electricity flowed through me, and I tried to hide the flush in my cheeks. Laura was going to make fun of me for this.

When the cab pulled up in front of the building, Matt hesitated getting out, and his hand landed on my thigh to brace himself. When he realized what he was doing, he removed his hand and locked eyes with me. "I apologize. Um... that was inappropriate and won't happen again."

As he extended his hand to help me out of the cab, I walked right into the building without looking behind me. This man was sending mixed signals, and he knew just how this could affect both of our careers.

I was so ready to go grab some drinks and sing some karaoke tonight. Laura would fish for information, like she always did, and at least I would have something good to tell her.

Matt's hands were soft, not calloused, and I wished it never left that spot.

9
Matt

The sun felt like a spotlight on me as I emerged from the sleek glass doors of the law firm. My feet were heavy, my blazer hung limp, and my tie was loosened hours before. As I reached for my phone, vibrating in my pocket, a chill ran down my spine. The number was the nursing home where my mother lived. The exhaustion of the twelve-hour day peeled off me as I answered, but the cheerful voice of my mother was on the other end.

As my mother told me about her minor accident, I felt a chill run through me. I wished I could be with her, to make sure she was really okay, but I was hundreds of miles away in New York City and had only been with the firm for a week. My heart raced at the thought of having to ask for an emergency leave so soon since starting work. I heard the fear in her voice. Every muscle in my body tensed. She said she was okay, and I wanted to drop everything, but I couldn't.

"I broke nothing, I swear," she said, a sigh of relief in her voice.

"Are you sure you're okay?" I asked, feeling my body tense up.

"I'm fine, sweetheart. Just take a few deep breaths and you'll be alright," she said in a soothing tone.

I inhaled deeply and let the air fill my lungs before slowly blowing it out. The tension in my body melted away. "I love you, Mom. Please be careful."

"I will, son. Love you too," she replied with a warmth in her voice.

I opened the door to the dive bar and the overpowering smell of stale beer, cigarettes, and bleach greeted me. A single light flickered in the corner while country music twanged softly from a jukebox in the back. The few customers that were there hugged their drinks tightly as they sat alone, staring off into space.

I stepped up to the bar and claimed a stool, my eyes scanning the room some more. A woman with a stern expression, thick arms, cropped dark hair, and a deep set of wrinkles came to take my order in a monotone voice. "What'll it be?"

I hesitantly asked for a lager, and when she placed it down before me with a clink of glass on wood, I wanted to smile, but I silently thanked her and contemplated my next move.

I was the only guy in a suit in a room full of pool tables and neon beer signs. It wasn't until I'd been watching the baseball game on the giant television for two hours, sipping my beers slowly, that people trickled in to fill the dimly lit space. People continued until it was shoulder to shoulder inside.

I ordered a whiskey on the rocks, and the bartender obliged. The glass touched my lips and the warmth of the liquid slid down my throat like a comforting blanket. My barstool swiveled, and a familiar voice came from the end of the bar.

I turned around on my barstool and there, illuminated by the neon lights, were Laura and Jennifer. They were in evening wear, laughing and smiling with each other, enjoying a carefree night out. I took a deep breath, feeling a strange mix of emotions, and I couldn't help but chuckle to myself. Of all the nights and all the places in NYC, they had to come to this one on the night I was here. *Go figure, that's my luck.*

Turning back around, I tried to make myself invisible, because if they saw me, then they would leave. Who wanted to hang out with their boss after work? Jennifer commanded attention in her black halter dress and red pumps. My throat tightened as I tried to avert my eyes from the vision of beauty. Her lips glistened from lip gloss, and she was smiling as she talked to her friend. I couldn't tear my eyes away from her.

The ladies had taken a seat at a table and were in the middle of an animated conversation when a tall, dark-haired man made his way over. I fixed my eyes on Jennifer as he sauntered closer, talking loud enough for the entire bar to hear. Without thinking, I crossed the room and took my place beside her, planting a swift kiss on the top of her head. "Hey, babe, you need another drink?"

The man's voice had a hard edge. He jammed his hands into the pockets of his fashionable jeans. It was clear he hadn't shaved in days. Jennifer's eyes darted back and forth between us like she was trying to detect a trap. She leaned close to my ear. "What are you doing?"

The man clenched his jaw, making a visible effort not to say a thing. He cast one last look of longing at Jennifer before delivering his critique. "So you have moved on already?"

Jennifer snuggled into my side and sent him a dismissive smile. "He's more of a man than you will ever be," she whispered. "Go handle your commitment issues and leave us alone."

As I watched him lumber out of the bar, the bitter taste of jealousy filled my mouth. My hand fell from Jennifer's shoulder and she slowly looked up at me, her eyes wide and questioning. "Why did you do that?" Offering an explanation seemed futile, but I tried anyway. "I thought he was bothering you. Figured I could help."

Laura filled him in. "That was her ex that just broke up with her... and now he is totally seething with jealousy." The corners of her mouth twitched upward.

My chest tightened as I watched another guy saunter up to her and flash a charming smile. Heat radiated through me, and I took a swig of bourbon, the amber liquid burning down my throat. No, it couldn't be—I was not pining over my assistant. The alcohol made the world feel hazy and malleable. But as she laughed at his joke, something inside me twisted with jealousy.

"I'm not looking for anyone tonight," she said. He stepped away without a word and scanned the crowd for someone else to flirt with. Pathetic.

"What is it about men and having what they can't have? As soon as Matt here sat down, now men are flocking to you. Come sit by me," Laura said, but rolled her eyes when Jennifer threw some shade her way.

"If your ex was dumb enough to let a woman like you go, then let him suffer," I said with a raised brow. "They should worship you."

Jennifer shook her head slowly as she stirred her bright-red mojito. "There are thousands of single girls in New York City. Men just move on to the next. It's all a game to them."

I leaned back. "What? You don't think you're a catch? Please tell me some man hasn't ruined your confidence because you are gorgeous."

A slight smirk crept up the corner of Laura's lips. Her best friend was enjoying this. She popped a maraschino cherry into her mouth. "That is the nicest thing she has heard this week."

I found myself captivated by Jennifer's presence. Every few moments, however, her gaze darted away from mine to Laura's. Suddenly I understood—the subtle flicking of Laura's eyes was an invitation that had nothing to do with me.

I stayed right where I was, next to Jennifer, soaking up her lavender perfume. Laura ranted about Jennifer's ex-boyfriend Peyton with a fiery sense of indignation, and the girl next to me was holding back tears that threatened to spill from the corners of her eyes. Laura declared he wasn't worth the time of day. I sipped my drink in silence and watched the game on the big-screen TV, not wanting to intrude.

"You deserve better," I agreed softly.

Jennifer's gaze locked with mine, and suddenly we were both blushing. "Thanks," she said quietly before quickly glancing away again.

The conversation moved on to other topics, but I couldn't help but still think about what I had said earlier. It had felt different from just a platonic comment between colleagues; it had been more personal than that. And it seemed like Jennifer had felt it too from how she had looked at me afterward.

The music began, and my heart sank. Jennifer had walked up onto the stage, and she was about to sing. The dress was hugging her curves perfectly, and I couldn't help but stare.

Laura said something that broke me out of my trance. "Oh no, there goes your foreign language."

I looked at her in confusion until the music became more clear and I heard Jennifer singing in French. It was beautiful. Her voice had a range like an instrument, hitting all the right notes without faltering or wavering even once. Every syllable was so precise; her voice made it sound like an angel had descended from Heaven to sing for us.

What other talents did my assistant have?

10
Jennifer

As I finished my last karaoke song, I scanned the room and my eyes met Matt's. He smiled at me, and I felt my heart soar. Onstage I felt exposed, but in a good way. I was wearing a beautiful dress, and I felt a surge of confidence course through me.

I watched as Matt walked toward me, making my heart sink even deeper for him. He stood in front of me, and I felt as if time had stopped. I wanted to say something, but I couldn't find the words. He just smiled at me, and I felt a spark of electricity pass between us. We were both able to see each other outside of our work element, and it was thrilling.

He held out his hand for me, and I took it. We started dancing together, and I felt as if we were the only two people in the room, moving to the music, and our eyes locked. We smiled at each other. I felt a warmth radiating from him, and it made me feel alive.

When we made our way back to the table, Matt undid his tie, and unbuttoned the top two buttons of his shirt... he was getting comfortable, which meant he wasn't going anywhere.

Laura was eyeing me, and I knew exactly what was running through her mind... she better not.

"Can you believe the jerk had the audacity to break up with her on their six-month anniversary and say that he wasn't ready for a commitment? I mean, look at her. He's an idiot." Laura's hands waved in the air.

He nodded. "Some men don't know what they have until it's gone. Looks like that's the case with... what was his name again?"

I laughed. "Peyton."

I felt a flutter in my stomach as I looked at Matt. Surely it was wrong to be sitting here next to my boss, looking this good while he was in such an intoxicated state. His eyes had been drinking me in since he had sat down, and my whole body was on fire. It was like we were doing the tango, and neither side was ready to take the lead.

He reached over and whisked away a strand of hair from my face, and I felt my heart skip a beat. He then grabbed my hand, his thumb caressing the back of it, and I felt the heat radiating through me. We stayed like that for moments before he finally spoke.

"You look stunning tonight," he said in a husky whisper that sent shivers down my spine. I smiled shyly as I looked away, not wanting him to know how much his words affected me.

"So, Matt, what brought you to New York City? Where are you from anyway?" Laura asked.

I swatted at her under the table. Right now wasn't the time to be asking personal questions.

"I'm from a small town in Montana called Amesbury," he answered, taking another sip.

He didn't look like a guy who grew up in a small town, especially looking so scrumptious in that suit and tie.

"It's the perfect place to be during the holidays. Everyone says Times Square is awesome, but nothing beats a small-town Christmas Square."

The way he talked about his hometown made it sound like a place I wanted to visit someday.

"The community rallies for one another. Everyone is like a big family, and when someone needs help, we all pitch in."

Laura's turn for karaoke came up, and she excused herself.

Matt and I locked eyes, and the hunger in his eyes told me all I needed to know. I broke the moment and looked down at the table. "So, what are you doing here, anyway?"

"Mr. Longford gave me the name of this place as a recommendation. My mom had a fall today and after getting the news, I thought I could use a beer, so I came here. I just live a block over."

When I heard his story, my heart sank. His mom was hurt, and he felt like he had to leave her side. I admired his dedication and loyalty which he obviously possessed for his family.

"That's really sweet of you," I whispered as I reached over and touched his hand gently. He looked up at me with a sad expression on his face, but the corner of his lips tugged upward ever so slightly when our eyes met again.

He seemed too good to be true—too perfect. Everyone had flaws, so where were Matt's? I took a sip of my beer to give myself time to think.

Before I could come up with any ideas, Matt spoke again.

"I don't talk about it often, but sometimes I can be a bit of a workaholic," he admitted as he shifted in his seat uncomfortably. "I get wrapped up in my job and forget what's important in life."

It was the flaw that I needed to see in him—that humanizing element that made him real instead of just some perfect Prince Charming who had just stumbled into my life out of nowhere. Suddenly all the walls that I had built around my heart came crashing down for this man who was looking at me with such depth and sincerity that no other person had done before.

11
Matt

Jennifer's vivacious spirit and independent attitude intrigued me. Over the next couple of hours, I learned a lot about her. Jennifer had grown up in Dallas, Texas, with her parents and two sisters. She'd spent her childhood in the city, with all the advantages. She was a self-confessed city girl who wanted to experience the hustle and bustle of life in a bigger city. After she graduated college, she moved to New York City, much to her parents' dismay. They weren't happy with her decision, but she did it anyway. I admired her courage and ambition.

I grew up in the small town of Amesbury, Montana. It was only a few thousand people, and something connected everyone. If you stepped out of line, you'd know it within an hour. We knew all our neighbors, and most people seemed to know each other by name. It was quite a change for me when I went off to college and had to adjust to the faster pace of life.

As our conversation went on, Jennifer asked me how I felt about growing up in such a small town. I told her I enjoyed growing up in a place where everyone was so close and connected. We could rely on each other for anything. I had grown up knowing my neighbors and being able to call on them for help if I ever needed it.

This intrigued Jennifer, so I gave her some examples. I remembered a time when I was in high school and had an emergency. My car had broken down, and I was desperate to get to a specific location. I did not know what to do, so I called one of my neighbors, who was a mechanic. He came to my rescue and fixed the car in no time. This impressed Jennifer and she asked me how it felt to rely on your neighbors like that. It made me realize how lucky I was to be living in such a small town.

We talked a bit more after that, and Jennifer eventually opened up about her own childhood and struggles.

She told me how she had grown up in a single-parent household until her stepdad came into the picture, which meant she had to take on a lot of extra responsibility. They often left her to take care of her siblings, and she had to learn how to be independent at an early age.

This was a troublesome thing for her, but she persevered and eventually made it to New York City.

Her courage to pursue the life she wanted inspired me. We had talked about the past, the present, and our dreams for the future.

I knew I couldn't act on my feelings, but it didn't make them subside. The more I got to know Jennifer, the more I wanted to show her how a woman should be treated. Yet I knew once Mr. Longford left, my life was going to be chaotic, and we would spend a lot of time together at the office. Maybe for now, I'd bide my time, have her as a friend, and one day when all was right with the world, maybe I could ask her out... but she was looking for her happily ever after and what would I do if she found it before I could ask her out?

I was about to suggest we leave for the night and head home when she mentioned Mr. Longford's retirement party the following day.

"Oh, yeah," I said, my mind suddenly absorbed with the thought of a retirement party. "Will I need to bring anything?"

"No," she answered, shaking her head. "I'm having coffee and breakfast delivered. And speaking of the holidays, since you don't know anyone in the city yet, I'm having a Friendsgiving with Laura. You should come. No one should be alone."

I hesitated for a split second, unsure of how to respond. "Are you sure?" I asked skeptically. "I don't want to intrude."

She waved her hand dismissively. "Nonsense. We'd love to have you. Besides, it's always more fun with more people."

I smiled. "Well, in that case, I'd love to join you guys. Thanks."

It was safe to assume why she wasn't going home for the holiday if she and her family didn't get along that well. I would give anything to see my mother, but I'd have to fly out on Thursday morning and come back Thursday night, which would give me like an hour with her at most.

No matter what, I was making it out to see my mom for Christmas. I talked the center into letting me take her home to Amesbury for the holidays. The small town wasn't for everyone, but she was a small-town gal and always would be. It was a surprise, so my mother doesn't know, but I had to clear it with the director before I planned anything.

Laura finally came back to sit with us after flirting with some guy who complimented her karaoke skills, and the subject shifted back to Peyton.

"I can't believe he had the nerve to show up here."

"At least he isn't as bad as Jonathan," Jennifer replied.

My head cocked to the side. "What happened with Jonathan?"

Jennifer opened up about the abuse she had endured with her first serious relationship in college, and for years she couldn't bring herself ever to allow anyone else in, but when she met Laura, things changed. She helped her restore her confidence and realize that Jennifer was deserving of a good man, no matter what some douchebag told her years ago. Knowing that some man had put his hands on her made my stomach turn. She was fierce, and no one should ever take her shine away.

No longer did she need to put on that protective armor; she could finally be the real Jennifer, with all her hopes and dreams, her fears and insecurities. She didn't have to be anyone else with me. I liked her the way she was, and any man who couldn't see what a catch she was—well, they were blind.

I stood up slowly and brushed down my shirt, collecting the last of my composure. We stood in silence for a moment, and then I heard a soft chuckle. I looked over and saw Laura grinning at us knowingly. She had obviously been watching our interaction even when she was flirting with that guy but was too polite to interject. We shared a brief, knowing look, and then I turned back to Jennifer.

My voice wavered, and I looked around the room for a distraction. She glanced down at her watch, her lips pursed in a thin line. "Well, I think it's probably best we get going," I said.

She bit her lower lip before responding, "Yes, I suppose we should."

We said our goodbyes, maintaining a professional air. As we walked out of the bar, I glanced back at Jennifer one last time, who was smiling and laughing with Laura.

Tonight was amazing and getting to know her on a better level would indeed help our professional and personal relationship. But the problem was, I wished that the personal relationship could come first.

12

Jennifer

The throbbing in my head was like a hammer pounding against my temples. With a groan of discomfort, I quickly grabbed the bottle of Tylenol from my bedside table and felt the smooth, cool texture of the tablets as I swallowed a couple with a gulp of water. Being aware that I had to get ready for the day, I knew I mustn't be late. Today was Mr. Longford's last day at the office, and I knew it was going to be a bittersweet day.

Mr. Longford had been my boss for the past decade, and I had learned so much from him. He had always pushed me to do my best, and I had grown so much under his tutelage. I would miss him, but I also knew that he had earned his retirement and deserved to spend more time with his family.

With a heavy sigh, I heaved myself out of bed and shuffled to the bathroom to wash the grime and sweat of the night before. I dried off and threw on a shirt and pants, feeling more alive with each passing minute.

I quickly got dressed and headed to the office. I had ordered blueberry scones and coffee, Mr. Longford's favorite. It was going to be our last breakfast together, and I wanted it to be special. As I waited for the delivery, I thought about all the years I had spent with Mr. Longford.

I had seen a lot of changes. Mr. Longford had kept every single client of his over his reign at the firm. He had dedicated so much of his time and energy to the company, and I admired him for that.

When the delivery finally arrived, I took the food and coffee into his office and set it down on the table in the right corner, so we could enjoy without having the sun right in our faces. I was determined to show my appreciation for all the years Mr. Longford was my boss.

When Mr. Longford and Matt finally arrived, I welcomed them with a big smile and asked them to take a seat at the table. Mr. Longford was shocked that I remembered his favorite blueberry scones and just to appease him, I ate one with my coffee. Matt looked like he had a rough night.

It wasn't my business to keep track of how much he drank last night, but it was a hefty amount. Yet he stayed in control, didn't act inappropriate, and got home okay. What happened last night would stay in the back of my mind today.

The atmosphere was quite solemn in the office. I could tell that Mr. Longford was feeling a little emotional. As we finished eating, he thanked me for the delicious breakfast and for the wonderful memories.

Mr. Longford stood at the office window, hands clasped together behind his back. He had been standing in the same spot for a few minutes. Then with a look of childlike wonder on his face, he recounted the plans his wife had made for their first cruise together. "We're going on a seven-day cruise to Cozumel next week," he said. "Can you imagine? I've never been on a cruise before. I'm so excited." A broad, proud smile lit up his face.

I glanced over at Matt, who shared my incredulity. While we had grown used to Mr. Longford's enthusiasm, this was a different level of delight. He practically radiated it.

"My wife has always wanted to travel the world, and I told her she'd have to wait until I retired," he continued. "Now that I have, we decided a cruise was the perfect way to start. We plan to go all around the Caribbean and then maybe head out to Europe this fall." Mr. Longford looked out the window at the darkening sky, his expression distant and dreamy. "I can't wait," he said. "It's going to be an amazing adventure."

The workday went by in a blur. Paperwork and emails kept me busy, but I didn't want the day to end because that meant Mr. Longford would leave for good.

"We better go," Laura whispered. "People are gonna start showing up soon."

We moved the retirement party into one of the bigger rooms because some of his long-term clients wanted to come and celebrate with him today. Thankfully, we did because people were already showing up and with all the firm's employees too, the other room wouldn't have sufficed.

I placed the microphone on the podium and made sure everything was set up correctly when the hushed conversations come to an abrupt halt and all eyes were on me. Mr. Longford had arrived in the room, so I rushed back up to the podium.

"Ladies and gentlemen," I whispered, my voice shaking. "I'm so pleased to welcome you here today to honor Mr. Longford's many years of dedicated service to this firm."

The crowd erupted into applause, the sound reverberating through the room. I looked out at the sea of faces and could feel the love and admiration they had for the man they were here to honor.

"Mr. Longford has been part of this firm since its creation and has been an integral part of its success," I continued. "Without his vision, dedication, and hard work, none of what we have today would have been possible. He has been a mentor and a friend to many of us here and for that, we thank him."

There was a loud cheer from the audience and I took a step back, letting Mr. Longford step up.

He cleared his throat and looked out at the crowd. "I'm overwhelmed by the number of people here today," he began, his voice shaky with emotion. "Being part of this firm for so many years has been a great privilege. I've seen it grow from a little family business to what it is today, and it's been a substantial source of pride for me. Thank you to everyone here for all the hard work they have put in over the years to make this the success it is today. I also want to take a moment to thank my assistant, Jennifer. She's been an absolute rock and I don't know what I'd do without her."

The crowd burst into applause, and I could feel my cheeks burning with embarrassment. But I also felt a sense of pride that Mr. Longford was recognizing my hard work.

Mr. Longford thanked all the partners at the firm and then introduced the new partner, Matt. Matt raised his hand in the crowd and there was a round of applause.

The applause died down, and Mr. Longford stepped back up to the microphone. "It's been an absolute pleasure working with all of you, and I will miss our time together, but I know the firm is in excellent hands and will continue to thrive. So thank you, and I wish you all the best of luck."

The crowd cheered again, and I teared up as I watched Mr. Longford step away from the podium.

The sound of laughter and clapping came from the hallway. Matt was shaking hands with Mr. Longford's colleagues. When he saw us, he waved us over with a smile.

Everyone was happy for Mr. Longford, but we all knew it would never be the same. Despite my sadness, I couldn't help but smile as I watched Mr. Longford beam with pride. He deserved this moment, to be surrounded by the people who had worked with him for so many years.

When the party ended, it was time for us to say goodbye. I hugged Mr. Longford tightly and wished him the best.

"Keep in touch and send pictures when you go traveling," I said. He smiled and promised he would.

I watched Mr. Longford step into the elevator. His salt-and-pepper hair was slick against his scalp, his boots polished to a shine. He had been my mentor, my advisor, and my friend.

A lump rose in my throat as the elevator doors closed. I had to fight back tears. Laura saw the tears in my eyes and stepped closer to me, putting her arm around my shoulders. Despite the pain I felt, I smiled at her.

"It's going to be okay," she said. "Matt will be a great boss," she said. "And Mr. Longford deserves to retire."

I knew she was right, but it didn't make it any easier to watch him leave. I took a deep breath and reminded myself that we would always have the memories of working together. It may be an ending, but it was also a new beginning.

In all my years in New York City, Mr. Longford had been the one constant in my life, a friend, mentor, and confidant—someone I could turn to when things got tough. I didn't normally get attached to bosses, but he was like a father to me and to see him walk out of this building for the last time broke my heart.

Now it's time for the new boss, Matt, to live up to his legacy. Despite the sadness of having to say goodbye to my old boss, I had to admit that I was curious to see what Matt had in store for us. It was a new beginning, one that I was both nervous and excited to see where it would take us.

13
Matt

As Thanksgiving approached, it filled me with anxiety at the thought of spending it with Jennifer, and my nerves were churning. Jennifer and I had been strictly professional since that night at the bar and it felt like there was a wall between us—a wall that made sense for both of our careers. Even so, her lavender perfume lingered in my mind, and as each moment passed, I wished I'd met her before I started working at the firm.

I ventured into the grocery store, my senses assaulted by the sweet and spicy scents of the holiday season. I grabbed a freshly baked pumpkin pie, its sweet custard oozing from the buttery crust. Red or white wine? They seemed to like red, so I threw one in my shopping basket. My mother taught me never to show up to a gathering empty-handed. A little liquid courage wouldn't hurt either.

I hugged my long wool coat tight around me as I trudged through the freshly fallen snow, feeling the icy chill of a day in New York City. The thought of missing out on Mom's annual holiday celebration weighed heavily on my mind as I walked. The wind whipped through the buildings, blasting gusts onto my skin. Even though I knew my mom understood why I couldn't make it home for the holiday, I still felt guilty. New York City was a stark contrast to the small town where I grew up, but at least I had somewhere to go when things seemed lonely during this holiday.

The air calmed as I arrived at Jennifer's apartment building and I paused outside. It was a nondescript building on the Upper East Side. Taking a deep breath to steady my nerves, I opened the front door and headed into the elevator. After arriving on her floor and finding her apartment, I lifted my fist and rapped on the door. Jennifer opened it with a radiant smile, her face framed by her brown locks and bright-blue eyes. She was dressed in a warm rust-colored sweater dress, her long legs finished with edgy black thigh-high boots with a small heel. Her eyebrows rose slightly in surprise at seeing me, her gaze flickering between the pumpkin pie and the bottle of wine before settling back into an understanding smile as she welcomed me in.

"You didn't have to bring anything," she said, her voice soft and a slight smile tugging at the corners of her lips.

I shrugged, my hands growing clammy as I looked down at pie and wine tucked into my arm. "My mom taught me better than that."

Jennifer stepped aside and opened the door wider. "Come in," she said, gesturing with a wave of her hand.

Stepping into the apartment, it was small and cozy. The savory smell of something cooking in the kitchen was an immediate comfort. I looked around, taking in the photographs on the walls—a smiling family at the beach, children playing in a field, and a newlywed couple embracing in front of a waterfall.

"I'm glad you could make it. There will be plenty of food. Laura is going a bit overboard. She's in the kitchen," Jennifer said, motioning to the hallway. "We are still cooking, but you can put those on the counter."

I stepped into Laura's kitchen and was surprised by how tidy it was. Not a single dish remained in the sink; the counters were spotless, and the smell of lemon cleaner lingered in the air. I smiled as I noticed all the details of her organization—her cooking utensils hung from hooks on one wall, pans separated by size on another, and she labeled all the cabinets with hand-drawn signs. This was not just a house to her, but a home. I smiled. It was clear to see that the same organizational skills she used at work translated perfectly into her home life.

Jennifer and I huddled around the sink, potatoes falling into the strainer from the boiling water. We sprinkled in heaps of butter and sour cream, topped with diced onion and bell pepper for a little color. We whisked it all together as we compared notes on our favorite recipes. Laura moved around the kitchen with an ease that suggested she had done this many times before. She worked quickly to mix the stuffing—tearing up bits of stray onion and celery stalks by hand, letting each ingredient simmer in its own juices before adding her special blend of spices. The sweet aroma of roasted turkey wafted through the air as the three of us made a magnificent Thanksgiving feast.

Laura told us about the time she and her family spent Thanksgiving with her grandmother in Mexico, while Jennifer recounted her favorite childhood Thanksgiving memory. We didn't just fix dinner; we crafted a moment, one that felt both intimate and comforting. By the time the dinner was ready, I had almost forgotten how much I had dreaded the evening. We put the finishing touches on dinner and the three of us stood back to admire our work.

We finally took our seats at the dinner table with the aroma of the freshly cooked food intoxicating us, and soon plates were piled high with the most delicious dishes I had ever tasted. Steam was rising from the succulent meats and vegetables, and the spices and herbs melded together to create a truly unique flavor. The conversation flowed freely. We shared stories about all the places we had visited and the hilarious experiences we'd each had in New York City. The entire room brightened as everyone's faces lit up with excitement and joy. Even the littlest details were fodder for laughter, making it a night to remember. They made me feel comfortable and at ease.

"Have you ever played Cards Against Humanity before?" Laura asked.

I shook my head. "Can't say I have."

She grabbed it off a shelf and plopped it onto the table, almost spilling my glass of wine. Laura explained the rules of the game while she was shuffling the white cards and gave us each ten. They did not know how badly I sucked at card games.

"So, whoever's turn it is to read the black card, the other two pick one of their white cards that fits the best."

After picking up my white cards, I almost doubled over laughing. These were dumb. Laura read the black card. "Having problems with blank, try blank. So for this one, you choose two white cards."

I sorted through my cards and put my two down. Jennifer looked like she was struggling. "Oh, come on, it can't be any worse than mine."

She laughed and put down two cards.

Laura picked up our two sets. "Having problems with your pet, try peanut butter." She looked straight at Jennifer. "Having problems with the hiccups, try shutting up."

Wasn't this supposed to be funny? Maybe we should play a different game, but I was just a guest. So, instead, I kept sipping my wine and playing along. The longer we played, the funnier things got.

Jennifer read the black card: *The year is 2150. The president is____*. I looked at my cards and put one down. These are ridiculous. She read out loud the cards we played.

The president is eating cat food and binging Law and Order SVU. *The president is returning all its money to the rightful owner, Jeff Bezos.* Literally neither of them made sense, but whatever. I guess that was the point of the game. She picked my cards because apparently she was not a Jeff Bezos fan, and I couldn't blame her. For the next two hours, we played this game, and by the end, they crowned me the winner.

I thanked Jennifer and Laura for the food, wine, and conversation before heading out into the night. It had been a while since I last enjoyed myself so much. As I walked home, my mind wandered back to the Cards Against Humanity game we had played.

We had all laughed hysterically at some answers that were read out loud, but it wasn't just about the funny answers; there was something else as well. We were connecting on a deeper level than we usually did and it made me realize how much I needed this kind of interaction.

The night air felt like a refreshing change from my usual routine and as I walked, I made a mental note to take more time for myself in the future. As soon as I arrived home, I quickly changed into my pajamas before snuggling up in bed with a book.

Although I was tired, my mind was still buzzing from all of tonight's events. It was amazing how one evening could change things —even if it was only temporary.

14
Jennifer

My desk was organized, my laptop open with a half-finished spreadsheet in front of me. The air smelled of freshly brewed coffee, the slightly bitter aroma of the java beans mixing with the scent of my colleagues' perfumes. I was just getting into the groove of my workday when Laura stumbled over, her face glowing. I could tell she had a good morning; her eyes were sparkling. She was wearing her favorite sweater, a soft pink number with little pearls adorning its neckline. She had never one to miss an opportunity to dress up, and she had put special thought into her outfit. Before I could even say hello, she was already spilling her plans for the holidays.

"So I've been thinking about what I'm going to do for Christmas this year and I've decided I'm going to go back to New Hampshire to be with my parents," she said. "My parents still have the old house in the countryside, and I'm sure they'd love to have me come home and spend a few days with them. I'm so excited," she said, her enthusiasm apparent.

As Laura continued to talk about her plans, I couldn't help but be jealous. Here I was, stuck in the city for yet another holiday season, while she was able to go back home and spend some quality time with her family. I wanted to do that too, to go back home and spend a few days with my parents, just like she was. But I made the tough decision to stay in New York this year.

My mom had been on my case about throwing my life away, staying with the firm this long. She thought my job was useless and when they let me go, I wouldn't be able to find another job. Why didn't she have any faith in me? So instead of going home and listening to that for a few days, *New York City, here I stay.*

Laura seemed to sense my envy and stopped talking. She smiled and put her hand on my shoulder. "Hey, why don't you come with me?" she suggested. "My parents would love to have you, too. And you know they'll treat you like family. It'll be so much fun."

I couldn't believe she was offering me the chance to join her. "That's okay. Your parents don't like me that much and if I wanted peering eyes on me, I'd just go home to my own family."

We sat there for a few moments, discussing the details of her trip. She knew her parents didn't care for me, which I still for the life of me didn't know why. They came into the city three years ago for the holiday, and they expressed concern for their daughter. They thought I was the bad influence. It made me laugh because if anyone knew Laura, they would agree that it was the other way around.

She showed me pictures of the White Mountains and then bragged about how she was probably going to gain so much weight being out there because her mother loved to cook.

Tears welled up in my eyes as I listened to Laura talk about all the wonderful things she'd get to experience together. A part of me was frustrated because this was the time of year that made me miss my family the most, but it wasn't worth the soul-crushing conversations. What child wanted to hear their parents tell them how disappointed they were?

When my mother called to inquire if I was coming home, I said no, and she didn't even try to convince to go. That broke my heart even more. I'd much rather just stay in the city, on the couch, curled up with a good book and some wine. At least then I knew my holiday wouldn't be spent crying.

Matt walked out and his eyes locked on mine. "Sorry to interrupt, but you shouldn't have to be alone during the holidays. This might be totally overstepping, but Amesbury is beautiful this time of year."

"Amesbury? Like your hometown?" Was he proposing what I thought?

"Yeah, I am going back to visit my mother and it's a great getaway. The lodge will be the perfect place for your binge-reading sessions. They even have a fireplace."

Laura didn't even give me a chance to reply. "Yes, she'd love to." My eyes flicked to hers. "She needs to get out of this city and enjoy her holidays. Being cooped up in her apartment is no way to spend Christmas."

Laura excused herself now, and I couldn't help but smile. She knew exactly what she was doing, and she would hear about it from me later.

"Why don't you come into my office and we can get a flight booked for you," Matt said.

I followed behind him but did not sit down once inside. We had been very good about keeping things professional since the bar, and even though Amesbury sounded wonderful, I wondered if this was a mistake.

"Are you sure this is okay? I mean…" I didn't lift my eyes. The burn on my skin told me he was looking my way.

"Don't worry, I will not cross that line. You made it clear, but that doesn't mean you should have to sit at home when you could enjoy yourself."

Wait? I made it clear? So did that mean he wanted to be more than just colleagues? This man was sending me too many mixed signals, and it was hard to keep up.

"So, the best flight would be the first one out. It'll get us to Missoula in time to get one of the earlier buses to Amesbury. I'll be able to get you settled in at the lodge before I have to go get my mom in Sikita."

So, now we were staying in the same place? As much as everything in me yelled to say *no*, I nodded. "That'll be perfect."

So now, instead of curling up on my couch, I would be stuck in a small town in a lodge with my hot boss. What could go wrong?

15
Matt

Okay, so maybe it wasn't the smartest idea to invite the assistant I had a crush on to my small hometown for Christmas, but what else was I supposed to do? When I asked her to come stay with me for the holidays, my heart was pounding in my chest. Even though I had a crush on her, this felt like a huge mistake. What if it ruined our friendship? But even as doubt reigned in my mind, I knew I couldn't leave her alone in the city. She had invited me to Thanksgiving, and now it was time for me to do the same. We would just have to prove that adults could behave.

I booked the first flight out of New York City so we could make it to Missoula in time to take a bus to Amesbury. We could take a cab, but it would cost a fortune. Jennifer was going to love the scenic route it took from the airport to my town.

It had been three weeks since I took over for Mr. Longford permanently, and chaos ensued. Clients were nervous about letting someone else take their cases. I have had to be more hands-on and accommodate their worries, which made me work longer hours. Being a good boss, I didn't require Jennifer to stay past six. Just because I had to stay didn't mean she should have to. I wasn't Mr. Curran.

It was a few minutes past seven when I closed out of my email and headed over to the boardroom. The sun was dipping closer to the horizon, casting its last rays of orange light on the city. A chill ran through me as I thought about my upcoming trip with Jennifer. The day after tomorrow, Jennifer and I would be leaving to spend a week in Amesbury. It would be interesting to see how this went.

I navigated the throng of people on the streets of New York City until I arrived at the dive bar. Music blared from speakers in the corners and colorful strings of multicolored Christmas lights hung from the ceiling. A group of men crowded around a pool table in one corner while others chatted in clusters around the room. The door opened and closed as new guests came and went. I ordered a draft beer and took a seat near the big-screen TV, watching unnoticed as the other patrons laughed and clanked their glasses together. I sipped my beer slowly and let the worries of the day fade away.

I felt a light tap on my shoulder, and when I spun around, I saw Jennifer. She smiled at me sheepishly, her hair pulled back and wearing the same designer dress from the office. "Guess you had the same idea, huh?"

She smiled softly, her lips curling at the corners. "Work has been so hectic these last few weeks," she said with a sigh. "I'm here to meet Laura, but she's running late... again." She took a sip of her wine and set it back on the bar.

I nodded. "Yeah, Mr. Curran sure keeps her busy." I cleared my throat, feeling an uncomfortable itch crawl up it. "At least you have me as a reprieve, right?" I tried to laugh, but it came out sounding forced even to my own ears.

She motioned to the bartender for another glass of wine. "Another glass, Helen," she said.

She slid onto the barstool next to me, and her intoxicating sweet perfume filled my nostrils. I felt my heart racing as I tried to avoid her gaze while adjusting myself in my seat, my cheeks burning. "So," I stammered nervously, "I don't want you to think..." I trailed off when my voice quivered, not sure how to phrase what I wanted to say without sounding too forward. "The trip to Amesbury is purely so you can get away from here if you want; there is no pressure on you to join us for Christmas or anything else. If you'd rather hole up at the lodge by yourself, that's totally fine." I swallowed hard and waited for her response.

With a trembling hand, she wrapped her slender fingers around the wineglass, condensation pooling at the base, and tilted it to her lips. As she swallowed, her eyes twinkled, and she leaned in closer. "I've been stalking your town online," she confessed. "You have one of those quaint town squares, like something out of a fairy tale or a Hallmark movie." Her eyes lit up as she described the main street with its old-fashioned shops and winding cobblestone paths.

It warmed my heart to see her excited about the trip. "It's not for everyone but for those of us who can appreciate a rustic main street, it's one of a kind."

A man's voice rang out through the otherwise silent atmosphere of the bar, his words dripping with venom. I turned to see Jennifer's ex-boyfriend Peyton, who had obviously had too much to drink, standing in the doorway with a menacing glare and accusing scowl. He jabbed an unsteady finger in my direction.

"You know this place only because I told you about it. Take your new boyfriend somewhere else," he spat bitterly.

My hands balled into tight fists as my jaw clenched. I had always kept my cool, but I was getting angrier by the second. A gentleman was trying to keep Jennifer from patronizing the pub because he thought she didn't belong there. "You think you can just show up here and push her around?" I said, my voice hard as steel. "She's welcome anywhere she pleases, and you'd do well not forgetting that."

"You think you are a tough guy? She's not worth it. You'll find out soon enough," the ex-boyfriend said.

The air was heavy with tension as the ex-boyfriend's words echoed through the bar. I could feel my rage boiling beneath my skin and before I knew it, I had lunged forward and landed a powerful punch to his face. The force of the impact sent him reeling back, colliding into the tables behind him and crumpling to the ground. The bartender, Helen, let out a laugh as she shook her head while wiping down the counter. "Finally, someone got him to shut up," she said with a smirk, glancing my way. "Don't worry about it, Jen. He had it coming."

Two of his friends grabbed him by the arms and yanked him off the floor. His eyes darted around the room, avoiding my gaze. The tension in the air was palpable as they dragged him out without saying a word. They obviously knew he was in the wrong.

Jennifer crossed her arms and furrowed her brow, shaking her head. "You didn't need to step in," she said.

I exhaled and rubbed the back of my neck. "He needs to learn that he can't talk to you like that—or anybody, for that matter." Even as I spoke, I clenched my fists at my sides.

As she sat back down, her hand fell to mine with a soft thud. She grabbed it gently and examined the wound on my knuckles—a deep cut caused by hitting one of his teeth. "You should put some ice on that before it swells. Don't think you want your mother to see that."

"On the contrary," I replied, a faint smile playing on my lips. "She was the one who taught me to stand up for women. She would probably give me a high five."

She chuckled, beginning to wrap a napkin around my injured hand as if she had done this many times before. She raised her other hand in the air to get the bartender's attention. "Can we get some ice for his hand, please?"

I longed to feel her body against mine, her lips brushing lightly against my own. I wanted to tell her she had a special place in my heart and show her how much I valued her, but then the wall was back up—professionalism. Something inside me broke, and my heart was telling me to be patient.

16
Jennifer

Hesitance and apprehension flowed through me at the thought of spending a week in Matt's hometown. On one hand, I wanted to stay out of his way and explore the little town and do my thing. I knew how much Matt missed his mother since moving to New York City, so I didn't want to take over their holiday together. I felt like I was stuck between two mindsets, not sure which path to take. I looked forward to exploring the unfamiliar streets and discovering new places.

When Matt told us he was planning a trip back to his hometown, I was excited for him. We had heard so much about it and the thought of being close to his family and reconnecting with his childhood home seemed like a dream come true. At the same time, I was filled with apprehension about spending an entire week in such close quarters with Matt. Would we get along? Would things go smoothly? All these thoughts raced through my mind as I tried to prepare for the upcoming visit.

I felt like an intruder in Matt's family affairs. Nevertheless, I wanted to make the most of it, to explore the small town and find something to keep myself from feeling like an outsider. Yet I found myself conflicted as I wanted to give Matt the space he needed to reconnect with his loved ones, and selfishly, I also hoped that maybe he'd be seeking some kind of solace in my presence, too. As much as I tried to remind myself that this getaway was for Matt and his mother, deep down, I knew I was still clinging to a shred of hope—that somehow there would be a place for me here, too.

I tried to concentrate on my task, but the words of Laura's optimism kept echoing in my head. She lay sprawled across my bed, seemingly oblivious to the fact that I was busy packing even though she spoke with such certainty about me finding a love in this small town. In my experience, holidays only brought disappointments.

"You can't get mad at me. That's what happens in small towns over the holidays."

There was uncertainty in my eyes and I tried to lighten the mood with an old classic, and said, "Said every single Hallmark Christmas movie ever!"

Reality struck. This was real life, and there was no assurance that anything between us would last longer than our weeklong escape. Though I wanted to be hopeful and optimistic, I knew all too well that sometimes this kind of thing just doesn't work out. The only thing that mattered was that I had an amazing time.

I sifted through my closets for sweaters, gloves, beanies, and a warm coat. I mentally prepared myself. Laura's words echoed in my head. What if this trip ends with Matt and me together? Would that be so bad? She acted like we were going to come back married, and I reminded her we were going to Montana, not Vegas.

I packed my warmest clothes for the trip, knowing it would be chilly in Matt's hometown. I had never been to a place like this before and wasn't sure what to expect. Laura seemed to think we were going to come back married, but we weren't going to Vegas. I carefully folded my thick sweaters and wool scarves into my suitcase. This would be the first time I left the city since moving here.

"You and Matt are meant to be together." She pressed her lips tight as she continued. "This could be the trip you need to figure it out, away from all the stress and chaos of work." Her eyebrows wiggled, emphasizing her point.

I carefully folded the last shirt and packed it, the smell of my grandmother's old leather suitcase filling my nose, then solemnly secured the locks. No matter what happened on this trip, I knew it was going to be an experience that would stay with me for a lifetime. I heaved it off the bed and carried it across the room to the door. What was I going to find on this trip? Joy or sorrow? Success or failure?

Laura put her hands on her hips, pulling up the straps of her dress and letting out an exaggerated sigh. "Seriously, stop all the anxiety. You're single, and you get to spend the next week with a handsome man for Christmas. Stop acting like you're headed off to prison."

I rolled my eyes and took one last look around the apartment, making sure I hadn't missed anything. "Alright," I said. "Chill. It's all your expectations that are giving me jitters. Just let me have a good time... Can't that be it?" I demanded, my arms crossed over my chest.

"Yeah, whatever, Mrs. Kneeland," Laura said with an exaggerated eye roll.

I rolled my eyes and grabbed my suitcase off the floor. My phone vibrated, signaling that the cab I had ordered was waiting out front. Laura, who had to board her flight an hour after mine, grabbed her suitcase and followed me out the door.

The streets outside the cab window were a blur of colored lights and decorations. I could make out festive wreaths adorning shop windows, glistening trees standing proudly on street corners, and brightly colored lights twinkling in the windows of shops.

As we arrived at the airport, she gave me an encouraging squeeze, her warm smile radiating confidence. I took a deep breath, feeling the butterflies in my stomach flutter as she headed off to get her boarding pass. I watched her go, taking in her determined stride and the way her long hair cascaded down her back. Gathering my courage, I followed suit, winding through the throngs of travelers until I reached Delta Airlines.

I shifted my weight from one foot to the other, fidgeting with the straps of my backpack. My stomach twisted into knots as I wondered if Matt and I would get along outside of work. What if this whole trip turned out to be a total disaster? The thought made me want to turn around and walk back home. Would we have anything to talk about over dinner? What if there were long awkward silences? But as Matt emerged from the cab and his eyes met mine, a smile spreading across his face, full of warmth and promise, my nerves were calmed. This could very well be a life-changing week after all.

He came right up to me. "I already checked us in, so let's drop our bags off with TSA and go through security."

My gaze lingered on him as I took in his new look—tight black jeans, a leather jacket, and scuffed combat boots. He was usually all buttoned-up at the office, but there was something different now. He had a rebellious edge that I hadn't noticed before and it made my heart skip a beat. I wondered if this was how he usually looked outside of the office, a far cry from the pressed slacks and crisp white shirts he preferred for work.

Maybe there was more to him... It was the right week to find out.

17

Matt

The gate was teeming with people, and the electronic board overhead said we should be boarding soon. I leaned closer to her, our shoulders touching as I took in the waft of her shampoo. She deftly maneuvered a finger across the glowing screen of her phone.

"Planning something?" I asked.

"Just looking at a few places in Amesbury," she said without looking up.

She was such a planner, and I loved that about her. Maybe I could get her to change her mind about crossing the professional threshold while we were there. Her long black joggers were tucked into her shoes, and her oversized cream sweater hugged her slim frame. Her chocolate-brown hair, tied up in a knot, accented her bright-blue eyes. Despite this, her beauty still shone through. Could I persuade her to take that risk?

A cheery female voice came through the speakers, announcing the beginning of boarding for Delta Airlines Flight 2122 to Minneapolis. I stood up, and she peered at me inquisitively. "What are you doing?"

"They're boarding," I said with a smile. "First class."

She gaped as realization dawned on her. Taking my hand, we made our way to the queue for first-class passengers.

The smiling ticket agent glanced at our phones, her eyes widening when she saw the upgrade to first class. She tapped away on the keyboard, and soon we were on our way down the jet bridge and into the cabin of comfort. Even with only three hours in the air, I was grateful for the extra leg room and plush seats that made settling in easy. The disappointment of not having a direct flight to Missoula faded away.

She shrugged as she pulled her sweater off, revealing a crisp black shirt with delicate silver buttons running up the front. Her eyes sparkled when the light from the window filtered through, casting a gentle glow on her porcelain skin. "You really didn't have to do this," she said.

"It wasn't that much extra, and you get free drinks," I replied, admiring how beautiful she looked in the soft light. "Plus, our bags were free."

As the flight attendants began their rehearsed safety demonstration, my eyes flickered to Jennifer. With each word they spoke, the blood was pounding my ears. This trip could make or break us. If only I had met her before the firm; we could have pursued each other without inhibition. But now, with so much to lose, it would take everything in me to make a move.

The drone of the engine pulling away from the gate was hypnotic and I got lost in thought again. But as our eyes locked for a moment, she was thinking the same thing. The possibilities stretched out before us like an endless road.

We both turned away, but not before sharing one last glance—a silent agreement that anything could happen on this journey.

Peyton and that other guy had hurt her so deeply, leaving her scared to be vulnerable again. But as I looked at her, all I wanted was for her light to shine brighter than ever before. On the one hand, I wanted to protect her, keep her safe. On the other, I wanted nothing more than for her to take big risks and find the courage to blossom.

The plane lurched forward, engines roaring as it raced down the runway. Jennifer squeezed my hand, her eyes wide with anticipation. I looked out the window, watching fields and buildings slowly shrink beneath us. The cabin lights flickered off, and soon we were suspended in a sky of pure blue. A thrill rose inside me. It was too late to turn back now—we were on our way. As the plane leveled off, the cabin lights came back on and flight attendants started pushing carts down the aisle with trays full of drinks. I ordered some red wine, but Jennifer shook her head.

A brilliant sun cast orange and yellow glows through the plane's window, illuminating my companion's face with a soft angelic light. As I looked into her eyes, I could feel the warmth of our tightly clasped hands resonating between us. Taking a sip from my cup, I said, "You're going to love it there." Her lips curled upward ever so slightly in a Mona Lisa-like smile as we sat contentedly, not needing words to be spoken between us as the plane flew on.

The plane touched down in Minneapolis with a jolt, and Jennifer and I hurried along with the other passengers to our connecting flight. We found our seats and settled in just as the engines whirred to life. Jennifer leaned against me, her eyes fluttering shut almost instantly. She smiled into my shoulder, her soft breaths tickling my skin. For the next three hours, I watched my movie on mute while Jennifer slept peacefully beside me.

As the plane began its descent, a gentle nudge woke Jennifer from her slumber. She reached up to wipe her mouth, but stopped short when she saw the wet spot on my shoulder. "Oh God, was I drooling?" she asked.

Amused, I said, "It's not a big deal. Happens all the time."

She laughed and leaned back in her seat, stretching her arms above her head. We chatted about potential shopping destinations while we waited for our gate to open.

"Laura said you liked to read. Caffeinated Bliss is just down the street from the lodge with stacks of books and all sorts of used gems too. And don't forget to pick up a cupcake from Frosted! I can you tell firsthand that it's some of the most delicious cupcakes in town."

We stepped off the plane and onto the jet bridge, stretching our legs for the first time in hours. As our eyes adjusted to the bright lights of the terminal, we heard cheerful voices welcoming us to our destination. We followed the signs to baggage claim through a throng of passengers eagerly awaiting their luggage.

We grabbed our suitcases and shuffled out to the shuttle bus. We were among the first in line, so we chose a seat at the very back of the vehicle, knowing it would be ours until Amesbury. As we settled into our seats and watched other travelers get on board, anticipation swelled. As the engine roared to life, we watched the city fade away in a blur.

Jennifer gazed out the window, mesmerized by the distant hills and valleys that seemed to stretch on forever as well as the lush trees and crystal-clear mountain streams. She sighed as she took in the wide-open space.

I fondly remembered the camping trips I used to take with my dad. "This is where I got my passion for hiking with my dad. Although, I don't have much time for it nowadays, especially being in New York City where it's not really an option."

She looked up at me through her lashes. "You're so lucky to have had a close bond with your dad."

I hated the fact that she was distant from her family, so unlike my own. I listened as she talked about her father spending all his time at work and when he was home, he would just sit in his old brown recliner watching sports on the television.

Her shoulders slumped in defeat as she recounted all the reasons to stay away from her family home over the holidays. My heart broke. Being stuck in the same room, watching her parents bicker like a tennis match or having to sit at the dinner table and listen to their disapproval of her chosen career path—too often the conversation ended with the suggestion that she move back home. A single tear rolled down her cheek as she shook her head and muttered. "It would be more of a burden than a vacation."

I put my arm around her, feeling the warmth of her body against mine. She felt so small and fragile. "I hate that for you," I whispered.

She asked me about my mom, and I could feel a lump forming in my throat. I cleared it and began, "Born and raised in Amesbury, she used to work at the Hideout diner until she got sick. She and my father met in high school and were together until he passed a couple of years ago." The conversation was quickly turning too dark, so I tried to lighten the mood by pointing out the mountains in the distance. "Look at the mountains," I said, gesturing with my free arm.

The majestic peaks of Glacier National Park towered above us, their summits adorned with a thick white blanket of snow. As we drove down the winding mountain roads, I could see the infinite meadows stretching ahead into the horizon, a patchwork of greens, browns, and grays. Jennifer leaned out the window and breathed in deeply, her eyes widening in wonder at the beauty surrounding us. Her face lit up with surprise and delight as we rode along, and that simple joy made me smile.

The shuttle bus rolled to a stop, and the doors opened with a loud hiss. A wave of cold air accompanied a cloud of exhaust from its tailpipe, sending a chill through the passengers. We stepped out into the unforgiving winter weather and onto the slushy street. The buildings and shops lined the street. Adorned with thin layers of snow, the sidewalks were littered with cigarette butts. On one corner, an older gentleman was gathering them up one by one using a handheld contraption, wearing an orange vest for visibility.

Stretching my neck, I counted the number of people ahead of me in line and sighed with resignation. Surrounding us were brightly painted storefronts, decorated with Christmas twinkle lights that shone with a festive allure. A few steps ahead of me, Jennifer spun around, her eyes wide with delight. "I can't believe I'm staying here!" she exclaimed as she reached out to touch one of the light strings.

After getting our bags, we shuffled down Main Street. An old

Ford truck sat outside Woodall's car repair, its hood propped open and a pair of oil-stained hands reaching into the engine. The windows of the vintage clothing store were filled with mannequins wearing colorful hats and flowing skirts. But then, the smell of roasted coffee beans filled the air when we passed the café. We finally reached the three-story cabin-style building at the end of the block.

Jennifer's eyes took in the property. "This place is just like a Hallmark movie... I can't believe you grew up here."

There was a lot about me she didn't know, but this trip could be the key to unlocking it all.

18
Jennifer

Amesbury was nestled in the rolling hills of Montana, its streets lined with old brick buildings and quaint Victorian homes. It was a picturesque oasis tucked away. Everywhere I looked, there was something new and delightful to see. The sky was a crisp winter blue, and the snow was piled high in the streets, the snowflakes shimmering in the sunlight. The quaint shops had festive wreaths; the bakery was adorned with strings of twinkling lights, and the streets were alive with people bustling about and spreading holiday cheer.

The Sterling Lodge was an aged Alpine-style building blanketed in a fresh layer of snow. Colorful icicle lights twinkled around the porch, and a welcome wreath hung from the door. I inhaled a sharp breath of chilly air as I opened the door, Matt close behind me, and my heart thrummed.

I stepped into the lodge, and a blast of warmth enveloped me. The room was large with high ceilings, and near the entrance was a fireplace lit with blazing orange and yellow flames. Around it, several brown leather sofas were arranged, surrounded by antler wall decorations. At the front desk, a woman with thin gray hair pulled back in a tight bun, with thick glasses perched on the bridge of her nose, her fingers rhythmically pounding against the keys of the computer until she noticed us. She then rounded the corner of the desk, her arms opened wide, ready for a hug, which was given to Matt before we were welcomed to the lodge.

"Jennifer, this is one of my mother's friends, Carina. She owns the place," Matt said, gesturing toward the woman.

Carina hugged him with enthusiasm. "I can't believe you're back! And for Christmas... how's your mama doing?"

Matt smiled, his brown eyes brightening. "It's nice to see you, too. Once I get Jennifer here settled, I'll be heading to get her."

"How wonderful," Carina said, clasping her hands together in delight.

She walked back around the counter, a huge imposing desk that seemed to swallow up the back side of the lobby, with two wooden chairs on either side and a coatrack with a cascade of hooks in the far corner. Carina handed him two keys. "Room 212 and 213. Let me know if you need anything at all."

Matt flashed a wide grin and grabbed my bag, taking the stairs two at a time. As he ascended the stairwell, I followed him up to room 212, where he gently set my belongings on the floor. "This is your room. I'm gonna put my stuff away and then head over to Sikita to grab my mom. You have my number if you need anything."

I nodded my thanks, opened the door, and stepped inside. The bright sunshine streaming through the window illuminated a cozy king-sized bed, its deep-blue comforter rumpled invitingly. I went to the window and pulled back the sheer curtains to reveal a stunning view of main street—perfect for watching the sun set over the town below.

I unzipped my bag and unpacked my belongings, placing them neatly in the wooden chest of drawers. After stretching my legs from the bus ride, it was time to explore the town. I fumbled for my phone.

Me: Made it. I'll send you pics. This place is as cute as you thought.

She would be so jealous of the snow-blanketed landscape below.

Anyone knew her obsession with Hallmark movies year-round, and this was something she would gaga for in real life. So with a snap of my camera to show the view from my room, three little dots appeared on the screen.

Laura: You have to be kidding me! Maybe I should ditch my parents and join you and Matt. =)

I rolled my eyes and slipped the phone and room key into my back pocket before hefting my backpack onto my shoulders. With a sense of excited anticipation, I descended the stairs and stepped out into the cold winter air. The snow was heavy, providing a soft cushion for each step as I breathed in deeply with delight. Ready for adventure, I marched forward.

My first destination was a small café bookstore. It looked like an older building that used to be a small bank and was converted. As I stepped inside, I was hit with the pleasant aroma of freshly ground coffee and warm pastries. The café was bustling with locals, everyone chatting and laughing over books. I chose a table by the window and looked out at the snow-covered streets, feeling the warmth of the fire radiating from behind me.

This place reminded me of Coffee Chaos because of the spaced-out bistro tables. They were almost the exact same tables. The Christmas tree sat right in the corner by the front door, making it the first thing you noticed when you walked in, giving it just that extra oomph of Christmas vibe.

The walls of the cozy bookstore were lined with bookshelves, which, during the holiday season, were elaborately decorated with twinkling lights and hearty evergreen garland. The shelves overflowed with books of all shapes and sizes from floor to ceiling, and in the back of the shop was a small counter where two men were busy making drinks for customers.

I scanned the bookshelves of the small café, patiently waiting for my turn in line. I spotted Amy Stephens' newest novel and my heart raced with excitement. Sparkling pink and teal lettering adorned the cover, declaring a romantic comedy involving a precious pup—it was perfect. Eagerly, I snatched it off the shelf and held it close to my chest like a priceless treasure as I approached the counter. *I'm so in! Take my money.*

The line snaked around the bookshop, and I was taken in by the atmosphere: conversations about books, debates about new authors. I opened the book, flipping through the pages of her creative prose. Every sentence was carefully crafted with metaphors and clever references. She knew exactly what kind of story to tell and how to make it come alive with words. It was like she had reached into my head and pulled it out of my wild imagination. A warm grin spread across my face as I took in each witty line. I had read every single one of her books. None disappointed! There was something about her writing that spoke directly to my heart, like she was tapping into my innermost thoughts. This was going to be perfect.

The counter was decorated with a beautiful festive display of cookies, small cakes, and other treats. The drinks menu was filled with delicious hot beverages, and I couldn't help but smile as I saw the Christmas-themed drinks like the Candy Cane Latte and the Gingerbread Mocha. Sold! Mocha was my favorite, and this was the place to try something new.

"Next!" the man shouted from behind the counter, his voice echoing off the tiled walls. At the sound of his gruff demand, I looked up. He was tall, with broad shoulders and a chiseled jawline that reminded me of one of the hunks in that romantic comedy Laura and I watched last year. He wore a red flannel shirt tucked into dark jeans. Steel-toed combat boots peeked out from beneath the hem of his jeans. The tight fit of his clothes revealed a lithe but powerful build. His name tag identified him as Cole.

"I'll take a mocha, hot please," I managed to squeak out, feeling my face flush with heat.

"That'll be four dollars," the man said in a deep rumble, his large calloused hand extended to collect the five-dollar bill. His eyes flicked over my outfit. "I don't think I've seen you around here before."

"Nope, brand new. Just checked into the lodge up the road." I glanced around his store, taking in all of its charming details. "Can't wait to see what all you have here."

"Do you intend on paying for that?" he asked sternly, pointing to the book clutched in my hand.

My palm hit my forehead in embarrassment. "Oh my God, of course. Here." I handed him another twenty-dollar bill and motioned for him to keep the change. His face softened as he took it from me and immediately bellowed out, "Next!"

Okay, that was my cue to get the heck out of his way so he could tend to more customers. Message received. He must be the broody type.

As I waited for my drink to be ready, I opened my book and nestled back into the armchair. The pages depicted a romantic scene in a park, where two characters were slowly falling in love as they watched their dogs play together in the sunshine.

"Gingerbread Mocha!" the man yelled, and I made my way up to the counter to grab it and his eyes peered at me. Maybe they didn't like outsiders. Hmm...

The first sip of coffee was always the best, and it didn't disappoint. Once again, another small store beat Starbucks by a long shot. As I made my way out of the store, I smiled to myself, knowing I would probably be back tomorrow to get another book.

19
Matt

My mother grinned from ear to ear as she took a few steps out into the sun. She looked very much like the woman I remembered. Her hair was still the same silver white, cascading down her back, and her eyes still held the same glimmer of mischief that had captivated me since I was a child.

Her eyes sparkled and her lips curled into a wide grin as we walked toward the car. She clapped her hands in joy, the wrinkles on her face deepening. A warmth filled me, knowing how lucky I was to give my mother the Christmas outside of that place that she deserved.

I had pulled the car up to the nursing home entrance and now I loaded my mother's bag into the back seat. I could feel the anticipation rising in my chest as I opened her door and helped her carefully settle in the passenger seat. I started the engine, relishing the low rumble that echoed from the exhaust. By this time, my mother had closed her eyes and was happily swaying her head to the soft melody coming from the car radio. The sun was shining, casting glistening rays of warmth on blankets of white on the ground as we drove away.

We drove for an hour, taking the more scenic route out of Sikita. The sun was making her skin glow, and she sang along to the songs on the radio. Every time I looked over, she had a smile on her face. This was a breakout that she desperately needed. Her smile only got bigger with each passing mile.

The nurses in the nursing home kindly warned me about what to expect when I took care of my mother over the holidays. The memories of her doctor's appointment when she received her diagnosis was still fresh in my mind, and I remembered how he had gently described every symptom she might succumb to due to her condition. I had spent months researching and consulting with her doctor. I would have never moved away if she hadn't forced me to.

That day she told me, "Giving up your life to take care of me isn't what I want." The weight of her words hung heavy. She knew how hard I worked. My journey to pass the bar exam, the years of long hours and sleepless nights I had spent preparing for it. Not using my degree would be detrimental to any future career, and she reminded me of that. I was willing to let it all go to take care of the woman who gave up so much to take care of me.

Dad's playlist was bringing joy to this trip, a tribute to all the times we took trips to Missoula. So many memories were embedded along with the songs playing, and by the looks of it, Mom agreed. Like the time when Dad had to pee so bad and there wasn't a gas station for miles, so he pulled over and stepped behind a tree in a meadow. Mom and I heard screaming, and then my father was running with his pants down, swatting at the air. Turns out, there was a beehive above his head and they thought he smelled sweet. Go figure. Mom made fun of him the rest of the trip after getting him some Benadryl. We never did make it to our destination, instead we turned around and went home. Dad felt so bad for ruining our trip to the zoo. Truth be told, it wasn't about the places we went, but the time I got. As long as I was with them, I had fun.

My mother turned down the folk music on the radio, and I could feel her gaze as she took me in. "So, you've been there for a while now. How are you liking it? You never seemed like the big city type."

I looked over toward her, letting go of the steering wheel with my right hand to take hold of hers. "Honestly, it would be better if you were there. Walking around Times Square just isn't as fun when you are alone."

She smiled and pinched my cheek gently. "Oh, Matt, baby, you need to get a good woman. A man as amazing as you are shouldn't be lonely."

If only my mom knew about Jennifer. Well, she knew about her, but not my feelings. It wasn't like I could tell her because then she would spend the next few days trying to push us together, and that could be uncomfortable for my sassy assistant. "Focusing on my career will always be lonely, but that's okay. Someday, the woman of my dreams will say yes, and lonely I'll never be again."

I turned the radio back up, so she didn't pry into that subject any further, because if there was one thing I wasn't good at, it was lying to my mother. She could spot it a mile away.

As I rounded the corner, the weathered Amesbury sign came into view and I took a right turn, approaching the town that held so many memories for us both. Being surrounded by her friends that she had known all her life might do her some good.

As we pulled into the lodge's lot, I knew I had made the right choice. Mom couldn't wipe the smile off her face as I went around and helped her out of the vehicle.

"I honestly never thought I'd see this place again," she said, grabbing her cane. "I can still get around... but I'm slower."

I wafted my hand at her and grabbed her bag from the back seat. She took off toward the front door, and I got there just in time to open it for her. "In you go."

Carina's face split into a wide grin when she saw my mom. "Leanne!" After a brief hug, Carina gushed about how long it had been since they last saw each other; they had known each other since their days in elementary school. Carina handed me the room key so I could get her bag into her room while they caught up. Thankfully, it was on the first floor, close to the lobby, so she wouldn't have too much difficulty getting around. When I returned, they were still talking, lost in conversation.

Mom released a yawn and stretched her arms as she spoke to Carina. "I'll stop gabbing now. Son, let me change out of my jammies and we can go grab a bite to eat," she said, scratching the back of her neck before walking away.

"Okay," I replied, nodding. I watched her silhouette disappear around the corner and headed up the stairs to my room. The hallway carpet was soft under my feet and scented with lavender. An old grandfather clock at the top of the landing ticked away the seconds as I made it to my door.

I collapsed onto the bed, my body ached from all the traveling today. My eyes caught on our adjoining room door. Was she out perusing? I didn't see her when coming down to the lodge, but she could've been inside one of the shops.

This town was amazing during the holidays, and I truly hoped she would enjoy herself. Her parents put so much pressure on her, and she wanted to make them proud, but if they didn't see what an amazing woman she was, they were idiots. From her words, they seemed harder to please. With each new accomplishment, their expectations rose higher and higher until she was being stretched beyond her limits. If they couldn't appreciate her for who she was, then maybe she didn't need their approval after all.

20
Jennifer

I reclined on the bed, immersed in Amy Stephens' novel, when my phone vibrated against the nightstand. Startled out of my trance, I saw that two hours had passed since I began reading. With a sigh, I picked up the phone and unlocked it, revealing a message that demanded my attention.

Matt: Mom and I are going to the diner for dinner. Wanna come? No pressure.

I lay on my stomach, feet crossed at the ankles. There were apparently only two places to eat an actual meal in this town, so it wasn't like we wouldn't run into each other eventually. My stomach growled.

Me: My stomach says yes, but my brain wants to finish this book I grabbed at the café today.

The meet-cute was always the part I needed to read before committing to buy a book. A book should be all about that. Amy was a professional at nailing the best of them. I picked up the book and read another couple pages before my phone vibrated again. No matter what, I needed to finish this by tomorrow midmorning so I could pick up another one from the café.

Matt: So you checked it out? Amazing, right? It reminds me of Coffee Chaos in a way. A small part of the city in this small town.

I smiled and bit my lip. The café might be my favorite spot because of the coffee and their selection of books. Being a small town, I thought it would be a tiny selection, but it was quite extensive.

Me: The coffee was delish!!!!! Guess I know where I'll be going every morning. The guy that works there was kinda off-putting, though.

Matt: If he was wearing flannel, then it must be Cole. He and his brother own the place. He's a good guy, just got a lot on his plate. Cut him some slack.

Once again, it slipped my mind that this was his hometown. He knew everyone. Heck, he and Cole probably played together when they were still in diapers.

Matt: If you want to join us, we will leave in five.

I put the phone down on my bed, grabbing my brush to get out any tangles, and then threw my hair up in a ponytail. There was no sense in changing since he already saw me in this. I threw on my winter coat, slipped my room key into my back pocket, and was on my merry way.

As I rounded the corner, Matt and his mother were waiting in the lobby. He smiled nervously and said, "Mom, this is my friend Jennifer." His mom gave me a once-over. Her lips curled into a polite smile. I could feel her eyes burning holes into my skin, trying to discern what our relationship was.

We walked slowly down Main Street, the evening air cool, but they were reminiscing about high school days. His mother pointed to the Hideout diner up ahead and recounted stories about how that spot used to be the place to be after every football game, the small diner packed with teenagers.

Matt heaved the weathered door open and ushered us inside first. The small booth seats were tucked in by the smudged windows, which looked out onto Main Street. Children of all ages mingled around the long countertop, lined with worn stools and laminated menus featuring breakfast, lunch, and dinner specials. My favorite thing was the black-and-white-checkered tile floor.

We all ordered the breakfast sampler, and then the conversation began. Leanne seemed very interested in me, and Matt looked scared.

"So, tell me about yourself, young lady. My son said you are the best assistant he's ever had..." she said.

"I'm the only assistant he's ever had... but I'll take it as a compliment, anyway. There's not much to tell. I live in the city, work my tail off, and love to read," I replied.

Gosh, my life sounded so boring. No wonder I was still single. Leanne probably thought the same thing.

"Well, my son here needs to settle down. Find himself a good woman, so be sure to keep an eye out for him. I'm not getting any younger," she said.

"Mom, Jennifer doesn't need to know all about my personal life. Some things I'd like to keep private," he nudged her.

The dynamic between Matt and his mom was amazing. They had a strong and healthy relationship, and I was jealous. A smile emerged. Didn't they say you can tell how a man is going to treat you by how he treated his mother? Well, if that was the case, whoever ended up with Matt was going to be a lucky lady.

"Don't worry, Leanne. Matt has a trove of women in New York City to pick from..." I looked right at Matt and winked. He shook his head.

Not once did I show his mother my feelings for him. We both needed to be careful around her, especially when she was this adamant about him finding someone, but what mother wouldn't? She just wanted her son to have someone. It was sweet.

The waitress brought us our food, and I took a sip of my Dr. Pepper. The conversation had taken a turn, but it was good to know where his mother stood. "So, Leanne, what is one thing I absolutely need to do while I'm here?"

She smiled. "'The square on Christmas. You think it's gorgeous now, but when the whole town gathers around and sings Christmas music, it's a sight for wonder. You won't find something like this in your big city."

I forgot she was a small-town girl through and through. This place was growing on me. Before, a big city was the only place I ever wanted to be, but now, seeing this beautiful and inviting town, I could imagine myself happy here. "Alright, it's on my list. Once Matt described the town a bit to me, I've been doing research. I don't want to miss a single experience."

A tall woman with dark hair glided up behind Matt. I raised my chin and tapped the table twice with my index finger to get his attention. When his eyes finally met hers, her gaze softened, and she smiled knowingly.

Who was this woman?

21
Matt

The surrounding air stilled as her eyes scanned my face. Standing before me was Nicole Peters. I watched as tears welled up in her eyes. "I can't believe it's you."

My throat tightened as I took in her unchanged beauty. "You look exactly the same."

Her voice quivered. "I didn't think I'd ever see you again."

"I didn't think I'd ever see you again."

She stood there with her arms folded, the tension between us tangible in the air. I couldn't look away from her; our shared history was like a magnet. Jennifer, unaware of what was happening, continued eating.

I stood and touched her elbow lightly and directed her away from our table. As we slowly made our way through the tables, she glanced around nervously, clearly uncomfortable, until we sat down at a faraway table.

"Do you remember the last time we saw each other?"

My throat tightened as memories of the disastrous evening flooded back to me. "I remember."

We were sitting outside on the grass, surrounded by a garden my mother had been tending for years. The sun was setting, painting the sky with soft pinks and yellows. I could tell from the conversations we'd had that day that it would not work out between us—our perspectives weren't aligning, and I couldn't take on another person's feelings right then. As I tried to explain why it wasn't working, her eyes became watery and soon tears were streaming down her face. Our fight escalated until we said things we'd regret later—my mother standing in the house's doorway, watching us silently. My dream was going to Harvard and I couldn't give that up after all the hard work.

"Listen, it's been years. Let's not worry about what happened then," I said, putting my hand on her shoulder. "How are you?"

Her entire body seemed to sag under the weight of years passed. Tears streaming down her cheeks, she spoke in a thick voice, "I've been okay."

I wondered what could make her cry after such a long time apart.

She looked up at me, her eyes still damp with tears, and squared her shoulders. "I just need to tell you one thing. Back then, I never understood why you had to go to Harvard, but I understand now. You had to follow your dreams, and it was worth it—I'm so proud of you for doing it."

"Thank you, Nicole," I said, warmth spreading in my chest.

Nicole's cheeks flushed and her eyes sparkled as she looked at me, and for a moment, it was like nothing had changed between us. We used to be good friends before we started dating. I smiled awkwardly, my heart still loyal to the woman sitting with my mother, and I tried to quash the spark by quickly asking about her new job. She lit up when telling me about how much she enjoyed working at the bakery around the corner and how moving back to Amesbury after her divorce had been a blessing in disguise for her son.

I caught Jennifer glancing our way, but she quickly averted her gaze and pretended to be eating. I wondered if she held feelings for me beyond that of a professional relationship, but perhaps she was too afraid to admit it to herself.

Nicole's face softened as she glanced at the booth where Jennifer was sitting, chatting with my mom. "Anyway, I must get home to my son. Would you like to grab dinner and catch up while you're in town?"

I shook my head apologetically. "Sorry, I'll be busy with my mother and Jennifer. It's her first time here for the holidays. So many things to do."

Nicole bit her lip. She gave me a rueful smile. "She's a lucky girl. Hopefully, she knows that."

I slinked back to the booth beside my mother, who shot me a sidelong glance. She'd always been fond of Nicole, and if the choice was hers, she'd marry me off without delay. Thankfully, this wasn't her call to make.

Jennifer kept her head down and wouldn't look at me. My mom shot her a quick glance before standing up and giving me a kiss on the cheek. Taking Carter by the arm, she said, "Carter is going to walk me to the lodge. You guys stay here for as long as you want. This old woman needs some rest."

This was an example of the difference from here to New York City. Someone willing to walk an older woman home wouldn't ever happen there. People didn't even stop when someone was getting beaten on the side of the road.

"Sorry about that. Small town means running into ex-girlfriends." I took a sip of my drink and asked for the check. The awkwardness in the air was palpable.

Jennifer wouldn't make eye contact with me. What was going on? Surely, she couldn't be upset. Something told me she was jealous, and a part of me enjoyed that. She might not want to be more than friends, but apparently her heart does.

After leaving the money to cover our meal, Jennifer and I stepped out of the cozy diner into the bitter, cold winter air. My teeth chattered as I pulled my scarf up over my neck and tugged my coat tighter around my body. We trudged along, our feet crunching in the snow as we made our way back to the lodge.

We took slow steps as we walked down Main Street, our feet in sync. The snow was coming down heavily now, and the Christmas decorations in the shop windows were barely visible through the snowflakes. I could feel her warmth radiating from her body, and it seemed like the distance between us had disappeared. I strained my ears to hear any sound coming from her; all I heard was the steady thump of her heart.

The streetlights highlighted the soft curves of her face, and I could feel my heart speeding up. She just stood there with crimson cheeks, snowflakes clinging to her eyelashes, making them look like tiny sparkles. I wanted to tell her how beautiful she was in that moment, but I couldn't find the courage to do so. All I could do was take in the sight of her as we stood there at the edge of Main Street.

"What is your favorite part of growing up in this town?" she asked.

"The community." I smiled fondly, recalling the abundance of potlucks we had attended over the years. "It's astounding to witness the power of a small, close-knit community come together whenever someone needs something."

We strolled along in comfortable silence, neither of us wanting to break the peace between us. I sensed a growing anticipation as the lodge came into view. Gradually, the steps to our rooms loomed ahead, and we gradually ascended, each step drawing us closer to each other. When we finally reached the top, we stood close, our eyes locked in an intense gaze. My heart raced and my stomach fluttered with electric energy as I yearned to feel her lips against mine. Yet I held back, afraid of disrupting the beautiful moment.

My gaze lingered on her face, finding a gentle warmth in her eyes. I wanted so badly to reach out to her, to confess my feelings and get it out in the open. But I couldn't move, not an inch, totally paralyzed by the overwhelming intensity. I eventually dropped my gaze.

The silence stretched out between us, and I nervously cleared my throat. "Good night," I said, making eye contact one last time before turning away. I felt her gaze on my back as I walked away, and when I glanced over my shoulder, she had disappeared into her room.

Just tell her how you feel...

22

Jennifer

I was back in my room at the lodge and couldn't breathe. We had been so close to kissing, something in the air was pushing us together. My hand went to my forehead, and I paced around my room. He was just in the next room, and I struggled to understand why I was so upset about his ex-girlfriend showing up while we were having dinner. It's not like he hadn't dated anyone else before. I was being ridiculous.

So I sent a text to my best friend, needing someone to talk to. She called me a few minutes later, and I told her everything that had happened. I tried to explain how I felt, but the words escaped me. I could hear the disappointment in her voice, but I couldn't help but feel relieved. She reminded me I wanted to find my one and if I kept pushing people away and keeping them at arm's length, I would never find them.

The room seemed to close in around me, and I felt suffocated. I stepped closer to the window and peered out, almost expecting to see someone. But no one was there. I felt my heart sink as I remembered why I came here.

The moonlight illuminated the trees, the stars twinkling like diamonds in the sky. I longed for something greater than I had ever felt before. I wished for the love that was shown in movies, and a part of me thought I found it, but everything in me told me it was a terrible idea.

I knew I could never go back to the way things were before we came here, but I wanted to move forward. I wanted to open my heart again, to let someone in and to live without fear, without hesitation.

I looked out into the night sky, and for the first time, I felt like I could breathe. I had a choice to make, to take a chance and find the courage or make things abundantly clear that something cannot happen between Matt and me. I took a deep breath and leaned my head against the window.

I closed my eyes and felt the night breeze on the cold window. The fireplace sounded like the perfect place, so I grabbed my book and a throw blanket and headed downstairs. There was nothing like a good book to put my mind into perspective.

I curled up on the corner of the couch nearest the crackling fire, my paperback resting on my lap. There was only a hundred pages until I reached the end. My heart ached as I read, wishing that life would replicate the unaccomplished perfection of the romance I was immersed in. Every page whispered of an ideal man who did not exist in reality.

I was twenty pages in when I heard a creak as Matt shuffled down the stairs. Anxiety knotted my stomach. Why did he have to come down here? Did he understand how hard this was for me, or was he just unable to sleep too?

He was wearing gray sweatpants that hung low on his hips, and his hands were tucked into the pockets. When he saw me, he stopped short in surprise. "Hey, I didn't think you'd be down here," he said, rubbing the back of his neck. "Didn't mean to bother you. The fireplace is a great place to come when I can't sleep."

He slowly lowered himself onto the opposite end of the couch, gazing into the fireplace. A soft glow from the flames illuminated his face, and his eyes were unreadable. We sat with only the crackling of cinders to fill the stillness.

I opened the thick book, desperately trying to focus on the words in front of me. But I could feel his presence like a tangible force that filled the room with tension as thick and heavy as fog. The air between us was charged, almost electric, as though we were standing at the edge of a volcano waiting to erupt.

I placed the book on the coffee table and turned to face him. "Thank you for dinner tonight. I'm so glad I decided to take a break from city life and come here for a change of scenery," I said.

His face softened as he shifted closer. His eyes were intense, like molten steel, and his gaze briefly flitted across my lips before meeting my own. "It has been nice having you around outside of work," he whispered.

His gaze moved slowly toward my lips, and I felt a fluttering sensation in my stomach. I wanted to get up and retreat to the safety of my room, but my body refused to obey. His head tilted slightly and our lips met, sending an electric shock through my whole being.

A split second after our lips touched, I yanked away with a gasp of surprise. My fingertips hovered near my mouth, my eyes wide with disbelief. His face had turned a deep shade of red as he glanced away.

He ran his hand through his hair. His eyes darted around the room, as if searching for an escape. He sighed heavily and reached out a trembling hand to touch my cheek. His breath caught in his throat as he spoke. "I'm sorry, I shouldn't have done that. You've been clear, but then everything besides your words tells me that you feel this... There's just something about you that draws me in." His gaze was intense.

There was a powerful electric tension between us that made my head spin and brought a flush to my cheeks. But I knew the reality of the situation. If I acted on my feelings, it would put both our jobs in jeopardy and cause far more harm than good.

"Listen, I'll admit it, and you seem like a wonderful man, but neither of us can afford to screw up our careers. Like you've said, you worked too hard to get where you are, and to jeopardize that for me, I won't allow it."

I picked up my book and rose quickly, the book held close to my chest like a shield. "We should both head up and get some rest," I said, avoiding his gaze. I took the stairs two at a time, unable to contain the whirlwind of emotions ricocheting through me as I heard his footfalls below. My room door closed with a resounding click, and my lips still tingled from our kiss.

My heart raced as I dialed Laura's number. No matter the hour, she was always my go-to confidant. When she answered with her usual bright greeting, I blurted out, "I have some tea..."

An excited gasp came through the phone line. "Dish!"

"Matt kissed me," I whispered.

"Girl, I knew this would happen. I warned you before about the small towns—why didn't you listen?" She sighed.

I stared at the bed, picturing his soft, warm lips pressed against mine, and heard myself replying, "It doesn't matter. How can I ever go back to work like nothing happened and act like everything is normal after feeling that? After tasting his kiss? Those sweet, luscious lips..."

"Come on! I know you too well. You're obviously head over heels for this guy, but you can't seem to let yourself fall for him. He got into a bar brawl defending your honor and now took you away for Christmas? The way he's showing you how much he cares is pretty clear!"

I responded, "It really isn't that simple. You know why."

"Actually, it is. New York City is huge and you could find another job if it came down to that. Are you telling me that finding the love of your life isn't more important than your job?"

She had a point. Even though I loved my job, the city was big and it might take me a bit of time, but I could find something.

"Plus, he's a partner. Trust me when I say they will not fire either of you. Now go to sleep. My mother has me getting up at the crack of dawn to go thrift shopping. Night."

The age-old question loomed through my mind: Is Matt worth putting it all on the line for?

23
Matt

I struggled to quiet my racing thoughts from the night before, knowing full well any sleep I would get would be occupied by her. My mother's words echoed in my mind—once the right girl came along, nothing else mattered. And now, as I lay there wondering how I could prove to her she was worth giving up the partnership for, I finally understood what she meant.

My mother and I wrapped our scarves tightly around our necks against the cold and navigated the sea of people out for last-minute Christmas shopping. I held the doors open for her as we made our way to the diner at the end of the block. The restaurant was bustling with activity, and a layer of snow glistened from the streetlights outside. We snagged one of the last booths and ordered the hamburger basket. I tried not to let on that something was amiss between Jennifer and me, but my mother's gaze lingered on mine for a moment; she had always been so perceptive.

"Just say it!" she said, setting down her steaming cup of coffee. Biting the inside of my lip, I looked away, suddenly feeling exposed and vulnerable. My fingers drummed on the tabletop nervously as I searched for the right words. "I... I don't know how to tell this girl how I feel," I finally said. "There are so many things I want to say but—"

She took both of my hands in hers. Her skin was warm and soft. She leaned closer to me, and in a quiet voice, she said, "Jennifer is smitten with you. It's written across her face like the stars across the night sky. I can see that you feel the same way about her, too." Her eyes were filled with wisdom beyond her years. "I know it's complicated because of your professional relationship, but finding someone who shares your passion, who understands every fiber of your being, now that's priceless." She paused for a moment and then added, "Don't let her go without fighting for her."

The waitress set our plates down in front of us, and I absentmindedly ate my food, barely tasting it as I ran through the things I had to say. I was done making excuses on why we couldn't be together any longer.

"I gotta go, Mama." I leaped up from the table and rushed out the door and could see Jennifer coming down the sidewalk to the café. My legs felt like lead weights as I stumbled toward her, and then my arms finally fell around her. Her body tensed at first, but then she let out a little sigh before I whispered, "Please give me five minutes."

As snowflakes collected atop of the shop sign and glistened in the streetlamps, she tightened her grip on my hand. I looked into her eyes. Her face softened, and I gently brushed a few strands of hair behind her ear and then took her inside Caffeinated Bliss.

"You have said that we can't pursue this because of work, but Jennifer..." I paused and looked deep into her eyes. "I will give up my job for you. That's how deep I know you are the woman for me. Even when I sleep, your presence is strong, your kiss lingers on my lips... and if giving up the firm is what it takes to be with you... then that's what I'll do."

Tears streamed down her cheeks and her lip quivered as she gazed at me. "You can't give up your career for me, Matt," she whispered. "That's selfish of me."

I reached out and cupped my hands around hers. "You aren't

asking me to... If the only thing standing in our way is my job, then I'll take it out of the equation." My voice was husky with determination, and I slashed my hand through the air for emphasis. "Easy, done."

She slumped into the chair at the bistro table, her elbows on her knees and her forehead resting in her palms. "But this is insane," she said. "Why don't we wait until we get back to New York City before deciding? You could be more rational by then, and I'd hate for us to make a rash decision." Her stubbornness was palpable, but I knew she wouldn't budge. "Okay," I said. "Let's compromise. When we get back to the city, I'll tell HR about us, and if they push the issue, I'll resign."

After ten years of loyal service, it would be an injustice to demand that she give up the job she had worked so hard for. My law degree gave me the opportunity to practice anywhere. If I wanted her by my side, I needed to make a change. I'd find a different firm willing to take me on and offer me a chance at success. She was worth it.

I grabbed her shoulders and looked into her eyes, willing her to understand my words. "Understand how much I care about you, Jennifer Jenkins. Nothing in this world matters more to me than your happiness." The intensity of my gaze broke through her resistance and she slowly lifted her gaze, locking eyes with me. With a single twitch of my finger, I pulled her closer and our lips met in a passionate kiss that said all the things that no words could express. Breaking away, I spoke with determination, "Now, let's go get my mother from the diner."

After retrieving my mom, she, Jennifer, and I had taken a stroll around town to support the local businesses, cheerful music playing in the distance.

We had eagerly entered the first shop, admiring the beautifully crafted ornaments, holiday wreaths, and Christmas cards. We browsed for a few minutes and then picked up a few items for our holiday decorations. My mom chose a set of red-and-white-striped candy canes, which we hung from our mantelpiece. Jennifer chose a set of colorful glass bells, which she hung near the window. I bought a festive wreath with silver and gold ribbons.

Next, we had stopped in at a cozy little boutique where we found an array of comfy sweaters and scarves. It was freezing outside, so we picked up a few cozy items to keep us warm. Jennifer found a lovely pink scarf with a matching hat, while my mom chose a thick cable-knit sweater.

After that, we headed to a small gift shop to pick up some Christmas cards. The shelves were lined with brightly colored cards with holiday messages, and we couldn't help but smile at the selection.

As we had made our way back home, we noticed the streets were even brighter and more inviting than before. The snow had stopped falling, but the twinkling lights still danced across the sky and illuminated the night. We had stopped to admire the Christmas tree that had been set up in the town square, sparkling with multicolored lights and ornaments.

Finally, we had returned to the lodge and entered the lobby, admiring the decorations. The room was filled with the warmth of love and joy, and the smell of freshly baked cookies filled the air. Carina loved Christmas and wanted the guests to feel welcome.

"Help yourself! I made plenty," she yelled from the lobby desk.

It was a Christmas Eve that we would never forget. Amesbury had shown us the power of holiday spirit, and it was a reminder of the importance of supporting local businesses. With the help of our small purchases, we had brought a little bit of holiday cheer to our community. We had created lasting memories, and we were grateful to have been able to experience all of it together.

Later, we headed to Christmas Even service, and the night air was crisp, yet comforting, carrying with it the faint scent of the evergreen trees that lined the streets. As we stepped into the church, the atmosphere immediately changed from one of winter's quietude to a festive holiday celebration.

Inside, they lined the walls with flickering candles, casting a gentle, golden light throughout the sanctuary. The pews were filled with people of all ages and backgrounds, united in their love for the season. The energy of the crowd was palpable as each voice joined in harmony to sing the familiar carols of the season.

My eyes then fell upon the altar, and the beauty of the scene left me breathless. A majestic Christmas tree, decorated with red and gold ornaments, glistened in the candlelight. At its base, they arranged a magnificent Nativity scene with intricate detail. My mother, standing next to me, let out a sigh of admiration. Jennifer's eyes never wavered.

When the service was over, we stepped out into the night. Children ran through the streets and town square, laughing and playing in the snow, and couples strolled hand in hand, taking in the season's beauty.

We continued on our way. I felt grateful for the powerful sense of community and belonging I had felt inside the church and for the reminder of the true meaning of Christmas.

This Christmas Eve was a special one. I had embraced my heart and went for it with Jennifer and there was no turning back. I intended to show her just how amazing she truly was and how a woman like her should be treated. All my worries went out the window because even if HR had a problem with us being together, they would lose a partner.

Jennifer Jenkins was the woman for me.

24
Jennifer

I quickly called Laura to wish her a merry Christmas and share Matt's confession that he would resign if HR pushed the issue. Afterward, I pulled on my festive holiday sweater and hurried downstairs.

Matt stood out like a beacon in the morning light, his simple white shirt unbuttoned just far enough to reveal a vivid tattoo. I felt my heart skip a beat as I took in my surroundings, and with each step closer to him, I could feel the ground beneath me shifting, beckoning me to take the plunge into the unknown.

He smiled, and I felt my stomach do a fluttery somersault. His eyes twinkled with warmth and a hint of mischief, but it was the hint of a dimple in his left cheek that made me smile back, our gazes locking as the air between us positively crackled with electricity.

"Good morning," he whispered. She looked up to meet his eyes, feeling the warmth radiating between them as they shared a moment of stillness. He finally broke the silence with a gentle reminder it was Christmas Day. "Merry Christmas. I've been waiting for you to get up so that we could cook together and spread some holiday cheer." Her heart raced at the thought of being near him for longer.

"I'd love to," she replied.

I followed him to the kitchen, where he set about gathering ingredients from the pantry and refrigerator. He chopped onions with a practiced hand, then cracked fresh eggs into a bowl with a deft flick of his wrist. As I watched, he fried bacon in one pan, simmered gravy in another, and mixed up a big batch of cinnamon rolls in between. He hummed a song beneath his breath as he juggled tasks. With each task he completed, my admiration for his cooking prowess grew.

We cut and chopped, stirred and simmered, as we talked and laughed. The kitchen filled with the aroma of spices and herbs, and the laughter grew louder when the food was done. We gathered around tables laden with steaming dishes, exchanging stories.

I placed my gift on the table and Matt gingerly untied the gold ribbon. He peeled back the wrapping paper, revealing an old wooden picture frame holding a photograph of his father. His eyes stayed fixed on the image as he ran his thumb over the edges of the worn frame. His breathing slowed, and a tear escaped his eye.

I attempted to clear my throat, hoping to break the silence and bring him back to the present moment, only to make things worse. "Your mom said that she had some old photos of the two of you together, but some were so faded that I got them restored," I whispered.

Matt's head hung low, and he was silent, his tears soaking into the front of his shirt. I stepped closer, resting my hand gently on his shoulder. Slowly, he looked up, tears still streaming down his face. With a deep breath, he stood and wrapped his arms around me. His voice was trembling as he said, "Thank you."

Gently setting down the photo on the coffee table, Matt walked across the room and came back, holding a small box wrapped in blue paper and tied with a white bow. He smiled softly at me as he handed it to me, saying, "This is for you."

I stared at the box in my hands, bewilderment and excitement tingling through me. With trembling fingers, I slowly opened the lid to reveal a slip of paper with an activation code for the EZ Planning software. Joy burst through me as I realized what it was. How did he know?

He smiled softly. "I heard you talking about it with Laura."

I wrapped him in my arms, pressing my face against his shoulder. My chest welled up with emotion, and I could hardly keep my feet on the ground. After three long years of anticipation, I couldn't believe it was actually happening. With a shaky voice, I thanked him. He had no clue how much this meant to me—more than words could ever express.

As we walked toward the town square, the crisp December breeze charged with holiday energy that made me feel like I had been wrapped up in a big festive hug. The streets were alive with families laughing and talking with each other as they wound their way toward the parade grounds. As we got closer, I could make out rows of bundled-up figures wearing thick winter coats and scarves, some sporting colorful earmuffs and pom-pom beanies to keep warm. There was an air of anticipation, of joy and celebration, that filled the area and my heart with Christmas spirit. It was easy to see why Amesbury was the perfect place to spend the holiday season.

The parade began with the thump-thumping of drums and the blaring of trombones, the sound rippling through the air like a wave. The marching band was decked out in their red and white uniforms adorned with shiny gold buttons, and they strutted proudly past the enthralled crowd. Next came the small floats, festooned with lights and glitter that glinted in the sun. Colorful figures danced on each float—miniature Christmas trees, reindeer, snowmen, and elves—all waving cheerily to the roaring crowd as they passed by. People clapped and cheered, pointing at their favorite characters and dancing in their seats.

The sky lit up with shimmering blues, purples, and reds. Explosions of color graced the night air, and my heart raced with excitement as I watched the grand finale to the parade. The cheers and clapping rose above the rumble of firework booms.

The only reason I was in town was because my family wouldn't accept me. The expectations they put on me were too much and instead of going home, I came here and found solace.

As we walked away from the parade, I couldn't help but feel a sense of hope and optimism. Maybe things would work out between Matt and me. Maybe the firm wouldn't push the issue and we could both keep our jobs. However, one other thought crossed my mind. What if he didn't want to stay in New York City? After all, he only initially agreed to a one-year contract.

All I could do was bask in the moment now and soak in the charm of this town before we left. I could see why he turned out the way he did. An amazing man with a wonderful heart.

25
Matt

As I helped Mom out of the car in front of Home Away from Home, all the walking we had done in the past few days had gotten to her and she was stiff. I blinked the tears away, trying to be strong for my mom. I hated to see her hurting like this, knowing I had to drive away and leave her here after spending Christmas together.

My mom reached out and grabbed my hand, giving it a gentle squeeze. "It's okay, love," she whispered. "We'll have plenty more Christmases together."

I smiled, but it was a weak effort. I couldn't bear the thought of having to leave her again. "I love you," I whispered, my voice cracking with emotion.

"I love you, too," she replied. "We'll see each other soon."

I nodded, my throat too tight to speak. I hugged her one last time and then walked her to the entrance of the nursing home.

My mom took a deep breath and smiled at me, her eyes filled with love. "Thank you for taking me home," she said. "It was the best Christmas I've ever had. Don't forget to bring Jennifer back next time. Although, I think y'all will be married before this time next year."

I nodded, my throat too tight to speak, giving her one last hug, and then watched as she strolled through the door of the nursing home. My heart felt like it was breaking in two as I watched her go.

As I drove away, even though it was a sad goodbye, I knew that no matter what, my mom and I would always have each other. And that was something to be thankful for.

I made it back to Amesbury in time for us to go to dinner. Tomorrow, we would take the bus to the airport and then begin our journey back to New York City. Would our relationship hold up once back in front of prying eyes?

I had been wasting away my life focusing on my career when none of that mattered without someone to share it with, and if I hadn't taken the risk of coming to this firm, I would have never met Jennifer.

As the sun set that evening, I held Jennifer close. I looked into her eyes, seeing the beauty and love that she brought into the world. I felt overwhelmed with emotion, but I wasn't sure how to express it.

I ran my fingers through her hair, caressing her cheek. She smiled, and I felt my heart swell with newfound hope. I knew that this moment was the one I had been waiting for. It was the moment where I could finally tell her how I felt.

I took a deep breath and exhaled slowly. I said the words I had been wanting to say for so long.

"Jennifer, I love you," I said, my voice breaking as I spoke.

She smiled, looking into my eyes with love and understanding. I meant every word.

"I want to be with you," I continued, feeling my courage grow with every second. "I want it all. Marriage, kids, a dog, a white picket fence. All of it with you. My job means nothing if I have to spend every day alone."

As I said the words, I could feel the emotion swelling in my chest. I wanted to be with her more than anything. I wanted to share my life with her, to make our dreams come true.

Jennifer smiled, her eyes misting up as she looked into mine. She reached out and took my hands in hers, squeezing them gently.

"I love you too," she whispered.

We stayed there in each other's arms, watching the sunset and basking in the moment's warmth. I felt like I could have stayed there forever.

We talked for an hour about marriage and kids, about a dog and a white picket fence, and most importantly, about a life together.

Finally, as the sun dipped below the horizon, I took her hands in mine, looked her in the eyes, and told her no matter what happened back in the city, we would be together and that was more important to me than anything else.

We held each other close, and my heart swelled, knowing I had finally found the person I had been searching for my entire life. As long as I had Jennifer by my side, I was ready for anything.

Epilogue
Jennifer

Laura and I had got our nails done before Matt and I went out to dinner tonight. We were both in need of a little pampering before a romantic evening, and the nail salon was the perfect place to get it.

The salon was bustling with activity as we arrived. Women were getting their nails done, their conversations lively and their laughter contagious. We took our seats in the waiting area, chairs lined up alongside the window overlooking the street.

Laura hadn't been able to wipe the smile off her face since she woke up and I couldn't help but wonder why? Was she seeing someone? I doubted it, since she hadn't mentioned it, but something was going on.

"Do you have something you need to tell me? I'm getting jealous of how happy you are right now."

She laughed. "No, we will talk about it tomorrow. Let's focus on your hot date tonight."

Matt and I had taken things to the next level. Laura didn't like that I moved out, but it was our next step and honestly things couldn't be greater between us. Things just felt right.

Once the firm got over themselves and Matt told them that if it came down to it, he would go to another firm so I could keep my job, they gave us their blessing but made us sign some paperwork so they weren't liable for any sexual harassment lawsuits down the line.

They didn't understand that what Matt and I had was special. It only came across once in a lifetime, and we weren't giving that up over something as idiotic as a job. We could both find another job. Once I got that through my head, our relationship flourished, and we had nothing else to hold us back.

"Jennifer?" the manicurist yelled and I jumped up, walked over, then sat down in front of her and let her do her magic.

My mind raced, wondering where he was taking me tonight. Work had been so crazy busy and his year at the company was almost up. Tonight, we would need to talk about what his plans were for the future. Did he plan on signing another contract with them? His mother wasn't doing so well, and as close as they were, I wouldn't be surprised if he opted to move back to Amesbury, and I wouldn't hesitate to go with him.

Sometimes sacrifices were necessary to get the result you wanted out of life and now that I had a man like Matt in mine, something as simple as moving would not stop me.

"All done," the lady said, and my phone buzzed against the desk.

Matt: I'm outside. No rush.

A smile tugged at the corners of my mouth and Laura was still getting hers worked on. "He's here. You gonna be okay?"

"Girl, it's not my first rodeo. Get out of here and go have fun with your man."

I paid the receptionist and walked outside, slipping into his car and giving him a quick kiss. "So where are we going?"

"Well, seeing as how it's the one-year anniversary of when we met... somewhere special."

He took off down the street until we arrived at LA VI, a fancy Italian restaurant. My heart fluttered as he pulled into the side parking lot. How did I get so lucky?

We walked into the restaurant and were immediately greeted by a hostess who led us to our table. As we were seated, I noticed the romantic vibes in the air. Candles were lit, low music was playing, and the atmosphere was intimate.

Matt took my hands in his and looked into my eyes.

"Laura," he drawled as he knelt, "I can't believe it's been a year since I laid eyes on you. I love you and I want to spend the rest of my life with you."

No way! He is not!

Tears burned my eyes, but I tried my hardest to keep them at bay. The man of my dreams was kneeling in front of me, my hand in his, and he was going to ask. I never thought this day would come. Finding your person was hard work, but now that I had him, I would never let go.

Matt reached into his pocket and pulled out a small velvet box. "Will you marry me?" he asked.

I nodded, unable to speak through my tears as he slipped the beautiful ring onto my finger, and then he pulled me into his arms.

The restaurant erupted in applause, and we didn't even notice. All I could do was look into his eyes and then at the ring. "Who knew that you coming to the city would change both of our lives?"

After that, we ended up not staying to order dinner. I wanted to shout the news from the rooftops and now I knew why Laura was so giddy all day. She had to have known what was going to happen tonight, and she didn't even give a hint.

As we left the restaurant, we both knew that our lives had changed forever. But we also knew that what awaited us was a life of love, happiness, and unforeseen blessings.

"Let's go home, Mrs. Kneeland."

Perfect For Him
Kaci Bell

1
Atlas

The steam from the cup of freshly brewed coffee rose as I took my seat behind my mahogany desk, ready to face the day. Ava Kennsington, my latest client, was due to arrive any minute now. The high-stakes divorce case against her husband, Mark, promised to be an interesting one. My fingers drummed against the desk.

"Atlas Harrington?" A sultry voice inquired from the doorway.

I looked up to find a woman with wavy chestnut hair and deep brown eyes. Her air of elegance screamed 'money,' even though she had none before marrying Mark. Ava Kennsington stood before me.

"Mrs. Kennsington," I replied, flashing her my disarming smile. "Please, have a seat."

"Are you going to win this for me, Mr. Harrington?" she asked, cutting straight to the point as she settled into the plush chair.

"Of course," I replied. "We just need to prepare you for the preliminary appearance in front of the judge."

"Good," she said, flicking her hair back over her shoulder. "Because I want everything."

"Everything?" I raised an eyebrow.

"Absolutely everything," she repeated, her voice dripping with entitlement. "Mark's fortune is rightfully mine."

"Mrs. Kennsington," I began, "it's important to approach the case with realistic expectations. Divorce settlements can be complex, and demanding everything might not be…"

"Atlas, darling," she interrupted, leaning forward with a smirk. "I did not hire you because of your good looks and charm alone. I expect results."

"Understood, Mrs. Kennsington." I sighed. "But we'll need solid evidence to support your claims and justify such demands."

"Then find it," she snapped, her impatience evident. "I didn't claw my way into this marriage for nothing."

Her arrogance rubbed me the wrong way, but I had a job to do. Everyone deserves someone to fight for what's fair, even the Ava Kennsingtons of the world.

"Very well," I replied, forcing another smile. "We'll start by gathering all relevant financial records and any proof of misconduct on your husband's part. But remember, Mrs. Kennsington, we have to play by the rules."

"Fine," she begrudgingly agreed. "Just make sure I get what's mine."

As Ava left my office, the weight of her demands settled on my shoulders. I knew the case would be challenging, but her entitlement added an extra layer of tension. Nevertheless, I was Atlas Harrington—undefeated, determined, and always ready for a challenge. I just hoped that Ava Kennsington's case wouldn't be the one to break my winning streak.

"Atlas, have you seen this?" my assistant, Ellen, burst into my office, brandishing a file folder like it was a weapon. "Larissa Montgomery is representing Mark Kennsington."

"Ah, Larissa," I mused, leaning back in my chair and steepling my fingers. "The courtroom pit bull herself. This should be interesting."

"Interesting?" Ellen's eyes widened. "She's ruthless, Atlas. We need to be prepared."

"Ellen, my dear, when have I ever backed down from a challenge?" I grinned, my blue eyes sparkling. "Besides, I've always been curious about what makes her tick."

"Fine." Ellen sighed, placing the file on my desk. "But remember, we're doing this for Ava, not because you want to play cat and mouse with Larissa."

"Of course," I replied, trying to suppress a mischievous smile. "It's all business. Now, let's get to work."

Later that day, I met with Ava to discuss our strategy against Larissa and her formidable reputation. As usual, Ava entered my office like she owned the place, her chestnut hair cascading around her shoulders as if in slow motion.

"Atlas, darling," she purred, taking a seat across from me. "I heard about our opponent. Should I be worried?"

"Mrs. Kennsington," I reassured her, my charm working overtime. "There's no need to worry. I've faced many tough opponents before, and Larissa Montgomery won't be any different."

"Good," she said, her deep brown eyes narrowing. "Because I expect nothing but the best from you, Atlas."

"Understood. Now, let's focus on the case at hand, shall we? We need to gather solid evidence to support your claims and make the best possible argument."

"Very well. I trust you, Atlas. Don't let me down."

"Never," I promised, my optimism shining through. "Together, we'll ensure that justice is served."

As Ava left my office, the realness of the challenge sunk on my shoulders. Not only did I have to contend with Ava's entitlement and demands, but I also had the opportunity to face off against the enigmatic Larissa Montgomery. The stakes were high, but I was more than ready to rise to the occasion.

"Alright, team," I declared as Ellen and the rest of my staff gathered around. "It's time to show Larissa Montgomery what Atlas Harrington is made of. She is a formidable opponent, but we're not going to let that intimidate us."

With a burst of laughter and a chorus of agreement, we dove headfirst into our preparations, fueled by determination, camaraderie, and just a hint of playful rivalry.

"Absolutely not, boss," Ellen chimed in. "We'll leave no stone unturned in our search for evidence."

"Good," I replied. "Let's start by digging into Mark's finances. I have a hunch there's something shady going on there."

"Already on it," Sam, our financial expert, said, tapping away at his laptop.

"Excellent. Now, we also need to gather proof of his infidelity and any abusive behavior toward Ava."

"Consider it done," Jill, our investigator, added, already dialing a number on her phone. "I've got some contacts who might be able to help us out."

"Perfect. Now, let's talk strategy. How do we throw Larissa off her game from the get-go?"

"Surprise witnesses?" Ellen suggested, raising an eyebrow.

"Maybe," I mused, rubbing my chin. "But I think we can do better than that. We need something unexpected, something she won't see coming."

"Like what?" Sam asked, looking up from his screen.

"Think outside the box," I urged them. "We need something that will make her question her own tactics and give us the upper hand."

"Maybe we could use some of her past cases against her? Show that she has a pattern of losing when faced with certain types of evidence or strategies?" Jill proposed.

"Interesting idea," I acknowledged. "Look into it, but let's not rely solely on that. We need a multifaceted approach."

"Got it, boss," Ellen replied. "We'll come up with a plan that's foolproof and, more importantly, Larissa-proof."

"Exactly." I grinned at my team, the thrill of the challenge coursing through my veins. "This is our chance to show her what we're made of. Let's leave her speechless when we present our case in court."

"Here's to victory," Sam declared, raising an imaginary glass.

"Cheers to that," I agreed, my optimism shining through. "Now let's get to work. We won't rest until we've done everything possible to win this for Ava."

We dove into our tasks, each member of the team driven by the desire not just to win, but to outwit and outmaneuver the formidable Larissa Montgomery. The days ahead would be filled with long hours and tireless dedication, but I knew that together, we were more than capable of rising to the occasion.

The sun had dipped below the horizon, casting a gentle purple glow across the city as I stood in my office, surrounded by stacks of evidence. My fingers traced the edge of a damning photograph with a surge of confidence. We had more than enough to build a rock-solid case against Mark Kennsington; I just needed to piece it together perfectly.

"Alright, team, let's go over our findings one more time," I announced, tapping the photograph on the table to punctuate my words. "We've got infidelity, financial misconduct, and abusive behavior."

"Exhibit A," Ellen piped up, holding up a glossy photo of Mark cozying up with someone who was most definitely not Ava. "Caught in the act."

"Excellent work, Ellen," I commended her, before turning my attention to Sam. "What about his finances?"

He grinned triumphantly, waving a stack of papers bound by a thick paperclip. "Found some questionable transactions in his business accounts. Looks like he's been siphoning off funds for personal use."

"Nice catch, Sam!" I said, giving him an appreciative nod. "And Jill, what have you got on the abuse allegations?"

"Plenty of texts and emails from Mark to Ava that show a clear pattern of emotional abuse," Jill revealed, scrolling through a digital folder on her tablet. "Enough to make your blood boil."

"Fantastic job, Jill." I clapped my hands together, feeling the excitement grow within me. "We're going to present this evidence in court so masterfully that Larissa won't know what hit her."

My mind raced with strategies and tactics, each thought flowing seamlessly into the next. I could practically see the courtroom, taste the tension in the air as Larissa and I squared off. The anticipation sent shivers down my spine—I had never felt more alive.

"Atlas," Ellen's voice broke through my reverie, "we've got this. Larissa has no idea what she's up against."

"Damn right," I agreed, smirking at the thought of catching her off guard. "But we can't get cocky. We need to stay focused and be prepared for any curveballs she throws our way."

"Absolutely, boss," Sam chimed in, his eyes locked on the evidence before him. "We'll be ready for anything."

"Remember," I cautioned as I rolled up my sleeves, eager to dive back into our preparations, "Larissa is a formidable opponent. But with meticulous attention to detail and unwavering focus, we'll come out on top."

"Here's to victory!" Jill raised her tablet like a toast, her expression filled with determination.

"Cheers to that," I echoed, my heart pounding with anticipation. "Now let's get back to work. We won't rest until we've done everything possible to win this case for Ava."

We poured over the evidence, each member of the team driven by the desire not just to win, but to outwit and outmaneuver the formidable Larissa Montgomery. The future was uncertain, but one thing was clear—we were a force to be reckoned with, and I couldn't wait to prove it in court.

2
Larissa

"Another one?" I muttered under my breath as I scanned the case file on my desk. Three years of law school, five years working my way up the ladder in this firm, and here I was—Larissa Montgomery, stuck with yet another cheating husband in a high-stakes divorce case. And to make matters worse, my hair appointment had been canceled because my stylist decided to take a last-minute trip to Bali.

"Seriously, what is it about me that screams 'unfaithful men magnet'?" I grumbled to no one in particular. The office was buzzing, papers flying faster than the gossip about my losing streak. As if I didn't already have enough pressure weighing down on me, now I had to deal with this monstrosity of a case.

"Ugh." I sighed, running a hand through my platinum-blond locks.

"Rough day, huh?" my coworker, Jenna, commented casually as she plopped down into the empty chair next to my desk.

"Understatement of the year," I shot back. "I'm starting to think I should just change my name to 'Larissa, Defender of Unfaithful Men.' It's got a nice ring to it, don't you think?"

Jenna chuckled. "Well, at least you can say you've found your niche."

"Please, don't remind me."

Another day, another adulterer.

"I've got to head over to meet with Atlas. Talk to you later?"

"Of course. Good luck."

I gathered up the materials and walked over to the conference room, ready for our fight to begin. I'd heard about him, of course—his movie-star good looks, disarming charm, and winning streak that made it seem like he had Lady Justice herself wrapped around his finger. This case would be anything but easy.

"Ms. Montgomery, allow me to introduce myself," said a voice that could only belong to the man himself. I turned to find Atlas standing before me, extending his hand. His brown hair was perfectly styled, and his vibrant blue eyes seemed to sparkle even under the harsh fluorescent lights.

"Atlas Harrington," he continued, a warm smile spreading across his face. "I've been looking forward to facing off against you."

"Likewise," I replied, shaking his hand with a grip that left no doubt who was in control. "But don't think your charm will work on me. I'm here to win."

"Wouldn't dream of it," he said, still smiling. "May the best lawyer win."

"Indeed." As we sat down at opposite ends of the table, my mind began racing with strategies to outwit this legal Lothario. He might have the charisma of Cary Grant and the looks of George Clooney, but I wasn't going to let that distract me from my mission.

"Alright, let's get down to business," I said, opening my laptop and pulling up my meticulously prepared notes. "Since I represent the husband, I'll begin."

As I launched into my case, I was hyper-aware of Atlas' gaze on me. It was unnerving, but also strangely exhilarating. A thrill of excitement shot through me at the thought of matching wits with someone as formidable as him.

"Ms. Montgomery, I must admit, you've done an impressive job gathering evidence," Atlas conceded when I finished. "But we both know that it takes more than a well-researched case to win. It's about telling a story that resonates."

"Are you suggesting I can't do that?" I shot back, my green eyes flashing with defiance.

"Of course not," he replied. "I'm merely pointing out the importance of understanding human nature—something I happen to excel at."

"Is that so?" I smirked. "Well, Mr. Harrington, I may not have your effortless charm, but I have a few tricks up my sleeve too."

"Really? Do tell." His interest seemed genuine, and I felt a little flattered.

"First and foremost, I never underestimate my opponent," I began, leaning back in my chair and crossing my arms. "I study their every move—their strengths, their weaknesses, their habits. And then, when the time is right, I exploit them."

"Interesting strategy," Atlas mused, raising an eyebrow. "And what, pray tell, have you discovered about me?"

"Wouldn't you like to know?" I teased, a sly grin playing on my lips. He chuckled in response, clearly enjoying our verbal sparring match.

"Very well, keep your secrets," he said, his blue eyes dancing. "But just remember: two can play at that game."

"Good," I retorted, relishing the challenge. "I wouldn't have it any other way."

As we continued to discuss—and occasionally argue—the finer points of our case, it became clear, this was going to be one hell of a battle. But as I glanced across the table at Atlas, his eyes twinkling with mischief and intelligence, I was more than ready for the fight.

Once he left, there were many things that needed to be done.

"Janai, I need you," I called out, my voice echoing through the empty hallway of our law firm. If anyone could help me dig up the dirt on Mark and Ava Kennsington, it was Janai Carlan—my loyal paralegal and best friend.

"Here I am, your legal fairy godmother!" she announced cheerfully as she appeared in my office doorway, her auburn hair pulled back in a messy bun, hazel eyes twinkling. "What's the plan, boss lady?"

"Operation: Take Down Atlas," I declared, motioning for her to take a seat across from me. "We need to uncover every last bit of information on Mark and Ava. I know there's more to their story than meets the eye."

"Ah, so we're going full Nancy Drew on this one, huh?" Janai grinned, pulling out her notepad and pen. "Where do you want to start?"

"Let's start with Ava. She's the one who's been playing the victim card, but something about her just doesn't sit right with me." I tapped my fingers on the desk, trying to recall the details of our previous encounters. "She's bold, brash, and rude—not exactly the damsel in distress she's trying to portray."

"Got it," Janai nodded, scribbling notes. "And what about Mark? Anything specific you want me to look into?"

"His infidelities, obviously," I replied, rolling my eyes at the thought of yet another cheating husband. "But also his business dealings. If he's hiding anything, that's where we'll find it."

"Consider it done," Janai said, snapping her notepad shut. "I'll get started right away."

"Thanks, Janai." I smiled, feeling a surge of gratitude for her unwavering support. "I don't know what I'd do without you."

"Let's not find out," she joked, giving me a small salute before disappearing down the hallway.

As Janai set to work investigating Mark and Ava, I began to prepare my arguments. Every so often, my thoughts would drift back to Atlas—his charisma, his confidence, that infuriatingly handsome smile. I shook my head, trying to focus on the task at hand. *No distractions.*

Alright, Larissa, you've got this. I cracked my knuckles, ready to dive into case law. "Let the battle begin."

The next morning, I walked into the office, coffee in hand, and immediately noticed the hushed whispers that seemed to follow me as I made my way to the conference room. In an attempt to ignore them, I took a deep breath and plunged headfirst into our firm's daily attorney meeting. As I sat down, there was some gossip about Atlas Harrington.

"Did you hear about his last case? He exposed that CEO's secret love child and won the entire settlement for his client," one attorney whispered to another.

"Rumor has it he's never lost a case," another chimed in, her eyes wide with awe.

"Please," I snorted, unable to hold back my disdain. "That's just a rumor perpetuated by his own ego. Besides, we all know how much he loves to dig up dirt on anyone who goes against him. I'm not worried."

"Really?" Jeremy asked, raising an eyebrow. "You should be. Atlas is known for embarrassing rival counsel by exposing their darkest secrets."

"Let him try!" I scoffed, rolling my eyes. "I've got nothing to hide. And I'll be damned if I let some pretty boy with a winning smile distract me from getting justice for my client."

"Bold words, Larissa," Jeremy replied with a grin, clearly amused by my confidence. "So, what's your plan?"

"Simple: two can play at that game." I leaned forward, my eyes narrowing with determination. "You think he's good at digging up dirt? Well, I have Janai on my side, and she's even better. Whatever he throws at me, I'll throw right back at him, tenfold."

"Ooh, I like this side of you, Larissa," Jeremy teased, smirking. "Just make sure you don't get too caught up in the battle and forget about winning the case."

"Trust me," I replied, taking a sip of my coffee and meeting his gaze with a smoldering intensity. "Winning the case is all I care about. Atlas Harrington won't know what hit him."

The room erupted in laughter, and I smiled, feeling a surge of adrenaline course through my veins. In that moment, I was ready to face whatever challenges lay ahead—even if it meant going toe to toe with the infamous Atlas Harrington.

"Alright, everyone," I said, clapping my hands together and standing up from the table. "Let's get to work. We've got a case to win."

The door to the conference room swung open with a flourish, and in strode Calvin Stockton, my boss and owner of Stockton & Associates. His tailored suit screamed expensive, his full head of salt-and-pepper hair impeccably styled, and his presence demanded attention. The temperature in the room dropped a few degrees as he entered; everyone knew when Calvin was around, it was time to put on your game face.

"Montgomery," he said, nodding in my direction as he made his way to the head of the table. "I trust you're ready for today's proceedings?"

"Of course," I replied, trying to keep my voice steady despite the sudden knot in my stomach. "I've been preparing nonstop."

"Good," he said, folding his arms across his chest. "This case is our opportunity to show the world what Stockton & Associates is capable of. We need to win, and we need to win big. The future of this firm depends on it."

I swallowed hard, feeling the weight of his words settle on my shoulders like a lead blanket. It was one thing to face off against Atlas Harrington for my own pride, but now I had the reputation of the entire firm riding on my performance in the courtroom. Talk about pressure.

"Understood," I managed to say, offering him a weak smile. "I won't let you down."

"See that you don't," he replied, his gaze piercing straight through me. "You've got the talent, Montgomery—now it's time to prove it."

With that, he turned on his heel and swept out of the room, leaving me to stare at the empty space where he'd been standing moments before. My heart raced as I tried to process everything he'd just said, my palms suddenly slick with sweat.

"Hey," Janai whispered, leaning over to give my arm a reassuring squeeze. "You've got this, okay? You're the best lawyer I know, and you've never let me down."

"Thanks," I murmured, forcing a smile even as my mind raced with doubts. *What if I wasn't good enough to win this case? What if I couldn't outsmart Atlas? What if I crumbled under the pressure and let everyone down?*

"Alright, everyone," I said, clapping my hands together and standing up from the table. "Let's get back to work. We've got a case to win."

As I strode out of the conference room, I tried to push those thoughts to the back of my mind, focusing instead on the task at hand. But no matter how hard I tried to shake them off, the weight of Calvin's words—and the pressure to succeed—hung heavy on my heart, threatening to consume me.

Ready or not, Atlas Harrington. Here I come.

3
Atlas

The morning sun streamed through my office window, bathing the room in a warm, golden glow. I leaned back in my chair, rubbing the fatigue from my eyes. My team and I had been through every detail, leaving no stone unturned. Now, it was time to put our hard work to the test.

"Alright, team," I called out, clapping my hands together to get everyone's attention. "Today's the day. How are we feeling?"

"Ready to rumble," Sam replied, cracking his knuckles with a grin. Ellen and Jill nodded, their eyes focused and determined.

"Great. Let's go over everything one last time before we hit the courtroom, okay?" I suggested, and they eagerly gathered around the table, ready to dive into our game plan.

We brainstormed strategies, pinpointing Larissa's potential weak spots and discussing how best to exploit them. We practiced our arguments, refining our lines and delivery to ensure maximum impact. And as we reviewed the evidence one final time, I reminded myself that our teamwork would be the key to staying on track and winning this case.

"Atlas, what do you think Larissa will try first?" Jill asked, chewing on the end of her pen.

"Knowing her," I mused, "she'll probably try to poke holes in Ava's credibility. But we've got this—we know how to counter her attacks."

"Speaking of which," Ellen chimed in, "I think we should watch out for any surprises she might throw at us. Larissa has a knack for pulling rabbits out of hats when you least expect it."

"Good point, Ellen," I acknowledged, making a mental note to stay vigilant in court. "But remember, we've got some tricks up our sleeves too."

With a final nod, we made our way to the courthouse, our determination palpable in the crisp morning air. The moment we entered the courtroom, the tension between Larissa and me crackled.

"Morning, Atlas," Larissa greeted me with a tight smile, her piercing green eyes daring me to underestimate her.

"Morning, Larissa," I returned the smile, my blue eyes meeting her gaze head-on. "Ready to dance?"

"Always," she replied, her voice dripping with confidence.

As we faced off in court, the air practically sizzled with our unspoken rivalry. Every objection, every rebuttal, every piece of evidence presented was another volley in our battle of wits. And as the day wore on, it became clear that neither of us was willing to back down without a fight.

During a short recess, I caught my reflection in the restroom mirror, noting the faint sheen of sweat on my brow. This case was proving to be more challenging than anticipated, but I refused to let doubt creep in. My team and I were prepared for this. We were ready to stand our ground and fight for Ava's best interests.

"Atlas," Ellen whispered as we reconvened in the courtroom, "remember what we talked about earlier. Stay focused, and don't let Larissa's tactics throw you off."

"Right," I murmured back, taking a deep breath to steady my nerves. "We've got this."

The trial resumed, and with each passing hour, the stakes grew higher. Larissa continued to press hard, but so did I. After all, I wasn't just fighting for Ava—I was also fighting to prove that when it came to matters of the heart, even the toughest opponents could be outmaneuvered by the power of love. My team and I would not back down, and we were determined to see this through to the bitter end just like every other case.

"Your Honor," I began, my voice strong and unwavering, "we have shown beyond a doubt that our client deserves at least half if not more of the husband's assets."

"Very well, Mr. Harrington," the judge replied, her eyes fixed on me. "Proceed."

I turned to face Larissa, ready for our final showdown.

"While it may be easy to get lost in the details, there's one thing that remains crystal clear: our client, Ava Kennsington, has been wronged."

Larissa watched from the other side of the courtroom, her piercing green eyes filled with determination. But I wasn't about to let her rattle me.

"Throughout this process," I continued, "we have demonstrated that my client's estranged husband, Mark Kennsington, has engaged in infidelity, financial misconduct, and abusive behavior. This is not only unacceptable, but it is downright despicable."

"Objection!" Larissa called out, rising from her seat. "We have already established that these claims are baseless."

"Overruled," the judge responded without hesitation. "Continue, Mr. Harrington."

"Thank you, Your Honor," I said, flashing a quick smile at Larissa before turning my attention back to the jury. "Now, as we've shown, Ava Kennsington is entitled to compensation for the emotional and financial damages she has suffered at the hands of her husband. It is our job—no, our duty—to ensure that she receives what she rightfully deserves."

"We have spent enough time here today. We will reconvene tomorrow. Adjourned."

"Atlas," Ava whispered, her eyes filled with gratitude, "thank you for fighting for me."

"Of course," I replied, giving her a reassuring squeeze on the shoulder. "That's what I'm here for."

As everyone filed out of the room, I couldn't help but steal one last glance at Larissa. She looked back at me, her expression unreadable. But beneath the surface, I saw a flicker of something else—perhaps admiration. Or even respect.

4
Larissa

"Your Honor, the evidence clearly shows that my client is entitled to a fair and equitable division of assets." My voice was steady and firm as I locked eyes with the judge. "My client has already offered a more than generous settlement, which Mr. Harrington's client stubbornly refuses to accept."

Atlas chimed in, flashing his million-dollar smile. "Generous? Your client is attempting to leave my client with next to nothing after twenty years of marriage. My client has dedicated her life to supporting her husband and raising their children. This isn't generosity; it's highway robbery."

"Mr. Harrington," Judge Phillips interjected, "please refrain from making inflammatory remarks."

"Of course, Your Honor," he replied.

How could he not see through Atlas's facade?

"Your Honor, I assure you that my client wants nothing more than to resolve this matter fairly and amicably so both parties can move on with their lives," Atlas said, his blue eyes practically twinkling as he spoke.

Ugh, those eyes. They were like pools of liquid charm, and they seemed to be working their magic on the judge.

"Thank you, Mr. Harrington," Judge Phillips responded. "It's refreshing to see a lawyer who understands the importance of civility in these proceedings."

"Your Honor, if I may," I interjected. "I understand Mr. Harrington's desire for civility, but we must not lose sight of what's at stake here."

"Ms. Montgomery, please," Atlas said in that infuriatingly condescending tone he'd mastered, "let's not resort to melodrama. We're all adults here." My blood was boiling as his disarming smile returned, making it seem like I was the one being unreasonable.

"Your Honor," I gritted out, trying to regain my composure, "I simply wish to remind the court that my client is seeking a fair and equitable division of assets, which is his legal right."

"Very well, Ms. Montgomery," Judge Phillips conceded, though I couldn't help but notice his gaze lingered on Atlas for a moment longer than necessary. I had to find a way to outsmart him before he won over the judge completely.

As we continued our verbal sparring match, I tried to focus on the facts, but Atlas's charm seemed to be clouding the judge's judgment. His laughter filled the room as he shared an amusing anecdote about a previous case, and my grip on the situation continued slipping away. I needed a new strategy, and fast.

"Your Honor, if I may," I began again, my voice wavering slightly as I tried to keep my nerves at bay. "Can we please return to the matter at hand? My client is depending on me and I refuse to let him down."

"Of course, Ms. Montgomery," Judge Phillips replied, his attention finally returning to the case. "I assure you that this court takes its responsibilities very seriously. Let's pick this up tomorrow."

"Thank you, Your Honor," I said, swallowing hard as I prepared to go toe to toe with Atlas once more. No matter how charming he was, I refused to let his charisma distract from the truth. I owed it to my client—and to myself.

The moment I stepped out of the courtroom, my heart raced as if it were trying to escape my chest. All I wanted was to put some distance between Atlas and me. The heavy oak door closed behind me with a thud, and I leaned against the cold marble wall, pressing my eyes shut. My thoughts swirled like a storm, each one more frustrating than the last.

"Rough day in there, huh?" Zoey's voice snapped me back to reality. She stood next to me, her dark curls bouncing around her face as she offered a sympathetic smile. No one knew me better than my best friend and fellow lawyer, Zoey Lofton.

"Atlas Harrington is infuriating," I growled, gripping my legal pad so tightly that my knuckles turned white. "He's all charm and no substance, but somehow, he still manages to win everyone over—even the judge."

"Hey, don't be so hard on yourself, Larissa," Zoey said, placing a comforting hand on my shoulder. "You're an amazing lawyer, and you've been preparing. You know every detail inside and out. No amount of charisma can change that."

"Maybe, but it doesn't help when the judge keeps getting distracted by his witty comebacks." I sighed and opened my eyes, meeting Zoey's concerned gaze. "I need to find a way to beat him at his own game."

Zoey's expression brightened as she nodded. "Remember when we first started practicing law together? We lost a case to him because of that same charm. But we swore that we'd find a way to beat him someday, and now's your chance."

"Right," I agreed, determination settling in my bones. "This time, I won't let his charm get the best of me. I'll focus on the facts and make sure that the judge sees the truth."

"Exactly!" Zoey grinned. "You've got this, Larissa. You're fierce, intelligent, and a force to be reckoned with. Atlas doesn't stand a chance."

"Thanks," I said, my lips curving into a small smile for the first time since entering the courtroom. "With you in my corner, I feel like I can take on the world—or at least, Atlas Harrington."

"Darn straight!" Zoey agreed, punching the air. "Now, let's grab a coffee sometime soon."

"Of course, good luck on your case," I said before she disappeared through the door.

I pushed open the heavy courthouse doors, my heels clicking confidently on the polished marble floor. *Bring it on, Atlas.* I was ready to face whatever challenges lay ahead. No matter how charming he was, I refused to let him win without a fight.

The sun beat down on my shoulders as I stepped out of the courthouse, momentarily blinding me with its harsh glare. I squinted and pulled a pair of sunglasses from my purse, sliding them onto my face. The cool metal frames helped to ground me, even though the persistent thrumming of my pulse threatened to drown out everything else.

"Ms. Montgomery," came that all-too-familiar voice, smooth as silk and rich as dark chocolate. Atlas Harrington leaned against the courthouse wall, his arms folded across his chest and a smirk playing at the corners of his lips. "I must say, I didn't expect you to put up such a fight today."

"Is that so?" I retorted, my voice dripping with sarcasm. "Well, Mr. Harrington, you should know by now that I'm not one to back down easily."

"Clearly," he replied, raising an eyebrow as he straightened up and closed the distance between us. "But tell me, do you always resort to personal attacks when you can't win a case fair and square?"

I bristled at the insinuation, my hands balling into fists at my sides. "Whatever it takes for my clients, Atlas. You might try it sometime instead of relying on your pretty face."

"Ouch," he said, feigning hurt as he placed a hand over his heart. "You know, Larissa, charm isn't everything. Sometimes you have to rely on your actual legal skills to make your case."

The condescending tone in his voice set fire to my anger. "Are you suggesting that I don't have legal skills? That's rich coming from the poster boy for 'style over substance'!"

"See, that's the problem with you, Larissa," Atlas shot back. "You're so busy trying to prove yourself that you can't even see when someone's giving you a compliment."

"Compliment?" I snorted, my rage bubbling over. "You have a twisted way of showing it, Mister 'I-Can-Win-Any-Case-With-My-Good-Looks'!"

"Is that what you think of me?" Atlas asked, his voice dangerously low. "Just some shallow pretty boy who doesn't take his job seriously?"

"Isn't that the image you project?"

"Maybe, but you shouldn't judge a book by its cover, Ms. Montgomery. There's more to me than meets the eye."

"Likewise," I hissed, feeling the heat rising in my cheeks. "And don't ever underestimate me again."

"Wouldn't dream of it," Atlas replied, his blue eyes flashing with an intensity that made my heart race. "Good luck, Larissa. You're going to need it."

"Thanks," I said through gritted teeth. "I'll be sure to remember that when I'm celebrating my victory."

My vision blurred as the red-hot rage surged through me. I clenched my fists, nails digging into my palms, and for a moment, I was completely out of control. My chest heaved with the effort to control my breathing.

"Fine. Just remember, you started this."

"Started what?" Atlas asked, infuriating me even more. "A friendly rivalry between colleagues? I thought that's what you wanted."

"Rivalry?" I scoffed. "This is not a game, Atlas. This is my career, my life. And I won't stand here and let you belittle me."

"Belittle you? Larissa, all I ever did was try to keep up with you," he said, his voice surprisingly gentle. "You're the one who made this personal."

"Keep up with me?" I echoed, my cheeks burning with embarrassment. *What had I done? Ugh, I was acting like a petulant child, not a respected lawyer.*

Atlas sighed, rubbing the back of his neck, clearly uncomfortable with the direction the conversation had taken. "Look, Larissa, I didn't mean to upset you. But we can't keep going at each other's throats like this. It's not good for either of us."

"Maybe not," I admitted, lowering my gaze to the pavement. "But don't expect me to go easy on you in court."

"Wouldn't dream of it," he repeated, the corners of his mouth twitching into the faintest hint of a smile. "Just promise me you'll keep it professional from now on."

"Fine," I muttered, my heart aching with the weight of my shame. "Professional."

"Good," Atlas said, his voice softening as he extended his hand. "Truce?"

"Truce," I replied, hesitantly taking his hand.

"Take care, Larissa," Atlas whispered, releasing my hand and turning to walk back into the courthouse.

"Wait!" I called out, my voice catching in my throat. He paused, glancing back at me expectantly. "I'm... I'm sorry."

"Apology accepted," he replied with a warm smile. "See you in court."

"See you," I echoed, watching as he disappeared through the heavy doors. My heart pounded in my chest, equal parts embarrassment and something else entirely, something I couldn't quite put my finger on.

As I walked away from the courthouse, my thoughts raced with uncertainty about how to proceed. The last thing I wanted was to be Atlas's enemy, but if we kept going down this path, we'd tear each other apart. I needed to find a way to win without losing myself in the process. And maybe, just maybe, I could do it without sacrificing the fragile truce we'd just established.

5
Atlas

As I walked down the courthouse hallway, my recent interactions with Larissa Montgomery came to mind. The woman was a force of nature, and her no-nonsense attitude challenged me in ways I'd never experienced before. I rolled my shoulders, trying to shake off the tension that seemed to linger after each encounter with her.

"Hey, Atlas, heard about what happened outside with Larissa," a fellow lawyer whispered as he passed by, giving me a sympathetic pat on the back. The hushed tones and stolen glances indicated that word had spread quickly about our heated confrontation. Oddly enough, no one seemed to blame me for what transpired.

Unbelievable. With the searing fire that flashed in Larissa's piercing green eyes during that conversation—somehow, she managed to make even anger look attractive.

"Atlas, my man," Richard greeted me as we both entered the courtroom together. "You know, you could use what happened with Larissa as ammunition against her in court."

I raised an eyebrow, considering it. "I appreciate the tip, Richard, but I think I'll try something a little more creative to gain the advantage. Besides, it's always good to have a secret weapon up my sleeve just in case."

"Suit yourself," Richard shrugged, clearly disappointed that I wouldn't indulge in some good old-fashioned legal mudslinging.

I took my seat and began reviewing my notes, and everything started swirling in my head. Larissa was tough, intelligent, and infuriatingly captivating all at once. I knew that winning over someone like her would be quite the challenge, but I was more than ready to rise to the occasion.

Bring it on, Montgomery. Whatever tricks she had up her sleeve, I was ready to play along and see where this game would take us.

"Nice suit, Atlas," Katharine said, her red lipstick perfect against her alabaster skin. It was Katharine James, the opposing attorney in this case. Now, she was dangerous.

"Thanks, Katharine." I flashed her my most disarming smile, wondering what she was up to.

"Look, I know we're on opposite sides today, but I thought you should know something about Larissa." She leaned in and lowered her voice, the sweet scent of her perfume wafting over me. "Ever since I started seeing her ex, Elliot, she's been acting... out of character."

"Jealous, is she?" I raised an eyebrow, trying not to let my surprise show. "I didn't think she was the type."

"Neither did I," Katharine replied with a smirk, her eyes glinting. "But people change. Anyway, if you want to undermine her, try something unconventional. Get under her skin. You know, like you do with everyone else."

"Interesting advice coming from the opposition," I mused, studying her closely. Despite the casual nature of our conversation, I could tell there was more to it than simple gossip. Katharine had never been one to share courtroom secrets without expecting something in return. And yet, the idea of getting Larissa to trust me, to see that I wasn't just another shark in the legal pool, was strangely appealing.

"Consider it a professional courtesy," Katharine shrugged. "Besides, isn't it more fun when we keep things interesting?"

"Perhaps," I admitted, my mind already racing with ideas. "But I'm not interested in getting involved in your little rivalry. Thanks for the tip, though."

"Your loss," she pouted, turning away to gather her things. "Good luck, Atlas."

"Thanks, Katharine," I replied, watching her walk away. As intriguing as her words were, I knew better than to play with fire. Larissa was a force to be reckoned with, and if she truly was jealous of Katharine and Elliot's relationship, there was no telling what lengths she would go to in order to maintain her professional reputation.

Instead, I decided to push just enough to make her retreat a little, to show her that I wasn't the enemy. My goal now was to charm her into trusting me, to believe that I had both Ava and Mark Kennsington's best interests at heart. If I played my cards right, perhaps we could even find a way to work together for the sake of our clients.

Game on, Montgomery. Let's see how well you handle a taste of your own medicine.

My heart pounded from the adrenaline in the courtroom, I stepped into the hallway and nearly collided with Larissa. The surprise on her face mirrored my own, and for a moment, we stood there speechless.

"Wow, fancy seeing you here," I said, breaking the silence with a small chuckle. "How've you been?"

"Uh, fine," she stammered, a hint of embarrassment coloring her cheeks. It wasn't like her to be so flustered. "I mean, aside from yesterday, obviously."

"Hey, no hard feelings," I assured her, shooting her a disarming smile. "We all have our moments, right?"

"I suppose. Thanks for being understanding."

"Of course." I leaned against the wall, allowing myself a moment to enjoy the lightheartedness between us. "You know, for what it's worth, I think your passion is one of your greatest assets. Makes things more exciting, don't you think?"

"Is that so?" She raised an eyebrow, a playful glint flickering in her green eyes. "And here I thought you were just trying to butter me up to gain the upper hand."

"Would I do that?"

"Absolutely," she retorted without missing a beat. "But nice try, Harrington. Dirty tricks won't work on me."

"Dirty tricks? I'm wounded," I replied, pressing my hand over my heart. Inwardly, though, I knew she was right—any attempt to manipulate her would likely backfire spectacularly. Still, I couldn't resist pushing the envelope just a little. "But if you ever want to grab a drink and discuss strategy... or anything else for that matter, you know where to find me."

Larissa's eyes narrowed, but the ghost of a smile remained on her lips. "I'll keep that in mind," she said coolly, before turning on her heel and striding away.

As I watched her go, something stirred within me—a mixture of admiration, intrigue, and a healthy dose of challenge. Larissa Montgomery was unlike any other attorney I'd ever faced, and despite our differences, I was drawn to her. She was a formidable opponent, no doubt about it, but perhaps there was more to her than met the eye.

6
Larissa

The office was a flurry of activity, papers rustling like leaves in the wind and hurried footsteps echoing through the halls. I stood by the window, scanning the bustling city below.

"Janai, are we missing anything?" I called out, tapping my foot impatiently. "I want to make sure Mark's case is airtight."

"Relax, Larissa," Janai replied, her quick wit shining through even as she leafed through stacks of documents. "I've got our bases covered. You're just wound up because you want to show off your mad lawyering skills against Atlas."

I scoffed, crossing my arms. "Hardly. He may be charming, but I can hold my own against him. I just need to win this case and prove to everyone that I'm the best lawyer in town."

"Alright then, Sherlock. Look what I found while digging into Atlas's past." Janai handed me a manila folder with a smirk on her face. "You won't believe what he did."

My eyes widened as she flipped through the contents of the folder. The pages revealed a surprising secret that could potentially give us the upper hand. A pang of guilt came for prying into Atlas's personal life, but it was all part of the game, and I needed to win.

"Janai, this could change everything," I whispered, stunned by the revelation. "I need some time alone to figure out how to use this against him."

"Sure thing, boss." Janai nodded, understanding the weight of the information we just uncovered. She slipped quietly out of my office, leaving me to contemplate the next move.

I sank into my chair, my mind racing with possibilities. It wasn't just about winning the case anymore. I had stumbled upon a vulnerability in Atlas that could be exploited. As much as I tried to dismiss it, there was also a hint of remorse for wanting to use this secret against him.

Get it together. This is about Mark's case, not your feelings.

I began to strategize, my eyes flitting back and forth between the incriminating documents and my notes on Mark's case. I would find a way to use this secret to our advantage, even if it meant sacrificing the tentative respect I held for Atlas. After all, I was a lawyer first and foremost, and nothing was going to stand in my way.

Ugh, Atlas Harrington. It would be so much easier to hate him if he weren't so infuriatingly attractive. I shook my head, snapping myself out of it. This was not the time for fantasies about my opponent.

Time to focus.

I rubbed my temples in frustration. This wasn't just about proving my abilities as a lawyer anymore; it was about untangling this mess.

"This complicates things."

"Complications can be fun," Janai mused, winking at me. "Especially when they involve Atlas Harrington."

"Janai!" I scolded, feeling my cheeks flushed. "This is serious. And besides, I'm not—" I hesitated, unwilling to admit how much Atlas had been on my mind lately. "It doesn't matter. I need to call him about this."

"Ooh, do I sense a heated phone call in your future?" Janai asked. "I'll leave you to it, then. Good luck, tiger."

"Thanks," I said, rolling my eyes as she sashayed out of the room. I took a deep breath, my heart pounding as I dialed Atlas's number.

"Hello?" His voice was smooth and confident, just like the man himself.

"Atlas, we need to talk about Mark."

"Ah, so you've discovered his little secret, then?" He sounded almost amused, which only served to stoke my growing anger.

"You knew about this, didn't you?"

"Perhaps," he replied. "But what difference does it make now? You're still going to represent him, aren't you?"

"Of course I am," I snapped, clenching my fists at my sides. "But don't think for a second that your knowledge of this situation will give you any advantage in court. I will fight tooth and nail, Atlas. And that includes bringing down anyone who tries to stand in my way."

"Such passion. Just one of the many things I find so... intriguing about you."

"Keep your flattery to yourself," I warned, my stomach fluttering despite my annoyance. "This isn't about me. It's about the case."

"Very well," he conceded, his tone serious once more. "I look forward to seeing how you handle this newfound information, Larissa. Just remember—secrets have a way of coming back to haunt us. Both in and out of the courtroom."

"Thanks for the warning," I replied, my mind racing with strategies and counterarguments. "But I can take care of myself."

"Of that, I have no doubt," he said before hanging up.

As I stared at the phone, my heart hammered. My feelings for Atlas would have to be set aside—at least until this case was over. For now, my focus had to remain on Mark and the battle ahead. And no matter what obstacles were thrown my way, I was determined to come out on top.

7
Atlas

"Risotto and reconciliation"—that's how I'd describe my last-ditch effort to save the case from going down in flames. It was time to make amends with Larissa Montgomery, that firecracker of a lawyer who had no qualms about taking me down a peg or two. I decided to invite her to Luigi's, an Italian restaurant near the courthouse that served up portions as generous as the owner's belly.

"Hey, Larissa," I said on the phone, trying to sound casual, "I thought we could talk things out at Luigi's. What do you say?"

"Fine," she replied, a hint of suspicion in her voice. "But I'm only agreeing because I happen to like their eggplant parm."

"Great, see you at seven," I said before hanging up.

When I arrived at the restaurant, Larissa stood outside, arms crossed tightly over her chest. The fading sunlight caught her green eyes in a way that made them shimmer like emeralds. She was stunning, and it was irritating to find myself so drawn to someone I was supposed to be at odds with.

"Hey there," I greeted, hoping to break the ice. "You know, I've always believed that the best conversations happen over a plate of pasta."

"Is that so?" she asked, raising an eyebrow, clearly not amused.

"Absolutely," I replied, holding the door open for her as we entered the bustling restaurant. "There's something about carbs that just brings people together."

We took our seats at a cozy table by the window, and I hoped that the warm ambiance of the place would help thaw the frost between us. As we perused the menu, I couldn't help but steal glances at Larissa—her hair framing her face perfectly, her eyes scanning the options with the same intensity she brought to the courtroom.

"Alright, Atlas," she said as she put down the menu, leaning back in her chair. "Why don't you cut to the chase and tell me why we're really here?"

"Can't a guy just enjoy a meal with a worthy opponent?" I tried to play it cool, but the truth was that I was desperate for an ally in this case—and who better than the person who knew all the angles?

"Save the charm for the judge, Harrington," she shot back, but there was a hint of a smile on her lips. Maybe my optimism was starting to work its magic.

"Alright," I said, waving away the hovering waiter, who seemed as eager to take our order as a vulture circling its prey. "I'll get the lasagna, and she'll have the eggplant parm. And a bottle of the house red to share and I insist on covering this meal. Consider it an olive branch."

"Fine," she relented, folding her arms across her chest. "But don't think that means you're off the hook."

"Wouldn't dream of it," I replied, raising my hands in mock surrender. The waiter retreated, no doubt relieved to escape the tension between us. I took a deep breath, preparing myself for what was sure to be a challenging conversation.

"Atlas," Larissa began, swirling the wine in her glass before taking a sip. "There's something I've been wanting to ask you. About your ex-girlfriend—the lawyer, right?"

My stomach clenched involuntarily as memories of my past relationship resurfaced. How had she found out? I tried to keep my voice steady. "What about her?"

"Word on the street is that she cheated on you while working on a case together. Is that true?" Her question was blunt, but her eyes betrayed genuine curiosity.

"Where did you hear that?" I asked, gripping my wineglass tightly, suddenly very aware of the weight of her revelation.

"Does it matter?" She leaned back in her chair, studying my reaction with those piercing green eyes. "I just find it interesting that you're so adamant about playing by the rules now. It's almost like you're overcompensating for something."

"Maybe I just believe in doing the right thing," I shot back, trying to ignore the uncomfortable feeling that she had struck a nerve.

"Or maybe you're afraid of getting hurt again," she countered. "And if that's the case, then it's going to be difficult for us to work together."

I took a slow sip of my wine, buying myself time to come up with a response. She was right—I didn't want to get burned again. But I also couldn't let her use that against me. "Look, Larissa," I said, meeting her gaze head-on. "What happened between me and my ex is ancient history. It has nothing to do with this case or how I conduct myself as a lawyer."

"Good," she replied, nodding slowly, apparently satisfied with my answer. Though I couldn't shake the feeling that she was still testing me, probing for weaknesses.

"Can we move on from psychoanalyzing my love life now?" I asked, forcing a light chuckle. "I thought we were here to talk about the case."

"Of course," she agreed, a sly smile playing at the corners of her lips. "Let's focus on what really matters."

Larissa's revelation had knocked me off-balance, and I was constantly second-guessing my motives. Was I really just trying to do the right thing, or was there something deeper driving me? And could I trust Larissa not to exploit my vulnerabilities?

Only time would tell. But one thing was certain—this case was about to get a whole lot more interesting.

We weren't friends, after all. We were adversaries, locked in a high-stakes legal battle. And as much as I wanted to enjoy this unexpected connection, I couldn't forget what was at stake.

"Atlas," she said suddenly, her tone serious. "Can I ask you something?"

"Of course."

"Promise me that whatever happens in court, we won't let it make us crazy."

"Deal," I agreed without hesitation, reaching across the table to shake her hand. "May the best lawyer win, Larissa."

"Indeed," she smiled, giving my hand a firm squeeze. "May the best lawyer win."

Desperate to shift the focus away from our professional rivalry, I decided to double down on the charm offensive. Inhaling deeply, I fixed her with my most dazzling smile and declared, "You know, Larissa, you really are stunning tonight. That dress brings out the fire in your eyes."

"Nice try, Harrington," she retorted, rolling her eyes playfully. "But flattery will get you nowhere with me."

"Really?" I challenged, raising an eyebrow. "So you're immune to compliments, huh? Well, how about this: not only are you one of the most beautiful women I've ever met, but you're also one of the smartest. If beauty and brains were a crime, they'd lock you up and throw away the key."

"Okay, okay," she conceded, a reluctant grin tugging at the corners of her mouth. "I admit, that was a good one."

"See?" I winked. "I knew I could make you smile."

"Fine, you win this round." She laughed. "But don't get too cocky, Atlas. Remember, I still know how to play dirty."

"Wouldn't have it any other way," I shot back, feeling the electric current between us surge once more.

As we continued to trade barbs and banter, I found myself

wondering if this game we were playing was worth the risk. What would happen if our flirtation spiraled out of control?

But as I gazed into her eyes, there was something genuine and real between us—something that went beyond the courtroom and our professional rivalry. And for now, that was enough to keep me hooked.

8
Larissa

The courtroom door swung open with a creak, and I strode in, my nerves buzzed under my skin, but my expression remained cool and collected. This was my stage, where I shone brightest. Winning this case for Mark.

"Miss Montgomery," Judge Phillips acknowledged me with a curt nod as I took my place at the table.

"Your Honor," I replied, giving him a tight smile.

Atlas Harrington, opposing counsel and my current headache, sauntered into the room next.

"Ah, good morning, Your Honor," he greeted Judge Phillips warmly. "I heard your golf game is coming along quite nicely! Congrats on that hole in one last weekend."

Judge Phillips' stern face cracked into a smile. "Thank you, Mr. Harrington. It was quite the surprise, I must say."

Ugh. How did Atlas always know just what to say?

"Shall we proceed?" I interjected, impatient to get started.

"Of course, Miss Montgomery," the judge said, his smile fading back into a neutral expression. "Mr. Harrington, you may begin."

"Your Honor," Atlas began, oozing charm from every pore, "my client has been nothing but a loving, devoted mother and wife. Unfortunately, Mark has refused to recognize her dedication to their family—"

"Objection!" I snapped, unable to let Atlas monopolize the conversation any longer. "We're here to discuss the division of assets, not to debate Mrs. Kennsington's character."

"Overruled," Judge Phillips sighed. "Please continue, Mr. Harrington."

"Thank you, Your Honor," Atlas beamed, not missing a beat. "As I was saying, Mark has been the primary breadwinner for their family, supporting Ava and their child in every way possible. It's only fair that she be awarded—"

"Objection!" I tried again, my face flushing with frustration. "This is irrelevant to the case."

"Miss Montgomery," Judge Phillips said, his tone icy, "I'll allow Mr. Harrington some leeway in presenting his argument. Overruled."

"Thank you, Your Honor," Atlas said, his grin widening. He continued on, spinning a fairy tale of his client's devotion and generosity while I stewed in my seat.

I clenched my fists under the table, biting back the urge to interrupt again. I couldn't let him get the upper hand, but it seemed as though the judge had already made up his mind.

"Your Honor—" I began, hoping to interject a point of my own.

"Miss Montgomery, please wait your turn," Judge Phillips snapped.

"Your Honor, I have evidence that will shed light on Ava's true motives in this divorce," I announced as we reconvened after the short recess, my voice steady and determined.

"Miss Montgomery, you may proceed," Judge Phillips said, his eyes narrowing slightly.

"Thank you, Your Honor." I stood up, clutching the papers that would reveal the truth behind Ava's insistence on a hefty settlement. Just as I was about to speak again, Atlas interrupted me.

"Your Honor, before Miss Montgomery presents her so-called

evidence, I'd like to remind the court that this is a matter of division of assets, not an inquisition into my client's personal life," he said, flashing that disarming smile of his.

"Mr. Harrington has a point, Miss Montgomery," the judge warned, his gaze stern. "Please ensure your evidence is relevant."

"Of course, Your Honor." I drew in a deep breath and launched into my argument. But every time I tried to present the crucial information, Atlas managed to interject, twisting my words and diverting the judge's attention back to the financial aspects of the case.

"Your Honor, if I may approach the bench?" I asked, hoping a face-to-face conversation might allow me to get my message across.

"Miss Montgomery, this is highly unorthodox," Judge Phillips said, clearly irritated by my request. But to my relief, he gestured for me to approach.

"Your Honor," I whispered urgently, leaning in close, "I have proof here that Ava's real motive is to ruin Mark financially as revenge for an extramarital affair. This isn't just about dividing their assets fairly; she wants to leave him penniless."

"Miss Montgomery," the judge hissed, "I've warned you before about bringing personal matters into this case."

"Your Honor, I must insist—" I started, but he cut me off.

"Miss Montgomery, return to your seat." His voice was cold and final.

"But Your Honor—"

"Enough!" Judge Phillips bellowed, slamming his gavel down with a resounding crack. The courtroom fell silent, all eyes on me. "One more outburst, Miss Montgomery, and I'll hold you in contempt."

Swallowing the lump in my throat, I returned to my seat, feeling the weight of defeat settling over me like a heavy cloak. I knew that without presenting Ava's true motives, my chances of winning this case were dwindling by the second.

As the hearing continued, I struggled to focus on the proceedings, my mind racing with possible strategies to salvage the situation. But one thing was clear: unless I could find a way to present my evidence, the truth would remain buried beneath Atlas's charm and the judge's disapproval.

As I sat in my seat, planning my next move, Ava and Mark suddenly erupted into a heated argument, their voices raised and full of venom.

"Mark, you can't seriously think you're going to get custody of our son after what you've done!" Ava spat, her chestnut hair whipping around as she turned to face her soon-to-be ex-husband.

"Me? You're the one who's trying to bleed me dry! You don't care about our son; you just want to punish me for your own twisted reasons!" Mark retorted, his face red with anger.

"Quiet!" the judge barked, but they ignored him, continuing their bickering. Their back-and-forth became a cacophony of accusations and bitterness that filled the courtroom.

"Enough!" The moderator, a woman with silver hair and glasses perched on her nose, threw up her hands in frustration. "This is not productive for anyone involved!"

As if on cue, Judge Phillips slammed his gavel down again, its sound echoing through the now silent room. "Order in the court!" he growled. "I have had enough of this circus."

Everyone froze, the weight of the judge's words sinking in. He glared at each of us in turn, his gaze like cold steel. "Attorneys, control your clients. If you cannot do so, I will have no choice but to hold all of you in contempt." He paused, letting the threat hang in the air. "We will reconvene tomorrow morning at nine sharp. In the meantime, I expect everyone to gain some semblance of decorum."

The hearing came to an abrupt halt. Ava and Mark begrudgingly retreated to their respective corners, leaving the rest of us to pick up the pieces. I tried to quell the disappointment and frustration bubbling inside me, knowing that I had to keep my emotions in check if I wanted any chance of winning this case.

As the courtroom began to empty, it felt like a tornado had just ripped through the room, leaving destruction and chaos in its wake. But amidst the wreckage, there was still hope. I just needed to find a way to present my evidence without inciting the judge's wrath. The stakes were high, and the clock was ticking. Tomorrow, I'd come back stronger and more prepared than ever before.

Ava stormed out of the courtroom. Mark followed close behind, muttering under his breath about the colossal waste of time this had been. They didn't even bother to glance back at us, their faith in their attorneys clearly shaken.

The heavy wooden doors slammed shut, leaving Atlas and me alone in the hearing room. For a moment, the silence between us was absolute, the weight of today's events hanging heavily in the air. I stared straight ahead, refusing to look at him, afraid that his smug smile would be too much for me to bear.

But when he finally spoke, it wasn't with arrogance or disdain. Instead, an unexpected chuckle escaped his lips, echoing through the empty room. I glanced over at him, irritation bubbling up inside me. How could he laugh after what had just happened?

"Can you believe it?" he asked, shaking his head and grinning. "We spend years studying law, working our asses off to become the best damn lawyers we can be, and then we're reduced to babysitting bickering clients like Ava and Mark." His laughter grew louder, and despite my annoyance, I couldn't help but crack a small smile at the absurdity of it all.

"Sometimes I wonder if we chose the wrong profession," I admitted, letting out a short, humorless laugh of my own. "Maybe we should have gone into couples counseling instead."

"Or marriage therapy!" Atlas added, still laughing. "We could have a joint practice—Montgomery & Harrington: Saving Marriages One Couple at a Time."

"Only if you promise to handle the golf-obsessed clients," I shot back, a genuine smile finally breaking through my frustration. "I've reached my limit for hearing about the intricacies of sand traps and putting greens."

"Deal," Atlas agreed, his laughter subsiding as he wiped a tear from the corner of his eye. "But seriously, Larissa, tomorrow's a new day."

"Thanks, Atlas," I nodded, grateful for his unexpected camaraderie. "You're right. Tomorrow, we fight another day."

"Wait, wait," Atlas gasped between laughs, holding up a hand. "You sounded just like this!" He mimicked my frustrated expression, complete with furrowed brow and clenched fists. "It was almost cute... if it hadn't been so infuriating."

"Ha! Very funny." I rolled my eyes, crossing my arms defensively. "Well, at least I wasn't fawning over the judge like some kind of lovesick teenager." I put on my best imitation of Atlas's voice, batting my eyelashes dramatically. "'Oh, Your Honor, I simply adore golf! Why, just last week, I made the most marvelous chip shot from the rough!'"

Atlas doubled over in laughter, clutching his sides as he struggled to catch his breath. "Okay, okay, you got me," he conceded, wiping tears from his cheeks. "I may have laid it on a bit thick with the golf talk."

"Thick?" I snorted. "You practically smothered us all in golf anecdotes. And for the record, I still have no idea what a 'chip shot' is."

"Hey, you gotta do what you gotta do to win a case." He grinned, raising his hands in mock surrender. "But let's not forget that you were the one who couldn't keep quiet long enough to even present your argument."

"Because you kept interrupting me!" I exclaimed, throwing my hands up in exasperation. "I've never seen someone so determined to monopolize the conversation."

"Guilty as charged," Atlas admitted, chuckling at our shared frustration. "But hey, at least we found some common ground, right? We both think the other person is unbearable."

"Speak for yourself," I smirked. "I'm a delight."

"Of course you are." He laughed, shaking his head fondly.

Our laughter continued, echoing through the empty hearing room. We were so caught up in our moment of levity that neither of us noticed the door swing open until a bailiff cleared his throat loudly.

"Excuse me," he said, his voice stern as he regarded us with a disapproving frown. "This is a courtroom, not a comedy club. I'm going to have to ask you both to leave."

"Of course, sir," Atlas replied, struggling to suppress another laugh as we gathered our things. "Our apologies for any disturbance."

The tension that had been coiled tightly within me seemed to dissipate as we walked down the hallway, leaving behind the echoes of our laughter. Just moments ago, I was ready to tear Atlas apart with my bare hands—and now, here we were, sharing a laugh like old friends.

"Thanks for... well, whatever that was," I said, turning to face Atlas with a genuine smile. "I didn't expect to leave that courtroom in better spirits than when I entered it."

"Likewise," he replied, his lips curving into a grin. "It's not every day you find a worthy opponent who can make you laugh."

"Is that a compliment?" I teased, arching an eyebrow as I tried to decipher his expression. "I'm flattered."

"Take it as you will." He shrugged, his eyes twinkling with amusement. "But don't get too comfortable, Larissa. When we return to that courtroom, I won't be holding back."

"Neither will I," I retorted, my determination surging back to the forefront. "Next time, I'll be prepared for your antics—and I won't let you derail me again."

"Bring it on," he challenged, his tone lighthearted. "I look forward to seeing what you've got up your sleeve."

"Trust me, you have no idea," I murmured, my mind already racing with strategies and tactics for the next hearing. This unexpected encounter with Atlas had given me clarity. It was as though a fog had lifted, allowing me to see the path forward more clearly.

"Until then," he said, extending a hand toward me. "May the best lawyer win."

"Agreed," I responded, taking his hand in mine and giving it a firm shake. The warmth of his skin against mine sent a shiver down my spine, but I quickly pushed the sensation aside. This was no time to be distracted by Atlas's infuriating charm. I had a case to win.

9
Larissa

As I stepped into the elevator, clutching my morning coffee, I checked my phone for any pressing messages. The scent of toasted bagels wafted up from the lobby café, momentarily distracting me from my task. Just as I reached for the button to close the doors and whisk me away to my office, my phone buzzed with an incoming call.

"Ms. Montgomery," a voice crackled on the other end. "I've uncovered something important. There are secret assets outside the country that you need to know about."

"Wait, slow down," I said, barely containing my surprise. My heart skipped a beat as the implications of this information began to sink in. This could change everything for our case. As the elevator doors shut, I somehow managed to keep my cool. "Let's discuss this further. I'll get back to you shortly."

"Very well," the client replied solemnly before hanging up.

My fingers danced across the screen of my phone, composing a quick text to Atlas. If anyone could handle a discovery like this, it was him.

"Urgent meeting needed. Coffee shop near the courthouse in thirty minutes?"

"See you there!" His response came quickly, accompanied by a smiley emoticon.

As I exited the elevator and entered the familiar chaos of my firm, my thoughts raced with the possibilities. With secret assets involved, this case could become even more complex than I had originally imagined. But at least I wouldn't be navigating these murky waters alone; Atlas would be right there with me.

I walked briskly toward my office, eager to gather my things and head over to the coffee shop. I couldn't help but smile at the thought of seeing Atlas again. Our professional rivalry kept us on our toes, but I'd be lying if I said I didn't enjoy spending time with him. His disarming smile and vibrant blue eyes were enough to brighten even the most stressful day.

"Morning, Larissa!" my assistant greeted me cheerfully as I passed her desk.

"Morning," I replied with a nod, trying to hide my excitement. "I've got to run out for a meeting. Hold down the fort, will you?"

"Of course," she answered with an understanding smile.

As I gathered my things and prepared to leave, my thoughts turned back to Atlas. What would his reaction be to this new development? Would he share my concerns and fears, or would his optimism win out once again?

Regardless of what lay ahead, one thing was certain: our lives were about to become much more interesting, and perhaps even more intertwined than ever before.

The aroma of freshly ground coffee beans filled the air as I took a seat in the corner of the café. A few minutes later, Atlas strolled in, looking every bit the charming lawyer that he was—sandy-blond hair perfectly styled and a confident smile playing on his lips.

"Hey, Larissa, hope you didn't wait long," he said as he sat down across from me.

"Only a lifetime or two," I quipped, rolling my eyes playfully.

"Alright, let's not waste any more of your precious time, then," Atlas said with a grin, opening his laptop and spreading out the documents we'd need to discuss. This was one of the many things I admired about him—his ability to dive right into work without hesitation.

As we analyzed the information regarding the secret assets, it became clear that this case was far more complicated than either of us had anticipated. We spent hours discussing possible strategies, dissecting legal precedents, and combing through every piece of evidence.

"Are you sure about this?" I asked Atlas, looking up from my notes. "The implications are huge."

"Positive," he replied, meeting my gaze with unwavering determination. "We've got to follow every lead, no matter where it takes us."

His confidence was contagious, and I couldn't help but feel inspired by his optimism. Together, we decided to spend the rest of the afternoon and evening at Atlas's office, bringing our teams together to tackle this unprecedented situation.

Atlas's office was a stark contrast to mine. Warm-toned walls were adorned with framed photographs of his loved ones and a large wooden desk that seemed like a relic from a bygone era. It was a space that felt lived-in and comforting, much like the man himself.

"Alright, everyone, we've got a lot to do and not much time," Atlas announced as we all settled in, phones in hand and laptops fired up. "Let's get to work."

The room buzzed with activity as we made phone calls, compared notes, and brainstormed possible approaches to the case. Despite the high stakes, there was an undeniable camaraderie that permeated the air; it was clear that both our teams were determined to see this through, together.

As the evening wore on, I couldn't help but steal glances at Atlas. There was something about the furrow of his brow as he concentrated, or the way he'd run a hand through his hair in frustration, that tugged at my heartstrings. It was a side of him I rarely saw, and I found myself increasingly drawn to him.

We continued to work late into the night, fueled by Atlas's optimism and the knowledge that, together, we could overcome even the most daunting of challenges. As the moon rose outside the office window, I couldn't help but think that, despite the chaos surrounding us, I wouldn't have traded this experience for the world.

As we finished reviewing the newly discovered assets, I couldn't help but feel a sense of urgency. "Atlas," I said, my voice tinged with determination, "we need to request an emergency hearing as soon as possible."

He looked up from his notes, his eyes meeting mine with equal intensity. "I agree," he replied. "We can't let this information go unnoticed. It could change the entire outcome of the case."

"Exactly." I nodded as we both got to our feet. The rest of our teams continued their diligent work, the office filled with the hum of focused activity.

"Let's get on it, then," Atlas said, and we moved in unison toward the conference room to prepare our arguments for the judge.

As I walked past the break room, I overheard two members of Atlas's team engaged in a hushed conversation. Their words caught my attention, my curiosity piquing as they mentioned Atlas's ex-girlfriend.

"Seriously, we have to make sure she doesn't show up here again," one said, a note of annoyance in her tone. "She's nothing but trouble for Atlas."

"Agreed," the other chimed in. "He's been so much happier since they broke up. We can't let her ruin his progress—or this case."

I hesitated by the doorway, biting my lip as their whispered words sank in. Did they truly believe that Atlas's personal life could jeopardize our case? Was there more to their concern than mere gossip?

My thoughts raced as I entered the conference room, trying to focus on the task at hand. Atlas was already there, pacing back and forth as he formulated his argument. He paused when he noticed me, offering a warm smile that momentarily chased away my concerns.

"Hey, Larissa," he said, his voice full of encouragement. "We've got this."

I forced a smile. "We do."

But as we continued to work side by side, our professional rivalry seemingly forgotten, I couldn't help but wonder about the conversation I had overheard. And as much as I tried to dismiss it, the thought of Atlas's ex-girlfriend—and my own growing feelings for him—lingered stubbornly at the back of my mind.

The words I had overheard echoed in my mind, but I decided to keep them to myself for now. There would be a better time for confrontation, once we'd won the hearing.

"Have you gone through all the documents?" Atlas asked, pulling me out of my thoughts.

"Almost. One more to go," I replied, focusing on the screen before me. My fingers flew across the keyboard while my heart pounded against my rib cage, an unsettling mix of anxiety and anticipation brewing inside me.

"Great. Let's wrap this up and celebrate with some takeout," he suggested, his blue eyes sparkling with excitement.

"Sounds good," I agreed, forcing a smile.

As the evening wore on, I couldn't shake the nagging feeling that I needed to address the conversation I had overheard earlier. Finally, after placing our orders for food, I decided it was time.

"Atlas, can I talk to you about something?" I asked hesitantly, my stomach churning with nerves.

"Of course, what's on your mind?" he responded, his brows furrowing in concern.

"Earlier today, I overheard a couple of your team members talking about your ex-girlfriend. They seemed worried about her showing up here and causing problems for you—and potentially for this case," I admitted, watching his reaction closely.

Atlas's face flushed with anger and embarrassment, his fists clenching at his sides. "Was it Rachel? Or maybe Jake?" He paused, his voice softer as he added, "I thought they knew better than to gossip."

"Does it matter who said it?" I snapped, my own frustration bubbling to the surface. "The point is, they clearly think she could be a problem for us. And if that's the case, I deserve to know about it."

"Fine," he conceded, his jaw clenched. "Yes, my ex has a habit of showing up unannounced and causing scenes. But she's out of my life now, and I won't let her interfere with our work. Happy?"

"Ecstatic," I retorted, rolling my eyes. "I just wish you could have been upfront about this from the start."

"Right, because you're always so open about your personal life," he shot back sarcastically.

"Maybe if you didn't have such a reputation for playing by the rules, I wouldn't have to worry about what your team says behind closed doors!" I exclaimed, my voice rising in anger.

"Is that what this is really about?" Atlas asked, his gaze narrowing. "Are you worried about your own reputation being tainted by association?"

"What if I am? We both know how cutthroat this industry can be," I argued, my heart pounding as I bared my concerns to him. "I've worked too hard to get where I am just to have it all come crashing down because of some ex-girlfriend drama."

Atlas sighed, his shoulders slumping in defeat. "Look, Larissa, I promise you. She won't be a problem. And if she does show up, we'll handle it together. Okay?"

"Okay," I agreed reluctantly, my anger slowly dissipating as I met his sincere gaze. "Thank you, Atlas."

"Anytime," he replied softly, his warm smile returning once more. And although I couldn't shake the lingering doubts surrounding us, for now, I chose to trust him.

The tension in the air slowly shifted as Atlas and I continued to exchange words. Instead of heated arguments, our jabs became playful, almost flirtatious.

"Really, Larissa? You're worried about my reputation?" Atlas grinned mischievously, his blue eyes twinkling. "I didn't know you cared so much."

"Please," I scoffed, feeling a smirk tug at the corner of my mouth. "I'm just looking out for my own interests here."

"Ah, there's the Larissa I know and love—always putting herself first," he teased, but there was warmth in his voice that hadn't been there before.

"Someone has to," I retorted, unable to suppress a chuckle. Although the laughter felt foreign, it also relieved some of the pressure building inside me.

"Is that why you're always so quick to challenge me in the courtroom?" Atlas asked, leaning closer. His proximity sent a shiver down my spine, and I found myself momentarily lost in the intensity of his gaze. "Afraid you might actually care about someone other than yourself?"

"Careful, Mr. Harrington," I warned playfully, though my heart raced at the implications of his words. "You might not like where this conversation is headed."

"Maybe I do," he whispered, and before I could process what was happening, his lips were on mine.

The kiss was passionate and intense—more than I ever expected from someone like Atlas. My hands gripped his shoulders, my fingers digging into the fabric of his suit jacket, desperate for something to hold on to as waves of emotion crashed over me. In that moment, all my doubts and fears faded away.

Atlas's hands moved from my waist to cradle my face, deepening the kiss further. The world around us seemed to blur and fade until all that was left was the two of us, locked in an embrace that threatened to consume us both.

As we finally broke apart, breathless and flushed, I stared into Atlas's eyes, my mind reeling from the intensity of what had just transpired between us. My earlier anger and frustration were now distant memories, replaced by a newfound connection that left me both exhilarated and terrified.

"Wow," I breathed, still feeling the lingering warmth of his touch on my skin.

"Wow indeed," Atlas agreed, a hint of awe in his voice as he traced his thumb gently along my lower lip. "I guess we should probably get back to work, huh?"

"Probably," I murmured, but neither of us made any move to break the momentary spell that had settled over us.

The cold reality of our situation began to seep in as I stared into Atlas's vibrant blue eyes, as we still held on to each other. My heart raced and my cheeks burned with embarrassment; I couldn't believe what had just happened between us. This wasn't like me—losing control and kissing a rival lawyer in the middle of his office. I could practically hear Janai scolding me in my head.

"Listen," I started, gathering my thoughts and trying to sound professional, "this... this can't happen again."

Atlas nodded, his expression serious but tinged with sadness. "You're right," he agreed quietly. "Our careers are too important, and we have clients relying on us."

"Exactly," I said, forcing myself to step back from him and create some physical distance. "This was a one-time thing, a momentary lapse in judgment. We can't let it interfere with our work."

"Of course not," Atlas responded, running a hand through his sandy-blond hair, looking almost as disheveled as I felt. "We'll just put this behind us and focus on the case."

"Right," I confirmed, straightening my skirt and adjusting my blouse as I tried to regain my composure. "Now, let's get back to work."

We both returned to our respective desks, the familiar sounds of phone calls and keyboard clicks filling the room as we attempted to refocus on the task at hand. I couldn't help but sneak glances at Atlas, remembering the feel of his lips against mine and the way his hands had cradled my face. It was hard to shake the memory, and even harder to ignore the lingering desire that stirred within me.

My mind kept replaying the kiss, making it impossible to concentrate. What if someone found out? How would this affect our reputations, our relationships with our teams? I forced myself to push those thoughts aside, reminding myself that it was just a kiss, and nothing more.

"Hey," Atlas called softly from across the room, drawing my attention to him. "Could you take a look at this document? I want to make sure I'm interpreting it correctly."

"Of course," I replied, grateful for the distraction as I crossed the room to join him. As we bent over his desk, our shoulders brushing slightly, I felt a pang of longing, wishing things could be different between us.

But as much as I wanted to explore whatever had sparked between us, I knew it was too risky. Our professional rivalry and the potential consequences on our careers simply outweighed any personal desires. So, with a heavy heart, I focused on the document in front of me, determined to keep our relationship strictly professional from that moment on.

10
Atlas

As I stood in the empty courtroom, a sea of wooden pews and the judge's bench before me, my heart pounded like it was about to escape my chest. It wasn't the emergency hearing that had me on edge—I'd faced countless high-stakes cases throughout my career—but rather my opposing counsel, Larissa Montgomery.

"Atlas, are you even listening?" Ava snapped, waving her manicured hand in front of my face. "I swear, if you're not going to take this seriously..."

"Of course, Ava," I assured her, forcing my attention back to the matter at hand. "I'm just running through some last-minute strategies."

"Damn right, you better be," she huffed, crossing her arms over her designer blouse. "I am not about to lose everything to Mark because you're too busy daydreaming."

The truth was, I wasn't daydreaming about winning or losing Ava's case. Instead, I couldn't help but steal glances at Larissa as she crossed the room, her dark hair cascading down her back and her piercing green eyes locked on a stack of documents. She was formidable, fierce, and utterly captivating.

"Atlas, focus!" Ava hissed, clearly annoyed by my lack of attention. "You seem... preoccupied. Is there something you're not telling me?"

My mind raced, searching for a convincing excuse. "No, Ava, I'm just trying to ensure we have all our bases covered. This is a crucial moment for your case, and I want to make sure we're prepared."

"Good," she replied, narrowing her deep brown eyes at me. "Because if I find out that you're holding out on me, we are going to have a serious problem."

I nodded, swallowing hard as I watched Larissa approach the table where we'd soon face off. The thought of pursuing a relationship with her sent a shiver down my spine, followed by an overwhelming sense of guilt. I was supposed to be focused on winning Ava's case, not fantasizing about the woman on the other side of it.

"Alright, then. Let's do this," I said with false confidence, straightening my tie and steeling myself for the battle ahead.

"Remember, Atlas," Ava whispered as we took our seats at the plaintiff's table, "I'm counting on you."

As the judge entered the room, I couldn't help but steal one last glance at Larissa. Her eyes met mine for just a moment before she looked away, her cheeks flushing ever so slightly. The stakes had never been higher—not only did I have to win Ava's case, but I also had to figure out what to do about my growing feelings for Larissa.

Later, as the judge called for a short recess, I seized the opportunity to escape the tension in the courtroom. My feet carried me down the hall, my mind a whirlwind of thoughts and emotions. I needed some fresh air—and fast.

"Atlas!" a familiar voice called out just as I reached the heavy double doors leading outside. I turned to find Tanner Dixon, my best friend and fellow lawyer, striding toward me with a grin on his face. "Man, you look like you could use a break."

"Tell me about it." I sighed, running my fingers through my hair. "This case is driving me up the wall, and I don't even want to think about Larissa right now."

Tanner clapped me on the back, easing the weight of the world off my shoulders. "Hey, I've seen you work miracles in the courtroom before. You'll get through this one too. Just take a deep breath and trust yourself."

"Thanks, man," I said, following his advice by inhaling deeply. But as I exhaled, Tanner's brows furrowed, and he eyed me with suspicion.

"Alright, spill it," he ordered. "What's going on between you and Larissa?"

"What? Nothing," I stammered, taken aback by his sudden question. Had I been that obvious? "Why would you even ask that?"

"Come on, Atlas," Tanner replied, rolling his eyes. "I've known you since law school, and I've never seen you this rattled over an opposing counsel before. Plus, your little glances across the courtroom haven't gone unnoticed. Are you sure there's nothing going on?"

"Absolutely not," I insisted, trying to keep my voice steady. "We're just adversaries in the courtroom, that's all. Besides, I have a duty to Ava and her case. I can't afford to get distracted by... feelings."

"Alright, if you say so," Tanner said, raising his hands in surrender. "But remember, dude, you're only human. And sometimes, the heart wants what it wants—even if it's not the most convenient thing for your career. Just think about it."

I nodded, though I couldn't help but feel a pang of unease at his words. Did my heart truly want Larissa, or was this just a fleeting attraction? Either way, now wasn't the time to dwell on it.

"Alright, I'll drop it," Tanner said, his eyes darting over my shoulder for a moment before meeting mine again. "But you might want to know that Larissa's been watching you this whole time we've been talking."

"Seriously?" I asked, trying not to let the surprise show in my voice. I resisted the urge to glance back at her, reminding myself that I had more pressing matters to focus on.

"Yep. She hasn't taken her eyes off you," Tanner confirmed, his eyebrows raised in amusement. "I'm getting the feeling there might be something mutual going on here, whether you want to admit it or not."

"Even if that were true," I began, keeping my voice low so only Tanner could hear, "it doesn't change the fact that pursuing anything with her would be... complicated."

"Ah, the classic 'opposing counsel' dilemma," Tanner mused, leaning back against the wall and crossing his arms. "I get it, man. But sometimes, life throws us curveballs. And sometimes, those curveballs are wrapped up in sharp-tongued, green-eyed packages that make us question our priorities."

I couldn't help but crack a smile at his description of Larissa. It was accurate, to say the least.

"Look, Atlas, I'm not saying you should throw caution to the wind and start making out with her in the courthouse," Tanner continued, chuckling at the thought. "But maybe, just maybe, it's worth considering the possibility that there's something real between you two—even if it means stepping outside your comfort zone."

"Isn't that a risk?" I asked, my mind racing with thoughts of jeopardizing my career and Ava's case.

"Of course it is," he admitted. "But what's life without a little risk, huh? Besides, I've seen the way you two spar in the courtroom—there's definitely some chemistry there."

I sighed, rubbing my temples as I tried to process Tanner's words. On the one hand, he was right—there was something undeniably electric between Larissa and me. But on the other hand, indulging in a relationship with her could potentially put both of our careers on the line.

"Maybe you're right," I conceded, looking back at Tanner. "But for now, I need to focus on Ava and her case. If... if there's something worth exploring with Larissa, it'll have to wait until this trial is over."

"Fair enough," Tanner said, nodding in understanding. "Just don't let your feelings cloud your judgment, alright?"

"Trust me, I won't," I reassured him, my mind already shifting gears back to the case at hand.

As I walked away from Tanner, I couldn't help but steal a glance at Larissa. Our eyes met for a brief moment, and I felt a flutter in my chest before quickly turning my attention back to my client. Tanner's words echoed in my mind, and while I knew I had to keep my focus on the case, the possibility of something more with Larissa lingered tantalizingly in the back of my thoughts.

Only time would tell if we'd ever find out what that something more could be.

I took a deep breath and squared my shoulders, feeling the weight of Tanner's advice bolstering my resolve. My chest swelled with newfound confidence as I strode back into the courtroom, ready to tackle the case head-on and reveal the secret that would secure Ava's victory.

"Your Honor," I began, my voice steady and unwavering, "I need to present some crucial evidence in this case."

"Proceed, Mr. Harrington," Judge Phillips responded, his piercing brown eyes studying me with curiosity.

"Thank you, Your Honor." I turned to face the opposing counsel, catching a glimpse of Larissa out of the corner of my eye. Her gaze was fixed on me intently, and for a moment, I felt a flicker of warmth amidst the cold tension of the courtroom.

"Objection, Your Honor," Larissa interjected smoothly. "We have not been made aware of any new evidence."

"Overruled," Judge Phillips declared. "Let's hear what Mr. Harrington has to say."

"Your Honor, I present to you Exhibit A," I said, holding up a stack of documents that had been hidden from view. As I caught Ava's shocked expression, I knew I was risking her trust, but it was a necessary gamble if we were to win this case.

"Exhibit A contains records of undisclosed assets held by my client's spouse," I explained, handing the documents over to the judge. "These assets were expertly concealed during their marriage, but our investigation has uncovered the truth. My client is entitled to a fair share of these assets in the divorce settlement."

Judge Phillips studied the documents carefully, his brow furrowed. The air in the courtroom crackled, and I stole a glance at Larissa once more. Despite the revelation that threatened her case, she appeared calm and composed—almost impressed.

"Very well, Mr. Harrington," Judge Phillips announced, setting the documents down. "The court will take this new evidence into consideration when determining the final settlement."

"Thank you, Your Honor," I said, feeling a surge of triumph as the gavel fell. It was far from over, but I could see the scales tipping in our favor.

Ava turned to me, her eyes wide with disbelief and gratitude. "Atlas, I... I don't know what to say. Thank you."

"Of course, Ava," I replied, giving her a reassuring smile. "It's my job."

As the courtroom began to empty, I couldn't help but replay Tanner's advice in my head. My heart raced at the thought of pursuing something more with Larissa—but for now, my focus had to remain on the case at hand. With a final glance in her direction, I allowed myself a small, private smile before turning away.

Whatever the future held for us, I knew one thing for certain: I was ready for whatever challenges lay ahead, both in and out of the courtroom.

As the courtroom began to thin out, I noticed Larissa gathering her belongings with a grace unmatched by anyone else in that dreary room. Her piercing green eyes met mine for a fleeting moment, and it felt like an electric current had jolted through me.

"Congratulations, Mr. Harrington," she said, her voice dripping with both sarcasm and a hint of genuine admiration. "You certainly know how to pull a rabbit out of your hat."

"Thank you, Ms. Montgomery," I replied, trying to keep my voice steady despite the pounding in my chest. "But as they say, all is fair in love and war—or in courtrooms, I suppose."

"Indeed," she said, allowing a small smile to touch the corners of her lips. Those lips... *focus, Atlas.*

"Though, I must admit, you surprised me today," she continued, her gaze lingering on mine as if she were attempting to decipher some hidden message in my eyes.

"Is that a good thing?" I asked, taking a step closer to her. The space between us seemed to crackle with energy, and I couldn't help but think back to Tanner's words.

"Perhaps," she said coyly, her eyes narrowing playfully.

"Then I'll take that as a win," I declared, grinning from ear to ear. Her laughter filled the air, causing a warmth to spread through me that had nothing to do with the stale air of the courtroom.

As she turned to leave, I couldn't help but revel in the excitement bubbling beneath my skin. Our future was uncertain, and yet, this was only the beginning of something incredible.

11
Atlas

"Your Honor," I began, my voice steady and confident, "I'd like to present a piece of information about Mr. Kennsington that has not yet been disclosed." My heart raced as I made the decision to reveal this crucial detail. I knew it could be risky, but it was the only way to counter Larissa's relentless assault.

"Very well," Judge Phillips said, nodding his approval. "Proceed, Mr. Harrington."

"Thank you, Your Honor." Taking another deep breath, I looked straight at Larissa, trying to gauge her reaction. "During our investigation, we discovered that Mr. Kennsington has a son from a previous relationship—a son he has never acknowledged or supported financially."

Larissa raised an eyebrow, her green eyes narrowing in suspicion. "And what does that have to do with the current case, Mr. Harrington?"

"Everything, Ms. Montgomery," I replied emphatically. "You see, the existence of Mr. Kennsington's son directly contradicts his claims of being a devoted family man. This new information is relevant to our case as it demonstrates that Mr. Kennsington has made a habit of withholding important facts and evading responsibilities."

"Objection!" Larissa shot back, her voice sharp and filled with venom. "This information is irrelevant to the current case and serves only to tarnish my client's reputation!"

"Overruled," Judge Phillips responded firmly. "The information is relevant. Continue, Mr. Harrington."

"Thank you, Your Honor." I could feel a surge of confidence coursing through me as I looked over at Larissa. For the first time since this trial had begun, she seemed genuinely rattled.

"Mr. Kennsington's refusal to acknowledge or support his own son," I continued, "demonstrates a pattern of behavior that we believe extends to his current situation. It is our contention that he deliberately concealed assets during the divorce proceedings in order to avoid splitting them fairly with his ex-wife."

Larissa clenched her jaw, clearly struggling to maintain her composure. But I wasn't about to let her off the hook.

"Your Honor, we request that the court consider this new information when determining the division of assets between Mr. Kennsington and his ex-wife."

As I sat down, I stole a glance at Larissa. She was glaring at me with an intensity that could have melted steel, but I could tell that her confidence had been shaken. And as much as I knew I shouldn't enjoy it, there was a part of me that reveled in this small victory against my fierce opponent.

The room fell silent as if someone had flicked a switch, cutting off all noise. The sound of shuffling papers ceased, pens stopped tapping, and even the ventilation seemed to hold its breath in anticipation.

"Ms. Montgomery?" the judge's voice broke the silence, though it was quiet and hesitant, as if she too was caught in the spell of the moment.

Larissa stared at me, her piercing green eyes narrowing. It felt like standing on the edge of a cliff, waiting for the ground beneath you to give way. But then, she straightened up, an icy smile spreading across her face. "Your Honor," she began, her voice deceptively sweet, "I must commend Mr. Atlas on his theatrics. They certainly make for a dramatic courtroom."

She paused, the smile never leaving her face, but her gaze only grew colder. "However, it is unfortunate that my esteemed colleague has chosen to use this stage to introduce unsubstantiated claims instead of following proper procedures."

As Larissa spoke, I could feel the air in the room grow tense, the electricity crackling between us like static. The spectators leaned in, eagerly anticipating the next move in this high-stakes game of chess.

"Ms. Montgomery, are you implying that Mr. Atlas's claims are baseless?" the judge asked, his patience clearly wearing thin.

"Of course not, Your Honor," she replied, feigning innocence. "I simply find it curious that this information is being brought to light now, in such a public manner, rather than during discovery, as protocol dictates."

Her words were like daggers aimed straight at me, and I couldn't help but wince as they found their mark. She was right—I should have brought this up sooner. But I had wanted to catch her off guard, to see her facade crack, even if just for a moment.

"Your Honor," I interjected, trying to regain control of the narrative, "I apologize if my actions seem unorthodox. But given the gravity of this new evidence and its implications on the case, I felt it was crucial to bring it to light as soon as possible."

"Atlas," Larissa cut in, her tone dripping with scorn, "your flair for the dramatic is truly commendable. But perhaps you should focus less on making a scene and more on doing your job—by the book."

Her words stung, but they also ignited a spark within me. I couldn't let her win, not like this. I had to fight back, even if it meant playing by her rules. As the room held its breath, I prepared for the next round in our battle of wits, knowing that the stakes had never been higher.

12
Larissa

Just as the courtroom was about to call it a day, the doors swung open with a dramatic flourish. In strode the surprise witness: a petite woman in her late forties, sporting a pixie haircut and wire-rimmed glasses. Dressed in a smart navy-blue pantsuit, she had an air of confidence that commanded attention. She took the stand, and the room fell silent, hanging on her every word.

Unbelievable!

As we prepared to cross-examine the witness, things were about to take a turn for the worse. A storm was brewing, and it threatened our case.

"Your witness, Ms. Montgomery," the judge said, snapping me out of my thoughts.

"Thank you, Your Honor," I replied, forcing a smile. As I approached the witness stand, I took a deep breath, trying to steady myself.

"Can you please state your name for the record?" I asked, my voice wavering slightly.

"Maria Reynolds," she answered, her voice shaking as well.

"Ms. Reynolds, can you please explain your relationship with

Mr. Kennsington?" I continued, my mind racing as I tried to focus on the task at hand.

"Um," she hesitated, clearly unnerved by our earlier argument. "I was... involved."

"Involved how?" I pressed, my heart in my throat as the tension mounted.

"Objection! Leading the witness!" Atlas barked, his voice strained.

"Overruled. The witness may answer."

"We had an affair," Maria finally admitted, tears filling her eyes.

"Thank you, Ms. Reynolds," I said quietly, feeling the weight of her confession settle heavily on my shoulders. As I walked back to my seat, I could feel the storm inside me growing stronger, threatening to tear apart everything I'd worked so hard to build.

"Your witness, Mr. Harrington," the judge announced, and I braced myself for the worst.

"Ms. Reynolds, isn't it true that you have a history of dishonesty?" Atlas asked, his voice tight. It was clear he didn't want to attack her character, but he had no choice.

"Objection! Character assassination!" I shot up from my seat, panic bubbling in my chest.

"Overruled. Continue, Mr. Harrington."

As Atlas continued questioning Maria, I couldn't help but think about the future, both of our case and our relationship. If things continued down this path, what would be left when the dust settled?

"Ms. Montgomery," the judge's voice interrupted my thoughts. "Do you have any further questions for the witness?"

"No, Your Honor," I replied, swallowing hard.

"Very well. You may step down, Ms. Reynolds."

"I will be taking everything into consideration and will give my ruling tomorrow. Court is adjourned."

As the courtroom began to empty, I stood frozen in place, my mind racing. The unresolved conflict between Atlas and me felt like an unbearable weight, and the storm inside me threatened to break loose at any moment.

"God, I hate cheaters." The hypocrisy of it all didn't escape me, given that Mark was the very man I was trying to protect. But then again, a lawyer can't always choose their clients.

"Ms. Montgomery, wait!" an intern called after me, struggling to keep up with my long strides.

"Handle it," I barked over my shoulder. "I've got things to do."

As if on cue, the lobby erupted into chaos. A crowd gathered near the entrance, their curiosity piqued by the spectacle unfolding before them. Security guards were scrambling to break up a scuffle between none other than Mark and a woman who could only be described as his mistress.

Who does he think he is? This isn't some trashy reality show!

"Mark!" I yelled, fighting my way through the horde of onlookers. "What do you think you're doing?"

"Stay out of this, Larissa! This doesn't concern you!"

"Are you kidding me?" My voice cracked. "I'm trying to save you, and you're out here brawling with your mistress like a caveman! Get it together!"

Ugh, men are such idiots!

The security guards were having a hard time separating the feuding pair, their efforts only adding fuel to the fire. It was obvious that they had no idea how to handle such a volatile situation—not that I could blame them. Mark Kennsington was a force to be reckoned with, but so was I.

"Enough!" I shouted, drawing myself up to my full height and channeling every ounce of authority I possessed. "Let the guards do their job!"

"Fine!" Mark huffed, finally allowing himself to be pulled away from his mistress. "But don't think this is over, Larissa. Not by a long shot."

"Atlas?" I blurted out, caught off guard by his unexpected presence. "What are you doing here?"

"Trying to help," he replied with a rueful grin. "But it seems I might have only made things worse."

"Join the club," I muttered, rolling my eyes.

"Look out!" Atlas suddenly cried, lunging toward me with outstretched arms. But instead of protecting me from some unseen danger, his sudden movement only served to startle me further.

"Ah!" I shrieked, instinctively swinging my fist in self-defense. Unfortunately, my impromptu haymaker found its mark square on Atlas's nose, eliciting a yelp of pain from the hapless attorney.

"Ow!" he groaned, clutching his face. "Larissa, what the hell?"

"Atlas, I'm so sorry!" I stammered, horrified by my own actions. "I didn't mean to—"

"Never mind that now," he interrupted, wincing as blood began to trickle from his nostrils. "We need to stop this before someone else gets hurt."

Blood blossomed from Atlas's nose like a crimson rose, and for a moment, we both just stared at each other in shock.

"Atlas, oh my God," I whispered, horrified at the damage I'd done to his perfect face. "I'm so sorry."

"Ah... it's fine," he said, trying to grin through the pain. The effect was more of a grimace, and he looked like he might pass out. "Just... didn't see that coming, that's all."

"Here, let me help you." I reached out, steadying him as he swayed on his feet. "You're bleeding pretty badly. Sit down, and I'll find something to clean you up."

"O-okay," he stammered, bravely attempting another smile. "Thanks, Larissa. I appreciate it."

As I guided him to a nearby bench, I couldn't help but feel a sudden rush of protectiveness toward him—a strange emotion, considering I'd just pummeled him in the face. But now that Atlas was injured, it was like some primal part of me had kicked in, demanding that I do everything I could to make things right.

"Here," I said, pressing a crumpled tissue against his nostrils. "Hold this while I find something better."

"Y-you don't have to do this, Larissa," he protested weakly, but I silenced him with a stern look.

"Of course I do. I hit you, remember? The least I can do is help patch you up."

"Right." He sighed, wincing as he applied pressure to his nose. "Fair enough."

"Okay, just sit tight," I told him, scanning the lobby for something—anything—I could use to stem the flow of blood. My eyes fell on a first aid kit mounted on the wall, and I hurried over, my heart pounding with a mix of adrenaline and guilt.

"Here," I said, returning to Atlas's side with gauze and antiseptic wipes in hand. "Let me take a look."

"Thanks," he murmured, gingerly removing the tissue from his face. "I hope it's not as bad as it feels."

"Only one way to find out." I gently tilted his chin up, my fingers ghosting over his jawline as I examined the damage. The sight of his bruised and bloody nose made my stomach churn with remorse, but I forced myself to focus. I was responsible for this mess, and I'd be damned if I didn't do everything I could to fix it.

"Okay, it doesn't look broken," I announced after a few tense moments. "But you're going to have one heck of a shiner tomorrow."

"Great," he groaned, wincing again as I dabbed at his wounds with an antiseptic wipe. "Just what I need."

"Sorry," I said softly, feeling tears prick at the corners of my eyes. "This is all my fault."

"Hey," he said, reaching up to squeeze my hand. "It's okay, Larissa. We're both caught up in this madness, remember? And besides... you were just trying to protect yourself."

"Still," I sniffled, blinking away the tears. "I never meant to hurt you."

"Accidents happen," he replied, giving me a lopsided smile. "Besides, now we have a great story to tell, right?"

"Right." I laughed, despite myself. "The time Larissa Montgomery decked Atlas Harrington in the middle of a courthouse lobby."

"Exactly." He grinned. "Now that's a tale for the ages."

"Maybe so," I agreed, smiling back as I finished bandaging his nose. "But let's try to avoid any more accidents in the future, okay?"

"Agreed." He chuckled, and for a moment—just a brief, shining moment—all the chaos around us seemed to fade away, leaving only Atlas, me, and the bond we'd forged in the heat of battle.

"Excuse me," I said, gently nudging a gawking bystander as I helped Atlas to his feet. We turned just in time to see security guards and police officers swarming Mark and Zippy like bees to honey.

"Mark Kennsington!" Zippy shrieked, pointing an accusatory finger at him as the authorities separated them. "You kissed Ava, you lying scumbag!"

My eyes flicked from Zippy's enraged face to Mark, who had the audacity to look sheepish. He tried to smooth out his disheveled hair and clothing, but the damage was done. Ava, meanwhile, stood off to the side with an air of smug satisfaction plastered across her face.

As the commotion began to die down, I realized that the responsibility of untangling this mess fell squarely on my shoulders. With a sigh, I turned to Atlas. "I suppose we should start figuring out what happened here."

"Agreed," he replied, touching his bandaged nose gingerly. "Though I must say, this is one of the more... interesting cases I've been involved in."

"Tell me about it," I muttered, scanning the room for any clues or witnesses who could shed light on the situation.

"Hey, Larissa?" Atlas said hesitantly, drawing my attention back to him. "You don't think this will affect our case, do you?"

"Unfortunately, I have no idea," I admitted, feeling a twinge of guilt for punching him earlier. "But I promise you, I'll do everything I can to make sure it doesn't."

"Thanks," he said, and I could tell he meant it. His faith in me warmed something deep within my chest, and I couldn't help but smile.

"Alright, let's get to work," I declared, rolling up my sleeves. "We need to talk to Mark, Zippy, and Ava, and then we'll see if any of these fine folks"—I gestured to the crowd that had yet to disperse—"witnessed anything useful."

"Lead the way," Atlas said with a grin. Together, we waded into the aftermath, determined to find answers amidst the chaos.

13
Atlas

"I might have underestimated how quickly things would escalate."

"Underestimated?" Larissa snorted, crossing her arms over her chest. "Atlas, what part of that didn't scream disaster to you?"

"Ah, but where's your sense of adventure?" I teased, nudging her gently with my elbow. Her laughter bubbled up then, infectious and bright, and I couldn't help but join in. Even in the midst of chaos, Larissa had a way of making my world feel lighter.

"Adventure," she muttered, shaking her head as our laughter died down. "You're going to be the death of me, Atlas Harrington."

"Wouldn't dream of it, Montgomery." I winked at her, trying to ignore the pounding in my chest. The truth was, I'd follow her on whatever adventure she chose. Even if it meant sitting on this cold floor, surrounded by police and security guards who were no doubt wondering how two lawyers had managed to land themselves in such a mess.

The metallic taste of blood filled my mouth, and I grimaced as I tilted my head back to stem the flow. My nose throbbed with each heartbeat, and I held my suit jacket against it, the once pristine fabric now marred by bright-red stains.

"Atlas, are you okay?" Larissa asked, her eyes filled with concern as she edged closer to me.

"Never better," I mumbled through my makeshift bandage, offering her a lopsided grin. "I've always wanted to see how I'd look with a crimson accessory."

"Very fashionable, I'm sure," she retorted, stifling a smile. "But seriously, maybe you should go clean up?"

I glanced around the hallway, noting the uniforms and walkie-talkies that surrounded us like a swarm of bees. "I think our friends in blue might have something to say about that."

"Can't hurt to ask," Larissa nudged me gently before raising her voice. "Excuse me, Officer? My friend here could really use a trip to the restroom."

One of the officers approached us, his face stern and unreadable. "I'm sorry, but we can't let Mr. Harrington leave this area. We need to preserve any potential evidence, and for safety reasons, we have to keep everyone contained."

"Even if I promise not to touch anything?" I tried, giving him my most charming smile despite the blood still dripping from my nose.

"Sorry, Mr. Harrington. Rules are rules," he replied, clearly immune to my charisma.

"Great," I grumbled as the officer returned to his post. "Looks like I'll be sporting this new look for a while." I sighed, trying to ignore the sticky sensation on my face as I focused on Larissa instead. She must have sensed my unease because she reached over and squeezed my hand reassuringly.

"Hey, don't worry. We'll figure this out," she said, her eyes shining with determination. "We've faced worse situations before, right?"

"True," I admitted. "But none of them involved me looking like a bad extra from a horror movie."

"First time for everything," Larissa winked, and I couldn't help but chuckle at her unwavering optimism. Together, we'd weather whatever storm awaited us—even if it meant sitting on this cold, unforgiving floor, my face a mess of blood and ruined dreams.

Suddenly, Mark Kennsington strode up to us, his face contorted with rage. He pointed an accusatory finger at Larissa and shouted, "I want my lawyer!"

"Uh, Mark," I said, trying to wipe the blood from my nose without smearing it all over my face, "Larissa is your lawyer."

"Exactly!" he yelled, not even bothering to lower his voice. "And she's supposed to be protecting me from this circus!"

As if on cue, a swarm of reporters descended upon us like vultures, their cameras flashing and microphones shoved in our faces. Some shouted questions, while others stayed eerily quiet, as if they knew something we didn't.

"Mr. Kennsington, can you comment on the allegations against you?" one reporter demanded.

"Ms. Montgomery, how confident are you in your client's innocence?" another chimed in.

"Atlas, how's your nose? Is it broken?" asked a third, her morbid curiosity almost comical.

"Okay, everyone, back off!" Larissa snapped, using her commanding presence to push through the crowd and create some space for us. I could tell she was just as annoyed by the chaos as I was, but her unwavering determination to protect both her client and me was admirable.

"This is a private matter," she continued, her green eyes blazing with defiance. "We will not be answering any questions at this time."

With the reporters momentarily silenced, I took the opportunity to share my own thoughts with Larissa.

"Hey," I whispered, leaning in close, "do you really think we can get out of this unscathed?"

"Of course," she replied, her voice firm but gentle. "We've faced worse situations before, right? Trust me, Atlas, we'll make it through this."

Despite the chaos around us and the blood still dripping from my nose, I couldn't help but smile at her unwavering optimism. Larissa was a force of nature, and with her by my side, I truly believed that we could overcome anything—even if it meant navigating a minefield of reporters and hostile accusations.

Just as the reporters began to fire off another round of questions, the elevator doors slid open with a soft ding. Judge Malcolm Phillips emerged, his salt-and-pepper hair perfectly coiffed and his piercing brown eyes scanning the chaotic scene before him. I held my breath, waiting to see his reaction.

"Judge Phillips," Larissa acknowledged, her voice steady despite the tension in the air.

"Miss Montgomery," he replied, his tone neutral and his expression unreadable.

As the judge's gaze landed on me, I could feel the weight of his scrutiny. Despite being well acquainted with his no-nonsense demeanor, I couldn't help but dread what might come next.

But then, out of nowhere, Larissa started laughing. It was the kind of laughter that built gradually, starting as a small chuckle and escalating into full-blown hilarity. Her green eyes shimmered with tears, and her body shook with each gasping breath.

I blinked, dumbfounded. This was not the time for laughter, and yet, there she was, nearly doubled over with glee. The reporters, equally stunned, ceased their questioning as they turned to watch her.

"Atlas, just look at us," she managed between giggles. "We're like some twisted Hallmark movie—the lawyer, the bleeding billionaire, and the grumpy judge!"

I had to admit, she had a point. The absurdity of our situation was almost comical, and the more I thought about it, the more I felt the corners of my mouth twitching upward. A chuckle escaped my lips before I could stop it.

"Miss Montgomery, are you quite finished?" Judge Phillips said, raising an eyebrow. His stern visage only served to fuel Larissa's laughter, inciting a fresh wave of giggles.

"Apologies, Your Honor," she said, wiping the tears from her eyes. "It's just... sometimes, you have to laugh at the absurdity of life, don't you think?"

"Indeed," he replied, allowing the faintest hint of a smile to grace his lips. "Now, if we could all return to some semblance of order..."

"Of course, Your Honor," Larissa agreed, her laughter finally subsiding. "We'll get this sorted out in no time."

As Judge Phillips turned to address the police and security guards, I marveled at Larissa's ability to find humor even in the darkest of times. Her laughter had been like a lifeline, reminding me that we were more than just pawns in a high-stakes game—we were two people who had found each other amidst the chaos.

"Let's just go grab something to eat until they get booked."

"Sounds like a plan. I've got an extra jacket in my briefcase."

14
Atlas

As I sat across from Larissa in the Mexican restaurant, my head was wrapping around the fact that The Kennsington family was a chaotic mess, like a tornado that had crashed into an erupting volcano. And now, here we were, two lawyers caught in the eye of the storm. Ava's determination to take everything Mark had, coupled with his unfaithfulness, made this divorce case a ticking time bomb.

"Have you ever seen a situation so impossible?" I asked, swirling my margarita around in its glass.

"Only when I try to find matching socks in my laundry," Larissa replied, her eyes twinkling with mischief. It was moments like these that I found myself drawn to her even more.

"Careful, Montgomery, I might just start believing you have a sense of humor," I teased as I took a bite of my enchilada.

"If I didn't have a sense of humor, I would've run for the hills by now." Her laughter was contagious, and soon we were both laughing, our worries momentarily forgotten.

Our eyes met, and for a split second, an electric charge seemed to pass between us. I couldn't deny the growing attraction I felt toward her—but there was also the case to consider. We were walking a fine line, balancing our personal desires against our professional responsibilities.

"Another round of margaritas?" I suggested, trying to distract myself from the intensity of her gaze.

"Only if you promise not to get too tipsy," she replied, her tone playful but firm.

"Deal," I said, signaling the waiter. As we sipped our drinks, I couldn't help but think about how easy it was to be around Larissa. Despite the high stakes of our case, we managed to find a sense of comfort in each other's company.

"Atlas," she said, her voice suddenly serious. "Do you ever wonder what it would be like if we weren't on opposite sides?"

"Of the courtroom or the restaurant table?" I asked jokingly, but my heart started to race at the thought.

"Both," she replied, a hint of vulnerability in her eyes.

"Truthfully? Yes, I do." Admitting it out loud felt both terrifying and freeing. "But we have a job to do, and as much as I'd love to see where this could lead, our clients need us to be focused for one more night."

"Agreed." Larissa sighed, her eyes drifting down to her plate. "I just wish things could be different."

"Me too," I whispered, feeling the weight of our unspoken desires settle heavily between us. The Kennsington case had brought us together, but it also threatened to keep us apart.

"Let's promise each other that once this case is over, we'll figure things out," Larissa suggested, her eyes meeting mine again.

"Promise," I said, sealing our pact with a smile.

As Larissa and I sipped our margaritas, the sound of mariachi music played softly in the background. The Mexican restaurant was the perfect escape from the stresses of the courtroom. We needed a moment to unwind, to enjoy each other's company without thinking about the Kennsington case.

"Did I ever tell you that Mexican food is my favorite?" I asked her, trying to lighten the mood as we ordered our meals.

"Really? I would have pegged you as more of a pizza guy," she teased, flashing me a playful smirk.

"Guilty as charged," I admitted, chuckling. "But there's just something about the combination of flavors and spices in Mexican cuisine that I can't resist."

"Same here," she said, nodding enthusiastically. "I love experimenting with different dishes at home, too. Cooking has always been a stress reliever for me."

"Seriously? Me too!" I exclaimed, genuinely surprised by our shared interest. "What's your specialty?"

"Enchiladas verdes. My grandmother taught me how to make them when I was a kid," she replied, a hint of nostalgia in her voice.

"Nice! I'll have to try your enchiladas sometime," I told her, feeling a spark of connection. "I make a mean chile relleno myself."

"Challenge accepted," she said with a smile, raising her margarita glass in a mock toast. "To good food and great company."

"Cheers," I agreed, clinking my glass against hers. As the waiter arrived with a bottle of red wine, we continued to share stories and laughter throughout the evening.

Our conversation moved beyond food, delving into our personal values and beliefs. It amazed me how much we had in common—from our dedication to justice to our passion for helping others.

"Atlas, I never thought I'd meet someone who understands me the way you do," Larissa confessed, her cheeks flushed from the wine.

"Likewise," I replied, my heart swelling with affection for this incredible woman. "You know, sometimes I think that if we put our heads together, we could change the world."

"Or at least the legal system," she joked, but there was a seriousness in her eyes that told me she believed it too.

No matter what challenges lay ahead, I knew that Larissa and I had something special worth fighting for—both in and out of the courtroom.

As we left the warmth of the Mexican restaurant behind us, a slight chill in the air made me pull my jacket tighter around me. The streetlights cast a soft glow on Larissa's face as she looked up at the starry night sky.

"You know," she said quietly, "it's been a long time since I've felt this... uncertain about the future." I glanced over at her, surprised by her candidness.

"Uncertain?" I asked, trying to gauge her thoughts.

"About everything—the case, us, life in general." She sighed, tucking a strand of hair behind her ear. "I guess it's just that I'm so used to having control, and right now, it feels like everything is up in the air."

I nodded, understanding where she was coming from. "I think that's part of what makes life interesting, though. The uncertainty, the potential for unexpected surprises."

"Maybe," she conceded with a small smile. "But surprises aren't always good, you know?"

"True," I admitted, remembering some less-than-stellar surprises in my own life. "But sometimes they can lead to amazing things. Like meeting someone who challenges you and makes you see the world differently."

"Or finding yourself on the same side of a courtroom with someone you never thought you'd get along with, let alone have feelings for," she added.

"Exactly," I agreed, chuckling. "And while I have my own fears—about the case, our careers, and what could happen between us—I also have hope. Hope that things will work out one way or another."

"Hope, huh?" Larissa mused, her expression softening. "Maybe that's what's been missing from my life lately. It's hard to hold on to hope when you're constantly fighting battles."

"Then let me be your hope," I offered earnestly.

She looked at me for a moment, her eyes searching mine before she finally nodded. "Alright, Atlas. Let's hold on to hope—and each other."

15
Larissa

"Guess who I ran into downstairs?" Mark said, grinning like a kid who'd just found the cookie jar. "Ava!"

"Of course you did," I replied, rolling my eyes.

"Turns out, we both had a lot to say to each other, some apologies here and there." He paused for dramatic effect. "And we've decided to give our marriage another shot."

The news hit me like a ton of bricks. "Are you serious? You absolute buffoon!"

"Hey, no need for name-calling," he said, feigning hurt, but his smile betrayed him.

At that moment, the guard stepped forward, observing their interaction with suspicion. "Everything okay in here?"

I forced a smile, as if my facial muscles were frozen solid. "Just peachy. Don't worry about us."

As the guard retreated, I took a few calming breaths before addressing Mark again through gritted teeth. "So, how did you get yourself in this mess? Why are you even behind bars?"

"Ah, well, it happened right after Ava and I shared hugged," he began, a dreamy look on his face. "We kissed... you know how these things go."

"Get to the point, Mark," I snapped, already regretting asking.

"Alright, alright," he conceded, chuckling. "So, while Ava and I were kissing, Zippy—you remember Zippy, right? My mistress?"

"Vividly," Larissa bit out. How many paramours could one man have?

"Anyway, she saw us and didn't take it too well. Started punching me in the back of the head—" He rubbed the spot gingerly for emphasis. "And it escalated from there."

My anger reached a boiling point, rendering me temporarily speechless. I wanted to be anywhere but here, listening to Mark describe his cavorting with Ava while his mistress attacked him. The man had no shame, no self-awareness, and it astounded me that I'd ever found him charming.

"Are you kidding me?" My voice cracked as I struggled to process this new information. The man had an uncanny ability to make every situation about him.

"Hey, don't look at me like that! People change, Larissa," he said. "We've both made mistakes, and now we're trying to fix them."

I stormed out of the jail cell, leaving Mark's pleading voice echoing behind me. The metal bars slammed shut with a satisfying clang, marking my exit from that infuriating conversation. My heels clicked against the linoleum floor as I marched down the hallway, fuming.

I pushed his voice to the back of my mind, focusing instead on the burning anger that coursed through my veins. How dare he make a mockery of our professional relationship like this?

My thoughts swirled like a tornado, each one more incensed than the last. The frustration bubbled up inside me until it threatened to burst forth in a stream of expletives. I had to find an outlet for this rage, and fast.

"Out of my way!" I snapped at a guard who was blocking my path. He jumped aside, eyes wide with surprise at my sudden outburst. I didn't have time for apologies; I needed air, space—anything to help calm the storm inside me.

I finally reached the exit, pushing the heavy doors open and stepping out into the sunlight. The warmth on my face did little to soothe my temper, but at least I could breathe again. "How does one man cause so much trouble?" I muttered under my breath, mentally preparing myself for the inevitable fallout from Mark's latest escapade.

"Rough day?" a familiar voice asked, startling me out of my inner turmoil. I turned to find Atlas leaning against the hood of his car, concern etched on his handsome features.

"Rough doesn't even begin to cover it." I sighed, feeling the weight of the day bearing down on me. I knew he'd be able to read the exhaustion and irritation in my eyes. "Mark just informed me that he and Ava have decided to give their marriage another shot. Oh, and he's currently behind bars for getting into a brawl with his mistress."

"Wow," Atlas said, raising an eyebrow. "I knew things were complicated with that case, but this is... something else." He pushed off from the car and came closer, offering a sympathetic smile. "Want to talk about it?"

"Later," I replied, suddenly feeling drained. "Right now, I just want to go home and take a long, hot bath. Preferably one filled with wine instead of water."

"Good luck. See ya tomorrow."

16
Atlas

I stood next to Larissa, my heart pounding as we faced the judge's wrath. Our clients, Ava Kennsington and her soon-to-be ex-husband, flanked us on either side. I could feel the heat of their anger radiating off them like an oven set to broil.

"Mr. Harrington, Ms. Montgomery," the judge addressed us, his brown eyes piercing our souls with every syllable. "I am extremely disappointed in the behavior displayed by both counsel and your clients during yesterday's proceedings." He paused, letting the weight of his words sink in. "This is a court of law, not a circus."

"Your Honor," I began, trying to muster whatever charm I had left after the previous day's disaster, "we apologize for any unprofessional conduct on our part. We understand the seriousness of the actions and will ensure that it does not happen again."

"See that it doesn't, Mr. Harrington," he warned. Larissa nodded beside me, her green eyes reflecting the same contrition I hoped was mirrored in mine.

"Moving on," the judge continued, flipping through pages of documentation before him, "I have reviewed the terms of the proposed settlement agreement and find them to be reasonable under the circumstances. Therefore, I grant Ava Kennsington ownership of the four properties she requested, along with everything else on her list."

Ava smirked, while her husband clenched his jaw in silent fury. This case had been a roller coaster from the start, and frankly, I just wanted off the ride.

"Thank you, Your Honor," I said, my voice betraying a hint of gratitude. Larissa echoed my sentiments, and together we vowed to uphold our end of the bargain, regaining control over the proceedings that had previously spiraled out of hand.

"Very well," Judge Phillips concluded, "court is adjourned." With a final resounding crack of the gavel, the room was dismissed.

I didn't even glance at Larissa as we rushed out of the courtroom, eager to put some distance between ourselves and the judge's disdainful gaze.

We arrived at the elevator bank, still not speaking. I tapped my foot impatiently while waiting for the doors to open, feeling the weight of our earlier embarrassment settling onto my shoulders. Finally, the elevator dinged, and we stepped inside, careful to keep a respectful distance between us.

"Floor?" I asked, my voice low and defeated as I reached for the control panel.

"Ground," she muttered, and I pressed the button without another word. Our descent was slow and agonizing, much like our collective pride that continued to plummet alongside us.

"God, that was humiliating," I confessed, running my hand through my hair. "I don't think I've ever been chewed out like that in court."

"Join the club." Larissa sighed, her piercing green eyes focused on the elevator floor. "I guess there's a first time for everything, huh?"

"Seems so," I agreed, trying to chuckle, but it came out more like a choked cough. We fell silent again, lost in our thoughts. My mind raced, replaying the judge's words over and over, each time feeling a new sting of shame.

The elevator jolted to a stop, and we stepped out into the cold, sterile hallway of the courthouse. The harsh fluorescent lights overhead did nothing to improve our moods as we trudged past the security guards, heads down, avoiding eye contact.

"Hey, have a good day!" one of the guards called out, his voice dripping with sarcasm. I forced a smile, but Larissa didn't bother to respond, her expression set in a steely resolve.

"You know," I began, suddenly desperate to fill the silence. "We'll bounce back. We always do."

"Sure," Larissa replied, but it was clear she didn't share my optimism. The weight of defeat hung heavy in the air as we continued onward, wondering what the future held for our bruised egos and reputations.

As we crossed the threshold to the parking garage, a wave of cool air washed over me. The transition from the cold, sterile halls of the courthouse to the dimly lit concrete jungle before us seemed to loosen something inside of me—something tightly wound and ready to snap.

"Atlas," Larissa suddenly said. I looked over at her, concerned, only to find her struggling to hold back a fit of laughter. In the juxtaposition of our solemn departure from the courtroom and the ridiculousness of our defeat, it seemed that she had found something infinitely amusing.

"What's so funny?" I asked, fighting the grin that threatened to spread across my face.

"Us!" Larissa gasped, finally giving in to her laughter. "We just got our butts handed to us by Judge Phillips, and all I can think is... what a spectacular show!"

Her laughter was contagious, and soon I found myself joining in, my own chuckle turning into a full-blown guffaw as I leaned against a nearby car for support. Our laughter echoed through the parking garage, bouncing off the walls and filling the space with a kind of cathartic release that only comes after holding your breath for far too long.

"God, you're right," I wheezed, wiping tears from my eyes. "I don't think I've ever been more humiliated in my life."

"Neither have I," Larissa admitted, her laughter slowly subsiding as she wiped her own tears away. "But it feels good to laugh about it."

"Absolutely," I agreed, feeling lighter and more relaxed than I had in weeks. It was as if being able to find humor in our situation had stripped away some of the weight of our failure, allowing us to breathe again.

As we stood there, still catching our breath and sharing the occasional residual chuckle, Larissa turned to me with a curious glint in her green eyes. "Do you have any place to be right now?"

"Uh, not really," I replied, my curiosity piqued. "Why? What's up?"

Larissa bit her lip. "Well, since we're both free, and we've just survived that disaster of a case together… I was thinking…"

Her hesitation only served to heighten my curiosity, and I eagerly awaited her suggestion—whatever it might be.

"Alright," Larissa said, her eyes sparkling with mischief. "I think you owe me dinner after the disaster we just went through together. There's this place I've been dying to try—Trattoria dell'Arte. You in?"

"Trattoria dell'Arte?" I echoed, my eyebrows shooting up in surprise. The restaurant was known for its exquisite Italian cuisine and warm ambiance, but it wasn't exactly the most affordable option in town. Still, the thought of indulging in a luxurious meal after the ordeal we'd just experienced was undeniably appealing.

"Are you sure?" I asked, still somewhat taken aback by her suggestion. "I mean, I'm all for treating ourselves after that fiasco, but that place is pretty pricey…"

"Consider it an investment in our relationship," Larissa replied breezily, waving off my concerns. "Besides, I have a feeling we could both use a little pampering right now."

Her words struck a chord within me. After weeks of tension, stress, and ultimately, humiliation, the idea of a lavish dinner at one of the city's finest establishments sounded like the perfect way to unwind and put the whole ordeal behind us.

"Alright, you've convinced me," I said with a grin at the prospect of spending more time with Larissa outside the confines of a courtroom. "Let's do it."

"Great!" she exclaimed, her face lighting up with genuine enthusiasm. "Meet me there."

"Alright," I agreed, watching as she strode away, her heels clicking confidently against the concrete floor of the parking garage. She had a presence that demanded attention, and even though we were leaving the courthouse with our tails between our legs, I couldn't help but be drawn to her indomitable spirit.

I made my way to my car and slid into the driver's seat, feeling the anticipation build within me as I started the engine. We may have been defeated in the courtroom today, but there was something about Larissa's invitation—and her unyielding determination—that made me feel like we were on the cusp of a new beginning.

As I pulled out of the parking garage and onto the city streets, I smiled, the lingering embarrassment from earlier already fading as I looked forward to a night of good food, laughter, and the unexpected company of a fierce and captivating woman.

17
Larissa

As the evening began to turn into a velvety night, Atlas and I found ourselves standing outside the entrance of 'Ristorante Amore,' a quaint little Italian eatery tucked away in one of the alleys off the city's bustling main street. A soft yellow glow emanated from the restaurant's windows, casting warm shadows onto the terracotta walls that seemed to wrap this place like a Tuscan embrace. The delicate scent of fresh basil and simmering tomato sauce filled the air, mingling with a faint hint of jasmine.

"Shall we?" Atlas asked, offering me his arm.

"Of course," I replied, linking my arm through his as we stepped into the restaurant.

Inside, the atmosphere was cozy and intimate, with tables adorned in white linens and flickering candles sitting beneath a ceiling lined with wooden beams. The rustic charm of the place made it feel like we had been transported to a small village trattoria, miles away from our urban lives.

"Table for two?" the maitre d' inquired, giving us a welcoming smile.

"Indeed," Atlas confirmed.

"Right this way." He guided us to a secluded table near the back of the restaurant, giving it a sense of privacy, the conversation from other diners only a low hum.

As we settled into our seats, I admired the way the candlelight danced across Atlas's striking features, accentuating the angles of his jawline and the sparkle in his blue eyes. There was something about his effortless charisma that always managed to draw me in, despite my usual guarded nature.

"Quite the romantic setting, don't you think?" he whispered, leaning in slightly across the table.

"Indeed," I agreed, a blush warming my cheeks. "I'm looking forward to whatever comes next."

"Did you hear about the latest case over at my firm?" Atlas asked, swirling a piece of bread in olive oil before taking a bite.

"Which one?" I replied, picking up my own slice and echoing his movements. "It seems like there's always something new happening."

"Ah, well..." He chuckled. "I'm referring to the one involving our rival firm and their client who tried to sue the city for damages after tripping on an uneven sidewalk."

"Ah yes, that one," I said. "They really thought they had a chance, didn't they?"

"Indeed, but it just goes to show how unpredictable our work can be." He took a sip of his wine, his eyes never leaving mine. "Speaking of which, how are things going outside of the office? Any exciting plans on the horizon?"

"Nothing too thrilling," I admitted with a shrug. "Just trying to find more time for myself, you know? Rediscovering hobbies and interests outside of the courtroom."

"Ah, that's important." He nodded. "What kind of hobbies are we talking about?"

"Believe it or not, I've been getting into painting recently," I confessed, feeling a sudden vulnerability as I shared this part of my life with him. "Nothing too serious, just a way to clear my mind and express myself creatively."

"Wow, Larissa, I never would have guessed," Atlas said, his surprise not judgmental. "You'll have to show me some of your work sometime. I'd love to see it."

"Maybe, if you're lucky," I teased, enjoying the unexpected turn in conversation.

"By the way," he added, looking me up and down with an appreciative smile, "you look incredible tonight. That dress is absolutely stunning on you."

"Thank you," I replied, heat rising to my cheeks at his compliment. "I thought I'd dress up a bit for the occasion."

"Ah yes, Italian food, my one true weakness," he admitted with a grin. "Though, to be fair, who can resist the allure of fresh pasta and authentic tiramisu?"

"Only a monster, I assume," I joked, reveling in our easy banter. "But really, you should branch out more, Atlas. There's a whole world of culinary delights just waiting to be discovered."

"Perhaps you'll have to show me some of your favorites," he suggested. "Consider it another way to expand my horizons outside of work."

"Maybe I will," I agreed, savoring the excitement that bubbled up inside of me as we continued to chat and laugh throughout the night, our connection deepening with every shared smile and stolen glance.

The warm glow of the candles flickered in Atlas's blue eyes as he shared a story about one of his more memorable legal victories. Watching him animatedly recount the tale, I admired the way his laughter lit up his entire face, making me feel an involuntary tug at the corners of my own mouth.

"Alright," I chuckled, placing my wineglass down on the table and gathering my courage. "I have a confession to make."

"Ooh, a confession?" Atlas asked, raising an eyebrow. "This should be good."

"Okay, don't get too excited," I warned, feeling the familiar sharpness of my tongue soften ever so slightly in his company. "It's just that... well, I've been thinking about this for a while now, and I—"

"Wait!" he interrupted, leaning forward with mock seriousness. "Before you continue, let me guess: you're secretly a superhero by night, fighting crime and saving the world?"

"Ha! Not quite," I replied, rolling my eyes. "Though I can see why you'd think that, given my many talents."

"Of course, of course," he agreed, grinning. "But please, do go on. I'm all ears."

"Right," I breathed, my heart pounding like a gavel in my chest as I prepared to reveal my true feelings. "I was just going to say that I... I would really like to go on a proper date with you, Atlas. Like, outside of work events and random dinner outings. An actual, intentional date."

There, I said it. The words hung in the air between us like a delicate, shimmering soap bubble, waiting to either burst or glide gracefully away.

Much to my relief, Atlas's smile widened, crinkling the corners of his eyes with genuine delight. "Larissa, I've been waiting for you to ask me that for what feels like ages," he admitted, reaching across the table to briefly touch my hand. "I would love nothing more than to take you on a real date."

"Really?" The surprise and joy in my voice was embarrassingly evident. Apparently, even a seasoned lawyer like myself could be caught off guard from time to time.

"Absolutely," he assured me, his eyes twinkling like the stars outside the restaurant window. "In fact, I already have a few ideas in mind for our first official outing."

"Is that so?" I raised an eyebrow, feeling the weight of my earlier hesitation dissipate into the dimly lit room. "Well, I do hope your plans involve something other than Italian food, Mr. Harrington."

"Trust me," he winked, leaning back in his chair with a confident air. "You're in for a treat."

A warmth spread through my chest, reaching even the tips of my fingers as they clutched the delicate stem of my wineglass. The relief was immense, like a heavyweight had been lifted from my shoulders.

My heart raced with excitement as I envisioned Atlas and me embarking on a real date, away from the confines of our professional lives.

"Atlas, you have no idea how much I'm looking forward to this," I confessed, taking a sip of my wine, its fruity notes dancing on my tongue.

"As am I," he replied, his eyes never leaving mine, causing a flush to creep up my cheeks.

The restaurant bustled around us, the sounds of laughter and clinking glasses filling the air. For a moment, I allowed myself to be fully present, absorbing the atmosphere without the nagging thoughts of work or the countless responsibilities that usually plagued me. It was liberating, like a breath of fresh air after being stuck in a stuffy office for too long.

All the years I'd spent burying myself in work, chasing success at the expense of my own happiness, and for what? The brief moments of pleasure were few and far between, often overshadowed by late nights at the office and weekends filled with paperwork. As I looked into Atlas's warm, inviting eyes, it was time for a change—time to start truly enjoying life beyond the courtroom.

"Atlas, I need to admit something," I began hesitantly, trying to find the right words. "All these years, I've been so focused on my career, on winning cases and building a reputation. But tonight, there's so much more to life than just that."

He nodded. "It's not always easy to find a balance. But I believe we owe it to ourselves to try."

"Exactly. I want to start enjoying life more—and I think this date is the perfect beginning."

Atlas raised his wineglass, the corners of his mouth lifting into a familiar, charming smile. "To new beginnings, then," he toasted.

"New beginnings," I echoed, clinking glasses with him, the sound ringing like a promise of better days ahead.

"Come on, Larissa," Atlas urged, his eyes twinkling with excitement and a hint of mischief. "Let's let loose tonight! I know the perfect place for our date." He leaned in closer, conspiratorially whispering, "There might even be... dancing involved."

Dancing? The thought thrilled and terrified me. My heart pounded at the prospect, the nerves tangling with anticipation like a knot in my stomach. But then again, wasn't that what new beginnings were all about?

"Alright," I agreed, chuckling nervously. "I'm up for an adventure."

"Trust me, you won't regret it," he promised, shooting me a reassuring wink that made the butterflies in my stomach flutter even more.

As we savored our desserts, I grew curious about the inner workings of Atlas's mind. He was such a captivating enigma, effortlessly charming clients and colleagues alike. I decided to test the waters, asking him a question that had been gnawing at me for a while.

"Atlas, between Max and Ava, who do you think was the worse client?"

He paused mid-bite, clearly caught off guard by the unexpected inquiry. A playful smile spread across his face as he considered his answer. "Well, that's a tough one," he mused, wiping a smudge of chocolate from the corner of his mouth. "Both have their... unique challenges, shall we say?"

"Come on, don't be diplomatic!" I teased, nudging him. "Give me a straight answer."

"Alright, alright," he conceded, laughing. "If I had to choose, I'd say Ava was the more difficult of the two. But that doesn't necessarily mean she was a bad client, just... challenging."

Challenging was certainly one way to describe Ava, though I would've used stronger language myself. Still, it was intriguing to see how Atlas viewed our shared experiences, his perspective shining a new light on the people who had become integral parts of our professional lives.

"Alright, then." Atlas leaned back in his chair, a mischievous glint in his eyes. "I've got the perfect Ava story for you." He took a sip of his wine, clearly relishing the anticipation.

"Go on," I urged, intrigued by the prospect of an amusing tale involving our notoriously difficult client.

"Okay, so picture this: it's the middle of a grueling negotiation session with her soon-to-be ex-husband's lawyers before he hired you. Tensions are high, and Ava is getting increasingly restless. Suddenly, she decides she's had enough."

I raised an eyebrow, already amused by the mental image of Ava Kennsington having a meltdown during negotiations.

"Instead of causing a scene, though, she storms out of the room and heads straight for the building's rooftop garden. Now, mind you, this garden is the pride and joy of the firm—impeccably maintained, filled with rare flowers and exotic plants. It's a sanctuary for stressed-out lawyers to find their zen."

"Let me guess," I interjected with a grin, "Ava decided to 'redecorate'?"

"Exactly!" Atlas laughed. "By the time I caught up with her, she was gleefully wreaking havoc among the prized flower beds. She had one hand buried in the soil, yanking out flowers left and right, while the other clutched a handful of petals like a floral bouquet of destruction."

My laughter bubbled up, mingling with Atlas's as we imagined the scene together. The absurdity of it all was too much, and the stress of our cases seemed to momentarily melt away.

"Did you manage to stop her?" I asked between giggles.

"Only after promising her we'd take a break from negotiations," he admitted. "But on the bright side, the gardeners were able to salvage most of the damage, and Ava did eventually settle down."

As we continued to enjoy our meal, the conversation flowed easily from one topic to another. We discovered a shared love for classic literature—Atlas was partial to Hemingway, while I favored Austen—and debated the merits of various vacation destinations, both dreaming of far-off places we longed to explore together.

The more time I spent with him, the more he changed my perspective on life. His optimism and warmth were infectious, making it impossible not to feel lighter in his presence. It struck me that maybe it was time to let go of some of my own cynicism and truly embrace the happiness that was blossoming between us.

"Alright, Larissa," he said with a mischievous grin. "You've impressed me with your encyclopedic knowledge of Jane Austen. Now, it's time for a real challenge."

"Bring it on, Harrington," I replied playfully, eager to see what he had in store.

"Who would you say is the most underrated character in all of literature?" he asked, raising an eyebrow and leaning back in his chair.

"Wow," I said, genuinely taken aback. "I wasn't expecting that one." I paused for a moment, considering my options before finally settling on an answer. "I'd have to say Elinor Dashwood from *Sense and Sensibility*. She's often overshadowed by her impulsive sister Marianne, but she's incredibly strong in her own right—always rational and dependable."

"Ah, a true testament to your affinity for Austen," he chuckled. "But I like it—a character who embodies quiet strength and resilience. I can see why you'd choose her. Let's just say our next destination is somewhere that I think will bring out an entirely new side of you," he teased, that irresistible grin spreading across his face once more.

"An entirely new side of me, huh?" I mused, intrigued by the prospect. "That sounds... interesting."

"Trust me, Larissa," Atlas assured me, his vibrant blue eyes sparkling. "You're going to love it."

18
Atlas

The weekend with Larissa had been nothing short of heavenly, and it was going to take more than the usual Monday morning blues to dampen my spirits. As I made my way through the walkway, I replayed the memories from our time together, each one sweeter than the last.

"Morning, everyone," I greeted my coworkers, who were scattered about the office, hunched over their desks or congregating in small clusters. The place was buzzing with activity—phones ringing, fingers tapping away at keyboards, and the gentle hum of the photocopier in the corner churning out fresh pages of legal jargon.

"Morning, Atlas!" came a chorus of responses, accompanied by knowing smiles and a few mischievous glances exchanged among my colleagues. It seemed like word of my romantic escapades had found its way around the office grapevine, and as much as I wanted to keep my blossoming relationship with Larissa under wraps for now, I wasn't ashamed of it either. If anything, I felt invincible—like it had given me a new kind of strength I never knew I had.

As I settled into my leather chair, feeling the familiar embrace of its well-worn contours, I took a moment to absorb the energy of the room. This was my sanctuary, the place where I felt most alive and capable. And now, with Larissa by my side, it seemed as though even the toughest cases and longest hours would be a breeze.

"Alright, let's get this show on the road," I muttered to myself, powering up my computer and diving headfirst into the day's work. But even as I busied myself with emails and legal briefs, I couldn't shake the persistent feeling of happiness that enveloped me like a warm blanket. As the sun continued to stream across the office floor, wonderful things were on the horizon—both for my career and my heart.

"Hey, Atlas! How was your weekend?" My coworker, Samantha, asked a mischievous glint in her eye. I looked up from my computer screen, feeling the corners of my mouth tug into a knowing smile.

"Great, actually," I replied, trying to keep my tone casual as I recalled the blissful moments spent with Larissa over the weekend. I could feel the warmth of her touch still lingering on my skin.

"Really? Just great?" Samantha nudged, raising an eyebrow. "Because, you know, Becky and I might have seen you and Larissa at that fancy restaurant on Saturday night. Table for two, candlelight... very romantic."

A few other coworkers who had been listening in snickered and exchanged knowing glances. Suddenly, I found myself at the center of office gossip. I knew there was no point in denying it—the cat was out of the bag.

"Ah, so you two were spying on me, huh?" I teased back, attempting to deflect the attention. But Samantha was relentless.

"Can you blame us? After all, we've never seen our golden boy, Atlas Harrington, so smitten before!" She grinned, winking at me.

"Did you guys share dessert?" another coworker chimed in, his voice dripping with innuendo. The office erupted in laughter, and I felt my cheeks grow hot.

"Alright, alright, enough with the third degree!" I exclaimed, trying to maintain my composure.

"Come on, Atlas, you can't expect us not to be curious!" Samantha said, grinning broadly. "You two certainly make quite the power couple."

"Thanks, I guess," I replied sheepishly, feeling the weight of their gazes upon me. In my heart, I knew that what Larissa and I had was special, and no amount of teasing or gossip could change that.

The laughter continued, my face turning as red as a ripe tomato. Clenching my jaw, I tried to keep my cool, but the teasing was really getting under my skin. My fingers tightened around my pen, threatening to snap it in half.

"Alright, guys, let's give Atlas some space," said Pete, noticing my discomfort. But his words only seemed to encourage others.

"Come on, Atlas, we're just having a bit of fun," chimed in Mindy with a sly smile. "Besides, isn't Larissa the one who usually puts people in their place?"

"Ha! You've got that right," I replied, managing a chuckle despite my irritation. My heart swelled with pride at the thought of Larissa—her intelligence, her confidence, and her unwavering determination. We were a formidable team, both in and out of the courtroom, and I wouldn't have it any other way.

"Look, I know you guys are just teasing, but I'm genuinely happy," I said firmly, making eye contact with each of them. "Larissa is an incredible woman, and our relationship is something I'm proud of. So yeah, we had a great weekend together, and I'm not ashamed to admit it."

There was a pause, and then everyone started talking at once, offering congratulations and expressing support for our newfound romance.

"See, Atlas, we knew you'd come around," said Samantha, giving me a playful punch on the shoulder. "Just remember, we're all here for you—even if we can't resist poking fun every now and then."

"Thanks, guys," I said, smiling genuinely. As the chatter died down and everyone returned to their work, I allowed myself a moment to take it all in. Sure, this office was filled with gossip and teasing, but at the end of the day, we had each other's backs. And as I settled back into my chair, my thoughts returned to Larissa when her name appeared on my phone.

Larissa: Can't wait to see you later tonight.

Me: Neither can I.

I immersed myself in a particularly complicated case file, trying to push away the lingering unease that still clung to the edges of my thoughts. But as the hours ticked by, I found myself increasingly lost in the depths of my own emotions, unable to shake the feeling that something was amiss.

As the day drew to a close and the office began to empty, I took a deep breath, letting the last remnants of tension dissipate into the air. My coworkers had shown their support for my relationship with Larissa, and any lingering doubts or concerns would have to be faced in due time.

19
Larissa

I glance at the clock for the hundredth time, as I anticipate my date with Atlas. Butterflies flutter in my stomach, leaving me feeling excited and nervous. It's funny how quickly things have changed between us since the divorce case ended. We've been seeing each other every night.

Get a grip, Larissa. It's just a date. It's just Atlas.

"Talking to yourself again?" My friend, Jess, teased from the doorway.

"Ugh, don't sneak up on me like that!" I exclaimed, startled by her sudden appearance.

"Sorry, I couldn't resist," she grinned. "So, this Atlas guy must be pretty special if you're this worked up about a date."

"Maybe he is." Since the case, Atlas had really opened himself up to me, showing a different side to him that I found incredibly endearing.

"Ooh, I want details!" Jess insisted, sitting on my bed and giving me an expectant look.

"Later, okay? I need to focus on getting ready," I said, shooing her out of the room before she could press any further.

"Fine, fine. Have fun, lovebirds!" she called out as she left, causing me to roll my eyes.

With Jess gone, I took a moment to remember the Atlas I'd come to know over these past few nights. His warm personality and disarming smile made it hard not to fall for him. But what truly captivated me was the way he listened intently when I spoke, making me feel as if I was the only person in the world who mattered.

I applied the finishing touches to my makeup, taking special care to accentuate my features without looking overdone. My piercing green eyes were framed by dramatic lashes, and I chose a bold red lipstick to complete the look. Then I slipped into the dress I chose earlier. Tonight felt different somehow—as if there was something new and exciting waiting just around the corner for Atlas and me.

Before leaving, I gave myself one last once-over. *Wow, Montgomery. You clean up pretty good.*

Okay, this is it. He's the one you've been waiting for.

The realization hit me like a ton of bricks, sending shivers up my spine. I'd always been so guarded, so focused on my career and success. The idea of opening my heart to someone had always seemed too risky, too vulnerable. But with Atlas, it suddenly felt worth the plunge.

As I arrived at the restaurant, Atlas was already waiting for me, his blue eyes lighting up when he saw me. God, he looked amazing in that suit.

"Wow, Larissa," he said, echoing my earlier thoughts. "You look absolutely stunning."

"Thank you," I replied, trying to sound casual while my heart raced. "You don't look too bad yourself."

"Shall we?" he asked, offering me his arm. I took it with a smile.

The restaurant's soft lighting cast a glow over the tables, each adorned with a white tablecloth and flickering candle. Atlas pulled out a chair for me.

"Thank you," I said, smoothing down my dress as I sat.

"Of course," he replied, his eyes sparkling with mischief. "I do have some manners, you know."

As we perused our menus, I was torn between the lobster risotto and filet mignon. Decisions, decisions. Though, honestly, I was more focused on the man sitting across from me than the food tonight.

"Have you decided?" Atlas asked, setting down his menu.

"Almost," I replied, still pondering. "What are you getting?"

"Salmon and shrimp," he said confidently. "You should try it; it's supposed to be their specialty."

"Alright then, salmon and shrimp it is," I agreed, grateful for the suggestion. The waiter took our orders, and we clinked glasses of wine in a silent toast.

"So, tell me more about your family," I asked, genuinely curious. "What were they like growing up?"

Atlas paused for a moment, considering. "Well, my parents... They've always been pretty hard to please, especially my dad. He's the main reason I became a lawyer, actually."

"Really?" I leaned in closer, intrigued. "How so?"

He sighed, swirling his wine around in his glass. "Growing up, it was all about making him proud. And since he's a lawyer himself, the best way to do that was to follow in his footsteps."

"Did it work?" I asked gently, wondering what kind of man would be so difficult to please.

Atlas chuckled bitterly. "Not really. As an adult, I've learned that nothing will ever be quite good enough for him."

"Atlas, I'm so sorry," I said, reaching for his hand. "That must have been really difficult."

"Hey, it's okay," he assured me, giving my hand a reassuring squeeze. "I've learned to accept it, and it led me to where I am now. Plus, look at the bright side—if it weren't for my dad, we might never have met."

I smiled, squeezing his hand back. "Well, I'm certainly grateful for that."

"Me too," he said softly, his blue eyes meeting mine.

"Atlas, you know what they say about playing with fire," I teased him.

"Only that it's incredibly fun," he replied with a cheeky grin.

"Fun until you get burned," I countered, raising an eyebrow as I glanced up at him from beneath my lashes.

"True, but isn't that part of the thrill?" he asked.

"Maybe," I conceded, smirking as I picked up a shrimp with my free hand and dangled it tantalizingly close to his mouth. "But sometimes, it's safer to just admire the flames from afar."

"Where's the excitement in that?" he challenged, capturing the shrimp between his teeth and biting down with a satisfying crunch. I laughed, the sound echoing through the softly lit room like tinkling glass.

"Excitement isn't everything, you know," I admonished, pretending to be serious as I sipped my wine. "There's something to be said for stability and predictability."

"Predictable? You?" Atlas chuckled, shaking his head in disbelief. "Larissa Montgomery, the woman who single-handedly dismantled an entire law firm and then danced on its ashes? I don't think so."

"Okay, maybe not predictable," I admitted, my cheeks flushing at the memory of my past exploits. "But I do appreciate a certain level of stability."

"Like having a handsome, charming lawyer by your side?" he suggested with a wink, causing my heart to race.

"Exactly," I confirmed, my voice barely a whisper as I leaned into him. "Someone who can keep up with me in the courtroom and out of it."

"Sounds like a tall order," Atlas murmured, his lips brushing against my temple. "But I think I might know someone who fits the bill."

"Really?" I asked, feigning innocence as I batted my eyes at him. "Who could that possibly be?"

"Guess you'll just have to wait and see," he teased, his laughter warm and inviting.

Epilogue
Atlas

Three years later...

Larissa and I stood side by side in our cozy living room, reflecting on how far we'd come, the happiness we shared made all the more radiant by the presence of our darling daughter, whom we named Serenity.

"Can you believe it's been three years already?" Larissa asked as she cradled Serenity, her green eyes sparkling with joy.

I grinned. "I know, right? It feels like just yesterday that we were two lawyers trying to outwit each other in court."

"Ha! And look at us now," Larissa teased, her sharp wit as quick as ever, softened by the warmth of her smile. "We moved in together, got married, and now we're raising this little bundle of joy."

I nodded, my heart swelling with pride as I watched Larissa tenderly stroke Serenity's cheek. It was true—we had taken our relationship to the next level, motivated by our shared desire to be good parents and devoted spouses. We combined our lives seamlessly.

"Remember the day we decided to move in together?" I asked,

reminiscing about our journey. "We spent hours debating whose apartment was better, only to realize that neither of them was big enough for both of us, let alone our extensive law libraries."

Larissa laughed. "Yes! We ended up finding this place, which is perfect for us. And I have to admit, I really love our home office."

"Me too," I agreed. "And I'll never forget our wedding day, surrounded by all our loved ones, pledging our lives to each other. It was the happiest day of my life."

"Mine too," Larissa confessed, her voice catching with emotion as she leaned in for a tender kiss.

As we pulled apart, Serenity let out a coo, reminding us of the joyous responsibility we shared. Together, hand in hand, Larissa and I faced the future, ready to embrace whatever challenges and triumphs life had in store for our little family.

"Being a father is the most amazing thing I've ever experienced," I said, looking into Larissa's eyes, searching for the same sense of wonderment I felt. "I mean, don't get me wrong—being a husband to you is pretty fantastic as well."

"Flatterer," she teased, but I could see in her expression that she felt the same way about our life together.

As I wiped Serenity's face clean, I marveled at the miracle of her existence—this tiny person who was equal parts Larissa and me, and yet so uniquely her own individual. From her golden curls inherited from Larissa to her feisty spirit that was unmistakably mine, Serenity was the living embodiment of our love.

"Her first steps, her first words, even her first tantrum... I wouldn't trade any of it for the world," I admitted, laughing as I recalled the infamous mashed peas incident of last month. "And the best part is knowing that we get to guide her through life together, as a team."

"Absolutely," Larissa agreed, reaching across the table to squeeze my hand. "We're in this parenting adventure side by side, and there's no one else I'd rather have by my side."

As Serenity babbled incomprehensible but enthusiastic words at us from her high chair, it was impossible not to feel an overwhelming sense of gratitude for the life Larissa and I had built together. We were a family, filled to the brim with love and laughter, and I couldn't wait to see what new memories we would create as the years continued to unfold before us.

"Atlas!" Larissa called out, her green eyes twinkling with mischief as Serenity wobbled toward me with open arms. "Our little monster is coming for you!"

"Ah! Save me from this terrifying beast!" I feigned terror, scooping her up into my arms and showering her with kisses as she squealed with delight. We had embraced our roles as parents wholeheartedly, finding joy in even the smallest moments of our daughter's life.

"Your turn, Mama." I grinned, gently tossing Serenity into Larissa's waiting arms. Her face lit up as she caught her, both mother and daughter sharing a moment I wouldn't trade for anything. This was what motivated us—being there for each other and for her, showing her how important family was, and knowing that we'd always be there to catch her if she fell.

"Alright, alright, it's time for bed, little monster," Larissa cooed, expertly balancing her on her hip. "Say good night to Daddy."

Serenity reached to me for a hug.

"Good night, sweetheart," I whispered, my heart swelling with pride as I hugged her tightly. She may have inherited her mother's sharp wit and fierce determination, but she also possessed a warmth that reminded me of her father—me.

"Come on," Larissa said, taking my hand. "I've got some wine chilling and a movie cued up for us."

"Sounds perfect," I replied, feeling content as we settled onto the couch together, our fingers intertwined.

As the evening wore on, with Serenity fast asleep and the soft glow of the television casting warm shadows on our faces, Larissa leaned her head on my shoulder, letting out a contented sigh.

"Atlas, I never imagined I could be this happy," she murmured, her voice filled with emotion. "But every day with you and Serenity just keeps getting better."

"Same here, love," I agreed, giving her hand a gentle squeeze. "We've come so far from those headstrong lawyers who couldn't stand each other, haven't we?"

"We certainly have," Larissa laughed softly. "And I wouldn't change it for the world."

Taming the Big Shot
Kaci Bell

1
Mario

My fingers tapped rhythmically on the mahogany desk. The evidence was laid out before me like a puzzle waiting to be solved. This high-profile case was mine to win and for weeks, anticipation had been building. New York City had announced me as one of the city's most successful lawyers. My intelligence and determination were unrivaled. A sly grin crept onto my face as I pieced together the perfect argument in my head, knowing that victory was within my reach.

"Mr. Vasquez," my assistant, Sarah, called from outside my door. "It's getting late. Are you sure you don't want to call it a night?"

"Thanks, but I'm almost done here," I replied, my brows furrowing. "I'll wrap up soon."

"Don't push yourself too hard."

As the door clicked shut behind her, my phone buzzed on the table, distracting me from my thoughts. I glanced at the screen and saw a message from my younger sister.

Celia: You didn't forget about family dinner tonight, right? Don't bury yourself in work!

How could I have forgotten about our monthly family tradition? I hastily typed back a response.

**Me: *Of course not, sis. I'll be there. Promise.*
Celia: *Great! See you soon!***

I sighed and leaned back in my chair, pushing away the legal documents I'd been scrutinizing for hours. As much as I wanted to win this case, I couldn't let my family down. After all, they were the ones who always supported me, believed in me, and cheered me on as I climbed the ranks to become a partner at West, Shure and Locke.

Alright, Mario, family time. I tried to shift gears from relentless lawyer to caring brother.

I stood up and grabbed my jacket. Even after all these years, I was proud of how far I'd come. But beneath the confident exterior, there were memories and emotions still haunting me. For now, I pushed them aside and focused on what really mattered—my family.

The moment I stepped into Celia's home, the smell of garlic and simmering tomato sauce greeted me like a warm embrace. Laughter bubbled through the air as my family mingled in the cozy living room. The familiar sight of my nieces and nephews playing on the floor brought a smile to my face. Because of my long hours, this was the one night every month I could interact with my family and put cases in the back of my head.

"Hey, big bro!" Celia called out from the kitchen. "You made it!"

"Wouldn't miss it for the world," I replied, giving her a hug before taking a seat at the dining table. The comfortable chatter of my family surrounded me, but something was different tonight. It wasn't until Celia clinked her fork against her wineglass, silencing the room, that I realized what was on her mind.

"Alright, everyone," she began, her cheeks flushed. "I know we're all excited about the upcoming wedding. Heather is officially in town and will be coming by tonight."

"Wait, Heather? As in... Heather Reese from high school?" I managed to choke out, my heart suddenly pounding.

Celia nodded. "Yes! She's been such a great friend to me over the years, and I couldn't imagine anyone else standing by my side on my big day."

I tried to force a smile, but all the memories of Heather that had been tucked away in a dusty corner of my mind came flooding back. The girl with the light-brown hair and captivating blue eyes who had left an indelible mark on my soul. The same girl who broke my heart back in high school. Honestly, I never thought I'd see her again.

"Wow, that's... that's wonderful," I stammered, struggling to find the right words. "I'm sure she'll be a great maid of honor."

"I knew you'd be happy for me," Celia replied, completely oblivious to the storm of emotions raging inside me.

As dinner continued, it was increasingly difficult to focus on the conversation. My mind was flooded with images of Heather: her smile that could light up a room, the way she always seemed to know exactly what I was thinking. After all these years, she was going to be front and center at my sister's wedding.

"Hey, are you okay?" Celia asked, her brow furrowed.

"Of course," I lied, forcing another smile. "Just... a lot on my mind with work, you know?"

"I understand. But try not to let it consume you," she advised, giving my hand a reassuring squeeze.

"Sure thing, sis," I nodded, making a mental note to keep my feelings about Heather hidden—at least for tonight.

My heart raced as I excused myself from the dinner table, pretending to head toward the restroom. The truth was, I needed a moment alone to process the news that Heather Reese would be my sister's maid of honor. The real question, though, is how didn't I already know this? Did she keep it from me deliberately because of our history? How could I face her after all these years? And why did it feel like someone had just sucker punched me in the gut?

As I splashed cold water on my face in the bathroom, memories of Heather continued to flood my mind. I closed my eyes, and suddenly, we were sixteen again, sitting under our favorite oak tree behind the high school.

"Hey, Mario," *she whispered, her blue eyes sparkling.* "*I have the perfect prank for Mr. Johnson's class tomorrow. You in?*"

"Always, partner in crime." I grinned, high-fiving her as she outlined her master plan.

Heather and I had been inseparable back then—best friends who shared everything. But there was one thing I never told her: how desperately I had fallen in love with her.

"Earth to Mario!" Heather called out. We were at the senior prom, slow dancing beneath the disco ball. Her brown hair cascaded down her shoulders, framing her beautiful face. My heart swelled as I looked into her eyes, knowing that this was the moment I had to tell her how I felt.

"Heather, there's something I need to say..." I began, but before I could finish, she placed a finger against my lips, silencing me.

"Just dance with me. Let's make this night last forever."

But the night didn't last forever. Instead, it ended with Heather telling me she was leaving town for college, breaking my heart in the process. I never got the chance to confess my feelings, and now, more than a decade later, they were still burning inside me like an unquenched flame.

"Are you alright in there, Mario?" Celia called through the bathroom door. "You've been in there for a while."

"Uh, yeah! Just... give me a minute," I stammered, trying to regain my composure.

I took a deep breath and stared at my reflection in the mirror. The successful lawyer staring back at me was a far cry from the lovestruck teenager I once was. But beneath the tailored suit and polished exterior, the same heartache lingered.

Get it together, Vasquez! It's just Heather. You can handle this.

But even as I thought the words, there was a gnawing feeling that seeing her again would either be the best or worst thing to happen to me since high school. And as I opened the bathroom door, bracing myself for whatever lay ahead, one thing was clear: I was about to find out.

As I stepped out of the bathroom, my heart raced in time with my thoughts. It was hard to believe that the same girl who had once left me breathless with a single glance now was coming back into my life.

I looked around the living room, taking in the cozy atmosphere Celia created for her dinner party. The warm glow of the candles illuminated the smiling faces of our family and friends.

The doorbell rang and Celia jumped up to answer it. When I heard her voice, my heart stopped. Celia and Heather walked into the dining room as everyone was laughing while they cleaned up their dishes.

"Your closing argument in the Johnson case was legendary," my cousin Luis said, snapping me back. "You've done well for yourself."

"Thanks," I replied, offering him a half-hearted smile. My success at West, Shure and Locke was well known among my peers, but tonight, it felt meaningless.

"Hey, are you okay?" Luis asked, his brow furrowing. "You seem like you are somewhere else tonight."

"Uh, yeah, I'm fine," I lied, trying to shake off the memories of Heather that threatened to consume me. "Just a lot of work on my mind, that's all."

"Come on, man," Luis pressed, clearly not convinced by my dismissive tone. "It's obvious something's bothering you."

"Alright." I sighed, knowing it was futile to hide from someone who knew me so well. "It's just... Heather. Seeing her again after all these years brought back a lot of memories."

"Ah, Heather Reese," Luis said, nodding. "The one who got away."

"Something like that," I admitted, feeling a pang of longing deep within my chest. Why couldn't I let go of the past? I had everything I ever wanted in my career, yet my heart still ached for the love I'd lost.

"Look, Mario," Luis said, placing a comforting hand on my shoulder. "The past is the past. You have a great life now. Don't let old memories hold you back from being happy."

"Maybe you're right," I conceded, knowing that he had a point.

But as my gaze drifted back to Heather, laughter lighting up her face, I wondered if there was more to our story than just memories.

"Hey, I'm going to grab another drink," Luis said, giving me an encouraging pat on the back before walking away. "You should go talk to her."

"Talk to her?" I repeated, feeling a sudden surge of panic. "What would I even say?"

"Tell her how you feel," Luis called over his shoulder, leaving me with no choice but to face the truth.

Okay, Vasquez. It's now or never.

As I approached Heather, my heart pounded like a drum. What if she didn't feel the same way? What if I was risking everything for nothing?

"Hey," Heather said, her blue eyes meeting mine with a warmth that both comforted and terrified me. "How have you been?"

"Good," I replied, trying to sound nonchalant as I desperately searched for the right words. "I've been... thinking..."

"Really?" she asked, her expression softening. "What about?"

"I guess I just wanted to say..." I started to say but then was cut off by none other than my sister.

"How's that big case going?" she asked.

"Uh, well, it's challenging," I admitted, attempting to shift my focus to something less heart-wrenching. "But I'm confident we'll win."

"Always the determined one, eh, Mario?" teased my sister, playfully nudging me with her elbow. Little did she know that beneath my calm exterior, an emotional storm was brewing.

"Ha, I guess so," I replied, chuckling nervously as I tried to swallow the lump in my throat. My gaze darted around the room, desperately avoiding Heather.

Throughout the night, I did my best to keep up appearances, engaging in small talk and laughing at jokes when appropriate. However, my thoughts were undeniably preoccupied with the girl who had once been the center of my universe and the possibility of rekindling what we'd lost.

"Is there more wine?" I asked, holding out my empty glass, eager for something to numb the ache in my chest.

"Slow down," Celia warned gently, raising an eyebrow. "You don't want to get too tipsy."

"Right. Of course," I murmured, my face flushing as I realized how obvious my distress must have been. The weight of my longing and regret threatened to crush me.

"Are you sure you're okay?" Celia asked once more.

"Positive," I assured her, squeezing her hand briefly before retreating back into my own private battle.

"Thanks for having me over," I said, forcing a smile onto my face as I stood up. "The food was fantastic, as always."

"Of course," she replied, returning my smile with a knowing glint in her eye. "I'm glad you could make it. Just remember, the wedding is almost here, so don't get too caught up in work."

"Wouldn't miss it for the world," I assured her, trying to keep my voice steady. As I hugged her goodbye, a thousand thoughts raced through my mind—memories of Heather and me, the what-ifs and might-have-beens, and the nagging fear that I was setting myself up for heartbreak once more.

"Drive safe," Celia whispered into my ear, squeezing me tight before letting go. I nodded, unable to speak as I felt the lump in my throat return.

As I walked out the front door, the cool night air hit me like a sudden wake-up call. The stars above seemed to mock me, shining brightly as if to emphasize the vast chasm between my present life and the past I'd left behind with Heather. I sighed heavily, running a hand through my hair.

Get it together, Vasquez. You're a partner at West, Shure and Locke. You've faced bigger trials than this. Are you really going to let a woman get you down?

This wouldn't be just another case to win or lose. This time, the stakes were personal, and the outcome would affect not only my professional life but also my chance at happiness.

As I slid into the driver's seat of my car, I realized that in order to move forward, I would have to confront the past—and Heather—head-on. No more running, no more hiding behind a polished façade of success. It was time to face the unresolved feelings I'd buried for so long and find closure, one way or another.

Alright, Heather Reese, here I come.

2
Heather

What am I going to do now? The man standing in front of me tonight wasn't the Mario I left behind after graduation. He wore a gray tailored suit and his hair a tad longer than he ever let it get when we were teenagers. The closer he got to me, the tighter my chest became. After all these years, he still had the same effect on me. Like anyone else, we had our ups and downs, but he was always there for me. Everyone thought we would end up married one day, and everyone around us could see our bond, but we both were too afraid to admit it back then. Mostly for the fear of rejection. Now, we were both living the lives we dreamed of, but the pressure was still there. I wanted to rip it to shreds.

The contrast between the idea of him being here and his physical presence was immense. The instant he realized I was in the room and our eyes met, the connection was undeniable. He stood there, gazing at the scene before him, his face bearing an expression that almost conveyed his disbelief. Did he not know about me being the maid of honor? Maybe there was a reason for keeping it from him. Celia couldn't have known that it would affect him, but catching him off guard wasn't in my plans.

"So, what's going on with him?" I asked, gesturing to the door. "Did he leave because of me?"

"No, he has a big case and he would rather be at the office working."

I might have looked him up once or twice. Articles popped up about the cases he won and lost, and then the announcement of Mario becoming one of the youngest partners at the firm in history. Something he talked about immensely in high school. He had big aspirations and to know that one of his dreams came true because of his hard work was gratifying. None of the articles talked about him dating anyone though. It shouldn't matter at this point. The thought of leaving my job behind and moving to New York City was just a harmless fantasy.

"He looks to be doing well for himself," I said to Celia, whose eyes never left me since he walked out the door. "That suit must cost a fortune from the looks of it."

Was she trying to read me? It was hard to keep anything from her, just like it was Mario, but this situation was far from normal. I didn't want to walk on eggshells around two of my best friends. Yet I had to. Celia knew how I felt about her brother, and even then, she kept things to herself and never told him. I respected that.

She laughed. "Yeah, my brother doesn't have much to spend his money on, so his clothes are over-the-top expensive. But one day, when he lets someone in, he'll be broke."

My awaited moment arrived. The confirmation of him being single. But did it matter? I am involved with a guy in a casual and undefined relationship. To be honest, since leaving Mario behind, nobody even came close to making me feel like he did. Understood. Appreciated. Most times, we were able to finish each other's sentences.

"He's not seeing anyone? I find that hard to believe, given his success. Girls must flock to him."

Celia deadlocked my eyes, and a grin took shape. "He's never found anyone worth giving up time for. He's very set in his ways and his career means a lot to him. How do you think he became partner so young? He has no life outside of work."

Unpacking our complicated history would be a daunting task. We didn't communicate well about our plans all those years ago, and I realize that now as an adult. But we also didn't reach out to each other. A deep regret of mine. Perhaps this wedding would be a successful way for us to reconnect, catch up on old times, and see if the same chemistry still burned inside of us.

"So how are things going with Lee? Still not official yet?" Celia asked with a grin.

She had been rooting for Lee and me. He was a nice guy, but for some reason, I couldn't see myself being with him long term which is why we were only seeing each other casually. "Same as the last time you visited."

"Girl, he is over the moon for you. Why haven't you taken the leap? You know he's just waiting for you to bring it up, right?"

I wanted to tell her that after seeing Mario tonight, the last thing on my mind was Lee. That my heart never yearned for him like it did tonight for Mario. That had to be a sign, right? Lee wasn't the guy for me.

"I'm in no rush. Shouldn't we be focused on you? You are the one getting married."

I started to yawn to try to signal that I was exhausted and maybe she would stop asking questions.

"Girl, what is going on with you?"

The situation demanded caution, so I needed to move slowly. Things would play out however they were supposed to with Mario over the next few days. Even though she was a friend of mine, Mario was her brother. She didn't need to be put between us or put her in the position where she would tell him something I said. So, I lied.

"Just tired. Traveling does that to a person, you know. I should go back to my hotel and get some sleep, so I'm ready for tomorrow."

I'm unprepared for tomorrow's rehearsal dinner. I didn't think seeing him would cause me such heartache and happiness, but it did. So, I need to spend some time unpacking before I see him again tomorrow.

This wedding was going on whether we were ready or not, and Mario and I would have to work together with him being the best man. The image of him walking me down the aisle came, and a smile took over my face. How many times did I imagine marrying him in high school? Yet, I was too stubborn to tell him my feelings. I knew what he was going to tell me on prom night, but I had already secured my plans to go to college thousands of miles away from him.

Someone would have said long-distance relationships work, but what if it didn't? We couldn't spend four years apart trying to make a relationship work. College is an opportunity for you to break free from your parents' watchful eye, socialize with new individuals, have some fun, and ultimately mature into an adult. Neither of us needed that hanging over our heads.

"See you tomorrow night." Celia draped her arms around me and jabbed me out of her front door toward my car.

Celia was good at reading people, and Mario and I didn't spend much time together tonight. But for good reason. The future of this trip was unpredictable. It would either be an incredible adventure or a complete catastrophe. I must proceed with caution and weigh my next moves.

I shuffled toward my rental car, got behind the wheel, adjusted the mirrors, and drove toward my hotel. Despite my tired eyes, my brain buzzed. Memories from the past flooded my mind. All of Mario and me. Our senior year, we spent every night together after school. Neither of us spoke our minds to be together, despite holding on to the fantasy.

Taking that path could have led to different outcomes. Would he be a partner at one of the most successful law firms in New York City? He would have moved or transferred schools to be closer to me? Mario and I deserved to go on and spread our wings separately.

Refraining from expressing our feelings on prom night was crucial. It paved the way for our success today. Although it caused me great pain, it was the best decision for both of us, although it remained one of my greatest regrets.

3
Mario

I adjusted my tie for the umpteenth time. Sure, I was successful—a hotshot lawyer with a sharp wit and an even sharper jawline. But beneath that polished exterior lay the jagged pieces of a heart that had been broken almost two decades ago.

Get a grip. You're a grown man, not some lovesick teenager.

But Heather Reese, the woman who shattered my heart all those years ago, was not easily forgotten. Her light-brown hair that seemed to defy gravity, her captivating blue eyes that could make any man weak in the knees—she haunted me like a beautiful ghost.

And now, this weekend, I would be spending most of my time with her as we prepared for my sister's wedding. It felt like fate was playing a cruel joke, forcing us together like this. Still, I was looking forward to it.

Okay. Let's do this.

"Hey there, stranger!" Heather greeted with a warm smile as I approached the rehearsal dinner venue.

"Hi, Heather," I replied, doing my best to sound casual. "Yeah, it's been a while."

As we joined forces to help set up the decorations, I stole glances at Heather. She still looked just as stunning as she did all those years ago.

"Remember when we used to hang out in high school?" Heather asked, breaking me from my thoughts. "We had some crazy times back then."

"Sure did," I agreed, a wave of nostalgia washing over me. "Feels like just yesterday."

"Time flies, huh?" Heather mused.

"Tell me about it," I replied, trying to keep my voice steady as we continued working side by side. We both wanted this to be perfect for my sister, and neither of us was going to jeopardize that.

As the night progressed, Heather and I were thrown together more and more—practicing our walk down the aisle as maid of honor and best man, helping the bride and groom with last-minute details, and even sharing a dance. It was almost as if we were reliving our past, but with an undercurrent of unspoken emotions that neither dared to address.

Maybe, just maybe, fate had brought us back together for a reason. But could I really risk my heart again after all this time? Not to mention the fact that besides a couple of women who didn't end up going anywhere, there hadn't been anyone in my life. My sister once told me I needed to let someone in, but how? I've heard horror stories from people at work about women who try to find a way to trap someone like us. So I've always been careful. After what happened with Heather, I never really understood a reason to let someone else in. Not in the same capacity. No matter what, they would never be Heather Reese. I know it was pathetic to still be comparing women to her decades later, but it was what it was. Things happened and my heart couldn't just move on. Even now, after being beside her, my heart knew. It still wanted her and until she told me that there was no chance of us being together again or giving us a chance, opening up to someone else was just not going to happen.

Of course, a part of me always thought about what would happen if we ever ran into each other years down the line. Fifty years old and still single, married to our careers... and we might not be fifty, but it was clear that we both put our careers before our personal lives. There was no other way that I would be named partner by my age. It just didn't happen.

Even watching her talk to others from across the room made me want to sneak away with her and tell her the truth. She might not have given me the opportunity all those years ago, but I was grown now. Until I said my piece, how would I ever move on? This was the perfect opportunity for me to figure out what was going on once and for all. Not tonight, but before she left back home after the wedding, I would have my answer.

Did Heather even feel the same way? *Only time would tell.*

The sun dipped behind the trees where the wedding was set to take place. It was the day before Celia and Jacob's big event, and I felt uneasy as I surveyed the preparations. White chairs lined the cobblestone path that led to an ivy-covered gazebo adorned with flowers.

"Hey there, Mario!" a voice called out from behind me. I turned to see Trevor, Heather's ex-boyfriend, approaching with a grin plastered across his face. He had that boy-next-door charm, with short sandy hair and bright-green eyes. He extended a hand, and I shook it firmly. "Been a while."

"Likewise," I replied, trying to sound as friendly as possible, even though I knew he still harbored feelings for Heather. It was evident in the way he looked at her from across the room, the longing etched into every line of his face.

"Beautiful setup, huh?" Trevor said, gesturing toward the gazebo.

"Absolutely," I agreed, forcing a smile. This wasn't the time nor the place for any drama.

As we continued exchanging pleasantries, Trevor's gaze kept drifting back to Heather. She was busy chatting with Lila and some of the other bridesmaids, looking radiant in a pale-blue sundress that matched her eyes. I tried not to let it bother me, but deep down, that familiar pang of jealousy rose within me. Heather and I had our own history, and seeing her with Trevor stirred up emotions I thought I had buried.

"Excuse me for a moment," Trevor said suddenly, his eyes still locked on Heather. "I need to check on something."

"Of course," I replied, watching as he made a beeline for her. As much as I wanted to intervene, I had to respect the unspoken rules of the wedding party. After all, we were all here for Celia and Jacob's happiness. The last thing I wanted to do was create unnecessary tension.

I focused on the beauty of the setting sun, allowing its warm embrace to soothe my frayed nerves. This was just one moment in time, and soon enough, the wedding would be over and life would go on. But as I watched Trevor and Heather share a quiet laugh together, I wondered what might have been if I had just taken that leap of faith all those years ago.

"Hey, Trevor," I called out to him as he made his way back from Heather. "Got a second?"

"Sure thing," Trevor replied with a nod, joining me near the wedding preparations. "Listen, I know things haven't always been smooth between us, especially considering Heather, but I just want you to know that I'm not here to cause any problems. I genuinely care for her and only want what's best for her."

"Same here," I admitted, swallowing my pride. "And I appreciate you saying that."

"Alright then." Trevor smiled, clapping me on the shoulder. "Let's make this weekend as perfect as possible for Celia and Jacob, shall we?"

"Agreed." I nodded, forcing a smile.

"Excuse me," a voice chimed in, interrupting our tense exchange. I turned to find Lila, one of my sister's bridesmaids, standing beside us. She had shoulder-length auburn hair, bright-green eyes, and an infectious smile. Her teal dress accentuated her curves, giving her an air of confidence that seemed to light up the room.

"Hi, Lila," I greeted, grateful for the distraction. "How are you?"

"Doing great!" she exclaimed. "I just wanted to check in and see how you're holding up. I know weddings can be a bit overwhelming, especially with old friends and unresolved feelings in the mix."

"Is it that obvious?" I chuckled.

"Only to those who know what to look for." Lila winked. "But don't worry, your secret's safe with me. Just remember, today is about Celia and Jacob. Everything else can wait."

"Thanks, Lila," I replied, appreciating her sage advice. "I'll do my best to keep that in mind."

"Good." She grinned. "Now, let's get this party started!"

With that, Lila twirled away, leaving me feeling slightly more at ease. As I watched Trevor mingle with other guests and steal occasional glances at Heather, I had to keep my emotions in check—for now. After all, there would be plenty of time to sort through my feelings once the wedding was over. For now, I'd focus on celebrating the love between my sister and Jacob, and hope that someday, I'd have another chance to find that kind of happiness for myself.

I watched Trevor and Heather share a lighthearted conversation from afar. My heart clenched at the sight, but thankfully, Lila's infectious laughter drew my attention back to the present.

"Come on, Mario, loosen up!" she encouraged me, handing me a glass of champagne. "It's a celebration, after all."

"Right," I replied, forcing a smile. "I just... I can't help but feel a little out of place, you know?"

"Of course," Lila said, her eyes sparkling with understanding. "But that's all the more reason to dive right in and enjoy yourself. Who knows? Maybe you'll find an opportunity to get closer to Heather."

"Maybe," I mused, taking a deep breath and steeling myself for the challenge ahead.

"Great!" She grinned, linking her arm through mine. "First order of business—dancing!"

As we made our way to the dance floor, I worried about the unspoken rules I had to navigate, especially when it came to Trevor. I needed to tread carefully if I ever wanted a chance of reconnecting with Heather. My thoughts raced as I considered how to keep things light and fun without crossing any boundaries.

"Hey," Lila said, snapping me out as we swayed to the music. "Trevor's been keeping a close eye on Heather tonight. Why don't you ask her to dance? It might show him that he's not the only one who's interested."

"Isn't that a bit bold?" I asked hesitantly.

"Sometimes you have to take risks." Lila winked.

"Alright, here goes nothing," I murmured under my breath, trying to quell the butterflies in my stomach.

With Lila's encouragement, I approached Heather, who was standing near the edge of the dance floor. "Heather, would you like to dance?" I asked, extending my hand.

"Sure." She smiled, taking my hand and allowing me to lead her onto the floor.

As we danced, I focused on enjoying the music and the warmth of Heather's presence, being careful not to overstep any boundaries. It seemed to work—our laughter and conversation flowed, and even Trevor's watchful gaze couldn't dampen my spirits.

"Thank you for the dance," I said as the song ended, still holding her hand.

"Of course," she replied, her eyes shining with genuine affection, making it hard for me to let go. "It was nice catching up."

I agreed, watching her walk away with a pang of longing.

"See? That wasn't so bad, now, was it?" Lila teased, appearing by my side once more. "You've got this. Just remember to keep your head in the game and your heart open."

"Thanks," I said, feeling a newfound sense of confidence. "I'll do my best."

With Lila's guidance and support, I continued to navigate the wedding party, always mindful of the delicate balance I had to maintain.

As the party continued, I engaged in conversations with various guests, all the while keeping an eye on Heather. Each time our eyes met, I reminded myself not to get too caught up in the moment.

"Hey, have you seen Trevor?" Lila asked me as she reappeared at my side, her brow furrowed.

"Last I saw, he was over by the bar," I replied, pointing in the general direction. We both spotted him easily enough, nursing a drink and looking forlorn.

Lila sighed. "He's taking this harder than I thought. Heather's really moved on, and it's about time he did, too."

"Maybe I should go talk to him," I suggested, feeling a strange sense of responsibility toward the man who still harbored feelings for the woman I loved. As much as I wanted Heather for myself, I didn't want to create drama by completely ignoring Trevor's pain.

"Be careful," Lila warned. "He might not take too kindly to you right now."

"Understood."

I approached Trevor cautiously, trying to gauge his mood as I neared. "Hey, do you mind if I join you?"

Trevor eyed me warily, then gestured to the stool next to him. "Sure, why not?"

"Look, I just wanted to say that I know things are... complicated between you and Heather," I began, choosing my words carefully. "But I'm not here to cause any trouble. I just want everyone to have a good time."

"Is that so?" Trevor asked, raising an eyebrow. "Well, that's mighty considerate of you."

"I hope we can all enjoy the night and put any past grievances behind us."

Trevor turned back to his drink, so I walked away.

"Oof," Lila said as I rejoined her. "That looked rough."

"Yeah, well, I tried," I muttered, rubbing my temples. "What's important is that I'm doing my best to keep the peace and not let anything jeopardize this day for happy couple."

"Good on you," Lila praised, giving me an encouraging pat on the back. "Now come on, let's go dance and try to forget about all the drama for a while."

"Sounds like a plan." As we danced, a roller coaster of emotions began—happiness at being close to Heather again, apprehension about Trevor's lingering feelings, and determination to navigate this delicate situation without causing irreparable damage. But with Lila being my sidekick, it was just the boost I needed.

As I waited for the rehearsal dinner to end, there was excitement and dread. We would be stuck together until after the wedding was over, and this would give me time with her that I might not get otherwise. It was an odd paradox—thrilling and terrifying at the same time.

"Ah, there he is!" the groom, my old Harvard college buddy, Jacob, called out, slapping me on the back as I approached the group.

"Jacob! How's it going, man?" I asked, trying to focus my attention on him and not on the stunning vision that was Heather.

"Fantastic!" he replied, his enthusiasm infectious. "I hope you're ready for a fun-filled weekend!"

"Of course!" I grinned, stealing another glance at Heather. "Wouldn't miss it for the world."

"Great! Now, let's get down to business. Heather, Mario, you two will be paired up, obviously. Hope that's alright with you both," Jacob said, completely unaware of our history.

I would have to fill Jacob in, eventually. Although I was shocked that my sister hadn't told him. Or maybe he just acting oblivious. Hmm...

"Sure, no problem," I managed to say, swallowing the lump in my throat as Heather simply nodded.

"Excellent," Jacob continued, oblivious to the tension between us. "Now, let's get back to enjoying the party!"

Heather and I shared small talk and subtle glances as we rehearsed our roles in the wedding and mingled with other guests.

How do I pretend that Heather Reese, the woman who shattered my heart into a million pieces, didn't affect me anymore? Every time she smiled or laughed, it felt like I was being punched right in the gut.

"Hey, we're setting up some tables outside. Could you give us a hand?"

"Sure thing," I replied, trying to sound nonchalant, even though my heart was doing somersaults. As we worked side by side, lifting heavy trays and adjusting tablecloths, I tried to focus on anything other than her intoxicating scent or the way her hair kept falling across her face.

"Remember that one time we stayed up all night studying for our final exams?" she asked, breaking the silence between us. "We were so delirious from lack of sleep that we started making up ridiculous stories about our teachers."

I chuckled. "Yeah, I remember that. We had some good times, didn't we?"

"Definitely," she agreed, her eyes meeting mine. It felt like an invisible hand was squeezing the air out of my lungs. How was I supposed to pretend that she meant nothing to me when every fiber of my being screamed otherwise? I wanted to reach out and bring her close, but I didn't. Controlling my emotions had always been my strong suit. In fact, it was basically required for my line of work. The first thing opposing counsel was going to do was try to get under my skin. So years of practice had finally come to some good use outside of work.

"Okay, break's over!" I announced suddenly, plastering a fake smile on my face. "Let's get back to work, shall we?"

"Sure," Heather replied, looking slightly taken aback by my sudden shift.

I did my best to keep up the facade that I was completely unaffected by Heather's presence. But as the twinkling fairy lights lit up the garden, casting a glow over everything, it was an impossible task.

"Can I talk to you for a second?" Heather asked, pulling me aside.

"Of course."

"Look, I just wanted to say... I'm sorry if I've made things weird between us this weekend. I didn't mean to dredge up any old feelings or anything. I just thought... well, that we could be friends again."

"Friends," I repeated, trying to wrap my head around the idea of being just friends with the woman I still loved. Was she crazy? Could she not see how madly in love with her I was? "Yeah, sure. We can do that."

"Great," she said, giving me a warm smile that made my heart ache.

I watched her walk away and join the others. I was torn. Was I supposed to take this opportunity to pursue a second chance with the woman who had once meant the world to me, or was it finally time for me to let go and move on? As I stood there, grappling with my emotions, one thing was for certain: this weekend was going to be a lot harder than I thought.

4
Mario

The sun began to dip below the horizon as I leaned against the railing of my balcony. With a glass of Cabernet in hand, I was relishing in my accomplishments—top-notch lawyer and house that would make even the most jaded New Yorker swoon. And yet, something was missing.

"You ready for my big day tomorrow?" Jacob's voice boomed from behind me, breaking my train of thought.

"Of course," I replied, forcing a smile.

As Jacob joined me, his carefree laughter filled the air. He was blissfully unaware of the storm brewing. The wedding of my best friend seemed to be the catalyst for my introspection, and there was no denying it now—my life felt incomplete.

"Can you believe it? Me, getting married!" Jacob said, clapping me on the back. "Feels like just yesterday we were graduating from Harvard and planning our future conquests."

"Time flies when you're having fun," I quipped. But deep down, I let something important slip through my fingers. Did I make the right choices in my life? Leave it to Heather to come back into my life and make me question everything.

"Hey, have you given any thought to your speech?" Jacob asked. "I want it to be perfect, like everything else."

"Always putting the pressure on me, huh?" I teased, shaking my head. "Don't worry, I have it under control."

"Perfect." Jacob grinned, confident in my abilities. "I'll be back in the morning to go over the rest of the plans."

"Night." I raised my glass in a toast, and he disappeared back inside.

Alone once more, I stared out at the city lights and wondered if I'd ever find that elusive piece of my life's puzzle. Jacob's wedding was forcing me to confront the truth—I prioritized my career over my personal life, and now, I stood on the edge of forty with a sense of dissatisfaction.

Is it too late for me?

As the sun began to come through the curtain, I groaned, burying my face in the pillow. Images of Heather danced behind my closed eyes last night—her warm, soft hair brushing against my cheek as we slow danced at prom; her laughter ringing through the hallways at school. In those moments, it felt like she was still here with me, but reality always found a way to claw its way back.

"Rise and shine, sleepyhead!" Jacob's voice boomed from the doorway.

"Ugh, it's too early," I grumbled, rolling to face him. "What happened to your beauty sleep?"

"Can't help it," he replied, plopping down on the foot of my bed. "Plus, you need to get up and help me."

"Fine, fine." I swung my legs over the edge of the bed, rubbing the sleep from my eyes. "But I want coffee. And lots of it."

"Deal." Jacob chuckled and headed downstairs.

"Hey, do you remember that time we went skinny-dipping in the lake?" Jacob asked as we carried boxes filled with wedding decorations. "Heather dared us to jump in first."

"Of course, I remember." I grinned, feeling the heat rise to my cheeks. "The mosquitoes had a field day with us."

"Good times." Jacob sighed.

"Hey, Jacob? Do you ever wonder what would've happened if things had turned out differently?"

"Like, if Heather hadn't moved away right after graduation? Nah, man. Life has a funny way of working itself out. Besides, we wouldn't be here celebrating my wedding if everything stayed the same."

Something was missing in my life. And deep down, I knew it was Heather.

My thoughts swirled around the choices I'd made in life, the paths that had led me to this successful career and comfortable lifestyle.

All these years chasing success... but have I lost too much of myself along the way?

Pondering the course of my life, I'd put all my energy into building my career, leaving little time for personal relationships or finding true love. The question gnawed at me: did I make the right choice? Was it worth sacrificing my own happiness in pursuit of professional success?

"Hey, you okay?" Jacob's standing in the doorway.

"Uh, yeah, just... thinking," I replied, forcing a smile.

"Ah, the dreaded existential crisis." Jacob chuckled. "We all go through it, buddy. But trust me, you have a lot to be proud of." He clapped me on the back, his easygoing demeanor bringing a temporary sense of comfort.

"Thanks, man," I said, grateful for his support. "It's just... sometimes I wonder if I made the right choices. Did I miss out on something more fulfilling by focusing so much on my career?"

"You know, there's no surefire answer to that. But maybe it's not about what you missed out on, but what you can still find. Life's not over yet. You can still make changes and chase after what truly makes you happy."

His words resonated with me. "Maybe you're right. It's time for a change."

"Darn straight," Jacob grinned. "Now come on. No more moping!"

"Deal." My heart still ached at the thought of Heather, but for the first time in years, I entertained the possibility of a future filled with happiness—one where I would finally confront the ghosts of my past and embrace the life I truly deserved.

"Wait, is this about Heather?"

"Who else would it be?" I reminisced, my voice tinged with regret. "That was the turning point for me, Jake. That's when I decided to focus on my academic and professional goals, and... well, look where it's gotten me."

"Wow, I didn't realize it still affected you," Jacob admitted, his expression turning serious.

"Every day, man," I confessed, feeling a knot form in my throat. "She was the one who got away."

"Listen, you can't live in the past. You've built an incredible life, and there's still time."

"Thanks."

I needed to find the perfect balance between my career and personal life.

The memory of our goodbye lingered in the air like the scent of freshly cut grass at our high school graduation—both a symbol of the end. Heather's tears mixed with the sweat on my face as we clung to each other, knowing that nothing would ever be the same again.

"*Promise me you'll make it big,*" she whispered into my ear, her voice wavering. "*Promise me you'll follow your dreams.*"

I nodded, choking back my own tears. "And I'll never forget you."

"Never," she echoed.

5
Heather

I never expected to feel like this coming back here. Deep down, I always knew that my feelings for Mario were still there. We had no real closure, but this? Since getting back to my hotel, I can't stop thinking about him. Flashes of memories from our childhood.

He lay next to me in my bed, his arms wrapped around me while I sobbed uncontrollably at the loss of my mother earlier that day. He wiped the tears from my eyes and kept me from going down a very dark road. I questioned how I could live a life without my mom. She had given up her career to raise me and was taken way too young. She would never be able to help me pick out my prom dress, walk across that graduation stage, get married, or meet my future children. Everything went through my mind that day and it just broke me. Mario understood the unshakeable bond between her and me.

"It's getting late. I think it's time you head out," my father said, popping his head inside.

"No disrespect to you, sir, but my place right now is here with her. She needs me and I can't leave her."

This was the moment that I truly knew there was more to us than just friends. It was our senior year and I had never told him how I felt, but after that night, everything in me knew the feelings were mutual.

Mario didn't leave my side for a week. My father tried to get him to leave that first night, but he refused. We had been friends for a long time, and honestly, my dad knew he would never try anything with him in the house. So, he let him stay and be there for me. It was one of the worst days of my life, but Mario made it just a little easier. The thing was, he had every single quality a girl could want, even back then. He listened and comforted me. Mario was smart and charismatic. He was everything to me, and walking away from him after graduation was one of the hardest things I've ever had to do.

Mario had always been the person I would run to when I needed to talk to someone, but since our separation, his sister had become that person. I couldn't talk to her about this dilemma. She had always been quite clear on her thoughts about Mario and me. When I left for college, she told me I was making a big mistake. And all these years later, I still think she was right. Going away was the right thing to do, but I regret leaving him behind. Sure, I loved him immensely, but he was so much more to me than that. He was my confidant, my shoulder to cry on, and my sounding board. He was the one person for a long time who I could count on for anything. Losing that person in a pivotal time in my life was detrimental. My freshman year of college, I thought about reaching out to him so many times, but I knew how he felt about me back then, and he was a selfless person. Young and in love. But something told me in my gut that our bond would still be as strong now.

The man I was currently seeing couldn't live up to Mario. It wasn't anything against him. If Mario wasn't in the picture at all, maybe Lee would be the right guy for me, but right now, my heart was telling me that I needed to pursue things further with Mario.

My phone vibrated against the nightstand.

Lee: *Can't wait for you to get back. I have a special dinner planned.*

Don't get me wrong, Lee was a good guy, but he wasn't Mario.

We had been casually dating for a little bit, but we never took the step to make things official between us because of our horrendous work schedules. My stomach was in knots. This wasn't fair to him.

As much as I wanted to find someone to make me happy, Mario had always been in the back of my mind, making it to where no man was ever going to live up to the challenge. Now, after seeing him again, it had only made it worse. Now I knew in my gut that Mario and I needed to give us a shot. If it didn't work out, so be it, but to keep tiptoeing around how I felt would be detrimental to any future relationship.

I typed out a couple different replies but kept deleting them and starting over. What should I say to him? The fact was, Mario walked back into my life and Lee was never going to be the man I wanted. Hard truth.

Me: *We will talk more when I get back.*

After the message was sent, I lay down on my bed, staring up at the ceiling, wondering how the rest of this trip was going to go. Would I work up the courage to tell Mario how I really felt before I left? I must. I couldn't go back wondering what life would be like with him. No, I needed to buck up. It was time to talk to him and say all the things that have been stacked up in my mind for two decades. I owed it to myself to give me an opportunity for happiness.

Lee: *Is something wrong?*

He might not be Mario, but he sure was good at reading situations. I didn't want to string him along; he deserved better. I might not love him, but hurting him wasn't something I wanted to do. Just like me, he deserved happiness. Someone who would move heaven and earth to be with him. That person wasn't me.

Me: *I think we need to end this.*

A tear rolled down my cheek and I wiped it away. Even though we weren't serious, it hurt me to end things because in an everyday world, he was a good man, someone's perfect husband. Just not mine. I had been playing this back and forth for months, wondering if I would ever fully be able to give myself to him, and the answer was enlightening. I wouldn't. There was no way to give my heart to him when it was still hung up on someone else.

When a fast response didn't come, it made my heart tremble. He was hurt. Caught off guard. Even though we hadn't ever made things official, he was only dating me. At some point, he was going to want more, and maybe I was hoping I would be ready when that time came. But then I came here, and my whole thought process changed. I shouldn't have to talk myself into wanting to be with someone.

Lee: Wait, what? Why? Did I do something wrong? Miss some kind of cue?

Now I felt worse. He thought that he was the reason I was doing this. That truly showed what a good man he was indeed.

Me: Nothing you did. We want different things. You deserve someone who jumps at the chance to be with you with no hesitation.

Now that I got that off my chest, it was time to decide what to do. The moment the wedding was over, I would confess my feelings to Mario, whether he felt the same way or not, and see what happened. I refused to go back home wondering what if?

6
Mario

A dusty photo album bound by worn leather sat on the bottom shelf of my bookcase, begging me to pick it up. The high school memories it contained were both fond and terrifying, but curiosity got the better of me. These were some of the best years of my life and there was nothing wrong with wanting to look back on things in life. In fact, it kept me grounded.

Alright, let's see what's in here. I flipped open the cover.

The first photo captured my attention immediately. There I was in all my teenage glory. My hair was a mess of dark curls, and my jawline hadn't quite reached its chiseled potential yet.

Wow, those baggy jeans really were something.

As I continued leafing through the pages, I smiled at the memories—the football games, the wild parties, and the friendships that still endured to this day. But as I turned the page, I sucked in a sharp breath.

There she was. *Heather*. The girl who'd stolen my heart back then and, if I'm being honest, had never quite given it back. She looked radiant, her smile bright enough to light up even the darkest corners of my mind. A wave of emotions threatened to knock me off-balance—the joy of our shared past, the pain of our present distance, and the uncertainty of our future.

I can't do this.

I slammed the album shut. It was easier to avoid these feelings, to bury them deep within and focus on my career. But the truth was, there was no escaping the memories of us.

Get a grip. She's just a part of your past. You need to let go.

As I stared down at the closed photo album, letting go wasn't so simple. And until I confronted my unresolved feelings, they would continue to haunt me.

The photo album quivered beneath my grip. Why couldn't I just forget her? Why did she have to keep haunting me? It wasn't fair.

Some things just never went away and she was one of them. Everything about her was seared into my memory. The way she looked on prom night. The way she bit her lip when she was nervous. The glint in her eyes when she smiled. The one time she laughed so hard at a movie, she snorted. Even all the weird quirks of hers, I loved. Maybe that was the reason I couldn't just forget about her. I loved her. Even now. After all this time. My heart was still tethered to my feelings for her and until I did something about it, I could never move on.

"Alright, dude, you need to talk to Heather," came the abrupt voice of Jacob, who had let himself in with my spare key. "It's about time to get some closure. And you haven't been the same since your sister told you Heather was coming."

"Did I ask for your help?" I grumbled, annoyed at his intrusion but secretly grateful for the company. Jacob knew about our past and how hard of a time I had after we went our separate ways. Besides my sister, he was the one person who saw firsthand the detrimental effect it had on me.

"Doesn't matter." He shrugged, flipping through the photo album that I'd abandoned on the coffee table. "You need it. And I'm not leaving until we figure this out together."

"Fine." I sighed, rubbing my temples as if it would somehow alleviate the chaos inside my head. "But what's there to figure out, really? Heather and I... we never got our shot... and that was a lifetime ago. We've both moved on."

Hopefully he couldn't tell I was putting on a facade because I hadn't moved on. I had been lying to myself for quite some time. The reason I hadn't gotten serious with anyone since coming to New York City was because my mind was still running rampant over her, but Jacob didn't need to know that. Jacob and Celia told each other everything and I didn't want her to know my business, especially with Heather being in town. How embarrassing if my sister was the one to tell her how I still felt. Not happening.

"Have you, though?" Jacob asked, raising an eyebrow as he held up the photo album, pointing at a picture of Heather and me from prom night. We looked so young, so happy. My heart ached at the memory. I wanted to tell her so badly how I felt that night, but she stopped me. Things could have been entirely different had I been able to tell her exactly how I felt.

"Look, man," I said, trying to sound casual despite my churning emotions. "I appreciate you trying to help, but talking to Heather again won't change anything. Our lives are in different cities now; it would never work."

"Stop fooling yourself," Jacob countered, his tone serious for once. "You've been holding on to these feelings for too long. And you'll never truly be happy until you confront them head-on. Loving someone isn't supposed to be easy."

"Ugh," I groaned, running my fingers through my hair. "Why does adulting have to be so complicated?"

"Welcome to the club, buddy."

At some point, I would have to tell Heather. If she left without knowing that I still cared for her, my heart would never fully move on and someday I wanted a family. I knew it was weird for guys to think about that sort of thing, but coming home to no one all the time was starting to get to me. After achieving all this success, it meant nothing without someone to share it with.

"I'll do it. But just so you know, if this all goes south, I'm blaming you."

"Fair enough." He chuckled.

Maybe, just maybe, I could find closure and finally set myself free.

It was the wedding day—the one I had been dreading—and I was the best man. My best friend was marrying his soulmate, and while I was happy for him, there was this nagging feeling in my chest that just wouldn't go away.

I rubbed the sleep from my eyes, took a deep breath, and reminded myself that this wasn't about me. This was about celebrating love and friendship. I begrudgingly put on my best man face and prepared to enter the special world of wedding festivities, where everyone seemed to be floating on cloud nine. I had to be at the venue in an hour to meet Jacob, so I rushed around to take a shower and speed there.

"Ah, Mario, there you are!" Jacob, grinning ear to ear, clapped me on the back as I walked into the bustling reception hall. "You ready for all the fun and games?"

"Of course."

The room buzzed as relatives chatted, children chased each other around tables adorned with fresh flowers, and event organizers flitted from one task to another. It felt as if the air itself was infused with romance and joy, which only served to amplify my already conflicted emotions.

Alright, best man, time to do your job. From ensuring the groom didn't lose the rings to making a speech, my duties were clear-cut. What wasn't so straightforward was navigating my unresolved feelings for Heather while maintaining a facade.

"Hey," Heather said, her eyes sparkling as she approached me with a clipboard in hand. "Could you help me with the seating chart? We have some last-minute changes."

"Sure thing," I agreed, my heart skipping as I took the clipboard from her. Her touch lingered for a moment, and it took all my willpower not to pull her into an embrace.

I sorted through the seemingly endless list of names and table numbers while Heather moved with such grace and purpose, making sure everything was perfect for her best friend's big day. It was one of the many things I loved about her—her unwavering loyalty and dedication.

As the day went on, I managed to fulfill my duties while keeping my feelings in check—for the most part. But every time Heather glanced my way or brushed past me, my heart would race, and I'd have to remind myself that this weekend wasn't about us.

Rows of white chairs appeared to shimmer as they stood proudly, awaiting their role in the ceremony. As I watched my best friend and sister inspecting the floral arrangements, a smile tugged at the corner of my mouth. The joyous occasion should have filled me with nothing but happiness; however, it was tainted by the unresolved emotions.

A subtle scent of lavender wafted through the air, and I knew without turning around that she was near. Heather. My chest tightened as her laughter danced across the breeze, mingling with the rustle of leaves and the gentle lapping of water from a nearby fountain. It was then that the realization struck me with full force: I needed to confront her about our past, to clear the air again and prove that I had grown emotionally since high school.

"Hey," Heather greeted me, her voice soft and melodic like wind chimes on a summer evening. Her blue eyes sparkled.

"Hey," I managed, swallowing the lump in my throat. "You know, I've been thinking… We need to talk."

Her gaze flickered away for a moment, a gentle crease forming between her brows before she met my eyes again. "I think so too," she admitted.

"Okay." I exhaled deeply, preparing myself for the ordeal ahead.

"I know things got complicated between us senior year. I wanted to tell you at prom how I felt about you..."

"I appreciate you saying that," she said, her voice wavering. "But I already knew. It took you that year to figure out what I knew for years. So, why bring this up now?"

"Because I want to show you that I'm not the same person I was back then. We have both changed, but..."

This conversation wasn't going how I expected. My hands were starting to sweat and the way her eyes were watching me made me nervous.

"Can we talk about this later? Not to be rude, but I need to take this in."

I nodded my head and watched her walk away, not knowing if I just scared her away.

7
Heather

The thunderous sound of my own heartbeat drowned out the vicious storm raging outside. It was my best friend's wedding day, and everything had to be perfect. The rain hammered against the windows, as if the heavens themselves were weeping with joy.

"Celia, you look stunning!" I gushed, eyes shining.

"Thank you," she whispered.

A deafening crack echoed through the air like a gunshot. We all froze, wide-eyed, as the ground trembled beneath our feet.

"Wh-what was that?" Celia stammered.

"Sounds like a tree came down," I said, rushing toward the window. My face paled as I took in the scene outside. "Oh, Heather... the entrance to the venue. It's... it's destroyed."

"What?" She joined Heather at the window. A massive oak had crashed onto the roof of the beautiful country manor where Celia was supposed to be married in mere hours, crushing the once-grand entrance beneath its weight.

"Okay, everyone stay calm!" I shouted over the din of panicked bridesmaids and groomsmen. But my words were lost in the chaos as everyone frantically scrambled to figure out what to do next. My mind raced, struggling to process the devastation. This couldn't be happening. Not today.

Celia was taking shallow gasps, and I tried to make her better, but any bride would have a panic attack if this happened hours before they were set to walk down the aisle.

"Celia," I said, gripping her arm. "We're going to fix this. I promise you."

"Everything's ruined!" she choked out, tears streaming down her face, smearing Celia's carefully applied makeup. We'd spent months planning every little detail, and now it was all crumbling around us.

"Nothing is ruined," I insisted. "You're still going to marry the love of your life today, no matter what. We'll figure something out. Together." I squeezed her hand.

Maybe there was still hope. Maybe, despite the destruction and chaos that had shattered her perfect day, she could still say "I do" surrounded by the people she loved most in the world.

"Everyone, listen up!" Mario's commanding voice cut through the chaos like a knife, instantly silencing the panicked murmurs and drawing all eyes to him. For a split second, I drank in the sight of him —his dark hair perfectly styled, his chiseled jaw set, and his eyes alight with purpose. This was a different side of him: commanding and authoritative.

"Obviously, we can't have the wedding here anymore," he continued, gesturing at the destruction that surrounded us. "But there is a solution. We will use my house. It's not far from here, and it's big enough to accommodate everyone."

A collective gasp went up from the crowd, followed by excited whispers. Mario's mansion was well known among our circle, often spoken of in hushed, reverent tones.

"That's incredibly generous of you," Celia said. "But we don't have enough time to redecorate. Everything's already set up here, and—"

"The decorations aren't what make a wedding special. It's the love between you and your fiancé, and the people who are here to celebrate that love with you. We'll make it work."

This was about more than just the perfect venue or the meticulously planned decor. It was about love, and that was something no storm could ever destroy. Mario understood that and just wanted to make his sister happy. And he did just that.

"Anything for you," he said with a genuine smile.

A dangerous thought crossed my mind: what if Mario was the one who got away? But I quickly pushed it aside, knowing that now wasn't the time to dwell on long-buried feelings. My mind was right. He was one hundred percent the one who got away, but pondering that right now wouldn't do me any good.

"Let's get moving, then!" I exclaimed, clapping my hands together with newfound enthusiasm. "We have a wedding to salvage!"

As we began the process of relocating to Mario's house, I marveled at how effortlessly he took charge, coordinating the efforts of friends and family alike with an unwavering confidence.

"I don't know how to thank you," Jacob told Mario, clapping him on the back. "You really saved the day."

"That's what friends are for, right?"

The chaos of last-minute preparations swirled around me as I watched Mario orchestrate the relocation. He moved with efficiency and purpose, like a conductor leading a symphony of frantic bridesmaids, flustered groomsmen, and bewildered family members. The scene was equal parts panic and determination, an odd yet fitting backdrop for today.

"Okay, we need to make sure everyone knows about the change," Mario said, his dark eyes meeting mine with a sense of urgency. "Do you have a list of all the guests' phone numbers?"

"Um, yes," I stuttered, fumbling with my phone as I pulled up the spreadsheet Celia had so meticulously compiled months earlier. It felt like a lifetime ago when our biggest concern had been choosing between peonies and roses for the centerpieces. Now, here Celia was entrusting her entire wedding to her brother. And knowing what I knew of him way back when, never in a million years would I have expected him to be able to pull this off.

"Great, send it to me, and I'll take care of notifying everyone," he said.

"Are you sure?" I asked. "I can do it if—"

"My assistant will reach out to everyone," Mario announced. "We don't have time for that. Right now, we need to get Celia and Jacob updated, and then we can go over and set up. We have a lot of work to do before everyone shows up."

"I don't know what we would have done without you."

"Hey, it's no problem," he replied. "Besides, I've always been a sucker for a good love story."

This man was nothing like I imagined. He had grown up to be a take charge type of person and he was proving that now. I didn't want to get in his way. I just let him do what he needed and did what he asked. My cheeks burned as the thoughts of his lips on mine took over and I quickly shook my head to get rid of them. *Not right now.*

I followed him back to Celia and Jacob, who, despite the bad luck, were clutching each other with him trying to console his bride-to-be. "You weren't supposed to see her. What is wrong with you?"

"Aw, that's all ludicrous. Listen, we are going to head over to my place. I have a couple of my people meeting us there and we will have it all ready to go by the time the guests show up," Mario said, taking Celia's hand. "Stop working yourself up. I won't let your wedding day be ruined on my watch."

He stormed out in a determined stride toward the exit but stopped and grabbed an umbrella from beside the door and opened it.

"Come on, that dress is too wonderful to ruin."

I smiled and stepped underneath as he opened the door and escorted me to his car, getting me inside and shutting the door before closing the umbrella. He didn't even try not to get wet at this point, but when you owned as many expensive suits as he did, I supposed it didn't matter if that one got wet. He could just change when we got to his house.

Here I was, on the way to his house to prepare for a wedding that I prayed someday would be ours.

8
Mario

It was strange to be here with her, in my home, after all this time apart, but there was also a sense of comfort from her presence. If there was anyone I wanted to be decorating for a wedding with, it'd be her.

"Where should we even start?" she asked.

Celia couldn't afford to hire a wedding planner, and even with me offering, she still refused. Now, I bet she was second-guessing that decision. Although, nobody could have seen this outcome. Who expected a tree to fall on their venue hours before their wedding?

"Okay, let's see," I said, unfurling the sheet of paper. "We need to get the altar set up over there by the window, and then we can start arranging the chairs." My eyes darted around, mentally mapping out the space. I wanted everything to be perfect for my sister. She had been dreaming about this day since she was a little girl. Heck, I still remembered the album she made with ideas for her future wedding at age eight.

"Wow, you've really thought this through, haven't you?" Heather remarked, her blue eyes scanning over my detailed plan. She seemed impressed, which secretly pleased me.

"Of course," I replied. "The bride and groom deserve the best, don't they?" I shot her a grin, but it only served to remind me of how much I missed her smile.

We got to work, moving furniture and setting up the decorations. As the room transformed before our eyes, it was impossible not to feel the weight of our past lingering between us. We both pretended that everything was fine, that we were just old friends helping one another, but our unresolved issues hung in the air like the delicate strings of the fairy lights we were hanging.

"I never took you for the wedding planner type."

"I'm full of surprises, aren't I?" I replied with a chuckle. "But really... They deserve a beautiful day."

"You always did have a knack for paying attention to the little details."

"Only when they matter," I said. Did she understand how much the little details mattered because of her? It was time to take charge—not just of the wedding preparations, but also of the lingering feelings between us. I clapped my hands together. "Let's finish this up and make it a wedding to remember."

Our eyes locked, and for a moment, time seemed to stand still. The air between us was charged, filled with all the words we never said and all the feelings we never shared. But now, in this quiet moment amidst the chaos of wedding preparations, we were finally acknowledging the truth.

"Look," I said. "I can't change the past, but I'm here now. If you're willing to give me a chance, maybe we can find our way back to each other."

Heather's eyes searched mine for a long moment, as if weighing the risks of letting me back into her heart. Finally, she took a deep breath and gave me a small, tentative smile.

"Let's finish setting up this wedding first," she said. "Then we'll see where life takes us."

"Deal," I agreed.

As we continued to work on the decorations, our conversation took a lighter turn. We reminisced about shared memories, laughing at silly moments and acknowledging the growth we'd achieved since then. It was as if the walls between us were slowly crumbling, replaced by a bridge built on forgiveness and understanding.

"I still love you. After all these years, after everything we've been through... my feelings for you haven't changed."

Her eyes widened. "I never stopped loving you either, Mario. Not for one second."

"Really?"

"Yes."

I reached out and took her hand. It was as if our connection had been reignited by her words, a bridge spanning the distance we'd created between us. This was all I'd ever wanted. To hear those words come out of her mouth. The pure joy my heart felt in that moment. Could anything ever top it?

"Can we try? Can we give ourselves a chance at happiness?" I asked.

"Only if we promise to be honest," she said, looking into my eyes. "No more hiding our feelings, even when it's difficult. No running away."

"Deal," I agreed, squeezing her hand. The tingles that shot up my arm at the contact confirmed what I already knew—this was right, and it was worth fighting for.

"Deal," she echoed, her smile radiant as she leaned in closer to me. Our hands were still clasped together. "Let's make the most of it."

With our hands still intertwined, we turned our attention back to the wedding preparations. As we moved around the room together, hanging garlands and arranging chairs, it felt like we were dancing a waltz of rekindled love, each step bringing us closer.

"Okay, I think that's the last of the fairy lights," Heather said, stepping back to admire her handiwork.

"Looks perfect," I agreed, taking in the scene before me. We had transformed my once-dreary backyard into a beautiful, enchanting space fit for a fairy-tale wedding.

"Wow, Mario, we actually did it!" Heather exclaimed, her face lighting up with pride. "It's been a roller coaster of emotions, but we managed to get everything done."

"Teamwork," I replied, giving her a playful wink. She grinned back at me.

"I guess we should go get ready ourselves."

The hard work was done, and now all that remained was the celebration.

The evening held so much promise, yet the uncertainty of what lay ahead left me slightly on edge.

With a final glance at each other, we parted ways to prepare for the evening ahead. As I stood in my bedroom, adjusting my tie and trying to tame my unruly hair, I smiled at Heather just down the hall, probably fussing over her own appearance.

You've been given a rare gift—a second chance. Don't let it slip through your fingers again.

9
Heather

The scent of roses and lilies filled the air, as delicate as the lace on my bridesmaid dress. I took a deep breath, trying to steady the butterflies swirling around in my stomach.

"Isn't it beautiful?" whispered Sarah, squeezing my hand. She was right; the wedding was picture-perfect, something out of a fairy tale. But the romantic tension that hung heavy between Mario and me was sharp enough to cut through even the thickest layer of frosting on the wedding cake.

As we stood across from each other in the wedding party lineup, Mario looked dashing in his dark suit, far too handsome for my own good. His chiseled jawline flexed as he clenched his teeth. It was like a dance we had been practicing for years, a waltz of longing and hesitation.

"Who gives this woman to be married to this man?" asked the priest, breaking into our silent exchange. As the bride's father answered, I reluctantly tore my gaze away from Mario, focusing instead on the bride and groom as they exchanged vows. With every word they spoke, I wondered if Mario and I would ever have the chance to declare love so openly.

"Speak now, or forever hold your peace," said the priest, and time seemed to slow down as my heart raced. I dared to glance at Mario once more.

The wedding ceremony concluded with a triumphant crescendo of music, and I exhaled. The guests erupted into applause.

The reception hall buzzed as people mingled, champagne glasses clinking merrily. The atmosphere was contagious, but beneath the surface, there was an undercurrent of anticipation—not just for the newlyweds, but for Mario and me.

"Can you believe it?" Celia gushed, practically glowing. "I'm finally married!"

"Here's to a lifetime of love and laughter," I toasted, raising my glass. "You deserve every bit of happiness."

"Thank you," she said. "But don't think this means you're off the hook! You'll be next, mark my words."

"Celia!" I protested, blushing. "Let's not jinx anything, alright?"

She doesn't even know about Mario and me yet. We might have agreed on giving each other a chance, but what does that mean? I don't live in New York City. The one good thing was I could do my job from anywhere as long as I had my laptop and camera. As happy as I was about this, there were things that needed to be fleshed out. Mario and I needed to talk about what step we were going to take or whether we thought we could handle a long-distance relationship for a while. I was only four hours away, but would we be able to endure that? A part of me wanted to say yes, we could handle it, especially since we went the last decade and then some being away from each other altogether and still held deep love for one another.

"Cheers!" Jacob boomed, lifting his own glass high. He caught Mario's eye and grinned, pulling him into a bear hug. "To my best man and best friend, thank you for everything."

"Anything for you," Mario replied, clapping him on the back. My heart ached at the genuine bond between them.

As the evening progressed, lively music sounded through the backyard, inviting guests onto the dance floor. Couples twirled, laughter bubbling up like champagne. Mario and I kept our distance, mingling with friends and family while stealing glances at each other across the room.

"Having fun?" Celia asked, sidling up to me with a raised eyebrow.

"Of course," I replied unconvincingly, watching Mario from the corner of my eye as he engaged in animated conversation with Trevor. "Your dream wedding is happening, what's not to love?"

"Uh-huh," she said skeptically, clearly sensing my internal struggle. "Just remember, life's too short for regrets."

"Is that advice from your Aunt Lucy or her favorite fortune cookie?" I joked, trying to lighten the mood.

"Both," Celia responded, grinning. "Now, go dance and enjoy yourself!"

Despite the merriment surrounding me, my thoughts were consumed by the possibilities that lay before Mario and me.

"Fine." I sighed, resigning myself to Celia's advice as I made my way over to the dance floor.

"May I have this dance?" Mario asked. His eyes sparkled mischievously.

"Only if you promise not to step on my toes," I replied playfully. Our hands clasped and he pulled me close, the electricity between us undeniable. It was like we were back at our prom once again.

"Wouldn't dream of it," he whispered, his breath warm on my neck as we began to move seamlessly. The music enveloped us, a slow, sultry melody that seemed to echo the beat of my heart.

Our bodies swayed, his strong arm wrapped protectively around my waist, while my hand rested gently on his shoulder. It felt like coming home. As we danced, his fingers brushed against mine, each touch igniting a fire within me that I struggled to contain.

"Remember when we used to dance like this?" Mario murmured, his voice laced with nostalgia.

"Of course," I breathed, lost in memories of simpler times. "We'd sneak into that empty ballroom and practice for hours."

"Until security kicked us out." He chuckled, his laugh rich and contagious. In that moment, I wished I could freeze time and stay there forever, wrapped in his embrace, forgetting the world outside.

"Hey, Heather?"

"Yeah?"

"Can I tell you something?"

"Sure," I replied.

"Whatever happens," he said, his sincerity shining through. "I don't want to lose you again."

"Neither do I," I admitted, my heart aching with the truth.

As the song came to an end and we reluctantly pulled apart, the applause of friends and family filled the air. The clinking of glasses signaled the start of the next toast, but all I could focus on was the man standing before me. Mario—the one who had captured my heart years ago and refused to let go, despite the obstacles.

And as we turned to face the crowd, their laughter and joy washed over us like a tidal wave.

The applause from the guests died down as Mario and I stepped away from each other, the warmth of his hand leaving mine. The room buzzed as I tried to process what happened, my mind a swirling mix of doubt and longing.

"Did you see that?" I heard someone whisper nearby, their curiosity piqued by our interaction.

"Wasn't Heather Mario's college sweetheart?" another voice chimed in, the gossip beginning to flow like fine wine at a party.

"Shh! They'll hear you!" a third cautioned, but the damage was already done.

I stole a glance at Mario, who seemed to be grappling with similar thoughts. His dark eyes met mine for a moment, uncertainty flickering within them, before he looked away.

"Alright, everyone, it's time for the bouquet toss!" called the DJ, his cheerful tone providing a welcome distraction.

As I moved toward the group of eager single ladies, Mario joined the men on the other side of the dance floor. Our gazes locked once more, as if pulled together by an invisible force, and I knew we were both asking ourselves the same question: What now?

Here goes nothing. Catch this, and maybe we can figure out where we stand.

"Alright, ladies, get ready!" the bride announced, her joyous laughter filling the room. "One... two... three!"

With a graceful flick of her wrist, the bouquet sailed through the air, its delicate petals shimmering in the soft glow of the fairy lights. My heart pounded as I watched it arc toward us, as if it held the answers to all our unspoken questions.

"Got it!" I cried out, triumphantly plucking the bouquet from the air.

"Looks like you're next in line for love!" someone shouted, a chorus of laughter and cheers erupting around us.

"Perhaps."

Mario and I stood in the eye of the storm—uncertain of what lay ahead, but determined to face it.

10
Mario

My mouth dropped open, seeing her with that bouquet in hand. She looked over and smiled. It was just a superstition. Even though we had a past, it didn't mean that we were going to rush into marriage even if we did work out. Don't get me wrong, I loved her, but marriage is a forever thing for me. When I asked a woman to marry me, it was meant for forever.

The way her eyes glinted as she smiled my way, surrounded by the other women, all jealous of her. Many had come with their boyfriends. They probably hoped they would be next. I shake my head and laugh.

Jacob leaned over. "Now's your chance buddy. Move it or lose it! I don't want to hear you being brokenhearted tomorrow."

He deserves to know the truth. I know we hadn't discussed telling anybody yet but he's my best friend. Surely, she wouldn't be upset with me. There was no reason to keep us a secret. "Heather and I talked and have decided to give us a chance."

"No way? You guys are finally giving in? Your sister will be ecstatic, especially to know that this happened on our wedding day. Nothing like a little bit of romance to kick-start the heart."

It had been a long time coming and now I had to make sure not to mess it up. She was wife and soulmate material. We both already knew most of each other's flaws and weaknesses. Now, we just had to get to know the updated versions of ourselves. What a breeze that would be.

Celia came over and looked at both of us before she put her hands on her hips. "What's going on?"

"Oh, your brother was just telling me some amazing news. Not sure you would want to know though." Jacob knocked my shoulder and then started laughing.

"You guys better tell me. Secrets don't make friends."

"I was just telling Jacob here that me and Heather decided to go for it."

"Oh my God! Are you serious? It's about time! You guys were made for each other. Ever since you met in the sandbox! Wait, why didn't she say anything to me all day?"

My guess was she didn't want to take away from her best friend's wedding day and I thought that was sweet of her.

Celia hugged me. "Don't mess this up. You're only going to get one shot!"

We shouldn't even be discussing this right now. It was their wedding reception and they should be in each other's arms out on the dance floor, not over here talking to me in the corner. "Y'all need to go enjoy yourselves. Congratulations again."

Celia pulled Jacob by the arm to the dance floor, laughing. I was happy for my sister. At first, it was a little awkward when my best friend and sister started talking, but they were perfect for each other. I knew he would treat her like a queen and had his stuff together. To see them tonight, so happy on their wedding day, it truly gave me insight that I could one day be as happy as them.

My eyes drifted over to Heather who was talking to a woman near the edge of the dance floor. Now that they knew, no reason to keep tiptoeing, so it was time to ask her to dance the night away with me. I didn't want to waste another second without being next to her.

I smiled and started walking toward her when out of the corner of my eye, I saw Trevor enter the room. Did he seriously just show up? He was friends with Jacob too, but he could have at least made it to the actual wedding. Showing up for the after-party seemed disingenuous.

I stopped for a moment and watched him, his eyes locked on Heather, and it made me squirm the way he was looking at her. Trevor might think he still had a shot with Heather, but tonight he would learn that I was who she wanted. They had history but no one was going to come between us. Not even him.

11
Heather

"Surprise!" Trevor exclaimed as he approached Mario and me. He feigned casualness, but his eyes betrayed a hint of desperation.

"What brings you here?"

"Can't I just drop by to see my favorite... friends?" Trevor replied, placing emphasis on the word 'friends' as he glanced between us.

I exchanged nervous glances with Mario, who seemed too lost in thought to fully register Trevor's presence. His jaw clenched.

"Alright, enough of this," Trevor said, frustration seeping through his easygoing demeanor. "I can see what's going on between you two."

"Wh-what do you mean?" I stuttered, feeling both guilty and defensive.

"Come on, Heather. Don't play dumb," Trevor snapped. "You've been spending a lot of time with Mario. It's obvious you two have rekindled your feelings for each other."

"Wait, that's not—" I began, but Mario cut me off.

"Actually, Trevor, that's true," he confessed, his voice firm with newfound courage. "I still love Heather, and I want to be with her."

Trevor clutched his chest. How could Mario declare his love so openly?

"Can't you see?" Trevor's voice filled the room, a low rumble like thunder building in the distance. "You two are betraying me."

My heart pounded as I looked from Trevor to Mario, feeling torn between the man I once dated and the one who had never truly left my heart. The air was thick with tension, like static electricity threatening to erupt at any moment.

"Look, Trevor, it's not what you think," I tried to explain, my voice wavering slightly. But deep down, I knew he wasn't entirely wrong.

"Isn't it?" he spat, his eyes blazing with anger. "I can see it, Heather. You're practically glowing every time you're around him."

"Hey, now," Mario interjected, stepping closer to me. His dark eyes were soft, full of understanding but also guilt. He could feel the weight of our shared history just as keenly as I could. "Let's all just calm down and talk about this like adults."

"Adults?" Trevor scoffed, his face twisting into a bitter smile. "You're the one sneaking around with my ex, and you want to talk about being adults?"

I could see the hurt behind Trevor's anger, the vulnerability that he tried so hard to hide. He still cared for me, despite everything, and it broke my heart to see him like this.

"Please, Trevor," I whispered, reaching out a hand to touch his arm.

But Trevor recoiled from my touch, his muscles tensing beneath his shirt as he clenched his fists. The charming smile that usually played on his lips was gone, replaced by a snarl that sent shivers down my spine.

"Stay away from me, Heather," he growled, his voice low and dangerous. "And you should stay far away from him too."

"Hey!" Mario exclaimed, his eyes narrowing as he squared up to Trevor. "You don't get to tell her what to do."

"Really?" Trevor sneered, his anger flaring. He took a step toward Mario, trying to assert his dominance. "Because it seems to me like she needs someone to protect her from people like you."

"Enough!" I cried, stepping between them as my heart raced in my chest. "I won't let you two fight over me like this. It's not fair to any of us."

"Maybe she's right," Mario said softly, his voice heavy with regret. "We should all take a step back and think about what we really want."

As the words hung in the air, I could feel the tension still simmering beneath the surface, threatening to boil over at any moment. But at least for now, we were willing to put our feelings aside and try to find a solution that would bring happiness to all three of us.

"Fine," Trevor muttered, his anger momentarily quelled. "But this isn't over."

And with those parting words, he stormed out the door, leaving me and Mario to face the fallout of our actions and the tangled web of emotions that lay between us.

My heart pounded as I watched Trevor storm out the door, leaving me and Mario standing in the wreckage of shattered emotions. The air was thick, like a storm cloud waiting to unleash its fury. I couldn't help but feel guilty for being caught in the middle of this love triangle, torn between my past with Trevor and Mario.

"Look, Heather," Mario began, his voice soft but firm, "I can't deny that the moment I laid eyes on you again... it felt like coming home."

The sincerity in his voice made my stomach flutter, but my loyalty to Trevor still tugged at me, threatening to unravel any chance of happiness with Mario. We all went to high school together, but after graduating, Trevor and I had a relationship at college. He wanted to get married and have a family before we even graduated and I wanted the opposite. My career needed to be built before I even contemplated having a family of my own. Nonetheless, seeing him like this tonight had really messed up my head.

Even back when we were dating, if Mario came up in conversation, he would get upset. He probably had an inkling that I still had feelings for him, but after him being around for the wedding, there was no doubt in his mind. We might have thought we hid it well, but we were wrong.

He called Trevor back over after giving him some time to cool down. Celia must have told him about us; otherwise, how would Trevor know?

"Listen, we aren't teenagers anymore. I might have been stopped at prom from telling her how I really felt, but I won't let anyone stand in my way ever again."

Trevor stared at him and then at me. We both knew what was coming.

"Heather, I love you. I've always loved you. I never stopped loving you, even after all these years apart. And I'm willing to fight for you if that's what it takes."

My heart swelled with a mix of joy and fear as I processed his declaration of love. Part of me wanted to leap into his arms and never let go, but another part of me held back, struggling to remain loyal to Trevor.

"Are you happy now?" I asked Mario, my voice trembling. "You've just poured your heart out in front of the man who still cares about me, who was there for me when you weren't."

"Because I want you to see that I don't care who knows. I'd give up my whole life to be with you. Don't you get it? I've been searching for what has been missing in my life and all along it was you."

As I gazed into his eyes, searching for any trace of doubt or hesitation, I realized Mario had changed. He had grown into a man willing to stand up for love, to face his fears and risk it all for the chance at happiness.

And maybe, just maybe, I could find the courage to do the same.

My eyes darted between Mario and Trevor, the room suddenly feeling much smaller. Mario's declaration of love hung in the air like a heavy fog, clouding everything else around us. My heart pounded as I felt my loyalty to Trevor being tested, but my feelings for Mario refused to be ignored.

"Is this some kind of joke to you?" Trevor growled at Mario, his eyes narrowed into slits. "You waltz back in here and expect Heather to just throw herself into your arms? You have no idea what we've been through."

"Hey, Trevor," I said, placing a hand on his shoulder in an attempt to pacify him. "Mario has said his piece, and now it's time for me to process what's going on. I need to figure out what I want." I glanced at Mario, whose eyes were full of hope and determination.

"Fine," Trevor spat, shrugging off my touch. He crossed his arms over his chest and glared at Mario, clearly not ready to let go of his anger anytime soon.

"Thank you," I whispered, feeling the weight of their gazes upon me. In the silence that followed, my thoughts raced, trying to weigh the consequences of following my heart or staying loyal to Trevor.

"Look, Heather," Mario began, his voice softening. "I don't expect you to make a decision right now. But I needed you to know how I feel. I'm not asking you to choose me without any thought, but please, think about our history, our connection, and consider giving us a chance. Because I promise if you do, there won't be a single day that you have to wonder how I feel."

"Connection?" Trevor scoffed, rolling his eyes. "You had your chance in high school, and you blew it. This is just a desperate attempt to claw your way back into her life."

"Enough!" I shouted, my emotions getting the better of me. "Can't you see how difficult this is for me? I care about both of you."

The three of us moved into the living room, straying away from the guests, still dancing the night away, but a thick tension filled the air like fog. It was as if time had stopped and the world outside ceased to exist, leaving only our intertwined fates hanging in the balance. My heart raced wildly in my chest as I weighed the consequences of my decision.

"Okay," I began, taking a deep breath to steady myself. " Here's what I've decided."

As the words left my mouth, I felt like I was standing on the edge of a cliff, preparing to jump into the abyss below. Mario's eyes were fixed on me, filled with hope and fear, while Trevor's expression was a mix of anger.

"First of all, Mario, your declaration really touched me," I continued, trying to put my thoughts into words. "It made me remember all the good times we had together, and how much we've grown since then. But most importantly, it showed me that you're willing to fight for us, even when it's not easy."

Mario's face lit up with relief, his shoulders relaxing ever so slightly. I could see the emotional weight of his confession starting to lift, replaced by a newfound sense of courage and determination.

"However," I added, turning to Trevor, "I also recognize that you've been there for me through thick and thin, and I'll always be grateful for your support. But this is not just about loyalty; it's about who I want to be with, who makes me truly happy. The person I could see myself growing old with and celebrating our forty-year anniversary."

Trevor clenched his jaw and stared at me, his eyes burning with frustration.

"Ultimately, I've decided... that I want to give Mario a shot," I said, my voice shaking but resolute. "I believe we can make each other happy, and I owe it to myself to take the chance on us that we never got."

"Are you kidding me?" Trevor exploded, his anger finally reaching its boiling point. "After everything I've done for you, you're choosing him? The guy who broke your heart once before?"

Even now, he had things wrong. Mario didn't break my heart. I was the one who chose to leave him behind to go to college. I was the one who stopped him from confessing how he felt at prom. However, instead of correcting him to make matters worse, I let it go.

"Please, Trevor," I implored, wincing at the raw pain in his voice. "I know this is hard for you, but it's what I want."

"If that's how it's going to be, then I'm out of here."

As Trevor stormed off, slamming the front door behind him, my heart ached with guilt and sadness. But I knew deep down that I had made the right choice. A man who acted that way, like a toddler who didn't get his way, wasn't the right person for me.

Turning to Mario, who stood by my side with a gentle smile, I reached out and took his hand, feeling the warmth of our connection instantly.

"I promise, I won't let you down."

"Here's to new beginnings," I said softly, as we embraced and started our journey together.

12
Heather

The warm glow of the setting sun bathed Mario and me in a golden light as we stood together on the terrace, watching our friends dance and celebrate inside. The wedding had been beautiful, and there was a sense of relief that it had gone off without a hitch. As the laughter and clinking glasses echoed behind us, I felt the weight of our own unresolved past.

"Beautiful day for a wedding, huh?" Mario said, trying to break the ice, his dark hair catching the fading sunlight.

"It really was. I'm so happy for them."

"Me too." He hesitated, searching for the right words. "So, can we talk about ourselves now?"

I looked at him, a hint of caution in my eyes. "What about us?"

"Look, I know we've both made mistakes, and I..."

My heart raced at the thought of a future with Mario. I sighed, my hair gently swaying in the evening breeze. "I've always cared about you, but I never thought we would ever get our chance. Are you sure?"

"More than anything," he replied firmly, his confidence shining through. "I want to be there for you, to take risks, and to make our relationship work. Even if it's from far away for a while. There is no one I would rather be with. So how are we going to do this?"

I wanted to believe that we could make it long-distance and after everything we have been through, the chances were in our favor. "Would you ever move?"

His eyebrow raised. "Would you?"

"I would move anywhere if it meant being happy."

Choosing to give ourselves a chance was only one step. We needed to have a discussion about how that was going to work. Would I move to New York City? Mario's career was based in the city and him moving meant he would have to give up being the youngest partner at the firm. He worked so hard for it. No way! I could take my job anywhere and have been looking for a change of pace. New York City might grow on me.

"Listen, all I know is that I love you, have since the first day I laid eyes on you, and if being with you means giving up everything, I would do it in a heartbeat. What I won't do, is watch you walk away from me ever again."

He pulled me in close and kissed me like I had been imagining for two decades.

"Wow," I said as he pulled away from me. "That's what twenty years of pent-up chemistry is like..."

"And just think we might be lucky enough to be able to enjoy that every day."

As we stood on the edge of a new beginning, Mario reached out to take my hand, his touch gentle and reassuring. I looked into his eyes, seeing the earnestness and determination that had always been a part of who he was.

"Alright," I said finally, my voice wavering. " Let's take the leap together."

"I promise you won't regret it."

With the decision made, we turned to face the future hand in hand, hearts filled with hope, love, and a newfound commitment to one another. And as the last rays of the sun dipped below the horizon, I knew that despite the risks, giving our relationship another chance was worth every ounce of courage it took to jump into the unknown.

Epilogue
Mario

Heather and I were standing side by side in the kitchen, attempting to make homemade pasta for the first time. The air was filled with the aroma of fresh basil and tomatoes, and a fine dusting of flour coated every surface.

"Okay, so we just need to roll this out and then cut it into thin strips, right?" Heather asked, her brow furrowed as she held up the dough between us.

"Sounds simple enough," I said, trying to hide my own uncertainty. My hands were covered in sticky dough, and I could feel the pasta machine mocking me from its spot on the counter.

As we rolled and stretched the dough, our laughter filled the kitchen, punctuated by the occasional yelp when one of us fed too much dough into the machine at once.

"Wait, wait, Mario!" Heather giggled, grabbing my hand as I reached for another ball of dough. "We're making a mess. Let's slow down and get this right."

"Alright, you win," I admitted, wiping my hands on a nearby towel. "I never thought making pasta could be so... challenging."

"Life is full of surprises." Heather smiled, squeezing my hand gently. "But we'll get through them together, won't we?"

"Definitely," I agreed.

After we had successfully made our pasta and enjoyed a delicious meal together, I sat on the couch with Heather curled up next to me. Her head was resting on my shoulder, and the steady rhythm of her breathing was audible as she dozed off.

"Hey," I whispered softly, nudging her awake. "I just wanted to say thank you, for everything. For giving us a chance, and for being here with me through the good times and the bad."

"Of course," Heather murmured sleepily, snuggling closer to me. "I love you, Mario."

I pressed a gentle kiss to her forehead. "I love you more than I can put into words, and I promise to always be there for you, no matter what life throws our way."

"Promise?" Heather asked, her blue eyes locking on mine.

"Promise," I confirmed, sealing our pact with a tender kiss that spoke volumes about our commitment to each other.

As we lay wrapped in each other's arms, I marveled at the incredible journey we had been on together. From the moment we reconnected at Celia and Jacob's wedding, Heather and I had faced our fears and taken a leap of faith, determined to give our love a chance.

And as we continued to support and encourage one another through both the challenges and joys of life, I knew that we were stronger together than we had ever been apart. Our love, once faded and uncertain, now burned brightly, fueled by the small gestures and acts of kindness that proved just how much we meant to each other.

"I got an email from Trevor earlier today."

"Really?" I asked, feeling a slight pang of jealousy. "What did he want?"

"Apparently, he's moving back to town, and he wants to meet to catch up and clear the air." She looked at me, her eyes searching for any sign of disapproval.

"Are you okay with that?" I asked, trying to sound casual even though my heart raced. It wasn't easy to hear her ex-boyfriend's name, but I knew that trust was vital in our relationship.

"Only if you're comfortable with it," she replied honestly. "I don't want to do anything that would make you feel uneasy."

"Go ahead," I said, swallowing my insecurities. "If it's important to you, then it's important to me." Heather smiled and squeezed my hand in gratitude.

"You've come such a long way from the jealous guy I used to know," she teased gently.

"Hey now," I chuckled, feigning indignation. "I prefer 'protectively affectionate.'"

"Of course," she agreed, leaning over to plant a soft kiss on my cheek. "And I love you for it."

"Love you too," I whispered back, wrapping my arm around her.

With every challenge faced and obstacle overcome, I knew we were building something truly special together. We were about to embark on the most beautiful chapter yet.

Saved by the Boss
Kaci Bell

1
Justin

I am a dreamer, with a positive attitude that's contagious. During the past five years, I have been providing freelance assistance to a range of businesses, helping them with their development and success. Helping struggling businesses has helped made a name for myself as someone who can turn even the most dire situations into success stories, and my clients are a testament to that.

Another day, another dollar. I sip my morning coffee, still warm from the artisan café down the street. My laptop screen has a dizzying array of email notifications and calendar appointments. It is going to be a busy day, but that is nothing new. Freelancing doesn't provide a set schedule, but sometimes that is what I like about it. When businesses are going under and they need help to figure out how to salvage their business, they call me.

Legacy Inc., my father's company, has grown tremendously in the last ten years, and soon it will be my turn to take over the reins. The desire and motivation to prove myself is more than just familial obligation. For me, taking over the family business means carrying on a legacy that extends far beyond my family's wealth and privilege.

Hard work and commitment can lead to greatness, even in a world of skepticism.

Legacy Inc... soon to be mine. I won't let you down, Dad.

I have been waiting patiently for my dad to retire, but he loves the company. He has been preparing me for it since I was ten-years-old. He used to bring me to work with him, explain what he was doing, and I still remember every word. Besides that, he sent me to a prestigious business school too. The weight of the world will soon be on my shoulders. After all, it is not every day that someone gets the chance to carry on their family's legacy, and I am more than prepared to rise to the occasion.

Legacy provides for my family, but my brothers have gone into another line of work, Law. It might be what gives us our wealth, but my father begged them to go a different direction. He didn't want them taking over the business, but instead focusing on something that will never cease. Lawyers will always be around.

Alright, time to get this show on the road. I crack my knuckles and dive headfirst into the daily tasks, analyzing graphs and spreadsheets for the next six hours. By the time it reaches five o'clock, my head is about to explode.

With a sigh, I close my eyes and lean back in my chair. It is time for the weekly family dinner at my parent's house, so I throw on a blazer and walk out the door, not sure what tonight will bring.

"Justin!" Mom calls from inside the house as soon as I step out of the car. "We've been waiting for you!"

"Sorry, Mom! Work ran a little late today." I try to catch my breath as I jog up the front steps. "You know how clients are."

"Your father will be happy you made it," she says, wiping her hands on her apron.

My mother catches me off guard a bit. The only time I have ever missed a family dinner is when I have been out of town. Who misses out on a home cooked meal?

"Hey there, kiddo!" Dad greets me with his signature bear hug. "How's my future CEO?"

"Working hard, as always." I grin.

"Good man," he says, patting me on the back. "But remember, this journey isn't just about skills. It's about passion and determination too. Don't lose sight of that."

"Never, Dad."

"Speaking of," Mom interjects with a playful smile, "let's get this dinner started before the lasagna turns into a fossil!"

"Your lasagna could never turn to stone." I joke, following them into the dining room. "It's a work of art!"

"Flattery will get you everywhere, dear," she winks, setting down a heaping plate of lasagna in front of me. "Now, eat up! You'll need all the energy."

"Thanks, Mom," I say, digging in. My mind wanders to the future as I eat, imagining myself sitting at the helm of my father's company, leading it to new heights.

"Anything interesting happening at work today?" Dad asks, snapping me back to reality.

"I had a breakthrough in a project I've been working on. It's going to make a tremendous difference for one of my clients."

"See? That's what I'm talking about!" Dad beams, his pride clear. "Keep working hard and learning, Justin. And remember, you've got your family behind you every step of the way."

"Thanks, Dad."

Garlic and basil in the air brings me warmth and comfort. It's remarkable that this weekly dinner tradition has been going on for years, and yet it never gets old.

"Justin, could you pass me the salt?" my sister, Cassie, asks.

"Sure thing," I say, chuckling as I hand her the shaker. The clink of silverware against plates and the hum of conversation fills the room, creating a symphony of family bonding. In between bites of lasagna, I catch my father's eye.

"Alright, everyone," Dad says, setting down his fork with a dramatic flourish. "I've got a very important announcement to make."

The table falls silent. All eyes lock onto him. Even Mom, who knows everything before the rest of us, seems taken aback.

"Justin, as you know, Legacy Inc has been my life's work, but it has come time to pass the torch."

My heart races as Dad pauses for effect, his excitement contagious. *Is this happening? Is he going to entrust me with the reins of the family business?*

"Your dedication and hard work have not gone unnoticed, son," he says, pride swelling in his voice.

"I've been working towards this for years."

My dad peers around the room. "It's important for everyone to understand just how significant this announcement is. The future of Legacy Inc—and our family's legacy — rests on Justin's shoulders."

As I grasp the significance of his words, a wave of responsibility comes over me. This is about carrying on a tradition, and proving to my family — and myself — I can step into Dad's shoes. Why do I even second guess myself when I help companies every day?

"Justin, are you ready?"

"Absolutely."

"Congratulations!" My older brother, Jake, joins in, reaching across the table to give me a hearty pat on the back.

Tears well up in my mom's eyes, and she dabs them away with a napkin before rising from her seat. She walks around the table and envelopes me in a hug.

"Honey," she whispers, her voice choked. "I'm proud of you. This is a new chapter in your life."

"Thank you, Mom," I say, my throat tightening as her words sink in.

Being the middle child, most times, makes me invisible. My two younger sisters get the most attention, obviously, and my two older brothers are the most harped on. Sometimes I'm left out altogether, but this is mine. Legacy Inc. is how I can make my father see me in a whole new light. Prove to my brothers that just because they have Law Degrees doesn't make them successful. Neither thinks that what

I do as a freelancer is truly making a difference, but the companies will say differently. Without me, they would have shut their doors. So, it's important that I help Legacy Inc. flourish and be more successful than ever before under my reign.

"Alright, enough with the waterworks!" Dad says, his eyes twinkling. Tears streaming down both my mother's face and his own. "This is supposed to be a celebration!"

"Of course, dear. We're all so proud of you. Now let's toast to your success and the bright future ahead!"

As we raise our glasses in unison, there will be plenty of challenges ahead. As the new CEO, it is an immense responsibility, but I am determined to do everything in my power to ensure its continued success—not just for me, but for my family.

"Cheers," I say, clinking my glass with those of my family members. "To new beginnings."

"Cheers!" they all echo, the clink of their glasses ringing through the air like a joyful chorus.

This is my chance to take charge.

"Alright, everyone," Dad says, his voice radiating with pride. "I know it's getting late, but how about we move this party to the living room for some celebratory dessert?"

"Ooh, that sounds wonderful!" Mom chimes in, her earlier tears now being replaced by a beaming smile. We follow her lead, our steps light as we make our way to the decorated living room.

As we settle onto the plush couches and chairs, a decadent chocolate cake adorned with candles is presented. My name and 'Congratulations!' is scripted in icing across the top, and the flickering candlelight cast a warm, golden glow upon his family's faces.

"Make a wish!" my other younger sister, Emily, squeals, bouncing up and down in her seat. She has always been my biggest cheerleader. She is the sibling I am closest to.

"Alright, alright." I blow out the candles, and the room erupts into applause.

"Here's to Justin!" Dad yells, raising his glass once more. "May you continue to build upon the legacy we've created and make us even prouder!"

"Here, here!" the rest of my family chimed in, their voices blending together into a harmonious swell of love and support.

"Can you believe it? You're going to be the CEO!" Emily squeals as she pulls me into a tight hug.

"Oof, easy there, Em." I chuckle, trying to catch my breath. "I'm excited too, but I'd like to make it to my first day in one piece."

"Sorry!" she releases me with a sheepish grin. "It's just so exciting. You finally got your dream... maybe one day I will too."

Mom wipes away her tears of joy and patting his arm. "We always knew this day would come. I couldn't be prouder, sweetheart."

"Thank you, Dad. I won't let you down."

Here's to the future. Let's make it one for the books.

2

Chloe

My heels click with authority as I stride down the hallway of Legacy Inc. My eyes lock on the door at the end. I have passed it countless times in the past decade, always with a sense of longing. The brass plate affixed to it read "Director"—a title I have yearned for since first stepping foot into this building ten years ago.

Determined and focused, I have spent countless nights poring over marketing reports, strategizing campaigns, and cultivating relationships with clients to ensure their loyalty to Legacy Inc. All of this effort is not just to excel in my current role, but to secure the coveted director position. A position that, until recently, has been occupied by the same person who hired me.

"Ten years," I mutter under my breath as I come to a stop in front of the door, my gaze unwavering. The weight of my ambition falling heavily on my chest, like a hummingbird tapping at my ribcage, urging me to push harder, reach further, and never settle for anything less than the best.

"Morning, Chloe," a colleague greets as they pass by.

"Morning, Susan," I reply, plastering a polite smile on my face before returning my focus to the door. How different will my life be if

I get this promotion and that office? No more playing second fiddle, no more biting my tongue during meetings when my idea is better. This is my chance to call the shots and lead the team to even greater heights.

Today's the day! I clutch my portfolio tighter. Inside are my crafted plans and proposals, the culmination of the tireless dedication to my career. They are the key to unlocking the life I have always envisioned for myself: one filled with success, recognition, and, yes, a bit of power.

"Excuse me, Chloe," a voice interrupts my thoughts. I blink and step aside as one of my team members rushes by, a stack of papers precariously balance in their hands. I watch them disappear around the corner, eyes narrowing slightly. Managing a team of 25 employees is no small feat, but once I have the Director title, they will be more inclined to listen and follow my lead.

For six days, I have been preparing for this interview. It's been a long time coming, and don't want anything standing in my way. From the internal candidates, I am the best person for the job with my experience and degree.

Alright, Jackson. I straighten my shoulders and fix my gaze on the door once more. *This is it. Time to show them what you're made of.*

With that, I take a deep breath, my confidence surging through my veins like liquid gold, and prepared to make my move. The door to my destiny is before me—all I have to do is reach out and grab the brass handle.

The interview goes on for about an hour, and I nail it. I am a person who is always over-prepared for meetings. I don't like not being able to provide adequate proof of my hard work. When I step out of the office, I go back to my normal office, waiting for their answer. They only have four people interviewing for the position, and I'm more than qualified. My unwavering loyalty has been to this company, and if they end up giving the position to someone else, I might need to start looking elsewhere.

My fingers tap against the polished mahogany desk, lost in

thought, as I gaze at the framed photographs adorning my office walls. These are visual testaments to my prowess in marketing: successful campaigns for Legacy Inc's top clients that have taken the company's revenues to new heights. Surely, they are going to take into consideration the amount of revenue I have brought in since my arrival or even in the last year. My marketing campaigns have seen some of the best engagement and ROI than any other person in the Marketing department.

Master's degree in Business and a decade of hard work. I muse, tracing my finger along the edge of my diploma that hangs on the wall. *I've more than earned my shot at Director.*

The phone on my desk rings. I wait a moment before pressing the speaker button.

"Ms. Jackson speaking," I say, trying to keep my voice steady despite the fluttering in my chest.

"Chloe! It's Ms. Johnson, Vice President of Human Resources." The voice on the other end is warm, but professional. "I have some news for you."

"Good news, I hope?" I ask, trying to inject some humor into the situation. My heart races, and I grip the edge of my desk with white-knuckled intensity.

"Indeed," Ms. Johnson says. "After reviewing your impressive track record and considering your expertise, we've decided to offer you the position of Director of Marketing at Legacy inc."

"Really?" I squeak. *Girl, get it together. Be professional.* A grin stretches from ear to ear.

"Absolutely," Ms. Johnson laughs. "We believe you're the perfect fit for the job, and we're excited to see what you bring to the table."

"Thank you so much, Ms. Johnson! I promise you won't be disappointed. I'm going to make Legacy Inc prouder and more successful than ever before!"

"Knowing you, Chloe, I have no doubt," Ms. Johnson says. "In fact, why don't you start moving your things into the designated

Director's office? We want you to feel comfortable and confident in your new role."

"I'll start packing my things now."

"The sooner, the better!" Ms. Johnson assures me with a chuckle.

"I'll get started right away."

As I hang up the phone, a triumphant whoop echoes through my office. *Chloe Jackson, Director at Legacy inc.*—it has a nice ring to it. My mind combs through the ideas and plans for the future as I'm ready to face challenges head on.

Here's to new beginnings. I raise an imaginary glass in toast too. After waiting a decade, I'm eager to show the world what I am capable of.

As I gaze around my current office, I pack my belongings—the framed picture of my family, the potted plant that somehow survived my less-than-green thumb, and the marketing awards that adorned the shelves. This is my chance to make a real name for myself in this business, and it starts today.

Time to make my mark. I collect my cherished items with care and placing them into a box, all while rehearsing the rousing speech I plan to deliver to the team.

With each item I add to the box, my confidence grows. This role will be a challenge of managing an ambitious and talented group of employees, knowing that together, we will propel Legacy Inc to even greater heights.

Here's to new adventures. I strut with purpose down the hallway toward the Director's office. *This is it.* Time to take my rightful place in the company and prove that I am more than deserving of this incredible opportunity.

The office is bigger than I remember, and the view to the city below is nothing short of amazing. As much as I want to celebrate, with this title comes many more responsibilities and as a woman, I need to be even more careful with everything I do. People are always watching, waiting for me to fail, so they can swoop in and take my spot. One man in particular.

Time to get to work. My fingers dance across the keyboard, composing a list of tasks I need to tackle on my first day as Director.

"Okay, let's see," I mumble. "First, review quarterly revenue targets... then, set up one-on-ones with each team member to discuss their goals and expectations..."

"Chloe, do you have a minute?" The soft voice of my now assistant, Lucy, pulls me from my thoughts.

"Of course. What's up?"

"Your calendar is filling up, and I wanted to make sure we're prioritizing your meetings correctly."

I laugh at first, thinking she is joking. It's been a whole hour since I became Director, how is my schedule already packed? Yet, I don't question her, because she is just doing her job.

"Ah, thank you for checking." I glance at the screen, noting the colorful blocks representing various appointments and commitments. I pause. This is just another obstacle to overcome.

"Alright, let's move my meeting with the creative team to later in the week. I want to make sure I have enough time to get settled in and meet with everyone before diving into strategy discussions."

"Sounds like a plan!" Lucy chirps, tapping away at her own keyboard to update my schedule.

"Thanks. I appreciate your help during this transition."

"Of course. It's going to be amazing watching you take charge as Director. You've got this!"

The words of encouragement warm my heart, and I look back at my task list. If there is one thing I know how to do, it is face challenges head-on. I have tackled countless marketing campaigns in my career, each more successful than the last. Managing a team and meeting revenue targets are not new puzzles for me to solve.

"Alright, back to it," I whisper, my fingers flying across the keys once more. "Next up: schedule team-building exercises and brainstorm ways to boost morale..."

With every task added to my list, I'm eager to tackle the new role. The obstacles ahead will be no match for my determination and passion. After all, love isn't the only battlefield—the world of marketing has its own share missteps. And I am ready to conquer them all.

As Director, it is important that I sit down with my employees and managers, and let them know what I expect from them. Weekly staff meetings. Daily updates with the campaigns analytics. It's important that I am on top of everything, especially when it comes to marketing strategies. Pouring money into a campaign that isn't working is detrimental and that can only be proven with digging into the analytics.

I hold my head high, trying to get all the nervous jitters out, and practice the speech I am to give to my employees.

"Good morning, team," I begin, my voice clear and steady. "As your new Director, I'd like to start by expressing how excited I am to work alongside each one of you."

I watch myself, noting the confident tilt of my chin and the genuine smile on my lips. This is the woman I have always aspired to become—a leader who can inspire passion and drive in others while maintaining a sense of humor and warmth.

"Of course, we have some big goals ahead of us," I continue, my hands gesturing to emphasize the points. "But I believe that together, we can not only meet our quarterly revenue targets but exceed them."

I see the determined marketing supervisor I have been for years, but now there is also the poised and powerful Director.

"Remember, collaboration is key," I tell my imaginary team, the words flowing now. "We'll face challenges along the way, but I know we can overcome them together—with creativity, hard work, and perhaps a bit of laughter, too."

With a deep breath, I conclude my speech, eyes shining with conviction. "Let's make this a quarter to remember!"

I allow myself a small chuckle, shaking my head at the slight absurdity of speaking to my own reflection. Yet, the exercise works wonders for my confidence. As I replay the speech in my mind, any lingering doubts about my ability to succeed in the new role evaporate like wisps of steam.

Alright, Chloe. You've got this. You're ready.

With a last nod, I head for the door. The challenges of the new role may loom large, but I'm more than prepared to face them head-on.

Laughter might dance around the edges of my professional life, but in the end, it is my unwavering determination and drive that will carry me through every twist and turn along the path ahead. And as Director Chloe Jackson, I can't wait to see just how far I can go.

3
Justin

The sun peeks through the floor-to-ceiling windows of my penthouse apartment, casting a golden glow on my tailored suit as I prepare for my first day as CEO of Legacy Inc. I adjust the tie with trembling hands. It is a big day—the day my father passes down the mantle of leadership to me. The weight of responsibility settles onto my shoulders like an invisible cloak.

First day jitters, huh? It isn't that I don't believe I can do the job, heck I do it for other companies all the time, but this is different. This company represents my family and will be passed down to our kids, so making it a success is far more important. There is a little more stress involved than freelancing with other businesses. It is all on me for Legacy Inc. It is my turn to keep the legacy alive and continue to build upon my father's success. The pressure to live up to his expectations gnaws at me.

"Morning, Mr. Myers," greets the doorman with a tip of his hat as I step out into the bustling city.

"Morning." My stomach churns with nerves, making it difficult to summon my usual optimism. I hail a cab and climb in, gripping the handle as the vehicle sped through the streets towards the impressive Legacy Inc. headquarters.

As the building looms closer, its glass facade reflecting the morning sun, I take a deep breath to steady myself. This is my chance to prove I am worthy of the title "CEO"—that I am more than just the son who has been chosen to take over the family business because my brothers went into Law instead.

"Here we are, sir," the cab driver announces, pulling up in front of Legacy Inc.

"Thank you," I reply, handing the driver a generous tip before stepping out onto the sidewalk. I gaze up at the towering skyscraper that will soon be under my command and swallow hard, trying to quell the butterflies in my stomach.

Alright. Time to make your mark.

With a final deep breath, I straighten my tie one last time and stride through the revolving doors of Legacy Inc., ready to face whatever challenges lay ahead and continue the legacy my family built.

As I step into the grand lobby, I take in the view. The lofty ceiling adorned with intricate murals depicting the company's humble beginnings. I stand there for a moment, taking in the scene, as both pride and trepidation swirls within me. This is it; this is the day I have been preparing for since I received that gleaming, embossed envelope from Harvard Business School.

"Justin!" a cheerful voice calls out from behind him, causing him to jump. Turning around, I greet my longtime friend and new assistant, Sarah, with an infectious grin.

"Sarah! Good to see you," I say, my nerves forgotten as we exchange pleasantries. "I still can't believe I'm here, taking over as CEO. Can you?"

She grins back, her eyes twinkling. "Well, after all those late-night study sessions and endless cups of coffee during your time at Harvard, I'd say you've earned it."

"Speaking of Harvard," I say, my shoulders squaring with pride, "I think all those lessons on business strategy and management are going to come in handy now. I just hope I remember everything."

"Of course you will!" Sarah reassures me, giving me a light pat on the shoulder. "You were a celebrity in the halls of Harvard. Everyone knew you were destined for greatness, and now here you are, ready to lead Legacy Inc. into a new era."

"Thanks. It's just... everything I've worked towards has led me to this moment, and I don't want to mess it up, you know?"

"Hey," she looked me straight in the eye, "you've got this. You're more than ready, and everyone here knows it. Now, let's go show them what you're made of!"

"Alright," I agree, my determination rekindled. "Let's do this!"

I have been coming to this place since seven-years-old. Many of the employees have met me over the years. Even as a freelancer, I still visit to stay up to date with whom is here, and see if there is anything I need to be aware of before taking over. The business is thriving, according to my father, and my only need is to make it even better. Find a way to make us more profitable and take us to a new level.

"Here goes nothing."

As we walk through the bustling halls towards my father's old office, a sense of awe at the sheer scale of the operation I am now responsible for. The weight of the responsibility, however, does not crush me; instead, it stokes the fire of enthusiasm that has been burning since I completed my master's degree. Since the day my father told me that I would be taking over someday. It has been stuck in the back of my mind all these years, and it's finally here.

"This just seems so surreal. Remember when we used to talk about this all the time?" I tell her. "And now I have you working alongside me. What could go wrong?"

"Keep your head up and go in there and make your mark, Mr. Myers," she replies, a warm smile spreading across her face as we approached the door to the CEO's office. My office.

With a nod and an optimistic glint in my eye, I push open the heavy door, stepping into the room where my journey as CEO will truly begin.

I step into the cavernous office, its walls lined with shelves upon shelves of leather-bound books and framed photographs of my father shaking hands with various business magnates. The room holds an air of importance that seems to whisper "Legacy" in hushed tones. It is here, in this very space, that I will make my mark on the family business.

"Hey, odd one out," a voice calls from behind. I turn to see my older brother, Daniel, leaning against the doorframe, a teasing smile playing on his lips.

What in the world is he doing here? Probably to rub something in my face or say some snide comment about how I got here.

"To what do I owe this pleasure? Aren't you busy with cases or something?" I ask, rolling my eyes but grinning.

"Couldn't miss my little brother's first day as CEO. Besides, I had to make sure you're not planning on turning Legacy Inc. into a clown college."

"Ha, hilarious," I say, though I can't help the twinge of insecurity at the jest. My brothers' careers in law had been our father's first choice—a fact they rarely let me forget.

"Relax, Justin," Daniel says, seeming to pick up on my unease. "You're going to do great."

"I just want to make everyone proud, you know? Prove that I can do this."

"Trust me," Daniel assures me, clapping a hand on my shoulder before leaving, "you've got this."

With renewed determination, I survey the office. The enormity of the task before me looms large, like the skyscrapers outside the window. I am responsible for thousands of employees, each depending on me to steer the company towards continued success. The pressure is immense, but I refuse to buckle beneath it.

My father already has a meeting scheduled for this morning. He says it's important for me and morale to meet with the directors and managers early on to show them my dedication and vision. He is right. It is important that everyone in the company trust me to lead. Most know my background.

Lucy pops her head inside. "Sir, you have about ten minutes until the meeting starts. Everyone is already in the conference room."

"Thanks. Be right there."

This meeting needs to go off without a hitch. I can't go messing things up on my first day here. There are so many things that I will need to catch up, but being upfront and approachable is important in any business.

I stand up and take a deep breath, preparing myself for the possibility of many questions and not having all the answers just yet.

Walking into the room, it's filled to the brim. Some aren't even sitting. All eyes are on me. I wipe the sweat from my brow and walk to the front of the room. *Don't let me intimidate you.*

"Alright, team, we've got a lot of work ahead of us. But I know that together, we can tackle any challenge and continue to build on the incredible legacy my father started."

Heads nod around the table, their expressions conveying a mixture of curiosity, skepticism, and cautious optimism. It is clear they are waiting to see if I can fill my father's shoes.

"Let's start by addressing our biggest ongoing project," I continue, my voice steady and confident as I outline the plan for the upcoming quarter. With each detail I provide, the room seems to relax ever so slightly. This presentation is one my father prepared knowing I wouldn't have enough time to prepare my own for today.

As the meeting draws to a close, I allow myself a moment to marvel at the path that has led me here—from Harvard Business School to the helm of Legacy Inc. There will be challenges, but this is my chance to prove not only to my family but also to myself that I can rise to the occasion. And with every decision, every triumph, and every hard-earned lesson, I will carry on the proud tradition of the company.

"Thank you all for your time," I conclude. "Now let's get to work."

Stepping out of the conference room, a surge of energy courses through me. I have just finished my first executive meeting as CEO of Legacy Inc., and despite the lingering doubts that haunted the corners of my mind, I can't help but feel invigorated by the challenge ahead. With every step down the corridor, my confidence grows stronger, fueled by the knowledge that I am where I belong.

"Mr. Myers," a timid voice calls out. Glancing over, I see Janice, the company's receptionist, approaching with a wide smile. "I just wanted to say how excited we all are to have you here. You're doing an amazing job already!"

Legacy Inc. isn't just a business; it is a beacon of hope for countless families who depend on the company for their livelihoods. The weight of this realization settles on my shoulders, but instead of crushing me, it only strengthens my resolve.

"You've got big shoes to fill, but there's no doubt in my mind that you can do it."

"Thanks, Janice. That means a lot."

"Janice is right, you know," chimes in Tim, the company's IT manager, who has been eavesdropping from a nearby office. "We've all seen the dedication you've put into preparing for this day. You've got the brains and the heart to make this work."

"Thanks." I haven't realized just how visible my efforts have been to those around me.

With every conversation, every encouraging word, my confidence continues to build. This will be filled with trials and tribulations, but I am surrounded by a team of hardworking individuals who believe in him—and in turn, I believe in them. Together, we will forge a new chapter in the story of Legacy Inc., one that will benefit not only their own families but also the community.

As I walk back to the office and settle into my father's old chair, I am ready to face whatever challenges lay ahead—head on, heart open, and determination unwavering.

"Your coffee is on your desk, just how you like it."

"Thanks, Sarah."

I chuckle at her enthusiasm, a stark contrast to the serious atmosphere I expect on my first day as CEO.

Time to show everyone that I have what it takes... here goes nothing.

4
Chloe

As the marketing director, I have learned to navigate the challenges that come with being a woman in a male-dominated industry with grace and determination. My focused gaze and squared shoulders telegraphed my authority to anyone who dares to question my ability to lead.

"Morning, Chloe," said a passing intern, trying to catch my attention with an eager smile.

"Morning," I say, not breaking stride. Time is money, and I didn't have any to waste on small talk. Efficiency is now my middle name.

My rise to the top is nothing short of meteoric. I started as an intern myself, fetching coffee for the senior executives and drowning in a sea of photocopies. But I proved my worth, my keen eye for detail and penchant for innovative strategies catching the eye of the superiors. I clawed my way up through the ranks, leaving a trail of impressed colleagues and envious rivals in her wake.

Of course, none of this would be possible if Mr. Myers didn't start the company with a simple design in mind. Legacy Inc. is a clothing brand that has skyrocketed. The biggest part of running a business is knowing where the trends are going and being able to adapt to the times. Right now, people want environment friendly and cruelty free products. You can charge more for them and they sell like hotcakes. Our biggest targeting success is twenty to thirty-year-olds in the United States. Our customer acquisition cost has gone down striking low in the past two years, but our marketing campaigns are successful.

As I settle into my office chair, I reflect on how far I have come. From intern to marketing director, I have built a reputation on an unshakable work ethic and razor-sharp wit. In this cutthroat world, my values of efficiency and avoidance of small talk have served me well.

Alright, let's get down to business. I open my laptop and dive into my emails, ready to tackle another day in the corporate jungle.

I survey the marketing team assembled before me, their eager faces illuminated by the soft glow of the morning sun. I need to tread carefully; one wrong move could send them all plummeting down the precarious tightrope of corporate survival. A thrill in my chest comes as I prepare to navigate another day on this high-stakes balancing act.

A meeting first thing in the morning is one of the things I want to implement on a long-term basis now.

"Alright, team. We've got our work cut out for us today," I begin, voice steady and measured. "Our competition is fierce, and we need to be smarter and more strategic than ever."

I pace across my office. In my mind, I consider each word, weighing its potential impact like an expert chess player contemplating the next move.

"Katie, I want you to partner with Alex on revising our social media strategy. Think about what's working, what's not, and where we can make improvements," I instruct, my eyes locked on the young marketer. "And remember: I expect well-reasoned suggestions backed by data, not just gut feelings."

"Understood," Katie replies, as she scribbles notes onto her pad.

"Michael, I'd like you to analyze our recent email campaigns. Look into open rates, click-through rates, and conversion rates. Identify trends and areas that need improvement," I continue, turning my attention to the next team member. "I want a detailed report by tomorrow morning."

"Of course, Chloe. I'll get right on it," Michael responds, already pulling up spreadsheets on his laptop.

I delegate tasks and challenge my team members to think critically. I craft every sentence, every directive, as a testament to my caution and strategic thinking. It is this very skill that has helped me climb the ranks in a male-dominated industry, and it is crucial in maintaining my hard-won position.

"Alright, everyone, let's make today count. I have faith in every one of you to deliver results. Now, get to work."

With that, the team dispersed, diving headfirst into their respective tasks. I watch them go knowing that their success—and mine—hinge on the delicate balance of power.

My eyes narrow as I scrutinize the mountain of data that sprawls across my desk, a kaleidoscope of numbers and graphs vying for my attention. A once steaming cup of coffee sits forgotten by my side, approaching room temperature as my focus remains laser-sharp on the task at hand. My fingers tap on the edge of my laptop, betraying my impatience as I wait for yet another report to load.

Come on! The spinning wheel of death on my screen disappears. The document materializes before me, and I dive in, my analytical mind working overtime as I sift through the raw data.

"Chloe, have you seen these projections?" John, a tall, broad-shouldered colleague who has been promoted to my old role as manager with a penchant for questioning authority, saunters over to my desk, waving a thick bundle of papers in his hand. "They make little sense. You think we should prioritize this campaign over the other?"

"John, I don't decide things on a whim," I say, not lifting my eyes from the screen. He is testing me, trying to see if I will waver under scrutiny. "Solid evidence backs every choice I make. If you have concerns, show me your data at the manager meeting. I'll be there in a minute."

He hesitates for a moment, surprised by my unwavering confidence. "Well, I just think we could put our resources elsewhere," John says, shifting his weight from one foot to the other. "But I will."

Shaking off the momentary distraction, I return to my work, delving back into the sea of information that awaits me. Because while I may have won this battle, but there will always be more challenges ahead, and I need to be ready to face them head-on.

I answer one last email before heading to the conference room. It's important I stay up to date on everything that is going on. Those above me expect me to keep us from bleeding money. Detailed reports are the only way for me to be able to determine the success.

I stand at the head of the conference table, my fingers tapping against the stack of research papers compiled. The team watches me, their eyes glinting like those of eager racehorses before the starting gun is fired.

"Alright, everyone, based on the analysis I've conducted, it's clear that we should focus our efforts on expanding our online presence through social media advertising and micro-influencer partnerships."

John leans back in his chair, studying me with narrowed eyes. "I'm not sure about that, Chloe," he says, his tone laced with skepticism. "In my experience, big-name influencers drive more traffic and sales. Are you sure this is the right direction for us?"

I resist the urge to roll my eyes at John's challenge, opting instead for a measured response. I flip open my binder, revealing a series of colorful charts and graphs. "John, our data shows that engagement rates with micro-influencers are higher than with more prominent figures because of their closer connection with their audience."

"Sure, but is that enough to make a significant impact on our bottom line?" John presses, not yet ready to concede defeat.

"Great question," I reply, my lips curving into a knowing smile. I gesture towards the graph, the lines dancing across the page like elegant ballerinas. "As you can see here, the return on investment for micro-influencer campaigns has exceeded that of larger influencer partnerships by 20%. And that's just the tip of the iceberg."

The room falls silent as my colleagues absorbed this new information, their gazes shifting between me and the data. Even John seems to grapple with this revelation, his defiant expression now clouded with uncertainty.

"Besides," I continue, seizing the opportunity to drive my point home, "it's not just about the numbers. We've all been in this industry long enough to know that trends change. By diversifying our approach, we're future-proofing our strategy, ensuring that we'll always be one step ahead of the game."

John sighs, his shoulders slumping in defeat as he nods. "Alright, you've convinced me. It's clear that you've done your homework, Chloe. I'm on board with the plan."

A ripple of approval spreads through the room, accompanied by nods and murmurs of agreement. I breathe a quiet sigh of relief, my heart swelling with pride at the hard-earned respect I'd garnered from the team.

I gather my belongings from the conference room. With every folder and document, I tuck into my sleek leather briefcase, the weight of their respect growing heavier.

"Great job today, boss," one colleague remarks, flashing a thumbs-up as they pass by. Chloe nodded in appreciation, a hint of a smile playing at the corner of her lips.

"Thanks, I appreciate it," I say, zipping my briefcase closed with a satisfying snap. I sling the strap over my shoulder and make my way toward the exit, the sun casting long shadows across the office floor.

"See you tomorrow, Chloe!" calls out John, his tone warm and respectful. The sound of his words solidified the victory that unfolded just moments before, filling me with renewed determination.

As the door clicks shut behind her, I pause for a moment, taking in the empty hallway.

In the silence, I allow myself a private smile, reflecting on the day's triumphs. Despite the odds stacked against me, I have risen above the challenges and proven my worth in the male-dominated world of marketing. But there is always more to conquer - more strategies to devise, more glass ceilings to shatter, and more hearts to win over.

My heart swells with pride at the thought of the barriers I have already broken down and the impact I am making in the industry, but there is still a rough road ahead. The reality of being a woman in my position is an ever-present challenge, but it fuels the fire and sharpens my resolve.

With a deep breath, I straighten my posture and walk through the corridors, my heels clicking against the polished floor. The day's accomplishments course through my veins, each step a testament to my hard-won success.

With plenty of day ahead and two meetings knocked out, I can finally focus on returning the hundred emails and go through my research. Now that I am the Director, I have to work hard every single day to make sure that no one doubts my ability to perform.

With every barrier I face, I vow to fight harder, think smarter, and never lose sight of what truly matters: breaking new ground for myself and the countless women who will follow in my footsteps. And as the elevator descends to go back to my office, so too does my resolve to challenge the status quo and carve out a brighter future for all.

5

Justin

I settle into the plush leather chair behind the desk, rolling up my sleeves, ready to get down to business. The company's policies and procedures manual sits on the desktop, accompanied by a stack of documents that seem to multiply each time I glance at them. With a deep breath, I open the hefty binder and begin poring over its contents.

As I flip through the pages, a stream of questions flood my mind, mingled with the perpetual optimism I try to maintain. *Surely, I can improve things around here, right?* I tap a pen against my chin. *Dad's been doing a great job, but there's always room for innovation, isn't there?*

A knock on the door interrupts my train of thought. Looking up, I see the department heads filing into my office. I smile, extending a hand to each of them as they introduce themselves again.

"Hi, I'm Chloe, Director of marketing," a woman with a tight ponytail and an even tighter smile says, giving me a firm handshake. "We're all eager to see what you have planned for us, Mr. Myers."

"Please, call me Justin," I reply, hoping to establish a rapport with the new team. "I'm just as eager to learn about your roles and how we can work together to make Legacy Inc even more successful."

The department heads exchange glances, not used to such enthusiasm. As we settle into our seats, I pull out a notepad and pen, ready to take notes on each of their responsibilities and insights.

"Alright," I begin, looking at the group. "Let's dive in. Chloe, why don't you start by telling me about some of the marketing initiatives you have in place?"

As Chloe launches into an explanation of their current campaigns, I listen, scribbling down notes and nodding along. My eagerness to learn is infectious, and soon the other department heads are chiming in with their own thoughts and concerns.

"Justin," interjects James, Director of HR, "we've been struggling with employee engagement. Any ideas on how we might address this issue?"

"Great question, James," I reply, rubbing my chin. "I think it's important that our employees feel valued and heard. We could try implementing regular feedback sessions, recognizing achievements, and organizing team-building events. What do you think?"

A murmur of approval ripple through the room. My optimistic attitude is winning them over.

"Alright, team," I say, closing my notebook as the meeting ends. "I know we've got a lot to tackle, but I believe in every one of you. Together, we're going to make Legacy Inc the best it's ever been."

As the department heads file out of the office, smiling and chatting amongst themselves, I allow myself a moment of pride.

I settle into back into my chair, ready to tackle the financials. I open the thick binder labeled "Legacy Inc - Financial Statements" and take a deep breath. The scent of ink on paper mingles with the faint aroma of cologne from the manila folder, a comforting reminder of my father's presence.

Let's dive in. I trace my finger down the income statement. As I read, my brow furrow, and the corners of my mouth tightened. The numbers are telling a story—one that isn't as rosy as I hoped.

Sales down by fifteen percent? And expenses are up? How did this happen?

I flip to the balance sheets, hoping for a reprieve. Instead, I discover that the company's debts have ballooned over the past year, casting an ominous shadow over its assets. I lean back in the chair, rubbing my temples as I try to digest the information.

"Hey, Justin!" calls out Chloe from across the hallway, the marketing director with a penchant for bold lipstick shades. "How's the thorough analysis going? Found any buried treasure yet?"

"More like a sunken ship," I reply, forcing a chuckle. "Did you know our sales have been declining? And our expenses are through the roof!"

"Yikes," Chloe winces, crossing the room and peering over my shoulder at the binder. "I knew things weren't great, but I didn't realize it was that bad."

"Neither did I," I admit, my optimism dampened. A sudden thought strikes me, and I turn to face her. "Do you think we could tie this to our high employee turnover rate? Maybe if we focus on improving morale and reducing costs, we can turn things around."

Chloe mulls it over, her fingers tapping on the binder's edge. "It's possible," she concedes. "I know a lot of our best people have left because they felt undervalued or overworked. And, well, we have been spending a fortune on recruitment and training."

"Alright, let's start there. We'll address employee engagement, cut unnecessary expenses, and get this ship sailing again. After all, it can't be all stormy seas, right?"

"Right!" Chloe agrees, her own smile returning at my contagious optimism. "We'll navigate these waters—and maybe even discover some treasure along the way."

"Sounds like a plan." I close the binder with newfound resolve. It won't be a simple journey, but with my steadfast optimism and the support of my dedicated team, I am confident that Legacy Inc will weather the storm.

My heart races as the weight of the companies struggles settles on my shoulders. The surrounding office buzzes with activity, oblivious to the storm raging inside me. I stand by the window, gazing at the cityscape below, feeling a sudden wave of vertigo.

"Is it selfish of me to wish my father had told me about all this?" I blurt out, clenching and unclenching my fists. "I feel like they have thrown me into the deep end without so much as a life jacket. I could have helped before it got this far."

Chloe put a hand on my shoulder, her touch gentle yet grounding. "It's not selfish, Justin. It's natural to feel overwhelmed by all of this, and a little betrayed too. You have every right to be frustrated."

"Thanks," I sigh. "It's just... I can't help but think how different things might be if I'd known sooner. Maybe I could've made some changes, helped turn things around."

"Maybe," Chloe concedes, a wry smile playing on her lips. "But you can't change the past—and besides, you're here now. And you'll do everything in your power to make things right."

"Darn straight." A flicker of determination returns. I turn away from the window, my posture straightening. "If I'm going to take charge of this company, I need to know every aspect, inside and out. No more secrets or hidden surprises."

"Agreed," Chloe nods. "I'll be right there with you, every step of the way. I've been with this company for a decade and don't want to see it fail."

"Appreciate it," I say, my gratitude genuine. It's time to prepare. "Well, there's no time like the present. Let's dive back into those financials and see if we can't identify some more areas for improvement."

"Already on it," Chloe grins, her fingers flying over her laptop keys. "I've started pulling together data on employee satisfaction, too. I think you'll find it... enlightening."

"Enlightening, huh?" His spirits lifting as we settle into the banter. "Can't wait to see what kind of Pandora's box that opens up."

"Trust me," Chloe winks, her eyes sparkling with mischief. "You ain't seen nothing yet."

"If we all work together, we'll make Legacy Inc something truly special—not just for us, but for everyone who believes in what we're capable of achieving."

"Here's to new beginnings," Chloe raises an imaginary glass, her eyes gleaming.

"Cheers to that."

Due to the recent information, I call a meeting. We are going to have to change some things if we are going to get back to where we used to be, and everyone needs to be on board. If our numbers continue like this, we won't be open for business in three years.

I stand at the head of the conference table, my fingers tapping rhythmically on the polished surface. The department heads sit around him, their expressions a mixture of curiosity and apprehension.

"Alright, everyone," I begin, my voice strong and steady. "It's time to create a plan of action to address the challenges we're facing."

Unlike my father, who likes to keep things like this private, in this instance, they need to know. Without everyone chipping in where needed, this won't work. If anything, I have learned that keeping employees in the dark about things only make it worse in the long run. When they are valued and are allowed to bring ideas to the table, they are more inclined to push through the hardships and come across the finish line more loyal than ever.

I gesture to the whiteboard, where I have written the main issues: declining sales, increasing expenses, and high employee turnover. As I explain each one, the energy in the room shifting from tentative to determined—a testament to the power of my optimism.

"First, let's prioritize these issues. I propose that we tackle declining sales and increasing expenses simultaneously since they're closely related. We'll then focus on employee retention once we've stabilized the financial situation. Thoughts?"

"Sounds like a solid plan," James chimes in. "If we can improve our financials, employees will feel more secure and be less likely to leave."

"Great. Now, we need to set SMART goals for each issue," I continue, my enthusiasm contagious. "For declining sales, how about increasing revenue by 10% in the next six months? And for expenses, let's aim to reduce them by 5% in the same timeframe. Will those work?"

"Agreed," nods Andrew, the finance director. "I think those are challenging yet achievable targets."

"Perfect. Now, let's assign tasks to the appropriate team members."

The room comes alive as we discuss strategies and delegate responsibilities, their excitement palpable. I watch the team rally together, each department head eager to contribute their expertise and ideas.

"I will be available for questions or concerns. No issue is too small right now."

Katie approaches me as others are filing out of the room. "I just wanted to say thank you," We've all been feeling the pressure lately, but your positivity and clear plan of action have made a world of difference."

"Thank you, but I couldn't do it without all of you. I know we can turn things around."

Not everyone understands the importance of making everyone feel valued, but that is where my focus will be. It's a true statement that people leave companies because they are undervalued or underpaid. In the future, I want to pay them well enough to where they won't want to leave and make sure we implement an employee recognition program. That is, if we survive that long.

6
Chloe

I stand at the head of the large conference table, my eyes scanning the impeccably designed meeting room. The comfortable chairs surrounding the table are unyielding beneath my colleagues' weight, just as I intend to be in presenting my innovative plan. My heart pounded with determination and ambition as I envision the positive impact my well-thought-out strategies will have on the company's future.

"Alright, everyone. As you know, I've been working to analyze our current marketing efforts and identify areas where we can improve." I take a deep breath, my chest swelling with pride and purpose. "Today, I'm excited to share with you my comprehensive plan that will not only revitalize our marketing strategies but also streamline our budget, ensuring our company remains competitive in this ever-changing market."

A hush falls over the room as my words echo, each syllable emphasizing my unwavering determination. I glance down at my prepared notes, pausing for a moment to center myself before diving into the details of the proposal.

"Let's begin," I say resolutely, my inner fire burning bright, ready to ignite the passion and drive of my colleagues—and perhaps even spark something unexpected within myself.

My gaze sweeps the room, taking in the diverse array of professionals gathered for the meeting. Among them is Justin, the new CEO, with a conservative reputation that seems to belie his youthful appearance. His trimmed beard framed a strong jawline, while his piercing brown eyes bear an air of authority and wisdom beyond his years. As I lock eyes with him, my heartbeat quickens.

"Thank you all for being here," I begin, my voice steady and commanding. "I'm confident that my plan will not only enhance our marketing strategies but also improve our financial situation."

As I launch into the presentation, I dissect the company's current marketing efforts, pinpointing areas of weakness and missed opportunities. The colleagues listen, their expressions a mix of admiration and curiosity—all except for Justin, who remains stoic, his arms crossed over his chest.

"By reallocating resources and tightening our budget," I continue, "we can invest in more targeted campaigns that will yield better results, giving us the edge we need in this competitive market."

A murmur of approval ripples through the room, but Justin remains unmoved, his expression unreadable. *What is going on inside his head?*

"Justin, I'd love to hear your thoughts on my proposal."

For a moment, he hesitates, his brow furrowing as he considers the question. Justin speaks up, his voice measured and calm. "While I appreciate the effort you've put into this plan, Chloe, I have concerns about the potential consequences of such drastic budget cuts. We don't want to compromise the quality of our work or our long-term growth."

A spark of irritation erupts at his skepticism. Still, I need to address his concerns head-on. "I understand your concerns, Justin," I reply, my voice firm but respectful. "However, I believe that by making these bold changes, we'll be positioning ourselves for even greater success in the future."

As our eyes meet once more, an unexpected flicker of attraction flutters through my chest. But now is not the time to dwell on such feelings; I need to stay focused and win over Justin—and the rest of the room—with the plan.

"Let me show you how we can achieve our goals without sacrificing quality," I say, diving back into the presentation. And as I make my case, I hope that, besides winning the debate, I might also capture something else—the elusive heart of a certain CEO.

Justin raises a well-groomed eyebrow, his skepticism clear as he studies my proposal. "I must admit, I'm not convinced," he begins, leaning back in his chair with a measured air of authority. "These budget cuts might have negative long-term effects on our business."

I clench my jaw, resisting the urge to roll my eyes. Instead, I focus on the smooth surface of the conference table, allowing myself a moment to collect my thoughts before responding. I need to make Justin understand the necessity of the bold strategy.

"Justin," I say, my voice steady and laced with determination, "our competitors are evolving and finding new ways to reach their target audiences. If we don't adapt, we'll be left behind. The budget cuts are a necessary part of that adaptation."

As I speak, my hands move, emphasizing each point. The passion for my plan is palpable, and I refuse to let Justin's conservative nature hold us back.

"Think about it—by reallocating resources from underperforming areas to those with greater potential for growth, we can ensure not only our survival but also our continued success in the market," I add, my gaze unwavering as I lock eyes with Justin.

He rubs his chin, a hint of amusement in his eyes as he regards my tenacity. "You don't lack conviction, Chloe. But I still worry about the unforeseen consequences of such drastic cuts."

I bite the inside of her cheek, my patience wearing thin. This is a battle worth fighting. "Justin, every decision we make comes with risks. However, I believe the benefits of my plan far outweigh those risks. We need to be proactive, not reactive, in order to thrive in this competitive market."

The two of us continue our verbal sparring match, each determined to prove the validity of our respective viewpoints. And though I know the stakes are high — both professionally and personally — the exhilarating thrill of engaging in such a spirited debate with someone who challenged me so completely.

"Alright, Chloe," Justin concedes, nodding his head slowly as he considers her words. "I'm willing to entertain the idea. But I want to be sure we're not jeopardizing our future for short-term gains."

"Agreed," I reply, suppressing a triumphant smile. "And together, I'm certain we can find the right balance to ensure our company's success."

As the meeting adjourns, a surge of pride and satisfaction renders through me at having stood my ground. But more than that, intrigued by the man who dared to challenge me—and wondering what other surprises Justin Myers might have in store.

7
Chloe

Papers scatter across my immaculate desk, the pen poised like a weapon, ready to strike at any moment. This is my battlefield, and my greatest weapon is my unwavering professionalism.

"Chloe, are you coming to lunch?" John asks, peeking into the office.

"Not today," I reply without looking up, "I need to finish this proposal."

"Alright, but don't work too hard," he calls out before disappearing down the hall.

I sigh, knowing full well that "working too hard" is my middle name. Despite my dedication to the job, there is one thing that threaten to distract me: Justin Myers. Even thinking his name sends a shiver down my spine, equal parts excitement and frustration.

Focus, Chloe! I try to shove thoughts of Justin to a dark corner of my mind.

But it isn't easy. The image of his charming smile and those piercing brown eyes haunt me. I steal glances at him when we cross paths in the break room or have a meeting together.

Ugh, why does he have to be so... captivating? I fight the urge to slam my head against the desk. This is not how things are supposed to go. I pride myself on the ability to separate my personal life from my professional one, but Justin is throwing a wrench into my balanced world.

Okay, think about something else. Think about the numbers, the graphs, the... the smell of coffee brewing in the break room.

"Chloe?"

I jump, startled by the sudden intrusion. Opening my eyes, I am face to face with none other than Justin Myers himself.

"Sorry, didn't mean to scare you," he says, grinning. "I just wanted to see if you had a minute to discuss the new marketing strategy."

"Of course," I reply, my heart pounding. I try to focus on the words coming out of his mouth, but all I can think about is how close he is standing, the warmth radiating from his body, and the subtle hint of cologne.

"Chloe? Are you alright?" Justin asks, concern etched on his face.

"Y-yes, sorry," I stammer, shaking my head. "Let's get back to the marketing strategy, shall we?"

As we discuss our ideas, I force myself to concentrate on the task at hand, even though my mind keeps drifting back to the conflicting emotions Justin stirs up.

"Could you look at these numbers for the marketing budget? I want to make sure I'm on the right track," he says, handing me an organized spreadsheet.

"Of course," I agree, trying to ignore the warmth creeping up my neck as I focus on the numbers in front of me. "I'll have this back to you in no time."

"Thanks, Chloe," Justin replies, his eyes lingering on me for a moment before returning to his office.

As I review the spreadsheet, I'm impressed by Justin's work. It is thorough and well-organized, clearly showing his intelligence and dedication. But even as my professional admiration grows, so did the nagging feeling that I am allowing myself to become too emotionally invested in our working relationship.

Stop it! This is ridiculous.

But as I hand the spreadsheet back to Justin, our fingers brushing ever so slightly, I can't deny that there is something between us—something I need to keep under control. If only my heart will listen to reason.

8
Justin

I find myself more and more intrigued by Chloe's strong work ethic and determination. I often catch myself observing her as she works diligently, her brow furrowed in concentration while she sips her coffee. There is an undeniable spark in her eyes that speaks of her passion for her job, a trait I admire. As we attend meetings together and cross paths in the break room, I see Chloe in a new light.

"Hey, Justin!" Chloe greets me with a bright smile as we bump into each other near the coffee machine. "How's your day going?"

"Better now. I just got some good news."

"That's amazing!" Her enthusiasm is contagious. "So, what's the secret to your success?"

"Optimism," I respond without missing a beat. "I always try to find the silver lining in every situation. Oh, and coffee. Lots of coffee."

I laugh, her melodic giggle filling the break room. "Well, you're in the right place for that," she says, gesturing towards the coffee machine.

As we fill our mugs and chat about work and life. She is so easy to talk to. She is intelligent, funny, and incredibly driven—all qualities I admire. And though it isn't exactly professional, I can't ignore the growing attraction.

"Hey, Chloe," I hesitate, rubbing the back of my neck. "Would you like to grab lunch sometime? You know, just to discuss work stuff and... maybe get to know each other better outside the office?" I mentally kick myself for sounding so awkward.

"Um, sure," she agrees, a hint of surprise in her voice. "That sounds like a great idea."

"Great!" I beam, trying to keep my excitement in check. "How about tomorrow?"

"Tomorrow works for me," she confirms, a soft smile playing at the corner of her lips.

"Perfect. I'll see you then," I say, unable to suppress the grin that spread across my face as we parted way.

As I return to my office, a sense of anticipation for our lunch date – even if it is just a casual, work-related meal. I need to tread carefully, not wanting to jeopardize either of our careers. But there is something about Chloe that makes me want to take a chance, and maybe, just maybe, she feels the same way.

9
Chloe

I unlock my phone and see the notification for a new email, but don't recognize the name, Clara. The email contains multiple attachment, and the body has a brief explanation.

Dear Chloe,
Now that George is gone, I feel it's best to reach out to you next. Let me preface this by saying that I know it might come as a shock, but he was stealing my designs and passing them off as Legacy Inc's. After trying to get him to compensate me for my work, and not coming to an agreement, it's best to reach out to someone new. I would like to give your company one last chance to make this right before I get a lawyer involved. The designs attached were used without my permission and have gained the company hundreds of thousands of dollars in revenue. Please review the information and get back to me as soon as possible. If I do not hear back from you by the 20th, then I will have no choice but to get my lawyer involved.
Thanks,
Clara

There are emails attached of correspondence between George and Clara. In these emails, he even admits to taking her designs, but shows no remorse. George was complacent in this? What are we going to do?

A knot forms in my stomach reading through all the attachments in the email. I have worked for George for a decade, and he has always been fair and professional, and I never would have expected something like this from him. The company is his livelihood, something he wants to pass down through his family for generations if possible, so for him to do something like this is out of character.

I quickly shut my email and start pacing around my living room, trying to clear my head and process all of this information.

If this gets out to the media, it can completely tarnish Legacy Inc's reputation. My mind races with possible solutions- can I confront George? Should I take the information to the new CEO, Justin, and ask him to take action?

The thought of bringing this to Justin makes me pause. We have only been working together a short amount of time, and we get along well, but how will he react? This is his father, which makes me hesitant to take this information to him. He shouldn't have to deal with something like this so soon after taking over. All I can do is bring it to Justin and let him decide what to do from there.

The next day, Justin and I are due to go to lunch today to talk about some projections, but that email is stuck in the back of my mind. Maybe this is the best place to drop the news. He will have time to process before going back to the office. This isn't something that needs to get out before we can find a way to diffuse the situation.

At eleven, Justin comes over and lets me know that the car is ready to take us to lunch, and I grab my purse, trying to give myself a pep talk for what I have to tell him.

Justin has been coming to this building since he was a kid,

waiting to take over the family business, and this is what his father hands him? What kind of parent would do such a thing?

The car maneuvers over to the curb to let us out, and as much as I want to just blurt out what's on my mind, I keep it inside until the right time.

I sit across from Justin Myers at a cozy bistro, the clinking of silverware and laughter from nearby tables filling the air. Our lunch meeting, focusing on the strategic marketing plan, turned into an enjoyable affair. The sunlight streaming through the large windows reflected off my stylish glasses as I discuss my ideas, while Justin listens.

"Alright, I think we've got this sorted out, but there's something else we need to talk about."

Justin raises an eyebrow, his easygoing demeanor faltering for a moment. "Sure, what's up?"

Taking a deep breath, I reveal the information that has been weighing on my mind since last night. "I discovered something unsettling. It seems he was complacent in stealing designs from other businesses."

A tense silence settles over our table, the previous jovial atmosphere evaporating like steam from the cup of coffee between us. Justin's eyes widen with disbelief as he stammers, "W-what??"

"An anonymous source sent me a series of emails and documents implicating your father and some designers in the company," I reply, my voice steady, despite the gravity of the situation. "It looks like it's been going on for years."

Justin takes a deep breath, trying to process the revelation. "If this is true, it could destroy our careers and the entire business. Our reputation would be ruined."

I nod, my heart heavy with the knowledge of the potential consequences. "We have a tough decision to make. If we expose the truth, we might save our own integrity, but it could cost us everything we've worked so hard for. If we keep quiet, we're complicit in the dishonesty, and it could come back to haunt us at any moment."

"God, I can't believe this is happening," Justin mutters, running his fingers through his hair. "We need to decide soon—if we wait too long, the information might become public anyway, and then we'll be powerless."

In that moment, a shared understanding of the high stakes we both face and the strength we will need to navigate our uncertain future.

I toy with the straw in my iced tea, the ice cubes clinking together like a nervous symphony as I glance at Justin, who is deep in thought, his forehead creased with worry. The sunlight streaming through the bistro window cast a halo around him, creating an ironic image of purity amidst this messy situation.

"Let's start by listing the pros and cons," I suggest, trying to make sense of the whirlwind of thoughts. "If we expose the truth...what are the benefits?"

"First, we'd be doing the right thing ethically," Justin says, tapping his fingers on the table. "And, well, our conscience would be clear."

"True, but if we keep quiet, we might save the company from going under, and our careers along with it."

"Is that worth it, though?" Justin asks, furrowing his brows. "I mean, can we live with ourselves knowing we're just as guilty as my father for keeping this secret?"

I bite my lip, torn between my ambition and my moral compass. "It's not a simple choice, but we have to weigh the repercussions of either decision."

"Alright," Justin sighs, taking a deep breath. "So, if we decide to expose everything, we risk losing our jobs, our reputation, and even the company itself. But, if we stay silent, we're going against everything we stand for—honesty, integrity, fairness."

"Maybe there's a middle ground," I offer, my determination shining through my conflicted expression. "What if we confront your father and give him the chance to come clean himself? That way, we're not directly responsible for the fallout, but we're not staying silent either."

"Would he do that, though?" Justin questions, skepticism clear in his tone. "I'd like to believe he would, but..."

"Then we need a Plan B," I say. "We have to be prepared for any outcome."

"Okay, so if my father refuses to come clean, then we can go to the board of directors with the evidence," Justin adds, his voice shaking at the prospect of betraying his own family. "We'll present our case and let them decide what to do next."

"Sounds like a plan. We'll give your father a chance to make things right, but if he doesn't, we're taking matters into our own hands."

As we discuss the strategy further, we are both committed to navigating this difficult situation together. Our shared ambition and passion for the work has brought us this far, and now we need each other more than ever to weather the storm ahead.

"Whatever happens, we'll get through this," Justin says, his hand reaching out to cover mine on the table, offering a comforting squeeze. "Together."

"Agreed," I reply, feeling the warmth of Justin's touch and allowing myself a small smile. "Together."

10
Justin

My foot taps, the rhythmic beat echoing. Will he tell me the truth? My father has always instilled ethical boundaries in our family, so this is out of character for him, but the proof is right here. As I sit down on the armchair, I am scared to hear his excuses. Finding out about this, it completely destroys everything I have learned from him. The man that raised me would never do anything like this.

"Father, we need to talk about something that has been brought to the marketing department."

"Aren't you supposed to be handling issues now? I'm retired, remember."

This conversation isn't going to end well. So, I grit my teeth, trying to keep myself calm.

"This has to do with you directly. A designer has come forward and brought up allegations that you are complacent is stealing their designs."

"Ah, yes," George replies airily, swirling the amber liquid in his glass, "the stolen designs. I've been meaning to discuss it with you."

So, he isn't even going to try to deny it? Who is this man?

"Discuss?" I exclaim, incredulity seeping into my tone. I have always been an optimist, believing in the inherent goodness of people, but this situation is pushing my faith to its limit. "Do you not understand how negatively this affects the company? Not just you?"

George takes a slow sip from his glass, his eyes never leaving mine. The silence hangs heavy like a suffocating fog, threatening to choke the truth that I so desperately need to hear.

"Look, I have proof," I press on, handing him a stack of papers. Photographic evidence of the stolen designs stare up at us, daring George to deny their existence. Even though, he doesn't deny his involvement.

"Where did you get these?" George asks, feigning surprise as he shuffles through the damning evidence.

"Does it matter?" I snap, frustration boiling in my chest. "What matters is that our company, our family legacy, is at stake because of your actions! What were you thinking?"

"Son, please," George begins, setting down his glass and leaning forward, the facade of nonchalance slipping away. "You must understand the pressures I was under. This business means everything to me, and I was simply trying to ensure its survival."

"By stealing?" I counter, feeling my heart fracture. I want nothing more than for him to tell me it is all a misunderstanding, that the accusations are false, but here we are, facing the undeniable truth. I can't even bring myself to look at him in the eye. My father has changed, and not for the better.

"Sometimes," George sighs, rubbing a hand over his face, "we have to make tough decisions in the name of progress."

"Progress?" I echo, stunned by my father's flippant admission. "We could lose everything! The employees, their families—they depend on us!"

"Justin," George says, as if trying to placate a spooked animal, "I know this isn't easy for you, but trust me when I say it was necessary."

"Was it?" I can't understand how the man who taught him right from wrong, who instilled in him a strong moral compass, can betray those values.

"Son, sometimes," George explains, his voice heavy with regret, "the hardest thing and the right thing aren't the same."

"Aren't they, Father? Being honest and ethical is the hardest thing to do in these situations."

The clock on the wall ticks away, filling the tense silence between us. My eyes flitted to it to escape the accusatory gaze of my father. Feeling cornered and suffocated, I force myself to focus on the bigger picture.

"Alright, let's say we can move past this. I have a plan that could save Legacy." I reach into the briefcase, pulling out an organized folder filled with papers detailing the proposal.

"Go on," George says, leaning back in his chair, arms crossed over his chest as if bracing for impact.

"First, you need to come clean about what happened. Admit your mistakes and take responsibility," I explain, feeling my cheeks flush at the thought of exposing our family's shortcomings. "Next, we need to reach out to the original designers you stole from and work out a deal to compensate them."

"Are you out of your mind?" George interjects, his face a mixture of disbelief and annoyance. "That would ruin us!"

"Better than being ruined by lawsuits and a tarnished reputation!" I shoot back, anger flaring. "We need to regain the trust of our employees—their livelihoods depend on us! This will come out in the media eventually, and either way your reputation will go down the toilet. Right now, my focus is on the company, not you."

"Oh, I see you. You are trying to be the hero. Swooping in to save the day from your big evil father?" George scoffs, waving a hand in the air.

"Of course not!" Hurt simmers in my chest, igniting a spark of frustration. "I'm just trying to do what's right – what you taught me to do! But now I don't understand how you could do something like this!"

"Justin, you're too naïve," George sighs, running a hand through his thinning hair. "This is business, not a fairy tale. You need take risks and make tough choices."

"Stealing isn't a risk, it's a crime!" I clench my fists to rein in my rising anger. "And it's not just about the business—this affects our family too!"

"Listen, I've built this company from the ground up," George argues, his eyes narrowing. "I know what it takes to keep it running. Don't lecture me about what's best for the business or the family."

"Maybe you knew once, but now, I can't help but think that maybe you've lost sight of what matters."

The words hang heavy in the air, echoing with the unspoken truth of our shared disappointment and frustration. As the clock continues its relentless march forward, both of us find themselves at a crossroads, unsure of where to turn or who to trust.

The air in the room grows heavier as George's defense grows stronger, like an invisible fog that threatens to suffocate me. I can see the desperation in my father's eyes as he tries to justify his actions. "Son, it was never about getting a leg up on the competition. It was about survival. If we hadn't used those designs, Legacy INC would have been left in the dust."

"Survival?" I scoff, my heart pounding. The sound of my voice seems foreign, tainted by the bitterness that now laces every syllable. "At what cost, Dad? Our integrity?"

"Integrity doesn't pay the bills, Justin," George shoots back, his tone pleading yet defiant. "You know how cutthroat this industry is. They backed us into a corner. I couldn't just stand by and watch our legacy crumble."

I pace the room, my polished shoes sinking into the plush carpet with every step. My mind spins with conflicting thoughts, each one battling for dominance over the others. Can I turn my back on the company that has given him so much—and on the man who raised me?

As I walk past the floor-to-ceiling windows, the face staring back at me is one I barely recognize—it is the face of someone grappling with the weight of a life-altering decision.

"Listen, there's still time to make things right. We can come clean, repay the designers you wronged. I know it's not ideal, but it's something."

For a moment, we stand in silence, our gazes locked in a battle of wills. The road ahead will not be an easy one—and that the future of both Legacy Inc and our relationship hang in the balance.

"Maybe we can't go back to the way things were," George admits, his voice heavy with regret. "But if you're willing to give me a chance, I promise I'll do everything in my power to make this right."

As I look into my father's eyes, whatever decision he makes will change the course of our lives forever. Life has never been about playing it safe—and sometimes, taking a risk is the only way to grow.

11
Chloe

It is best to keep this information between Justin and I for now. The legal department will need to know eventually, but if he wants to get his father's side of the story first, then why not. Information like this can completely destroy Legacy Inc., but Justin seems determined to try to salvage what he can. It's important we stay in front of this, but do we agree on the path?

Information like this can be potentially damaging and have serious implications on the company. I just received my promotion and the last thing I want is to ruin her career.

Sitting at my desk, I wonder how things are going on Justin's end. He left lunch to confront his father, and all the years I have known Mr. Myers, something like this never came to mind. He seems like an honest and caring man. Why would he do something like this?

We will need to make a plan and get the legal department involved, but need to be careful how we handle it. A sound and well thought out plan is best.

The first step is to find out as much information as possible about the stolen designs. How did George get the designs in the first place?

While Justin is busy with his father, I go back to the email and pull up the signature at the very bottom, providing Clara's number.

As soon as the line connects, I inquire about the details of the situation. I want to know how George had access to the designs in the first place.

"I initially interviewed for a position at the company years ago and brought in some designs to present. A couple of months later, my designs were on your products, but not accredited to me."

Clara is understandably outraged by this, and I don't blame her. George should have never done anything like this.

"Well, I would like to say that we had no idea. Why didn't you go to the media or file a lawsuit?"

Okay, so maybe I shouldn't have said that exactly.

"I've been mulling over my options, but I don't want to take down a company I believe in. It was only a matter of time before he retired. I have heard great things about his son. Hopefully he will do the right thing by his family legacy."

She deserves compensation, and George needs to be held accountable for his actions. "I will get with our legal department who will reach out to you to get this resolved. I do appreciate you coming to me with this, instead of going to the media. Justin and I will do the appropriate thing. Unlike his father."

My phone drops to my desk, and I put my hands on the top of my head. This is bizarre. How many designs have been stolen this way? We are going to need to launch a full investigation now. There is no telling how many designers have been ripped off. How did no one catch this? Did my predecessor know?

I can't imagine how Justin is handling this. To think, he has been brought up to take over this company, and a couple days after, he finds out his father has been stealing designs. Heart-crushing. How is the public going to react to this? Will they boycott the company? Cancel culture is growing in this new generation and if that happens, it's likely Legacy Inc will not survive.

My office door swings open.

"I can't even believe this!" Justin closes the door behind him. "He doesn't even seem sorry for what he did. Didn't even try to deny it."

I gesture for him to bring his voice down. "I know you are furious, but we need to keep this from getting out for now."

"Sorry, I'm just in shock. The man that raised me would never do something like this. How am I supposed to carry on the family legacy when this is what is left to me? Utter disrespect for intellectual property. He should know better. No matter what pressure he was under."

I get up from my chair and walk over to him. "Take a deep breath. No need to go ninety to nothing just yet. I spoke with Clara."

"Why on earth would you do that?"

"To get more information. Do you want to know how your father got the designs in the first place?"

He nods and takes a seat. "Spill it. Please tell me it's not that bad."

"She interviewed to be a designer here. The designs were her pitch to get hired. So, he stole from designer instead of just hiring her. Why would he do that?"

"That's a very good question, but now that opens a whole new issue. How many designers have interviewed here in the past decade? We could be using more than just her designs without their permission."

I clap my hand down on his shoulder and he looks up at me. "I think it's time to take what information we have to the legal department and have them sort it out from here. We can try to come up with a plan to try to keep the company afloat."

He puts his head in his hands. "How do we do that? This information is going to ruin us. I'm usually one for optimism but this is a crap show."

I smile. "Honestly, we have so many young adults on the marketing team that they may be able to help us. You haven't done anything wrong. We can make sure everyone knows that you don't tolerate this."

Justin is going to have a rough time over the next week as we determine the best course of action, but he is going to have to be strong. His father is going to be knocked down, dragged through the mud, and he might even face legal action.

"I need this company to survive, Chloe. He can't hand the company over to me and it go under. I'll be the laughingstock of my family."

He is in such a hard position. Justin seems to be a very strong-willed man, and nothing like that of his father. It speaks volumes that he is so upset about the situation and still willing to take the allegations to the legal department. It would have been easy for him to sweep it under the rug, but he is an ethical man.

"Don't beat yourself up over this. You couldn't have known. You are a wonderful man, and we as a company are very lucky to have you as a boss."

Justin looks up at me, a half-attempted smile. "That's very kind of you to say, but it doesn't change the situation. My father may very well never speak to me again after this. It makes it all the more difficult."

The fact he will go against his father speaks volumes to his character. If under different circumstances, he is exactly the type of man I would want in my life. Yet, he is my boss, and things need to stay professional.

"You are doing the right thing. The rest of your family will surely see that. If they want this company to survive, it must come to light and then we work on getting over the hurdle. You aren't alone in this. My department will do whatever it takes... I promise you that."

I rarely say those words, but, I have every intention on keeping it.

12
Justin

My head is spinning leaving Chloe's office. I have to make this right for Clara. Wasting no time, I gather up all the evidence I have about the former CEO's misdeeds and take it to the legal department before I leave for the weekend. If I wait until Monday, it's possible that it gets leaked into the media before they have resolved the matter.

The team of lawyers gather round a large conference table, all eyes on me. "I have made copies of everything I have and they are in front of you. My father stole her designs and has been passing them off as ours. I do not know if there are more out there that were used illegally, but we need to get in front of this. Clara has agreed to talk to you to remedy the situation."

The lawyers start asking me questions, not giving me a break in between, but I answer each one with the knowledge I had. They all seem surprised to hear that my father would do something like this, and it seems I'm not the only one he has been fooling.

"How did he get access to the designs?" one lawyer asks.

"Clara came to interview here and as you know many when they come bring their designs to show the department what they can do.

Apparently, my father took it upon himself to take that as permission to use them without her permission."

The lawyers are appalled and agree that this is a very serious matter. "He will most likely face legal action. However, we will do our best to keep the matter out of the public eye, depending on what is agreed upon with the designer."

The lawyers discuss the different legal options that are available for Clara. She can either sue the former CEO for damages, or she can try to negotiate an out-of-court settlement with him. These included compensatory damages, which cover her lost wages and any financial losses she suffered due to his actions.

No matter what, Clara deserves compensation for the loss of being able to use her designs. My father used her property without her permission.

"She can also ask for punitive damages... basically punishing him and deter him from doing it again in the future, but with him not being with the company anymore - I think she will find that isn't necessary."

It's out of my hands and everything depends on Clara now.

"Clara is expecting your call, and she seems to just want compensation. You might be able to get her to settle. Please keep me in the loop. The marketing team is going to have to keep a close eye on social media."

As I leave the room, a sense of relief washes over me. It is no longer in my hands. Those guys have been to school for this sort of thing and they should be able to handle it with ease.

As I drive home that evening, the implications of my father's wrongdoings weigh heavily on my mind. Until this moment, I haven't fully realized the impact of. his decisions might have on me. Not only will it hurt the company, but it diminishes me as a whole. All the companies I worked with prior to coming on as CEO might not want to work with me again, and if this does go south and I can't keep Legacy afloat, what am I going to do?

Instead of focusing on that, I need to focus on how to make sure nothing like this happens again. Without designers, our industry can not survive. Clara has my utmost respect. Stealing designs doesn't just hurt the victim—it hurts our entire industry. It makes it hard for people to trust each other and it discourages innovation and creativity.

After arriving home, I send a quick text to Chloe to let her know the legal team has all the information. Chloe has been by my side every step of the way since Clara reached out to her, and I'm thankful. Without her to talk to, or vent, this situation would have been much worse.

Chloe: Good. I'll tell my team to watch our socials just in case over the weekend. We will need to meet first thing Monday morning to talk logistics. We need to stay ahead of this.

She has a good point. We do not know how Clara is going to react. Our lawyers might try to offer her some tiny settlement. Why didn't I think about this?

Me: Yes, first thing Monday. Have a good weekend.

Wait! My family. He will not come clean about this willingly, and they don't deserve to be blindsided by the media. How are they going to react? This is going to cause a rift between the family, but I am not the one that did this. He needs to face the consequences. I can see the disappointment is my mother's eyes already.

I step into my family's home with a heavy sense of dread. As I walk down the hall, the delicious scent of my mother's cooking comes through the air, momentarily distracting me from the looming confrontation that I am about to face.

For a fraction of a second, I consider turning on my heel and fleeing back out the door, but eventually I force myself to keep going, my feet carrying me forward against my own will. I reach the dining room. My father is already seated at the head of the table, my mother next to him. Sisters and brothers scatter around the table, and they all look up as I enter the room. There is an awkward silence, and a knot tangles in my stomach. When I sit down, my father's gaze does not meet mine. Matter of fact, he is looking everywhere but at me.

Did he want me to tell the family? Did he want me to burst at the seams? How long can I keep the truth about my father from the rest of my family?

Everyone fills their plates, then eat in silence, with the only sound being silverware clinking against plates. Am I sitting on a ticking time bomb? The truth is coming out, eventually. Keeping information like this to himself is detrimental to the entire family, and even though my father doesn't think what he did is wrong, things will change once it's public. The scrutiny that will be lashed out at him, will have him changing his mind quickly.

Why should I be the only one dealing with this?

"I've got something I need to tell you all."

My father's eyes lock on mine and he shakes his head. If he thinks he is going to intimidate me, especially now, he is mistaken.

"Dad was caught stealing designs and passing them off as Legacy's. The designer might even being suing for damages."

The room erupts into chaos after the words leave my lips; with everyone talking at once trying to figure out how something like this can occur and questioning if the information is accurate or not.

Out of the corner of my eye, I see Jake's jaw drop. My mother is frantic that he would do something so foolish; my sisters argue whether our father even di it; Daniel goes even further challenging my father asking if he did the despicable act - an action that can hurt us all financially while hurting the company as well.

My father remains silent throughout the outbursts - caught off guard from the whole family questioning him.

Finally, my father speaks up.

"I did what I had to do for the company. We were on our last leg and something had to be done to keep it afloat. Without it, there would be nothing left of the family business."

Jake and Daniel are both lawyers and know the road ahead. "Depending on how badly this goes, it won't just bankrupt you, but all of us. Was it worth it?"

Tears start in his eyes. "Yes, even if it meant sacrificing my morals, it's important that the company survive. You kids deserve something to hand down to your kids someday."

Jake steps in. "George must accept responsibility for his actions now so that we can all move forward together as a family."

I see Jake and Daniel exchanging glances; they understand that this is serious if a lawsuit ensues.

Everyone goes quiet as if waiting for me to explain further. "You all deserved to know instead of finding out in the papers. It's only a matter of time before someone picks up on this."

The entire family is staring at my father who can't seem to shake his... what is it? It's not remorse. He doesn't enjoy disappointing his family, but it's not the same as remorse.

"You don't understand how close we were to bankruptcy. Creditors breathing down my neck calling every day asking when payments are expected- something drastic had to be done fast."

My mother stands up after being quiet this whole time. "And instead of coming to us, your family, and letting us help, you did something that jeopardizes everyone instead? Something like this doesn't just effect you. Now Justin has to pick up the pieces with everyone wondering if he is just like you. No matter what, he didn't deserve that. Your sons are lawyers - why not ask them?"

My father hangs his head in shame. We all know that whatever we do moving forward has to reflect more positively on the family business - otherwise, it could spell doom for Legacy Industries.

As if sensing what I'm about to say next my mother breaks the silence. "Justin, you don't have to do anything..."

But before she can finish I interrupt her. "I'm going to go into an interview and discuss what steps we need to take so that this doesn't happen again."

Jake nods. My sisters gives me a look of encouragement while

Daniel just looks at me, waiting for something else from me; they both understood there is no other way out now - not when it's my face people will associate with Legacy Industries now because of this fiasco caused by our father's mistake.

My father gives my mother a sad smile. "When it comes to business, I do what I think is the best course of action - and quickly. I get results." He turns his attention towards me now. "You are my youngest son, but you weren't born yesterday. I want you to go to the interview and just tell the truth. I'll handle the backlash. Just make sure the company survives - It's your face people will see for the company now. I know you can do it."

I give a curt nod in response and walk out of the dining room, my thoughts heavy with responsibility. It will not be easy getting people to trust that Legacy Industries is still an honest business after this gets out into the world, but if there is anyone who can do it, it's me.

My father's actions are going to cost us either way; whether we fight it legally or accept what Clara counters. I hope we can move forward and bring Legacy back to where it should be.

Stepping outside, I take a deep breath as I approach my car parked in front of the house and get inside. My head is spinning as I drive towards home. Thinking about Clara, who has to decide how much money covers the damage my father has done. None of us would be in this mess right now if my father would have just stuck to his morals.

13
Chloe

Sundays have always been a day that I don't get out of my pajamas. I like to lounge around the house, catch up on shows and relax. The weekends always go by so fast. The past week has been stressful to say the least, especially with everything going on with George and the designs. What are the employees going to think when this gets out? So many of us have a good relationship with him, and this information completely contradicts the man I know. Although, sometimes people will do anything to get ahead in business.

This next week is going to be crucial in keeping the business running and my department will be at the forefront. It is time for me to put my skills to use as well as everyone in the marketing department to take care of this online. Cancel culture is very real and many businesses have gone under do to a viral video or post. Legacy Inc. doesn't deserve to go out of business because of what George did. Justin is proving to be more than capable of running this business, and has a good head on his shoulders. His nobility of going against his father, which might result in legal action, proves that he wants what is best for the company overall.

My phone vibrates against the coffee table and I hesitate to pick it up. I stare at it, trying to stay strong, but end up getting it anyway.

Justin: Can you meet for dinner? My treat.

Things between us seem to have gotten more on the personal side lately, not that I am complaining about getting to know him on a much deeper level, but I need to keep myself in check. Having feelings for my boss isn't exactly a good thing. It's the old saying. You can't control who you fall in love with. In this case, helping him through this difficult time, I have been able to see a different side to him. A side that intrigues me.

My career has always come first. Sure, I have dated, but nothing serious in the last ten years. To be honest, my focus has always been on getting the big promotion and now that I have it, I am starting to realize all the things I have put on the backburner. Some nights I come home and miss having someone to talk to. A partner. It might be time for me to open myself up to finding someone.

Me: Sure. Where? When?

This is a strictly professional dinner, of course. It isn't like he is asking me out on a date. Right now, I am the only person besides the lawyers that knows about the issue. So, it's natural for him to talk to me about it. Or is there something more going on?

Justin: Italiano's. 30 minutes?

Yeah, it's definitely not a date if he is only giving me thirty minutes. I pull up the Uber app and request a driver. I scramble to my bedroom closet, and pick out a simple black dress and heels. Nothing fancy, one I usually wear to work. I don't have much time to do something with this awful hair of mine, so I throw it up into a high bun and call it good.

My phone dings and I grab my bag and head downstairs to find my Lexus waiting for me. "Italiano's please. Appreciate you getting here so fast."

Me: On my way.

I try to calm myself on the way to the restaurant, but I can't help my thoughts from running away. What if the company does go under? Her feelings for Justin wouldn't be against the rules. Although, I am not sure there is actually anything in the employee handbook about dating within the workplace.

I hand the driver a twenty dollar bill for a tip for getting me here on time and walk in with grace. The restaurant is bustling, so I scan the room until my eyes fall on Justin, hunched over a table with a phone in his hand, and a look of deep concentration on his face. He glances up at me when I approach and breaks into a relieved smile.

He jumps up to give me an embrace, then gestures for me to take the seat across from him. The waiter comes right over, not wasting a moment, and takes my order before scurrying away.

Justin leans back in his chair and gives a heavy sigh. His eyes are wide with apprehension as if he is about to explode. "So I did it," he says with conviction. "I told my family about my father stealing designs."

My mouth drops open with surprise. "Wow... how did they take it? As shocked as I was, I can't imagine your mother's reaction."

He nervously ruffles his hair with one hand. "Yeah, everyone was taken aback by the news. It's so out of character for him, but I think I made the right decision to stand by my principles no matter what choices he made." His face softens as he adds, "He may hate me for life, but that doesn't mean I should cover his tracks. He raised me better than that."

Though George has certainly made his fair share of mistakes, he can take pride knowing that he raised Justin to be a morally strong man. Standing up for your convictions takes courage though, especially when you have to face family members who may not agree with you.

He exhales a shaky breath and runs a hand through his hair. His eyes are downcast. Fear is radiating off him, but also a deep gratitude.

"It's all out in the open now," he says. "I just wanted to thank you for supporting me through this disaster. I know it's been difficult, and I appreciate you being open to listening to me."

My own smile widens in response. His trust is touching, and I reach out to squeeze his arm.

"You're welcome," I say. "We'll get through this."

The server brings our food and we start to dig in. Somehow, I forgot to eat lunch and being here has my stomach grumbling. "You are a wonderful man. Many people would have covered for their father, but you didn't."

"Why should I? All my life he has told me to never forget my morals, but it seems like he wanted to forget all that because it was him. The way he looked at me when I told my family. Like I was a monster."

"You are anything but... and don't let him make you question yourself."

Justin's eyes lock on mine and for a split second, I think there is definitely something more going on here.

"It's not easy to find an honest person anymore," he says.

I nod, my cheeks growing warm. He's right.

"So, what now?" I ask. "We need to figure out how to move forward and start creating a plan of action." Justin nods in agreement before taking another bite of his food. We discuss the way he's feeling toward his father and whether or not there is any potential for reconciliation down the line.

We both start to plan out the next steps. We brainstorm ideas on how a formal apology can be issued. To truly make amends, it's important that George understands the enormity of his actions and takes responsibility for them while making an effort towards reconciliation with those he wronged. We talk about setting up some kind of compensation or restitution fund so that people impacted by the theft could have some recourse. There is a a formal investigation into any designer who interviewed with Legacy since inception to confirm that no one else's designs were used without permission.

Justin takes notes while I talk passionately about ways we could expose this situation without completely destroying George's reputation; finding a balanced middle ground somehow between compassion and justice so that everyone feels comfortable with where we end up.

Facing this kind of challenge takes courage and a clear plan of action.

"I think that before making any decisions," I say slowly. "It would be best to talk it through and figure out all the different possibilities."

I take a long sip from my water glass then set it down firmly on the table, trying to give him strength with that small gesture of determination. "What are our options? Who might potentially help us - people inside the company perhaps? If they know about his involvement in stealing designs?" I continue on with more questions until we both come up with ideas concerning how move forward and create a plan of action which will hopefully lead us towards resolving this dilemma in an ethical way while maintaining justice for everyone involved.

We come up with some potential recommendations and solutions, but we both know that it'll take much more than a few ideas for this to get resolved fully. In the end, I suggest that George writes out an official apology. After discussing all options thoroughly Justin agrees and begins to craft a formal letter of apology on his father's behalf based off our conversations about what should be included in the document.

The final draft consists of various elements designed specifically by us: He expresses personal remorse over his involvement in stealing designs from designers who put their hearts into their work; acknowledges how wrong he was whether intentional or not; apologizes multiple times for any harm caused; pledges to never make such mistakes again in thought or action—and promises restitution where appropriate as well as coming forward with applicable details regarding anyone else potentially involved.

This is only just scratching the surface but it's an important start — one which takes courage but also demonstrates humility by admitting wrongdoing and showing others genuine respect.

By the time we finish discussing all of our ideas, it's already late into the evening. With a heavy heart I realize that I must take my leave and head home soon. We both are relieved and hopeful after talking through the plan. Justin pays the bill, insisting that I not worry about it, before offering to drive me home since he knows don't have a car of my own. It's New York City, I walk or take a cab everywhere.

On the ride home there is silence as we contemplate this difficult journey ahead. When we arrive at my house, Justin gets out of his car and walks me all the way up to my front door.

"Thank you for your time tonight. I will sleep better tonight knowing we have a plan in place. See you tomorrow." He pecks me on the cheek. "I'm sorry - I shouldn't have done that."

My palm rubs the spot his lips touched. "That's okay. See you tomorrow."

I shut the door behind me and grin.

Is it possible that Justin shares these feelings?

14
Justin

The office is eerily silent, the only sound the faint ticking of a wall clock and my own heart pounding in my chest. I have spent the past few hours trying to piece together what happened: my father, the former CEO of Legacy Inc., has been implicated in a large-scale fraud. Despite his reputation and the thorough vetting process his father created, he somehow managed to dupe hundreds of designers out of their designs.

I shake my head, still unable to wrap my mind around the scope of his deception. I always trusted his judgment, but somehow he managed to pull off such a sophisticated and intricate scheme without anyone suspecting a thing.

The evidence is piling up against my father, and I need to take action. He might have been able to fool everyone else, but I am determined to get to the bottom of this. Taking out my phone, I begin making calls.

One after another, I speak with the designers who have been scammed out of their work. While some are understandably suspicious of my motives – they seem relieved that an investigation is being launched and a compensation package offered.

I receive countless emails from these same designers thanking me for looking into the matter and ensuring their rights are being respected. With each message, it becomes clearer that there is something seriously wrong with the way Legacy Inc has been operating for years.

After an entire fourteen hour day of hard work and digging through thousands of records and financial statements, I uncover enough information to publicly expose my father's frauds for what they are: a massive theft of intellectual property that can no longer be ignored or swept under the rug.

With one final push, I make sure everyone knows exactly what happened - and how reckless Legacy Inc's leadership has been in allowing such an injustice to occur.

I am proud of what we have accomplished - together, we helped restore justice and integrity to Legacy Inc - but more than anything else, it's good to know that these talented designers finally get the recognition they deserve.

When I finally finish, I slump in my chair and sigh. We are facing the consequences of my father's actions. Now all I can do is wait for the legal team to sort out the details.

I sit in silence for a moment, processing everything. My father is a thief, but he will face the consequences. I lean back in my chair and look out the window. The sun is setting, and the skyline of the city is off in the distance. It is a beautiful sight that allows me a moment of peace before returning to the reality of the day. There is so much work to do.

It is going to be a long night, but I am determined to make it right. He will do whatever it takes to ensure that every designer is compensated for what they have lost. It's up to me to make amends for my father's mistake—it is the only way I can live with myself.

The next day, I call the legal team to get their help in sorting out the details of my father's fraudulent activities. It is a big job and will require coordination between multiple departments to ensure everyone affected gets compensated for what they have lost and that justice is served.

My lawyer assures me they are determined to get to the bottom of it, so I take a deep breath and settle in for what will certainly be an intense time. As I wait for updates from the legal team, I spend my day fielding questions from those designers who were affected by this mess and doing my best to answer them with as much clarity as possible.

I know that all we can do now is stay positive and allow the lawyers to do their work - no matter how long it takes.

Before going home, my PR team has set up a press conference to get in front of the stories that will be in the papers tomorrow. I need to make sure everyone has accurate information of the subject and not here-say. They need to know about how operations will now be run - what went wrong in the past, and how we are correcting our mistakes now and why they should believe in us again.

So I draft a statement outlining what has been uncovered about my father's exploitation of designer's works and how Legacy will make amends by properly compensating them for their hard work - along with other initiatives set up towards protecting intellectual property rights from now on.

After hours of fine-tuning every sentence so that its message can truly resonate with people's hearts, I distribute this piece of writing far and wide across print media outlets as well as online platforms so everyone understands exactly who we are at Legacy.

"This is just a first step though. We are going to have a hard time getting customers to trust us after this comes to light. No doubt there will be videos about it. Everything is taken to social media anymore," Chloe says. "We will need to get in front of that too."

"I need people to realize that I am not my father and I will operate this company with integrity and respect. I think it's time we speak with the marketing team about damage control."

Chloe nods and gestures for me to follow her.

15
Chloe

My ambition has always driven me, but I worry for Justin, who is so optimistic by nature. Will he be able to handle the fallout? I study his face, noting the firm set of his jaw. He's decided.

"Are you sure about this, Justin?" I ask, concern lacing my words. "Going public might cause a bigger rift between you and your father."

He sighs, rubbing the back of his neck. "I know, but it's the right thing to do. We need to save the company's reputation and show that we're not like him." He pauses, his eyes searching mine, seeking reassurance.

I reach out and squeeze his arm, my heart swelling with admiration for his courage. "I've got your back."

"Thank you," he whispers, a smile tugging at the corner of his mouth. "That means more to me than you know."

As we brainstorm our plan of action, the magnetic pull between us grows stronger. The shared responsibility and our mutual determination to right the company's wrongs seems to draw us closer by the minute, blurring the lines between professional and personal. I shouldn't entertain thoughts of anything more than friendship, but with each passing moment, it becomes difficult to resist.

I stand in front of a whiteboard, tapping my marker against the surface. The office is tense and under a cloud of gloom, almost suffocating. The recent scandal will leave the company's reputation in ruins.

"Alright, everyone," I begin, my voice firm. "We have a monumental task ahead of us."

At this, Justin Myers—the eternal optimist—raises an eyebrow, his eyes twinkling with curiosity. "Social media? How so?"

"Simple, we'll leverage every platform we can think of to create a unified message that emphasizes our commitment to innovation and quality."

Throughout the room, heads nod, including Charlotte—my longtime employee and confidant. However, Thomas Crawford, who always seems to have an ulterior motive, smirks. He doubts my plan but says nothing.

"Start researching influencers we can partner with. Let's get them talking about us positively," I instruct, and he types away on his laptop.

"Charlotte, you work with Lila Peterson and the rest of the design team to ensure that everything we put out is fresh, authentic, and worthy of our brand's name."

Lila's fingers tremble as she jots down notes. The junior designer is talented, but her insecurities sometimes hold her back. I offer a reassuring smile, hoping to boost her confidence. "You've got this, Lila."

"Thomas, I need you to coordinate with our PR team to make sure our messaging is consistent across all channels." I stare him down.

The team dives into research, scouring social media platforms for suitable influencers.

"Okay, I've got a few names," Lila Peterson announces, her voice wavering. I glance at the junior designer, noting her insecurities and offering another reassuring smile. "These influencers have strong followings and excellent engagement rates."

"Perfect, Lila. Let's reach out to them and start discussing collaborations," I say. "Now, we need a content calendar for the next month. We'll need eye-catching graphics and scheduled posts that highlight our new designs and commitment to innovation."

"Leave it to me," Charlotte says with a grin. "I've already got some ideas brewing for engaging content that will grab people's attention."

The team buzzes with activity, putting together the pieces of their social media strategy.

With every graphic designed, post scheduled, and influencer collaboration confirmed, the weight of the company's future resting on Justin and I's shoulders. But as I watched our team work to save our reputation, I know we are creating something special—a new beginning forged from the ashes of the past.

"Look at this!" Chloe exclaims, pointing to the analytics dashboard on her laptop screen. They fill the room with an air of electric excitement as the team gathers around to witness the fruits of their labor. "Our engagement rate has doubled already!"

"Wow," Lila breathes, her eyes wide with astonishment. "And look at all those positive comments and shares! People are loving our new designs."

"Of course they are," I say with a grin, my eyes sparkling with pride as I glance over at Lila. "You did an amazing job coming up with those, after all."

"Thanks, Chloe," Lila replies, blushing under the praise. "But it's not just me. It's all of us working together—your brilliant marketing strategies, Charlotte's engaging content, and the entire team's commitment to turning things around."

"True," I agree, feeling a swell of gratitude for the people surrounding me. "But let's not forget that we still have a long way to go. Our work is far from over."

"Right," Lila nods, steeling herself for the challenges ahead. "We need to keep pushing forward and continue showcasing our company's commitment to innovation and quality."

"Let's use this momentum to fuel our next steps. We'll need fresh designs for our upcoming collection that will set us apart from the competition."

"Leave it to me. I won't let you down."

"You'll rise to the challenge. I believe in you, Lila."

"Alright, team. Let's keep up the hard work and continue winning hearts, one hashtag at a time!"

This has to work.

16
Justin

Taking over the reigns of a company so recently rocked by scandal is no small task, and as the new CEO I'm well aware of the challenge. But I also believe that with the right steps and an unwavering commitment to ethics and transparency, I can restore the public's trust in our company and make Legacy stronger than ever. The weight of the scandal is like an anchor around my neck, dragging me down into the depth of the murky abyss. I'm aware of the monumental task before me, but I will not falter. With unwavering dedication, I will lead Legacy out of the fire and back into the light. The public's trust will be restored, and our company will emerge from this stronger than ever before.

Since taking the helm, I have been working diligently alongside my team to make sure we are putting our best foot forward in the public eye. This includes taking responsibility for the wrongdoings committed by my predecessor and making a strong commitment to ethics and accountability. We have been making sincere apologies to our customers and those affected by my predecessor's actions in the press and on social media, and have been very open in communicating our plan to ensure that something like this never happens again.

My team and I have also been working hard in the realm of public relations to rebuild our reputation and make sure that our new values and mission are clear. We have been actively engaging with the public on social media, responding to questions and concerns and making sure that our commitment to transparency is understood. We have also taken the initiative to create content that is both entertaining and informative, such as videos and blog posts, so that we can keep our audience informed about our progress and mission. We have also been utilizing influencers to our advantage, making sure that we are partnering with people who share our values and can help spread the word about our commitment to doing better.

On top of our external efforts, we have also been putting a lot of work into our internal policies and procedures to make sure that our commitment to ethics and accountability is reflected in our daily operations. We have implemented a zero-tolerance policy for any form of unethical behavior and have instituted rigorous checks and balances to ensure that our employees are acting in the best interests of our customers and the company. We have also re-evaluated our training and onboarding programs so that our new hires are well-versed in our values and expectations for ethical behavior.

We understand that rebuilding trust and restoring a positive reputation takes time and effort, and we are committed to doing the work necessary to get us back on the right track. To this end, we have been engaging with our stakeholders and partners to ensure that we are taking their concerns and suggestions into consideration as we move forward. We have also been working with outside experts and advisors to help us develop new initiatives and programs that will further strengthen our commitment to ethics and transparency.

We have come a long way in a short amount of time, and I am proud of the progress we have made. I am confident that with my team's dedication and hard work, we can make Legacy Inc. an example to the rest of the corporate world. My goal is to make sure our customers and stakeholders can be proud of the company they are associated with, and I will continue to work hard to ensure that we remain true to our values and mission.

To further reinforce our commitment to ensuring that we are always held accountable, I am proud to announce the introduction of an external review board composed of industry experts. This team will be tasked with evaluating our progress and policies, providing insightful feedback on what we can do better and helping us stay true to the commitments made by legacy inc. We look forward to their input and ideas as they play a key role in making sure that legacy inc is on the right path towards being known for its ethics, transparency, accountability - both internally and externally.

At the press conference, I am told to keep it to the facts and nothing more, but sometimes it's better to upfront and honest than follow instructions. So instead, I say what I feel is necessary.

"Along with the external review board, I would also like to take this opportunity to address another key issue - one that is very close to my heart. As you know, we discovered when conducting our internal audit that the former CEO had been engaging in unethical practices - namely stealing designs and using them for their own gain. My father was at the helm of legacy inc at the time these incidents occurred and will be issuing an apology statement at this time."

My father has been working on his statement all morning, but he wouldn't let me read it. All I can hope is that he takes full responsibility.

"Good morning, my name is George Myers, former CEO of Legacy Inc, and I would like to issue an apology to all of the designers caught up in this mess. I take responsibility for my devious actions and have learned fully from my mistakes. I will covering the compensation packages of all the designers I implicated. Going forward, my son, Justin Myers, is the one who launched this investigation and has high standards for Legacy Inc. moving forward. Thank you."

His eyes say it all – guilt and sorrow over something so heinous as stealing ideas from hardworking individuals who entrusted him their creative passions so freely. My heart races as I process each word.

Everything shifts as my father looks at me. He apologizes for his wrongdoings, admits the faults of handing the company over in it's current state, but then comes a powerful statement.

"I believe you have what it takes to restore the family legacy - maybe even make things better than they ever were. I'm proud of you, son."

His worlds fill me with inexplicable warmth despite all we have gone through. Regardless of what transpired here today, this is still our family's business - My company now - and for once in my life I am carrying that weight on my shoulders. There may be obstacles along the way, but one thing remains true. I will always be honest and act with integrity. Never expect any less.

17
Chloe

I look out the floor-to-ceiling window of my office, sipping a lukewarm cup of coffee as I gaze out at the bustling city below. The clatter of typing fingers and the gentle hum of the photocopier provided a familiar soundtrack to my thoughts.

"Morning, Chloe," Justin Myers greets with a warm smile as he strolled into my office, hands tucked into his pockets.

"Morning, Justin," I reply, feeling a sudden flutter in my chest. I hate how easily he makes me feel that way. As a marketing director, I built a reputation for determination and focus - and yet, here I am, contemplating the potential risk of falling for someone who can jeopardize it all.

"Big day today. We've got to complete the presentation for the board," I remind myself, shaking off my thoughts and trying to refocus on my work. This is no time for distractions or daydreaming about the handsome man standing before me.

"Of course," Justin agrees, his eyes twinkling with enthusiasm. "I've been working on some new ideas I think you'll love."

"Great, let's get started." I need to focus on the task at hand and prioritize my career goals, but the growing feelings for Justin are becoming harder to ignore.

As we sit down to work, I steal glances at Justin. His optimism and energy are contagious, making it difficult for me to maintain the professional distance I have always prided myself on. *Remember the consequences of dating someone who you work with? Oh yeah and he's also your boss!* The temptation to explore my feelings for Justin grow stronger each day.

"Are you okay, Chloe?" Justin asks, noticing my hesitation in discussing a particular idea.

"Um, yes, sorry. Just... thinking."

"Let me know if you need help with anything," he offers, his genuine kindness making it even more challenging for me to keep my emotions at bay.

I attempt to bury my feelings deep within and concentrate on the work. But even as I force myself to focus on the presentation, my thoughts keep drifting back to Justin.

A relationship with Justin might damage my professional reputation, but the thought of never knowing what could have been weighs on my mind.

"Chloe, we did it! The presentation is ready!" Justin exclaims.

"Great job."

"Couldn't have done it without you," he says, our eyes locking for a moment before I glance away.

"Teamwork!"

The sun sets as I stare at my computer screen. The numbers and charts from our presentation blur together, reflecting my scattered thoughts.

"Chloe!" Justin calls from across the room. "You're still here? It's getting late."

"Uh, yeah," I reply, rubbing my temples. "Just trying to tie up some loose ends before the big meeting tomorrow."

I fidget with the pen, my thoughts swirling like a whirlwind as I try to focus on the spreadsheet. In the past few weeks, our plan to compensate the designers has been set into motion, and Justin's heartfelt confession to the press garnered an outpouring of support. The company's reputation is on the mend.

"Hey, Chloe," Justin says, leaning against the doorframe of my office. I look up, and my heart skips a beat at the sight of his disheveled hair and endearing grin. "Got a minute?"

"Of course. What's up?"

Justin walks over, perching on the edge of my desk and giving me one of those looks that make my insides melt – a mixture of vulnerability and hope. "I've been thinking. We've been through a lot together, and I feel like we've grown closer because of it."

I nod, my pulse quickening as I sense where the conversation is going. "I feel the same way, Justin. We make a great team."

"Exactly," he agrees, his smile broadening. "So, I was wondering if you'd like to grab dinner with me tonight. You know, outside of work." He scratches the back of his head, bashful.

A rush of warmth floods my cheeks. It is foolish, perhaps, to mix business with pleasure, but my heart argues that sometimes, the most significant risks lead to the greatest rewards.

"Are you asking me on a date, Mr. Myers?" I tease, my eyes sparkling with amusement.

"Guilty as charged," he chuckles, his own cheeks tinted a light shade of pink. "So, what do you say?"

My ambitious nature screams for caution, but the part of me that longs for happiness and connection urge me to leap into the unknown. As I gaze into Justin's eyes, the answer is simple. The heart's desires outweigh logic and reason.

"Alright, I say. "Let's give it a shot. Dinner sounds lovely."

"Fantastic," Justin beams, his smile lighting up the room. "I'll pick you up at seven?"

"Seven it is."

As Justin leaves my office, exhilaration fills my chest, chasing away my earlier doubts. We are venturing into uncharted territory, but there is something thrilling about exploring the unknown with someone who makes my heart race like no other.

"Here's to taking chances," I murmur, raising an imaginary glass in toast before returning my attention to the spreadsheet, my mind already racing with possibilities for the evening ahead.

Sunshine for the Boss

Kaci Bell

1

The alarm shrieks at 6 AM, jolting me awake as sunlight streams through the blinds. Time for the daily grind. I groan, dragging myself out of bed and into the shower. As hot water slides over my body, a picture of the unending pile of paperwork waiting on my desk clouds my head. Another day, another dollar.

After ten years as a legal assistant, it etched my routine into my bones. File this, email that, schedule a meeting here, push back a deposition there. Lather, rinse, repeat.

After a deep sigh, I switch off the faucet and use a towel to dry off. I crave something more. A new challenge. Growth. Adventure.

Anything but the same old, same old.

By the time I arrive at the office, I plaster a smile on my face. "Morning Mr. Curran! Your schedule for today: 9 AM meeting with Smith and Doe re: the Johnson case, lunch at noon with prospective new client Mr. Collins, and a 4 PM call with the partners to discuss the acquisition."

"Fantastic. Thank you, Laura. I don't know what I'd do without you." Mr. Curran gives me a warm smile, patting my shoulder before disappearing into his office.

Weird. He isn't hands-on like that. After working for him for almost a decade, he has never patted me on the back. What is going on?

I settle into my desk and open the floodgates, emails pouring in and demanding my attention. But my mind drifts as I work, dreaming of new worlds to explore beyond these four walls.

Someday.

For now, I have files to organize and phone calls to make. I crack my knuckles and dive in, embracing the familiarity of the daily grind. The usual morning tasks are becoming dull. They put my organizational skills to good use as I schedule meetings, answer emails, and file away important documents, but I still crave more.

The desk phone rings, pulling me out of my task. "Mr. Curran's office. How may I help you?"

"Hi Laura, it's Sandra from Jenkins & Morris. I have Mr. Curran's 2 pm deposition rescheduled for next Thursday. Will that work with his calendar?"

I pull up his schedule, scanning for conflicts. "Next Thursday would be perfect. Thank you for letting me know. I'll update his calendar right away."

"You're a lifesaver! I don't know how he'd manage without you." Sandra laughs. "Talk to you later!"

"Goodbye!" I hung up the phone, a smile playing on my lips. Being able to juggle so many moving parts and ensure everything runs smoothly gives me a deep sense of satisfaction.

My eyes drift to the LSAT study guide peeking out of my bag. Maybe I didn't need to leave this job behind to pursue my dreams after all. Perhaps there is room for growth here too, a way to challenge myself and gain new experiences without sacrificing the familiarity of a place that has become my second home.

"Do you think you could pull the Jenkins contract for me before the meeting? I want to review a few clauses."

"Of course, I'll have that ready in just a moment."

After the meeting begins, Sandra from Jenkins & Morris calls again, her tone urgent.

"Laura, I'm so sorry, but Mr. Curran's deposition has to be rescheduled again. Our client had a medical emergency and won't be available next week."

I check the calendar, wincing at the lack of open slots. Mr. Curran has been looking forward to resolving this case. "I understand. When would you like to reschedule for then?"

"The next opening we have is December 12th. I know that's not ideal but—"

"That won't work," I interrupt. "Mr. Curran is going on vacation that week."

Sandra sighs. "I was afraid of that. Let me talk to my team and get back to you then. I appreciate your patience, Laura."

"Of course. Speak to you soon." I hung up the phone, staring at the calendar. This is turning into a logistical nightmare. But I am determined to find a solution. All it took is rolling up my sleeves and getting to work.

I comb through the calendar, searching for any open slots or ways to rearrange meetings. After an hour of attempts, one possibility emerges: if I push back a few client meetings by a day or two and ask Mr. Curran to postpone a mediation, we can fit the deposition in on December 5th.

Despite being far from ideal, it is our best chance. I call Sandra back with the proposed date, holding my breath.

"December 5th could work," she says. "Let me double check with the client and get back to you within the hour."

"Wonderful. I'll keep that day booked for now."

I hang up and lean back in my chair. Moments like this remind me why I love my job. The obstacles that seem insurmountable at first are now falling into place, allowing the case to move forward. While the life of a legal assistant isn't always glamorous, I take deep satisfaction. The impact of our cases stretches far beyond the office walls, helping clients in ways both big and small.

Sandra calls back with confirmation, and I solidify the plans. The deposition is on. I add the details to the calendar, smiling as I did so. Challenge overcome. Mission accomplished.

I continue to smile as I pack up my things and head out of the office for the day. It has been another successful day full of challenges and victories, both big and small. But they all add up to progress - for my career, for the cases we are working on, for the clients we are serving.

As I walk down the street, contentment settles over me. I have found my adventure, my growth, my impact in the unlikeliest of places.

My work might not make headlines, but in my small way, I am changing lives. As the subway train rattles down into the tunnel to take me home, I smile, knowing I have found my calling. We can find adventure every day, and I won't trade the joy for anything.

2

The morning sun hits my face before I walk into the law firm. As soon as I walk in, the strange atmosphere seems off. Everyone is talking in hushed whispers. What is going on? I look around before placing my handbag on my desk. My heart beats faster. Why is everyone whispering amongst themselves? This isn't high school.

I sit down and log into my computer, and the announcement is already there. Mr. Curran, my grumpy and strict boss, has proclaimed his retirement and I'll be going under Mr. De La Cruz. I can't believe it. His wife has been pressuring him to retire for the last couple of years, but I never thought he would do it. The man doesn't know how to relax and is all work, all the time. I have never gotten along with him, but from the gossip around the office, Mr. De La Cruz is even worse. How am I going to handle another tough boss? Guess I'll just have to pull up my big girl panties.

"Did you see?" Jennifer says, taking a seat on the edge of my desk, her feet dangling. "I mean, I knew his wife was pressuring him, but I never thought he would do it. Aren't you over the moon?"

I peer at her. "Okay, so I have been waiting for this day since my first week, but they are assigning me to Mr. Office Grump. Why would they do that to me?"

She laughs, leaning toward me so the others around can't hear. "At least he won't make you work twelve-hour shifts. Just brush him off when he's being over the top and just do your job. No one here can say you aren't good at what you do."

She has a point. I might complain to Jennifer because she is my best friend, but Mr. Curran pays me well. Rent in this city is a fortune and a necessary evil. As awful as he is, at least he has given me a substantial raise every year. "We will see how this goes."

"Are you ready to move? I still can't believe you're leaving me."

Jennifer met the love of her life right here in this very office, and now he has convinced her to move back closer to his hometown of Amesbury. For someone who always planned to live in a big city, love changed her.

"You act like I'm going to move away and never see you again! Don't get all crazy."

It's her last week here and I'm going to miss the heck out of her.

I try to stay focused throughout the rest of the day with the gazillion emails that have come in over the weekend, but my mind keeps going back to De La Cruz. He is notorious for firing his assistants. I don't need that drama. After two more cups of nasty coffee, I'm in a groove and it's already seven. Mr. Curran wastes no time working late again. By nine, he allows me to go home and to be back bright and early in the morning. The man doesn't know how to take a break.

"Goodnight, see you in the morning."

I grab my purse and take the elevator to the ground floor. My heels click against the pavement as I come to the Subway steps. On the way to board, my mind keeps going back to De La Cruz. What if he is as bad of a boss as everyone says? I can't afford to lose my job, especially with Jennifer moving out and leaving me with the full amount of the rent. I'm already feeling the pressure and stress of the changes, and I don't know if I have the energy to handle another difficult boss.

Once home and after my bath, I spend the night tossing and turning, unable to find a moment of rest. The worry about my future is at the forefront of my mind and what if I can't keep up with the demands of the job?

The next morning, I get ready for work after not sleeping a wink, trying to put on a brave face and not let my worries show.

"Laura, can you come to my office, please?" Mr. Curran says as I set my coffee down on my desk.

"Yes, sir. What can I do?" I stop right outside the door, realizing it's not Mr. Curran.

I have heard plenty of office gossip, so I'm interested to see if he really is the big bad wolf.

When I enter his office, I am surprised to find a semi-friendly face and not the stern one I am used to on Mr. Curran.

"Good morning, you must be Laura. I'm De La Cruz. Have a seat."

I didn't expect him to take over Mr. Curran's office, but with him just wrapping up paperwork, he can do that from home without even coming to the office if he wants. "Nice to meet you, sir."

"So, let's get right down to the business. I have heard about you from Mr. Curran, and I think we will work well together. He tells me you are okay with staying late and that's a must for me. With the amount of clients I have, sometimes I am here until ten. Are you going to do that?"

The question catches me off guard. If I say no, will he fire me? I don't want to stay until ten every night, especially since I am the only assistant on record that has to do so. The only way that is happening is if I get another raise. "Can we discuss a raise? I have worked very hard for Mr. Curran, but with more hours, I should be compensated fairly."

De La Cruz interlocks his fingers and leans on his desk. "I show you just got a raise six months ago."

This is where I need to lie on my charm and know my worth. Companies will not pay you more unless you prove to them why you are worth it. "If you look at my schedule, I have worked late every single night since that raise. Also, I could never use all of my vacation time since starting here because of the importance of keeping the clients happy. If we will be working later into the night and adding more hours to my schedule, then compensation is required."

I try to keep my face straight, even though my head is telling me I'm getting fired. This man doesn't know me from Eve and I'm here telling him it is imperative that he give me a raise. What the heck am I thinking? I don't backtrack though, because being weak isn't my thing.

De La Cruz pulls something up on his computer and clicks a few buttons. "It looks like I have some extra money on my AOP. The most I could do is a 7% increase."

I place my hand on my knee and think about it. The increase is more than I got last year and will help me afford the apartment on my own, but I don't want him to know that. You never take the first offer. "I was thinking more like 9%."

He leans back in his squeaky chair. "You were, huh? How about we meet in the middle and do 8%?"

I stand up and extend my hand out to him. "That'll do. If you'll excuse me, I have many emails to answer and the phone has been ringing nonstop since I walked in here."

If there is one thing no one at this office has ever said about me, it's a lack of work ethic. I have worked hard for everything in my life, and this is no exception. Without this job, I wouldn't have a place to live or clothes on my back.

"Of course, we will have another sit down later."

I stroll out of his office and sit down at my desk, squealing inside. Mr. Curran would have never given me another raise, so maybe I like my new boss a little more now. He doesn't seem to be all that bad, so maybe the rumors are wrong.

He doesn't seem so bad, but maybe he is keeping his crazy under wraps for the first couple of days.

"I heard he made his last assistant cry every day for a month before she quit," Jenny says.

"Utter slave driver." Mark babbled. "No lunch breaks, no personal calls. I'd start looking for a new job if I were you."

I swallow hard, clutching the box of files to my chest like a shield. So much for my perfect attendance record and employee of the Month awards. According to the stories, these meant nothing to the likes of Mr. De La Cruz.

The walk down the hallway to his office is like heading to the gallows. My hands are clammy, and my mouth has gone dry. You can do this. Just keep your head down, don't cry, and try not to hyperventilate.

When I step through the doorway, Mr. De La Cruz glances up from his desk, blue eyes peering out from under heavy brows. I brace myself for the barrage of insults and unreasonable demands.

Instead, he gives a curt nod and says, "Take a seat."

I hesitate, waiting for the other shoe to drop, but it seems the worst is over. At least for now. I sink into the chair across from him, clutching my box like a life raft in a churning sea. My new boss may have been less awful than expected, but surviving at Shark Island is going to take a lot of luck.

Mr. De La Cruz leans back in his chair, steepling his fingers as he studies me. My heart thumps wildly, like a caged bird desperate for escape.

"Let's see if you live up to the hype." He nods at the box in my lap. "That contains the Wilson file. I want it organized, cross-referenced, and summarized by the end of the day."

My mouth falls open. The Wilson file is legendary, passed down for decades and containing enough documents to fill a small library. Organizing that in a single day is impossible.

Panic surges. This must be some kind of test. But what is the right response? If I argue, he might fire me on the spot. If I agree, I'll fail and be fired, anyway.

Honesty is the best policy, even if it means walking into a trap.

"Sir, that file contains hundreds of thousands of pages. Organizing and summarizing it in a single day is impossible." My voice shakes, but I hold his gaze.

One eyebrow rises. "Is that so?" His tone is mocking, challenging.

I grit my teeth. "Yes, sir. I'm afraid it is."

He watches me, unblinking, and then the corner of his mouth quirks up. "Good. I want assistants who tell me the truth, not what they think I want to hear."

I blink. Did I pass the test then? But his stern expression didn't change.

"Get to work," he barks. "I'll expect a report on my desk by five, and it had better impress me."

He swings around and stalks back to his desk, dismissing me. I stand frozen in place, panic and confusion warring in my mind.

How on earth am I going to do this? Even with an army of assistants, organizing that file in a few hours is impossible.

Failing isn't an option. There has to be a way to get this done, somehow. Then it hits me.

I grab the box and rush back to my desk, flipping through the files at breakneck speed. Most are decades old and irrelevant. I can ignore those.

The more recent files are a mess, but if I focus on the key cases and documents…yes, that might work.

I spring into action, sorting files into the trash, "irrelevant," and "priority." The priority pile grows at an alarming rate, but it is coming together.

Doubt and panic continue to war in my mind, but I push them aside. I have a plan now, and that is enough.

As the clock ticks down to five, I finish the final case summary and report. My hands shake as I place the work on Mr. De La Cruz's desk. I did the impossible.

3

The next morning, I walk into the office with a mix of dread and determination. Is Mr. De La Cruz satisfied with my work? Or have I made some fatal error that will get me fired?

When I reach my desk, I find a single red pen sitting on top of the case file. My heart sinks. Of course it wasn't good enough.

I steel myself and knock on Mr. De La Cruz's office door. He looks up, his face as stern and unreadable as ever. "The file. You wanted to see me?"

"Yes." He stands up and circles his desk. "Do you know why I asked you to organize this file yesterday?"

I shake my head, unsure of the answer he is looking for.

"I wanted to see what you were made of," he says. "And you did not disappoint. You accomplished in one day what it takes most assistants weeks to finish. Well done."

I blink, stunned. A compliment? From him?

"Th-thank you, sir," I stammer.

The corner of his mouth quirks up. "You're welcome. I look forward to seeing what else you can accomplish here."

He sits back down, effectively dismissing me, but I leave his office with a grin. Maybe this new boss won't be so bad after all.

My colleagues are waiting when I emerge, questions and concern on their faces. I just smile mysteriously and get to work. Let them wonder—for now, I am content knowing I have proven myself. The impossible task has been possible after all.

I sigh and rub my temples, staring at the mess of papers strewn across my desk. Finding those missing documents has been like searching for a needle in a haystack, and the conflicting accounts from witnesses give me a headache.

But I did make a promise to Mr. De La Cruz I will get this done, and I am not about to go back on my word.

My stomach rumbles, reminding me I haven't eaten since that granola bar at breakfast. I glance at the clock—already after 5 pm. The others have already left for the day, off to enjoy happy hours and home-cooked meals.

I dig back in, piecing together clues and connections until the words blur on the page. It is 8 pm when I straighten the last file, satisfaction flooding me. I did it.

I stumble out of the empty office into the dark lobby, fatigue hitting me all at once. But underneath the exhaustion is a spark of pride at a job well done.

Mr. De La Cruz has been right to put his faith in me. I am stronger than even I have realized.

Once home, I sit on my couch with a glass of wine and contemplate calling Jennifer. She has always been my voice of reason, but I didn't know if I want to hear what I need to say this time.

With a sigh, I pick up my phone and dial her number.

"Laura!" Her cheerful voice filters through the line. "How's it going?"

I take a large swig of wine before answering. "I'm not sure. My boss is...difficult. Demanding. Impossible to please."

"That doesn't sound good," Jennifer says. "Is he worse than Mr. Curran was?"

"Maybe." I slump further into the couch. "I feel like I'm in over my head. Everyone says he cycles through assistants every few months. What if he fires me?"

"Laura, listen to me." Jennifer's voice is firm. "You are one of the most capable, hardworking people I know. Don't doubt yourself—I know you can rise to the occasion."

"You think so?" I ask.

"I know so. Now stop overthinking this and go in there tomorrow like you own the place! You've got this."

I smile, feeling warmth spread through me. "Thanks, Jen. I needed to hear that."

"Anytime. You can do this, Laura. I believe in you."

We chat for a few more minutes before hanging up, and I go to bed with renewed determination. Jennifer is right—it is time to rise to the challenge. Mr. De La Cruz didn't know it yet, but I am here to stay.

The next morning, I stride into the office with my head held high. Mr. De La Cruz is already barking orders at the paralegal, but he pauses when he sees me. Our eyes meet for a moment, and I give him a confident smile.

For the first time, I see a flicker of surprise in his expression. Then his lips twitch, and he gives me a curt nod before returning to his tirade.

My heart swells. I render the formidable De La Cruz momentarily speechless. This is a victory, however small, and it strengthens my resolve.

I settle in at my desk and get to work, fielding his requests and demands with efficiency and poise. By the end of the day, I prove myself invaluable, and Mr. De La Cruz gives me an approving look as we pack up to leave.

"Good work, Stevens," he says. "Keep this up."

"Thank you, Mr. De La Cruz," I say. "I intend to."

He blinks at my boldness, but says nothing else. I walk out of the office with my head high, a spring in my step. Jennifer has been right to encourage me to take a leap of faith. I am going to rise to this challenge—and maybe, just maybe, I will get the chance to glimpse the man behind the mask. The game is on.

"Stevens, in my office. Now." His tone is brusque, but I detect a hint of curiosity behind the command.

I follow him in and take a seat across from his desk. He studies me for a long moment, his expression inscrutable. I meet his gaze, waiting.

He pauses, watching me. "I've got a new case that requires a deft, diligent touch. The clients are high profile and demanding. Do you think you're up for it?"

My heart races, but I keep my expression neutral. This is the opportunity I have been waiting for. "Absolutely, Mr. De La Cruz. I won't let you down."

He studies me for another long moment. Then he nods, a glint of challenge entering his eyes. "Good. The files are on your desk. Get to work."

I stand, barely able to contain my excitement. "Right away, sir."

As I leave his office, I catch the ghost of a smile on his lips. The game is still on—but for the first time, we are playing on the same team. This is going to be an interesting partnership indeed.

Today has been a weird day. He still seems dissatisfied, quick to criticize me, and always seems irritated. It can't be anything I have done, because I have been working my butt off.

He has been in his office pacing for the last twenty minutes, and I swear he keeps staring out here at me. What did I do?

"Laura, please come into my office."

My shoulders tense and I take a deep breath, walking inside and taking a seat in front of his desk. He is still pacing around the room. He bites his lip.

"Why did you reschedule the meeting from today to tomorrow?" His nostrils are flaring.

"Sir, the meeting before it would take at least two hours, which would run into that meeting, so instead of rescheduling for after office hours, I moved it to tomorrow."

"Don't you think you should have asked?"

Oh, so we are going to play this game, huh? I don't even respond.

"That meeting was very important, and I needed to get it done today. It's too late to change it back now."

"It's my job as your assistant to take care of your schedule and make sure there are no overlaps. If I have to ask you every time, then what is the point of even having me here? That would slow down my ability to work tremendously."

He runs his fingers through his hair. The man is good looking in a dark and brooding kind of way. I don't know anything about this man besides that he seems to have anger issues.

"Sir, I don't need you micromanaging me. I'm a grown woman who has been doing for many years. I have work to get back to." I stand up and walk out of his office. If he thinks that I am going to sit around and ask him for permission every time I need to do my job, he's sadly mistaken. If he doesn't trust my judgment, then maybe it is time to start looking for another job.

"What was that?" Jennifer asks, trying to be quiet from her desk.

"He told me I should ask him before rescheduling meetings..."

She laughs. "You're kidding, right?"

I shake my head.

"Wow, you got a real winner there."

I am grateful for the raise, but not being able to do my job is a big red flag for me. If he can't trust my decisions, then this is most definitely not going to work.

You know what? I need to stand up for myself. My chest heaves and I walk back into his house, where he is still pacing. "Sir, if you can't trust me, like Mr. Curran could, then please tell me so I can look for another job. I bust my butt for this company and don't deserve to be questioned like that."

"What are you talking about? Now you want to quit? I just gave you a raise yesterday?" he asks, eyes big.

"I understand, sir, but my job is all about making things easier for you, so if I have to ask permission, then I'm pointless."

He sighs big and then sits down at his desk and crosses his hands. "Listen, I'm having a rough day today, and maybe it's best if I just don't talk to anyone. There is no need for you to leave."

"What can I do, sir? Are you okay?"

He runs his fingers through his hair again and puts his hand down on his desk. "Just... reschedule all my meetings today."

I nod and leave his office.

What is going on?

4

Mr. De La Cruz is the grumpiest man in the office, and I'll be stuck dealing with him. He is grouchy and complains at the slightest provocation - or even without one. He snaps at me for no reason, leaving me wondering what I did wrong.

Despite all his gruffness, I am determined to stick it out with him. After all, he has to be tolerable underneath all that grumpiness, right? Even if it didn't seem so in the present.

I try to find something to like about him - I mean, he can't be that bad, can he? - but it is hard to focus on anything else. He is gruff, impatient with the minor tasks, and doesn't seem to see the value in anything I do.

Still, I keep at it to make the best of the situation. I didn't want to give up, and I refused to let his poor attitude get to me. What is it with grumpy men in this office?

So I listen more closely when Mr. De La Cruz speaks and tries to see things from his point of view. I understand the source of his grumpiness, the struggles he is facing, and his daily frustrations.

Why is Jennifer so lucky? She has had two incredible bosses. Jennifer has been so lucky with both bosses - they have been patient, professional, and understanding. She is now marrying one, Mr. Kneeland. I'm over here with back-to-back grumps.

"How's the grumpy one doing today?" Lisa says, referring to De La Cruz.

"He's not the easiest person to work with, but I don't think he's worse than Mr. Curran."

I laugh.

"Laura!" De La Cruz yells from his office.

"The Acme account files—where are they?" he barks. "I told you I needed them first thing this morning!"

"My apologies, sir," I say, swallowing hard against the lump forming in my throat. "I haven't received them yet, but I'll get right on that."

He let out an exasperated sigh, pinching the bridge of his nose between his fingers. "Honestly, do I have to do everything around here myself?" His glare is icy enough to freeze flames. "Don't just stand there like a mindless drone. Get to work!"

I duck my head to hide the hot flush creeping up my neck and make a beeline for my desk. Some days, his criticism stings more than others, but I am determined not to let him get the better of me. I have dealt with worse than De La Cruz before.

Even if it kills me.

I sit down to calm my frayed nerves. The last thing I need is to lose my composure in front of him—that will only give him more ammunition.

Instead, I focus on the task at hand, sifting through emails and phone messages to track down the missing Acme files. My hands shake slightly as I type residual tremors from his biting tone, but I push onward. There is work to be done, and I won't let his foul mood slow me down.

When I find no trace of the files in my inbox, I ring up the courier service we use for inter-office deliveries. Of course, the files have been delayed, caught up somewhere in the mid-morning traffic. I relay the information to Mr. De La Cruz, bracing myself for another outburst.

He throws his hands up with a wordless shout, sending papers flying. "Unbelievable! Do I pay those imbeciles to twiddle their thumbs all day?"

I bite down on my lip, hard enough to taste copper. "I apologize for the inconvenience, sir. Shall I have the files couriered over as soon as they arrive?"

"As if I have any other choice," he grumbles, righting the papers that have drifted to the floor. He sinks into the chair behind his desk, pinching the bridge of his nose again. The fight seems to drain out of him all at once, leaving behind bone-deep weariness.

Despite his foul temper, I can't help but have sympathy. The stress of his position must be enormous, dealing with high-profile cases day in and day out. No wonder he is so irritable all the time.

I clear my throat gently. "Would you like me to bring you a coffee or reschedule your morning appointments, sir?"

He waves me off without looking up. "Just...get back to work. And get those files here as fast as humanly possible." His voice is rough with exhaustion.

"Of course, sir. Right away." I stand and gather my notes, hesitating for a moment. The urge to say more tingles on the tip of my tongue This is not the time or place to overstep my bounds.

With one last glance at his hunch form, I slip out the door and set to work. The files will come when they come, but in the meantime, there are still tasks to complete and chaos to wrangle into order. If nothing else, this job keeps me on my toes.

As I sort through paperwork and field calls, my thoughts keep drifting back to Mr. De La Cruz. It is becoming clear why he goes through assistants—that fiery temper and abrasive manner will wear anyone down.

But I am not just anyone. After ten years with Mr. Curran, a little rough treatment will not scare me off. Mr. De La Cruz can bark and snap all he likes; I've faced far worse.

Besides, there are glimpses of something more beneath this gruff exterior. The exhaustion in his voice, the way he deflated all at once...those aren't the reactions of a heartless man.

Mr. De La Cruz might not know it yet, but he is stuck with me. I'll crack that tough shell of his if it kills me and show him that not all assistants are cut from the same cloth.

The phone trills again, dragging me from my thoughts. "Mr. De La Cruz's office, this is Laura speaking."

"It's Sandra from Records. I have those files Mr. De La Cruz wanted, but they're quite substantial. Shall I bring them up or would he prefer to review them downstairs?"

"I'll check and get back to you." I stand, straightening my skirt, and stride over to Mr. De La Cruz's office. It is time for round two. After all, I have a point to prove.

I knock on the doorframe. "Mr. De La Cruz, Sandra from Records, is on the line. She has the files you requested, but says they're quite substantial. Would you prefer to review them downstairs, or shall she bring them up?"

Mr. De La Cruz glares at me over the top of his glasses. Irritation etches into the lines of his face. "Well, what do you think?" he snaps. "Haven't I taught you anything yet?"

I bite back a retort, clenching my jaw. Deep breaths. Patience. "I apologize, sir. Given the size of the files, reviewing them downstairs in Records may be more efficient."

"At last, a flicker of common sense." Mr. De La Cruz waves a hand at me. "Tell her to bring them up. If I'm to be saddled with an incompetent assistant, the least she can do is save me a trip downstairs."

Heat rises in my cheeks, but I keep my expression neutral. "I will inform Ms. Williams to bring the files up."

With a curt nod, Mr. De La Cruz dismisses me. I duck out of the room, closing the door behind me.

Once at the safety of my desk, I exhale through my nose, trying to release the tension gathering between my shoulders. That man is insufferable. But I won't give him the satisfaction of knowing how deeply his barbs cut.

I call Sandra back and relay the message, then busy myself with menial tasks as I wait for her arrival. There has to be a chink in Mr. De La Cruz's armor; I just need to keep looking.

When Sandra steps out of the elevator, I hurry to meet her. "Here are those files for Mr. De La Cruz," she says, passing me a stack of folders a foot high. "Tread carefully, Laura. I know how he can be."

"Believe me, I'm well aware." I offer her a wry smile. "But I appreciate the warning all the same."

Sandra gives my arm a quick squeeze. "You've got this. If anyone can bring him to heel, it's you."

"I wish I shared your confidence." I balance the teetering pile of files against my hip. "But I do have one advantage."

"Oh?"

"Stubbornness." I grin at her. "And Mr. De La Cruz does not know who he's up against."

I return to my desk and dive into the stack of files, searching for anything that might give me insight into the enigmatic Mr. De La Cruz. But aside from a few scribbled notes in the margins, there is little personal information to be found.

When he emerges from his office a few hours later, I steel myself for another barrage of insults. But to my surprise, he grunts and waves me into his office.

I follow him in, clutching my notebook and pen at the ready. "Yes, Mr. De La Cruz?"

He is staring out the window, hands clasp behind his back. "I'm heading out for the evening. I trust you can handle any urgent matters until tomorrow?"

"Of course." I blink, nonplussed by his abrupt change in demeanor. "Enjoy your evening."

For a moment, he seems poised to snap at me again. But then he sighs, shoulders slumping forward. "Thank you, Miss Stevens. I will do my best."

Without another word, he gathers his briefcase and coat and leaves the office. I sink into one chair opposite his desk, stunned into silence. So there is a human being underneath that prickly exterior, after all.

5

At work the next day, he seems different. Something is going on and he isn't the best at hiding it. Barking orders, getting angry with others over nothing... what is his problem?

The piercing ring of the telephone shatters my concentration and I wince, glancing over at Mr. De La Cruz. His jaw is clenched as he barks into the receiver, one hand clutching at the papers on his desk.

I study him through my lashes, taking in the furrow between his brows and the tension radiating from his broad shoulders. There is something almost predatory about the way he prowls around the office, all coiled energy and restrained aggression. What will it take to crack that impenetrable facade of his?

"This is unacceptable!" Mr. De La Cruz slams the phone down, startling me from my thoughts. I jerk back, eyes widening at the fury etched into his handsome features. My heart lurches into my throat.

He rakes a hand through his hair, mussing the dark strands. I bite my lip, fighting the ridiculous urge to smooth them back into place. Get a grip, Laura! This is your boss, not some heartthrob.

Mr. De La Cruz pins me with a glare, chest heaving. "Did you finish reviewing the Thompson briefs?"

I swallow hard, scrambling to compose myself. "Y-yes, sir. I left them on your desk with my notes and recommendations."

For a moment he just stares at me, dark eyes inscrutable. Then he sighs and the fight seems to drain from his body. He slumps into his chair, all the bluster and bravado fading away to reveal a glimpse of the man beneath.

"I'm sorry you had to see that, Ms. Stevens," he says.

My lips curve into a wry smile. "No need to apologize, sir. I'm familiar with difficult clients." After all, I had plenty of experience dealing with the most difficult client of all.

"Even so." A ghost of a smile flickers across his face and my traitorous heart skips a beat. "It's unprofessional."

"With all due respect, you're only human." I shrug, aiming for nonchalance. "We all have our moments."

For a long moment, he gazes at me with an unreadable expression. I fidget under the weight of his stare, wondering if I overstepped. Then he huffs out a soft laugh and shakes his head.

"How on earth did I get so lucky as to get you, Ms. Stevens?"

My cheeks flush with pleasure at the compliment. Maybe I am getting closer to cracking that tough exterior after all.

I clear my throat, willing my blush to fade. "Shall we order in some dinner? I'm afraid it's rather late and we still have more work left to do."

"An excellent suggestion. Chinese?"

"Perfect." My stomach rumbles. In the day's rush, I forgot to eat lunch.

It takes twenty minutes before the savory aroma of garlic, ginger and chili envelopes the office. We order several dishes to share, and when we eat an awkward silence falls between us.

"So, how did you first become interested in law?"

He pauses, as if deciding how much to reveal. "My father was a lawyer. He always hoped I would follow in his footsteps, so I felt obligated to pursue a law degree to please him. But I never enjoyed it."

"Then why did you stick with it?" I ask, tilting my head. This is the most he's ever opened up about his personal life. I hang on his every word, eager to learn more about the man behind the intimidating facade.

"Family obligations. Duty. Pressure to meet expectations." He shrugs, a wry twist to his lips. "The usual reasons people end up in careers they don't find fulfilling, I suppose."

His words strike a chord in me.

I bite my lip, hesitating, then say softly, "I can understand that. My parents always wanted me to become a teacher, like my mother. But I never really felt passionate about it. I just went along with their plans because I wanted to please them."

Mr. De La Cruz's gaze sharpens, and for a moment we simply look at each other with a kind of quiet understanding.

"So why did you become a legal assistant instead?" he asks.

I smile. "To rebel, I suppose. After graduating, I realized I couldn't face a lifetime in a classroom. I wanted to break free, find my own path. Even if it meant disappointing my parents."

"And do you regret your choice?" His tone is neutral, but his eyes are intensely focused on me, as if my answer matters a great deal.

"Not anymore," I say. "Working at this firm has been challenging, but it's helped me discover what I'm passionate about. What I'm good at." I duck my head, feeling shy. "It's made me realize I don't need my parents' approval to find fulfillment and purpose in my life."

When I glance up again, Mr. De La Cruz is looking at me with an expression I can't quite read. But for the first time since I met him, I sense the hardness around him softening, revealing a glimpse of the vulnerability beneath. My cheeks warm, but I can't tear my gaze away from his.

At that moment, something shifts between us. An understanding passed, fragile yet profound, and the distance I always sensed narrowed into something that feels almost like intimacy.

I clear my throat and look away, breaking the spell. But the feeling lingers, and when I risk another glance at Mr. De La Cruz, I find him watching me with a curious half-smile.

"What is it?" I ask, self-conscious.

"Nothing." He shakes his head. "I was just thinking..."

"Thinking what?" I prompt when he doesn't continue.

He sighs, running a hand through his hair. "That maybe I misjudged you. I expected an eager young woman desperate to please. But you're not that at all, are you?"

My heart swells at the compliment, spoken so grudgingly yet with such conviction. "I just want to do good work," I say. "To contribute something meaningful. I think we both want the same things, in the end."

"Do we?" He arches an eyebrow, but his tone is light, teasing. "Well, I suppose there are worse faults to share with one's assistant."

I laugh, the sound bright and airy in the cozy confines of the office. When is the last time I laughed like that with Mr. De La Cruz? If ever?

The thought sobers me, and I glance at the clock on the wall with a start. It is midnight, and we still have a full day ahead. Yet despite the late hour, I am less tired than I have been in weeks.

As I gather the empty takeout containers, I catch Mr. De La Cruz's eye again and we share a private smile, full of promise and understanding. Yes, something has shifted between us tonight. And as I make my way home through the empty streets, I hope, perhaps for the first time, that it is only the beginning.

The next morning, I arrive at the office with a spring in my step and a latte in each hand. When I enter the lobby, Mr. De La Cruz is already there, poring over a stack of case files.

He looks up at the sound of my footsteps, and for a moment we just gaze at each other, a wealth of unspoken thoughts passing between us. Then he clears his throat and looks away, a hint of color touching his cheeks.

"You're late," he grumbles, but there is no real irritation in his tone. I hide a smile and hold out one latte in offering.

After a brief pause, he takes it with a muttered "Thank you." Our fingers brush in the exchange, and a spark of electricity shoots up my arm at the contact.

Mr. De La Cruz's eyes flick to mine, dark and fathomless, and I wonder if he feels it too, the subtle charge in the air between us. But he only takes a sip of his latte and says, "We have a meeting with the partners at nine. Be ready."

I nod, suddenly flustered. What am I thinking, bringing him coffee like we are friends? Like anything has really changed? Mr. De La Cruz will always be my demanding, abrasive boss, no matter how much I might wish otherwise.

With a frown, I retreat to my desk and immerse myself in work, trying to ignore the confused tangle of emotions inside. But every so often I glance up and find Mr. De La Cruz watching me, a pensive look on his face, and a traitorous warmth blossoming in my chest.

Whatever this is between us, it is far from over. The bonds we forged last night, over cold sesame chicken and confessions whispered in the dark, have woven us. And try as I might, I can't shake the feeling that everything is about to change.

6

"Get in here now."

My heart skips a beat. I straighten my skirt and smooth my hair as I walk into his office, steeling myself for whatever tirade he is about to unleash. His reputation as the firm's most demanding partner isn't earned by chance.

Mr. De La Cruz stands by the window, gazing pensively at the city below. My eyes trace the sharp lines of his suit, hugging broad shoulders and a trim waist. For a fleeting moment, I allow myself to admire how the sunlight brought out hints of gold in his dark hair.

Then he whirls around, pinning me in place with a glare. I swallow hard. So much for wishful thinking - it is time to face the dragon.

"The Acme account is a disaster," he growls. "We're losing them to Blackwell and Marks."

My heart sinks. The Acme account is one of our most prestigious. We can't afford to lose them. I wrack my brain, searching for a solution. This is my chance to prove myself. If I can win them back, it will cement my value to the firm. To him.

An idea flickers, then ignites into a flame. It is risky, but it just might work. I meet his gaze and say with more confidence, "Give me a week and I'll bring Acme back to the fold. Just trust me on this one."

One dark eyebrow rises skeptically. My pulse races as he contemplates my words. Please let him take the bait.

After a long moment, he gives a curt nod. "You have one week, Stevens. Don't disappoint me."

I breathe an inward sigh of relief, hoping I haven't just signed my own death warrant. But the opportunity is too good to pass up. I have everything to gain - and everything to lose. The stakes are high, but so is the reward.

This is the chance I have been waiting for. Now all I need is a plan.

I pace the floor of my apartment, wracking my brain. How am I going to win back the Acme account and prove my worth to the firm —to Mr. De La Cruz?

Then it hits me. A charity gala. We can host an extravagant charity gala and invite Acme as the guest of honor. It is the perfect opportunity for schmoozing and will showcase the firm's generosity and community spirit.

My mind whirrs with the details. Finding the right venue, choosing a theme, handling the catering and entertainment. It will be a massive undertaking. I can already picture the look on Mr. De La Cruz's face when it is a rousing success. The admiration in his eyes when he realizes I saved the account.

The risks are enormous, but the potential rewards are even greater. I smile, feeling a surge of excitement. My week is going to be busy, but if I succeed, it will be life-changing. Now, all I need is his approval for the idea.

I rehearse my pitch on the drive to work, anticipation and nerves battling in my stomach. When I enter the office, Mr. De La Cruz glances up, his eyes sharpening. "Well, Stevens? Do you have a proposal for me?"

Here we go. I take a deep breath and launch into my idea, injecting as much enthusiasm and confidence into my voice as possible. His expression remains impassive as he listens, arms folds across his chest. My heart pounds, waiting for his reaction.

When I finish, he is silent for a long moment. Then a smile tugs at the corner of his mouth and he nods. "I'm impressed. It's bold and unconventional. Exactly what's needed here."

I sag in relief, a grin breaking across my face. "You won't regret this, sir. I'll make it an event no one will forget!"

His lips quirk. "See that you do. The Acme account is riding on this."

No pressure then. I swallow hard, already feeling the weight of responsibility settling onto my shoulders. But I won't fail. Not this time. The future of my career at the firm depends on it.

The next week flies by in a blur of activity as I organize the charity gala. I tour over a dozen venues, haggling with the managers over prices and availability. I spend hours on the phone chasing down vendors, trying to find the best deals on everything from catering to decor. And in between, I am recruiting volunteers from the firm to help on the actual night of the event.

It is exhausting, frustrating work at times. The florist keeps changing their mind about what flowers will be in season, the band is making constant demands, and several people back out of volunteering at the last minute. I am ready to tear my hair out.

But with each obstacle overcome, I could my confidence growing. I am learning how to navigate tough conversations, handle crises, and motivate people to rally behind a common goal. Mr. De La Cruz checks in on my progress, his gaze sharp, and I know he is testing me, watching for any signs of weakness or incompetence.

I am determined not to crack under the pressure. This is my chance to prove I have what it takes to advance in my career, and I refuse to mess it up. Each time I smooth over another issue, my satisfaction grows. I am going to knock this gala out of the park if it kills me! And when Mr. De La Cruz sees the results of all my hard work, he will have no choice but to see my true potential.

7

The chandelier crystals tinkles above as I step into the grand ballroom, my heels clicking on the marble floor. I smooth the front of my red satin dress and take a steadying breath.

After a week of planning, the charity gala is here. But my nerves aren't because of the event itself. No, they are all thanks to the man walking in beside me.

Mr. De La Cruz cuts a dashing figure in his tux, his tall frame filling out the classic cut to perfection. I risk a glance up at him and had to stifle a gasp. He shaved for the occasion, revealing a firm jaw and dimpled chin I've never seen before.

Good grief, he looks like a movie star. How am I supposed to concentrate when my boss turned out to be secret eye-candy?

I tear my gaze away and survey the room, desperate for a distraction. Crystal chandeliers light up the high ceilings in a warm golden glow and round tables drape in ivory linens to fill the space, each set for eight.

"Quite the production," Mr. De La Cruz rumbles, glancing around with an approving eye. "You've outdone yourself, Stevens."

I flush under the praise, equal parts pleased and annoyed at how easily he can discompose me. "Thank you, sir, but it was a team effort. Shall we greet the guests?"

He tucks my hand into the crook of his arm, an intimate gesture that makes my heart stutter. "Lead the way."

As we make our rounds, I grow aware of how well we complement each other. His presence is commanding yet unobtrusive, allowing me to shine as a hostess while still deferring to him as my escort.

I face the truth. Against all odds, the man I once found so intimidating now feels like a perfect partner in crime. And as the first strains of music fill the room, I hope the night would never end.

We take our seats at the head table as the first course is served, a seasonal salad with goat cheese croquettes.

"This is lovely," Mr. De La Cruz says, eyeing his plate. "You have excellent taste, Stevens."

"As do you," I say before I can stop myself. His gaze flickers up, a smile tugging at his lips. My cheeks flame and hastily add, "In music, I mean. You were right about the string quartet being a perfect choice."

"Were we not just discussing your penchant for Tchaikovsky?" he asks, a teasing lilt to his voice. "I believe you compared his symphonies to 'audible chocolate.'"

I groan, mortified he remembered my fanciful turn of phrase. "Please forget I said that. I'm afraid I get a bit carried away at times."

"Nonsense. I find your passion refreshing." His eyes glint with amusement and something warmer, more intimate. "And your analogy was quite apt. His music is decadent, layered, meant to be savored."

My heart stutters at the intent in his gaze. I duck my head to hide my blush, fiddling with my napkin to buy time. Is it possible he views me as more than his assistant? The idea both thrills and terrifies me.

Our conversation turn to lighter topics as the meal progresses. Beneath the polite veneer, something is simmering between us, waiting to be uncovered. The thought makes me tremble with nerves and anticipation. By the time we rise to open the floor for dancing, I can scarcely breathe. Whatever this is between us, the night is no longer ending soon enough.

As the band begins the first strains of Moonlight Sonata, Mr. De La Cruz turns to me. "Would you care to dance, Ms. Stevens?"

I stare up at him, stunned. "I'm afraid I don't know how."

"Nonsense." He grasps my hand and waist, pulling me close. "Just follow my lead."

His cologne envelopes me as we move across the floor, my heart pounding so loudly I am certain he can hear it. But if he did, there is no indication, gazing down at me with a soft smile.

"You're a natural," he murmurs. My steps falter at the praise, warmth flooding my cheeks.

"Only because I have such a capable partner," I say. His hand tightens on my waist and I bite back a gasp.

When the song ends, I expect him to release me. Instead, he draws me closer. "The auction begins soon. Why don't you go freshen up while I see to the final arrangements?"

I nod, disappointment warring with relief as he steps away. My skin still tingles where he'd held me and I press my hands there, trying to contain the sensation.

What am I doing? This is my boss, a man known for his aloofness and indifference. I am reading too much into simple politeness, letting my imagination run away with me.

With a sigh, I make my way to the restroom to collect myself. By the time I emerge, the auction is in full swing and Mr. De La Cruz is engrossed in conversation across the room. As if sensing my gaze, he glances up, offering a brief smile and nod before returning his attention to his guest.

The earlier warmth fades, replaced by stinging embarrassment. I have been a fool to think, even for a moment, that I am special enough to pierce his detached facade. My place is by his side as his assistant, nothing more. Resolved, I straighten my shoulders and move to join him, shielding my hurt behind a professional mask. The rest of the evening passes in a blur, and before I know it, we are saying our goodbyes in the parking lot.

The ballroom is awash with color and sound. Crystal chandeliers cast a warm glow over the crowd, the light glinting off jewelry and champagne flutes. Classical music plays in the background, the melody light and airy. Laughter and conversation flows together, a sea of mingled voices.

Mr. De La Cruz guides me through the throng, his hand a warm presence at my back. I swallow, hyperaware of his touch and the scent of his cologne. Get a grip, Laura. He is just being polite.

A few attendees greet us, complimenting the event. Mr. De La Cruz accepts their praise with a gracious nod, though his eyes remain cool and detached. I plaster on a smile, making small talk and steering the conversations back to the charity and its mission.

One couple scrutinizes me with unveiled curiosity, their gazes flickering between me and Mr. De La Cruz. The woman's lips curl in a knowing smirk that makes me blush. I clear my throat, eager to escape their avid stares.

"If you'll excuse us," Mr. De La Cruz says. He guides me away, irritation etched in the tight line of his mouth.

"Nosy socialites," he mutters. "Pay them no mind."

"Of course." I resist the urge to look back at the couple. "The important thing is we raised a good amount for the charity tonight."

"We did." His expression softens. "You did well, Ms. Stevens. I don't say it enough, but your work is invaluable to me."

Warmth blooms in my chest at his praise. I duck my head, hoping the dim light hides my pleased smile. "Thank you, sir. I'm happy to help in any way I can."

His hand squeezes my back for a moment. "I know. And it's appreciated."

Our gazes catch and hold, a wealth of unspoken words hovering between us.

He glances away, the shutters closing over his eyes once more.

The memory of his touch fades, and I am left with only the lingering ache in my heart.

I shake off the strange melancholy and force a smile. "Shall we mingle some more, or would you like to head out?"

"I think we've done our duty for the evening." He checks his watch. "Unless there's someone else you need to speak with?"

"No, I'm ready to call it a night." I stifle a yawn behind my hand. It has been a long day preparing for the gala, and the heels I chose are pinching my feet into something awful. All I want is to kick them off, change into pajamas and veg out in front of the TV.

Mr. De La Cruz nods and steers us toward the exit. I bid goodnight to a few more guests on our way out, but my heart isn't in it.

Outside, the driver hops out of the town car to open the door for us. The cool night air is a relief after the stuffy ballroom, scented with the promise of rain.

Mr. De La Cruz hesitates, glancing between me and the car.

"Goodnight, Ms. Stevens. Thank you again for all your hard work."

"Goodnight, sir." I duck into the car, hiding my disappointment. It seems I will enjoy a pint of mint chocolate chip ice cream instead of a fancy cocktail tonight.

As the car pulls away from the curb, Mr. De La Cruz is still standing there in the glow of the streetlights, gazing after us with an unreadable expression.

What is that about? I lean my head back with a sigh, realizing I am no closer to figuring out my enigmatic boss than when I first started working for him. The man is an absolute mystery.

One I find myself determined to solve.

―――

The next day at work, I am distracted by thoughts of the previous evening. Mr. De La Cruz has been in a good mood, complimenting my work and crack a few jokes.

My boss is mercurial on the best of days. There is no point trying to analyze his behavior or search for hidden meaning.

When Mr. De La Cruz summons me into his office, I brace myself for his usual brusque manner to have returned. But he greets me with a smile and says, "The charity reported that last night's event raised over $200,000. I wanted you to be the first to know, since you worked so hard to organize it."

"That's wonderful news!" I say, stunned. "Thank you for telling me. I'm so glad it was such a success."

"As am I." His gaze turns soft. "You did an excellent job, Ms. Stevens. I'm proud of you."

Heat floods my cheeks at the praise. Coming from a man as demanding and sparing with compliments as Mr. De La Cruz, those words mean the world. I didn't know how to respond, so I say, "Thank you, sir. I appreciate you saying so."

"You're most welcome." He clears his throat and shuffles some papers on his desk, the moment of vulnerability passing. "That will be all."

I nod and make for the door, unable to keep a smile from my face. It seems I will have to revise my view of Mr. De La Cruz. There are hidden depths to the man yet to be explored.

I leave the office in a haze of giddy excitement, my heart doing cartwheels in my chest. All the stress and hard work organizing the charity event paid off in more ways than one. Not only had it been a rousing success, but it gave me a glimpse into the complex man behind the imposing figure of my boss.

As I walk to the elevator, our bond last night over a shared love of classical music, laughing and chatting with an ease I never would have expected. The memory of his proud smile and praise makes me blush again.

The elevator doors slide open, interrupting my reverie. I step inside, leaning back against the wall with a sigh. What is happening here? I have never felt this way about a boss before. But then, Mr. De La Cruz is unlike any boss I've had.

The doors open again on the ground floor, and I make my way out of the building, deep in thought. By the time I arrive at my apartment, I realize that both thrills and terrifies me: I am developing feelings for my demanding yet fascinating boss. What that might mean for our working relationship, I do not know.

8

The aroma of brewed coffee wafts through the air as I step into the break room, my mind still swirling with thoughts of Mr. De La Cruz and those piercing blue eyes.

I pour myself a mug of coffee, hoping the caffeine will knock some sense into me. This is ridiculous. He is my boss, for crying out loud. I have to stop this nonsense before I make a fool of myself.

As I add creamer to my coffee, Valerie breezes into the room. "Morning Laura! You're in early again today." She flashes me a knowing smile and grabs a mug from the cabinet.

Here is my chance. I have to tell someone before I burst. "Can I talk to you for a minute? In private?"

Valerie's eyebrows rise, but she nods, following me to a corner of the break room. I take a deep breath, wondering how to even say the words aloud. "I think I'm developing feelings for Mr. De La Cruz."

Valerie inhales sharply, nearly dropping her mug of coffee. "Oh honey, that's not good." She bites her lip, searching for the right words. "You know he has a reputation for being tough on his assistants. If something happened between you two and then didn't work out, he might make your life miserable. I don't want to see that happen."

She is right, of course. This is a terrible idea that can end in disaster. But how am I supposed to ignore these feelings when I see him every day? I sigh, stirring my coffee pensively. Valerie places a comforting hand on my shoulder. "Just be careful, okay? Guard your heart."

That afternoon, I find it impossible to concentrate on the stack of briefs in front of me. My mind keeps wandering to Mr. De La Cruz, remembering the way he smiled at me this morning and thanked me for the coffee.

When Valerie walks by my desk, I can't contain myself. "We have to talk about this. I can't stop thinking about him!"

Valerie glances around. "Not here," she whispers. "Meet me in the break room after work."

The minutes tick by slowly until 5 o'clock rolls around. Valerie is already waiting in the break room, two mugs of coffee in front of her.

"Laura, listen to me," she says. "Getting involved with Mr. De La Cruz is a terrible idea. Remember what happened to Jenna in accounting?"

I wince, recalling how Jenna dated one partner before things ended badly. She was demoted and ended up leaving the firm.

"Or Tom in HR?" Valerie continues. "He dated his manager, and she completely destroyed his reputation after they broke up. He's still trying to pick up the pieces."

"I get it," I say with a groan. "Workplace romance is a nightmare."

"Exactly." Valerie squeezes my hand. "You're too good at your job to risk it all for a fling. Promise me you'll avoid acting on these feelings."

She is right, as usual. My career is more important than some crush.

"I promise," I tell her. "I'll stay far away from trouble."

Valerie smiles, relieved. "Good. Now, do you want to get dinner? We can find you a nice, single man with no power to ruin your life."

I laugh and loop my arm through hers. "Yes, please. Save me from myself!"

Valerie laughs, her eyes sparkling with humor. "Alright, let me tell you about my own mistake so you can learn from it."

She takes a sip of coffee and gazes out the window, her expression turning wistful. "A few years ago, I dated this lawyer from the Mergers and Acquisitions team. Thomas. He was charming, smart, and we had great chemistry."

Valerie shakes her head with a rueful smile. "After we broke up, he started spreading vicious rumors about me. He said I only got my job by sleeping with the partners and that I didn't do any work."

I gasp, shocked at the malice. "That's awful! What did you do?"

"At first, it devastated me," she admits. "My reputation was damaged and people treated me differently. But then I marched into HR and reported his behavior. They investigated and found out he'd done it before to other women."

Valerie's eyes hardens. "Thomas was fired, and the partners issued an apology and statement clearing my name. It was still difficult, but I refused to let some jerk ruin my career."

"I'm so sorry you went through that," I say. My heart ached for my friend, even as I admired her strength.

Valerie gives me a wry half-smile. "The point is, you can't predict how people will react after a breakup. No matter how charming or kind they seem, it's just not worth the risk. Protect yourself and your career, Laura. Don't make the same mistake I did."

Her words echo in my mind, a sobering reminder of what is at stake. Valerie is right—when it comes to Mr. De La Cruz, I will stay far away from trouble. My career depends on it.

Valerie watches me, gauging my reaction. "I can tell this is sinking in for you. That's good—you're too smart and dedicated to throw it all away for a fling."

"You're right," I say. "I value my job and reputation too much. No man, no matter how charming, is worth jeopardizing that."

Valerie smiles, relieved, and squeezes my hand. "I'm glad we had this talk. You know I only want the best for you."

"I know," I say, "and I appreciate your honesty more than I can say. You've helped me gain some much-needed perspective."

My friend has done me a real favor, even if the message is hard to hear. While the idea of a romance with Marco has seemed thrilling and irresistible before, now I see it for what it truly is—a recipe for disaster that I am better off avoiding altogether. Valerie has saved me from myself, and for that, I will be forever grateful.

9

The fluorescent lights flicker above as I stride into Mr. De La Cruz's office, clutching a steaming cup of coffee in one hand and a stack of case files in the other. My heels click against the tiled floor, fueled by the three shots of espresso I downed on my way into the office.

I am ready to tackle anything. Bring it on Monday.

As I set the files on Mr. De La Cruz's desk with a satisfied thud, a glint of gold catches my eye. There, beside his laptop, is a framed photo of a woman with wavy brown hair and a radiant smile. She looks familiar. A sister? Cousin?

My curiosity spikes. I haven't heard him mention any family. He is tight-lipped about his personal life, but he has to have someone. A wife? Girlfriend?

I lean in for a closer look, tilting my head. The woman's smile seems almost melancholic, as if she is gazing into the distance at something long gone.

Who is she? More importantly, who is she to him?

My heart races as I contemplate snooping through his desk drawers for more clues. This is dangerous territory, I know, but when has that ever stopped me before? I live for adventure, and this mystery woman is proving irresistible.

Just then, the door bangs open behind me. I jump, upending my coffee, and spin around to find Mr. De La Cruz looming in the doorway. My face burns under his flinty gaze.

Busted.

Mr. De La Cruz strides past me without a word and sinks into the leather chair behind his desk. I stand frozen in place, unsure if I should apologize or pretend nothing happened.

After a long moment of silence, he picks up the photo frame and runs a finger down the edge. His stony expression softens into something I can't quite decipher. Sadness? Longing?

I clear my throat. Now or never. "Sir, I hope you don't mind me asking, but who is the woman in this photo?"

His gaze flickers up to meet mine. "My wife, Amelia, she passed away ten years ago."

My eyes widen. His wife? He had a wife? All this time, I assumed he was a lifelong bachelor, married only to his work.

Mr. De La Cruz runs a hand over his face, looking older and more careworn. "I don't speak of her often. It's still...difficult." His Adam's apple bobbed as he swallowed hard.

My heart squeezes with empathy. I know that kind of pain all too well. "I'm so sorry for your loss," I whisper.

He waves a hand, blinking back the sheen of tears in his eyes. "It was a long time ago." But his tone says otherwise. The wound is still raw, still bleeding.

"Some losses stay with us forever."

Mr. De La Cruz meets my gaze again, his eyes soft with understanding. In that moment, I feel our roles of boss and assistant fade away, leaving only two people bonded by the deepest, most profound connection of all: loss, and the love that comes after.

He gazes at the photo, lost in memory, a sad smile touching his lips. "She always knew how to make me laugh. We used to love going dancing together, even after all those years. Every night when I came home from work, she'd greet me at the door with a kiss."

His voice catches, and for a moment he can't continue. A lump rises in my throat, imagining the depth of love and loss in his words. This is a side of my boss I never could have imagined—a glimpse into the tender heart beneath the stern exterior.

"I'm so sorry," I say. I want to reach out and comfort him, even though we rarely share any personal contact. He seems so alone in his grief, holding onto the memory of a love cut tragically short.

Mr. De La Cruz's pain mirrors my own, and the barrier between us crumbles. He isn't just my demanding boss anymore; he is a man who has suffered a terrible loss. Against all odds, I realize we have a connection—and the beginnings of an understanding.

I clear my throat, self-conscious. We shared something deeply personal, and now the normal boundaries of our working relationship felt blurred.

Mr. De La Cruz seems to sense my discomfort. He straightens in his chair and folds his hands on the desk, adopting his usual formal manner. "Thank you for your condolences, Miss Stevens. Now, was there something you needed to discuss?"

I nod, grateful for the return to familiar territory. "The Hartman brief. I've reviewed the documents and believe I've found a loophole in the language of the original contract that could strengthen our case."

"Excellent work," he says with an approving nod. "Please elaborate."

As I launch into an explanation of the details, I find a newfound respect for the man across from me. My boss has depths I never suspected, layers of love and loss and longing beneath the polished professional exterior. It makes me see him in a whole new light—and realize how much more there is to discover about the complex, multi-faceted person he is. Mr. De La Cruz isn't the stern, demanding figure I have always seen him as. Beneath the intimidating exterior is a man who felt as deeply as I did, who had loved and lost in the way only those who have lived can understand.

Gone is the barrier between boss and employee, melted away by the fires of shared grief and the balm of mutual understanding. I see into his soul, and he into mine, and when I leave his office, I carry with me a newfound respect for the complexities of the human spirit. Mr. De La Cruz is no longer simply my boss—he is a friend.

Maybe this job will be an adventure after all. I smile, already looking forward to the next surprise Mr. De La Cruz might have in store.

Another long night is ahead of us to find these financials. He wasn't kidding when he said he doesn't get out of here until ten almost every night. The circles under my eyes are getting worse.

I settle in for another long night of paperwork. I stifle a yawn, steeling myself for the barrage of demands that are sure to come from Mr. De La Cruz the moment I stride through the door.

"I, uh...I brought you a coffee. Hazelnut latte, right?"

I blink. He remembers my coffee order? "Yes, thank you," I say, a bit stunned.

He has dark circles under his eyes and the slump in his shoulders. It seems the notorious workaholic hasn't been sleeping well lately either.

We aren't so different, he and I. Two restless souls chasing purpose through the daily grind.

When he pokes his head out a few minutes later, I venture a hesitant smile. "Everything alright, Mr. De La Cruz?"

He runs a hand through his hair and sighs. "Please, call me Marco."

My smile widens into a grin. "Only if you call me Laura."

A ghost of a smile flitted across his lips. "Touché."

I take a sip of the latte, savoring the burst of hazelnut flavor. Maybe this won't be such a long night after all. Marco and I...we have an understanding now. A spark of hope that this job can turn into something more. A partnership, even.

"Any leads on those financial records?" Marco asks, stifling a yawn.

I shake my head, blinking blearily at the stacks of papers strewn across the conference table. "Nothing yet. But there has to be a money trail somewhere. People like this always slip up, eventually."

"You're right," he says. "Let's keep digging."

Despite the late hour, a surge of determination rushes over me. Marco trusts my judgment. He sees me as an equal, not just an assistant. I am not about to let him down.

As the hours drag on, we fall into an easy rhythm, trading theories and ideas. Marco's razor-sharp mind complimented my own, and together we are able to connect dots that previously seemed disparate.

By the time we stumble upon a crucial discrepancy at 3 AM, exhaustion has given way to exhilaration. We exchange a triumphant grin, the thrill of the chase bonding us together.

"We did it!" Marco says, a rare smile lighting up his face. "I couldn't have solved this without you, Laura. You're a heck of a worker."

I flush with pride at the compliment. "Back at you, Marco."

He claps me on the shoulder, and for a moment his hand lingers there, his eyes soft with unspoken warmth.

My heart skips a beat. A partnership, indeed. Maybe there is something more to be found here after all.

10

I arrive at the office early as usual, a fresh cup of coffee in hand for Mr. De La Cruz. But when I enter his office, I find him hunched over his desk, massaging his temples.

"Sir? Are you alright?" I ask.

He looks up, eyes bloodshot, a scowl etched into his features. "Does it look like I'm alright?" he snaps. "Stevens, must you ask such stupid questions?"

I recoil at his harsh tone, a flush of embarrassment heating my cheeks. So much for hoping yesterday had been an isolated incident. When will I learn that there are no "good days" with Marco De La Cruz?

Biting my tongue to avoid a retort I will surely regret, I set his coffee on the desk with a trembling hand. He didn't even glance at the offering, too absorbed in the papers scattered before him.

I stand for a moment, unsure whether he requires anything further. But it seems I have already proved incompetent enough for one day. Best to make a hasty retreat before I make things worse.

With a quiet "Let me know if you need anything else, sir," I turn to leave, clutching at the door handle like a lifeline. His irritated sigh follows me into the hall, grating against my frayed nerves.

Once the door closes behind me, I lean back against the wall and closed my eyes. How did I get myself into this mess? When I pictured my dream job, this isn't what I had in mind. But I am committed to this path, and I won't give up . Even if it kills me.

I take a deep breath and steel my resolve. If Mr. De La Cruz wants to treat me like his personal punching bag, he has another thing coming. I won't cower at his temper or shrink under his criticism.

Squaring my shoulders, I march back into his office. He glances up at my entrance, one dark eyebrow rising in surprise.

"Yes, Miss Stevens? Have you lost something else so soon?" His tone is biting, meant to cut me down to size.

But I won't give him the satisfaction. "I won't tolerate being spoken to this way," I say.

He blinks, taken aback by my nerve. "I beg your pardon?"

"Yelling at me, snapping at me, criticizing me at every turn," I continue, meeting his gaze without flinching. "I understand you may have impossibly high standards, but there's no call for rudeness. I am not a mind reader, sir. If I'm not meeting your expectations, you'll need to communicate that to me clearly and directly."

Mr. De La Cruz opens his mouth as if to issue a scathing retort, then seemed to think better of it. He studies me for a long moment, dark eyes probing. I refuse to look away, willing him to see I mean every word.

He leans back in his chair with a considering hum. "Miss Stevens, you continue to surprise me." His tone softens, the harsh edge gone. "My apologies."

I release a breath, relief washing over me in a flood. My gamble has paid off. I can tame the beast, after all.

"I'm not accustomed to being challenged in such a manner," he admits, rubbing the back of his neck. "It's no excuse, but I've been under a great deal of strain as of late. I took it out on you, and I'm sorry."

His words ring with sincerity. Remembering the rumors of troubles at the firm and setbacks with important clients makes me stop for a second. He is only human, after all.

"Apology accepted," I say. "I understand this job can be stressful. Perhaps we can start over?"

I extend a hand across the desk. After a brief hesitation, he clasps it in his own forceful grip, the ghost of a smile lightening his features. "A fresh start would be most welcome. I look forward to a more harmonious working relationship, Miss Stevens."

"As do I, Mr. De La Cruz."

As I leave his office, a warm glow suffused my limbs. The beast had been tamed, and the adventure is only just beginning.

After our heart-to-heart, the animosity between us has vanished, replaced by a newfound understanding and camaraderie.

Mr. De La Cruz greets me with a nod and a "Good morning, Miss Stevens," his tone friendly instead of brusque. I smile at him, noticing again the gold flecks in his eyes.

"The Anderson files for the merger need to be reviewed by this afternoon," he says. "Would you join me for lunch so we can discuss the details?"

My heart skips a beat at the invitation. "I'd be happy to."

Over sandwiches from the deli down the street, we talk and laugh like old friends. The chemistry between us is undeniable, a crackling energy that leaves me breathless with delight.

When he reaches across the table to brush a stray crumb from my lip, the simple touch sends a jolt of electricity through me. I freeze, catching in his smoldering gaze, my lips parting in invitation.

For a moment we stay there, poised on the edge of something

new, full of promise and passion. Then he pulls away, a flush staining his cheeks, and clears his throat.

"We should, um, head back. Much work left to do."

I blink, struggling to regain my composure. "Yes, of course."

This is inappropriate. Mr. De La Cruz is my boss. No matter the attraction between us, a relationship can never happen.

I take a deep breath and steady my nerves. Back to business as usual, though the memory of almost-kiss will linger, a bittersweet taste of what might have been.

As we leave the cafe and head back to the office, a new tension hums between us. Things have shifted, a line crossed that can't be uncrossed, though we didn't speak of it.

When the elevator doors slide shut, trapping us in the small space, my heart stutters. I stare at the floor numbers, hyper aware of his body mere inches from mine.

The doors open, releasing the pent up energy between us in a rush. I hurry to my desk, burying myself in the stack of files that awaited.

Through the rest of the afternoon we dance around each other, the memory of that charged moment as an elephant in the room. More than once I glance up to find Mr. De La Cruz watching me, an unreadable expression in his eyes.

I leave work that day feeling off balance and confused. Never did I experience such a visceral reaction to someone, and to have it be my boss, of all people!

Yet there it is, this undeniable attraction I can't ignore.

11

I arrive at the office to find Marco already immersed in paperwork. Dark circles hung under his eyes, and his usual impeccable grooming was slightly unkempt.

"Rough night?" I ask gently.

He blink up at me, eyes clouded with pain for a moment before he schooled his features into their usual stern mask. "I'm fine. Just have a lot of work to get through."

I hesitate, then say, "I know it's not my place, but if there's anything you want to talk about…I'm here to listen."

For a long moment, he is silent. Then, gaze fixes on the papers in front of him, he speaks in a low voice.

"Today would have been my wife's birthday." He swallows hard.

My heart aches for him. I can't imagine losing someone so close, especially not after so long together. "I'm so sorry," I say.

"She was." Marco's eyes shone with tears for a brief second before he blinks them back. "Strong, kindhearted, brilliant. She made me want to be a better man." He sighs, shaking his head. "I'm afraid I haven't been doing a very good job of that lately."

"You're too hard on yourself," I say. "Grief is difficult, and it's a process. Be patient with yourself."

For the first time, Marco offers me a small, sad smile. "Wise words. Thank you, Laura. Your kindness means a lot."

My cheeks warm at the unexpected praise. I smile back, hoping to offer him some comfort. "You're welcome. And if you ever want to talk about her, I'm here."

He nods, gaze softening. "I appreciate that."

All day, I can't stop thinking about our conversation. Marco's raw honesty and grief has struck a chord deep within me, and I worry about him. He seemed so alone, so lost.

After that, a new ease and camaraderie develops between us. Marco spent his childhood in Spain. He has a love of classic literature, and his dream of one day retiring to a villa in Tuscany. In turn, I share details of my life, my hopes, and my dreams.

My gaze drifts to Mr. De La Cruz's office, where he is pacing and gesturing wildly while talking on the phone. His sharp, angular features are creased in a frown, but then he glances up and catches me watching him. For a moment, his stern expression softens into something warmer, almost fond.

I jerk my eyes away, heat flooding my cheeks. What is that about? My heart races as I rifle through the files without seeing them.

Ever since I start as Mr. De La Cruz's assistant, he's been brusque and demanding. But I noticed these little changes—the way his voice is gentler when he speaks to me, how he squeezes my shoulder in passing. And those looks, like the one he just gave me.

My thoughts spin in circles until a sharp knock on my desk makes me jump. Mr. De La Cruz looms over me, brow furrowed in concern. "Are you feeling alright, Miss Stevens? You seem distracted."

"Just tired, Mr. De La Cruz," I say, hoping my voice didn't shake.

"In that case, let's go to lunch." He straightens, glancing out the window with a frown. "You work too hard. It's important to take breaks."

Panic and longing war within me. Spending time with him outside of work will only make my feelings more complicated. But when he looks at me with those dark, fathomless eyes, I find myself saying yes before I can stop myself.

This is a terrible idea. But as Mr. De La Cruz guides me into the busy restaurant, his hand a warm pressure on my back, I can't bring myself to regret it.

The maitre d' seats us in a secluded corner booth, lit by the soft glow of a stained glass lamp. Looking around at the other patrons leaning close together, speaking in hushed tones, my face grows warm. This is meant to be an intimate setting.

Mr. De La Cruz didn't seem to notice my discomfort. He sits back with a contented sigh, studying the menu. "Everything here is excellent. I hope you'll allow me to choose for you?"

"Please do," I say, pulse racing. How am I going to make it through this meal?

After ordering a bottle of red wine and two plates of osso buco, Mr. De La Cruz sets the menu aside—and looks at me. My mouth goes dry under the intensity of his gaze. "I'm glad we could do this, Laura. I've been wanting to spend time with you outside the office for a while now."

He wants to spend time with me. The words echo in my mind, and I clutch my napkin to hide their trembling. "R-really?" I manage. "Why?"

A slow smile spreads across his face. "Because I find you fascinating," he says. "And I think we have a connection that goes deeper than a working relationship."

My heart stutters. This can't be happening. But the warmth in his eyes tells me it is all too real.

"Ever since you came to work for me, I haven't been able to stop thinking about you." He reaches across the table, covering my hand with his. "I want to get to know you better, Laura—not as my assistant, but as something more."

I stare at our joined hands, a storm of emotions churning inside me. Surprise. Confusion. A dangerous flutter of excitement I didn't dare acknowledge.

When I find my voice, it comes out breathless. "I don't know what to say."

"Say you feel the same way about me." His thumb traces slow circles on the back of my hand, sending tingles up my arm. "That there's something here worth exploring."

His touch, his words—they unravel my composure until I'm utterly exposed. Vulnerable. And though alarm bells are ringing in my mind, warning me of the perils of a relationship with my boss, I can't deny the connection.

I offer him a hesitant smile, my cheeks flushing hot. "I—it's complicated."

"Why?" He leans closer, his eyes searching mine. "We're both single, we're attracted to each other. What's so complicated?"

"You're my boss." I pull my hand from his grasp, losing contact, bringing a strange ache. "If we started something romantic, and it didn't work out, it could get messy."

"I understand your concern." His expression softens. "But I don't want you to think of me as just your boss anymore, Laura. When I'm with you, I feel happier and lighter than I have in years." He gives a self-deprecating chuckle. "I suppose you could say you bring out the best in me."

"I'm willing to do whatever it takes to make this work, if you'll give me a chance." He leans closer still, his breath warm against my cheek. "Will you take that chance, Laura? Will you take a chance on me?"

My heart swells at the tenderness in his tone, the vulnerability etched into the lines of his face. He is putting himself on the line for me, and I want, more than anything in that moment, to say yes.

But doubts creep in. What if we fight, and he fires me in a fit of anger? What will people at the office say about me sleeping my way to the top? I worked too hard to get where I am to throw it all away on a fleeting romance.

"I'm afraid this could end badly for me." I avert my gaze, staring at the white tablecloth. "If we break up, I could lose my job. People might think the only reason I got promoted was because we were together."

"I would never fire you out of spite." He places his hand over mine, the warmth of his touch chasing away my doubts. "And anyone who thinks you didn't earn your position through hard work and skill alone isn't worth listening to. You know that."

I want to believe him. But can I risk everything I have worked for on the chance we might find happiness together? If it didn't work out, will the heartbreak be worth the memories we might make?

My heart and head re at war, desire battling with reason, longing with logic. In the end, the choice comes down to whether or not I will take a leap of faith.

Did I dare?

I look up, meeting his gaze. The warmth in his eyes nearly undid my resolve, but I steel myself. This isn't about what I want - it is about what is best for my career, my future.

"I'm sorry," I say. "But I can't. Not now."

His hand tightens around mine. "Why not?"

I sigh. "You're my boss. If we pursue a relationship and it ends badly, it could damage my career. I've worked too hard to get where I am."

"I understand." He releases my hand, the loss of contact like a physical ache. "I want what's best for you. Even if that means..."

"I care about you," I say. "But I have to put my career first. I hope you can understand."

"Of course I do." But the smile he gives me didn't reach his eyes. "You're one of the most pragmatic and level-headed people I know. I shouldn't have expected anything less."

He pays the bill and walks me back to the office, the comfortable silence now strained. We part with a stiff nod, the memory of what might have been hanging between us.

I did make the right choice, the responsible choice. But that didn't make the longing in my heart hurt any less. The future is unclear, but one thing is certain - nothing between us will ever be the same again.

12

I scramble to get ready, mad at myself for staying up so late researching case law. But it paid off. The idea is risky, but it can help win De La Cruz's impossible case.

I race into the office, clutching my files, and burst into his office. "Sir, I have an idea for the Pemberton case."

De La Cruz peer at me over his reading glasses, one eyebrow raised. My cheeks flush under his scrutiny. "This better be good, Stevens. I don't have time for nonsense today."

I swallow hard and steady my nerves. Now or never. "We argue the illegal search violates not just Pemberton's right to privacy, but his right to freely practice his religion. The police seized several religious artifacts along with the drugs."

De La Cruz leans back in his chair, steepling his fingers. My heart pounds so loudly I am sure he can hear it. After a long moment, he nods. "That's...not bad, Stevens. Unconventional, but it just might create enough reasonable doubt for the jury."

I relax as a smile creeps across my face. He likes the idea! I have taken a risk, and it paid off. Maybe this is the breakthrough I need to prove myself as more than just another assistant. Maybe, just maybe, De La Cruz will see I am capable of more. Growth and improvement—here I come!

The next few weeks fly by in a flurry of activity. I throw myself into preparing for the Pemberton trial, working long hours to gather evidence and build our argument. But instead of feeling overwhelmed like I have in the past, I thrive under the pressure. Streamlining the process and delegating smaller tasks to the interns making the work seem less daunting.

When the trial starts, I was at De La Cruz's side every step of the way. My suggestions and questions prove invaluable, and more than once I provide a key piece of evidence or insight that strengthened our case. We make a good team, playing off each other's skills.

After the jury announces their verdict of "not guilty," De La Cruz turns to me with a grin. "We make a heck of a duo, Stevens. This win is as much yours as it is mine. Drinks are on me tonight!"

I flush under the praise, hardly able to contain my joy. The risks I've taken, the long hours, the setbacks and struggles along the way—they have all been worth it. De La Cruz's words echo in my mind, spurring me on to greater heights. Growth and improvement—the future is mine for the taking. I proved myself, and nothing seems out of reach. What an adventure this is turning out to be!

The next day at work, I stride into the office with newfound confidence. My heels click decisively on the tiled floor as I make my way to De La Cruz's office, a fresh mug of coffee in hand.

He looks up from his desk as I enter, surprise flickering in his eyes before a smile creeps across his face. "Well, good morning, Stevens. Aren't we chipper today?"

I grin, setting the coffee down next to him. "I wanted to thank you again for the opportunity to help with the trial. It meant a lot, and I learned so much. If another challenging case comes up, I'd love to assist in a similar capacity."

De La Cruz studies me for a moment, brow furrowing. I hold his gaze, refusing to back down or stammer like I might have in the past. He nods. "You more than proved yourself, Stevens. Consider yourself on the shortlist for any complicated cases in the future."

"Wonderful," I say, unable to tamp down my smile. After a slight hesitation, I add, "I was also hoping we might grab dinner again sometime, when we're not quite so busy."

Again he seems startled, though not displeased. Rubbing the back of his neck, he averts his eyes with a cough. "Yes, well, I enjoyed your company too, Stevens. Dinner would be...amenable."

My grin widens as I go back toward the door. "Great. It's a date, then. I'll check your schedule and let you know when I'm free."

With a jaunty wave, I step out of the office, closing the door behind me. I lean against it for a moment, eyes closing as I take a deep breath.

A couple of hours later, I am buried under a mountain of paperwork when he strides to my desk. "Stevens, I've got it. The missing piece of evidence we've been searching for."

I jump up, heart pounding. "Really? What is it?"

"Come see for yourself." He grabs my hand and tugs me to his office, shutting the door behind us. There on his desk are photos of the crime scene we've been scrutinizing, but these are taken from a different angle. And in one shot, partially hidden behind an overturned chair, is a glint of silver.

"A letter opener," I breathe. "The murder weapon."

De La Cruz grins. "Exactly. This is exactly what we needed to conclusively prove the wife's guilt. You've done it again, Stevens!"

Before I can respond, he sweeps me into a hug, clutching me close. I melt against him, intoxicated by his rare display of excitement and affection. When he pulls back, we are both breathing hard, faces inches apart. For a long moment, we simply stare at each other, the tension thick between us. I lick my lips, watching his gaze drop to follow the movement.

He swallows, eyes darkening, and lean in. I close my eyes, heart pounding—

The shrill ring of the phone on his desk shatters the moment. We jump apart as if scalded, heat flooding my cheeks. De La Cruz clears his throat and snatches up the phone, turning away to answer it. I slip out the door on trembling legs, unsure whether to curse or bless the poor soul on the other end of that call.

13

The shrill ring of my phone startles me from my daze. I glance at the caller ID and my heart skips a beat. Mr. De La Cruz.

I take a deep breath and answer, "Hey, how are you?"

"Ms. Stevens, I was hoping you'd join me for dinner this evening. I made reservations at Chez Antoine at 8 pm. Will I see you there?" His deep voice sends a thrill through me.

I hesitate, warring with myself. Did I dare go? But there is something about his vulnerability, revealed in unguarded moments, that intrigues me.

Pro: The chemistry between us was undeniable.

Con: If it ended badly, I'd be jobless.

Pro: He seemed different with me, softer. Vulnerable, even.

Con: He was still my boss. Totally inappropriate.

Pro: When was the last time a man had sparked my interest like this?

Con: I could read this all wrong. He could just see me as a conquest.

"Ms. Stevens?"

"Yes, I'll be there," I say, my cheeks flushing. What am I getting myself into?

After we hung up, I race to my closet, flinging dresses and shoes everywhere. What does one wear to a date with their boss? I settle on a little black dress, modest but figure-hugging, and a pair of killer red heels.

As I did my makeup, my nerves jangled. Is this a mistake? But the memory of his smile surfaces in my mind, melting my anxiety. I want to see where this leads. I am tired of playing it safe. It is time for an adventure.

I glance in the mirror and don't recognize the woman staring back - a woman ready to take a chance on love. With a smile, I grab my purse and head out the door. The night is full of promise. Mr. De La Cruz better be prepared. I am not his assistant tonight.

We meet at an upscale Italian restaurant, all white tablecloths and low lighting. I spot him at a corner table, dressed in a sleek suit that emphasizes his broad shoulders. When he sees me, he stands and smiles. Not his usual smug grin, but something warmer, shyer.

"You look stunning," he says, pulling out my chair.

"Thank you." I sit, formal. "You look very nice yourself."

"Shall we order some wine?"

Over antipasto and red wine, we chat about work, our families, hobbies. He is an excellent conversationalist, listening and asking thoughtful questions. I find myself relaxing into the familiar rhythm of our banter, realizing how much I enjoy his quick wit and challenging mind.

When the waiter brings our main courses, Mr. De La Cruz says, "I'm interested in getting to know you better."

My heart skips. So this is an actual date. I take a sip of wine to hide my smile. "I think this will make working together quite interesting."

He chuckles. "Your trouble, Ms. Stevens."

Our lively debate over certain cases segues into a walk in the nearby park. The air is crisp, scented with blooms. Moonlight filters through the trees, dappling the path.

Marco takes my hand, his fingers warm and sure around mine. I glance at him to find his gaze already on me, soft with tenderness. My heart skips a beat.

Perhaps sensing my sudden shyness, he says, "I apologize if I've made you uncomfortable. I should have asked before taking your hand."

"No, not at all," I say. "I like it."

He squeezes my hand and we continue walking, shoulders brushing. I steal glimpses of his profile, struck by how content I feel strolling with him under the stars. It is as if I've known him for years rather than months.

We pause on a bridge overlooking a pond. Marco leans on the railing, gazing out at the rippling water. "I haven't felt this way about anyone for a long time," he says.

I turn to him, heartbeat quickening. "Me either."

"But I think it's best if we take things slow."

Disappointment flickers, but I appreciate his restraint. "You're right." I squeeze his hand. "Thank you for a lovely evening."

"The pleasure was mine." He gazes at me with a tenderness that makes my knees weak. "Goodnight, Laura. I'll see you tomorrow."

"Goodnight." I watch him go, heart full and tingling with anticipation of what the future may hold. What an adventure this is turning out to be indeed.

14

The sun dips behind the trees in Central Park. I tuck a strand of hair behind my ear and glances over at Mr. De La Cruz, my stomach fluttering with nerves.

After weeks of casual flirting over case files and coffee runs, we have been seeing each other. I can't believe this is happening.

We walk in comfortable silence for a while, enjoying the tranquility of the park at dusk. The only sound is the crunch of gravel under our feet and the chirping of crickets beginning their nightly chorus.

When we emerge onto Central Park West, the sun has nearly set, bathing the city in shades of purple and rose.

Mr. De La Cruz glances down at me, eyes gleaming. "Dinner?"

I squeeze his hand, warmth flooding my chest. "Definitely."

This is turning out to be an evening of many firsts, in the best way.

We choose a cozy Italian bistro, drawn in by the aroma of garlic and herbs wafting from the entrance. Inside, dim lighting and red checkered tablecloths created an intimate ambiance.

Over antipasto and wine, we delve into more personal topics. Mr.

De La Cruz describes his large, boisterous family and some of their hilarious cultural misunderstandings. I share stories of my close-knit group of friends from college and our adventures exploring the countryside.

"You seem so carefree and full of life," he says, studying me. "Not at all what I expected."

I swirl the wine in my glass, self-conscious. "What did you expect?"

"Someone more serious. Reserved." He pauses. "Not someone who would turn my world upside down."

My heart skips a beat at the tenderness in his tone. "I didn't mean to disrupt your universe," I tease.

"I don't mind." His eyes gleam with warmth and affection as he reaches across the table to brush a stray curl behind my ear. "Not one bit."

Heat rises in my cheeks at his touch. I clear my throat, hoping to dispel the sudden tension. "So, favorite books. What are yours?"

"The classics. Dickens, Tolstoy, Hemingway." He shrugs. "I like stories about the human experience."

"Me too. There's nothing quite like getting lost in a vivid tale of love and heartbreak and redemption."

"Spoken like a true romantic," he says with a grin.

I duck my head, embarrassed to be caught. I do believe in love. And for the first time, I can imagine finding it in the unlikeliest of places.

The next week flies by in a blur of long workdays and stolen moments together. We meet for coffee on our lunch breaks, text constantly, and see each other nearly every evening. The more time we spend together, the more at ease I feel in his presence.

One night, we go for a hike at a nearby nature preserve. The trail wounds through a forest of towering pine trees, their branches intertwining overhead to form a leafy canopy.

As we walk, our hands brushed together once, then again. On the third time, his fingers interlace with mine, squeezing gently. I glance up to find him watching me, a soft smile on his lips.

Heart pounding, I step closer so our arms touched, thrilling at the contact. He responds by draping an arm around my shoulders and pressing a kiss to my temple.

We stop walking then, turning to face each other in a sun-dappled glade. His other arm encircles my waist, pulling me flush against him. I slide my hands up his chest and around his neck, losing myself in the warmth and strength of his embrace.

"You've turned my world upside down," he whispers, gazing down at me with eyes full of tender affection. "And I don't want to be set right again."

I swallow hard against the rush of emotion swelling inside me. "Good," I say. "Because you've become my world, and I never want to leave it."

He makes a sound low in his throat and lowers his head. Our lips meet in a kiss that is soft, then deepened into something more - a kiss full of longing and promise, sealing our hearts forever.

We break apart, hearts pounding, cheeks flushed. I press my forehead to his chest, listening to the rapid beat of his heart while he strokes my hair.

"I'm nervous," he admits with a self-conscious chuckle. "More nervous than I've ever been in my life."

I smile, tilting my head back to meet his gaze. "Why's that?"

"Because you mean a lot to me." He takes a deep breath. "And I want this - us - to work. I want a future together, with all the ups and downs and imperfections that come along with it. I want to face every challenge life throws at us, side by side and hand in hand."

My own heart swells at his words. "I want that too," I say. "I want to share every moment with you, no matter what comes. The good and the bad, the laughter and the tears, today and always."

The smile that lights his face is brighter than the sun. He leans down and kisses me again, sealing our promise.

When we part, I lace my fingers through his and we continue down the trail. The woods are alive with birdsong and dappled sunlight, but my world has narrowed to the man at my side.

I glance up at him, at the joy and affection in his eyes, and smile. My heart is full of a peace and contentment I've never known before. Together, I know we can face any challenge and overcome any obstacle. As long as we are together, that is all that matters.

15

The weekly staff meeting drags on as per usual, but today I gaze out the window with a goofy grin plastered on my face.

Jake elbows me, "What's with the smile? Did you win the lottery or something?"

I shake my head, feeling my cheeks heat. "No, nothing like that."

"Come on," he nudges. "Spill."

I glance around. "I've...been seeing someone."

Jake's eyes grow wide. "No way! Who is he? When did this happen? Why didn't you tell me?"

"Shh! Keep your voice down." I swat his arm, trying to stifle a giggle. "We've been dating for only a little bit."

Jake hisses. "And you're only telling me now?"

"I wanted to make sure it was serious before I said anything. But..." I bite my lip, feeling almost shy. "Things have been going well."

"I can tell." Jake gives me a knowing look. "You've been in a great mood. And you're dressing nicer, doing your hair more. Not to mention you've been bringing homemade lunches instead of going out with the rest of us. If I didn't know any better, I'd say you were in love."

My face feels hot enough to fry an egg on. "I don't know about love yet," I say, trying to sound nonchalant. "But I am happy. Happier than I've been in a long time."

Jake smiles and pats my arm. "I'm glad to hear that. You deserve it."

I smile back, a flood of warmth and affection for my friend rushing over me. Maybe I haven't won the lottery, but at that moment, I am the luckiest woman in the world.

"So come on, give us the details!" Jake says, leaning in. "What's he like?"

I take a bite of my salad, savoring the memory of Marco's bright smile and mischievous eyes. "He's charming, intelligent, has a great sense of humor..." I trail off with a dreamy sigh.

Jake snorts. "Sounds like you've got it bad. But what does he do for a living? Where did you meet? How did he get past that fortress you call a heart?"

I swat his arm again, fighting back a blush. "That doesn't matter."

"A meet cute!" Jake clasps his hands together. "How romantic. So when do we get to meet this paragon of charm and wit?"

"Soon, I promise." The thought of Jake and Marco meeting makes me smile. He'll never believe it.

"It's a date!" Jake pumps his fist in victory. "I'm dying to give this guy the third degree and make sure he's good enough for my best friend."

I batt his arm again, but I appreciate his protectiveness.

"Don't worry," I say. "He can hold his own. And..." I bite my lip, feeling almost shy. "I think you'll like him."

"If he makes you happy, that's all that matters." Jake smiles and squeezes my hand. "I'm thrilled for you, Laura. You deserve all the best."

"Thanks, Jake."

I find my thoughts drifting to Marco more often than is probably appropriate. His texts fill me with warmth and make me smile at random moments. I catch myself gazing out the window during meetings, lost in daydreams of our next date.

My coworkers notice the change in me, of course. As much as I try to rein in my distraction, it is impossible to hide how smitten I am.

"Earth to Laura!" Maya waves a hand in front of my face during our lunch break. I blink at the concerned looks on my friends' faces.

"Sorry, I was...off in my own little world there for a minute." I duck my head, knowing I've been caught.

"Thinking of lover boy again?" Maya raises an eyebrow and the others laugh.

"Maybe." I can't deny it and see no point in trying. "We have another date this weekend and I guess I'm just excited."

"Just excited?" Jen scoffs. "Girl, you look like you've been transported to another planet."

I smile.

"Just don't forget we exist now that you have your dream man," Jen says, nudging me with her elbow.

"I won't." I shake my head. "You're still my friends. It's just..." I struggle to find the right words. "Being with Marco makes me happy in a way I've never experienced before. The intensity of it surprises even me sometimes."

"Wait, Marco? He's the guy you've been seeing?" Jen asks.

I nod.

Maya rolls her eyes. "You look at that man like he hung the stars in the sky."

"Does it bother you?" I ask.

"Not at all." Jen squeezes my hand. "We're happy you found someone who makes you light up like that. Even if it means less gossip time for us." She winks to show she is joking.

"Besides," Maya adds. "Any man who can make our Laura this disgustingly sweet has to be a keeper."

"He is." The words come out softly but with conviction. Marco is a keeper, and the more time we spend together, the more I realize he might just be the one.

I laugh, warmth flooding through me. My friends might give me a hard time, but their teasing is all in good fun. They want me to be happy, and if Marco is the one putting that ridiculous smile on my face, they are willing to put up with it.

"All right, all right." I wave my hands in surrender. "Enough with the third degree. We have work to do, remember?"

"Fine, fine." Jen holds up her hands in mock defeat.

This weekend can't come soon enough.

With the teasing over for now, we disperse to our respective desks. I sit down and open my email, but find myself gazing out the window instead, lost in daydreams of the future. One that might just include a tall, dark, and handsome lawyer who's stolen my heart.

16

I walked into the bustling office seeing Marco's unreadable expression, but there is a tenseness to his posture that puts me on edge.

"A word in my office, please."

Dread coils in my gut as I follow him into the spacious room. He closes the door behind us, and I brace myself for the inevitable end to our brief romance.

Instead, Mr. De La Cruz turns to me with a sigh. "I heard there's been talk about us. Ugh. I shouldn't have put in this position."

What does he mean? "I'm the one who should apologize."

"You did nothing wrong. I'm the one who asked you out, and I should have considered how that might impact you here." He runs a hand through his hair, looking contrite. "If you'd prefer to end this now to avoid further gossip, I understand."

His words stun me. He will sacrifice our relationship to spare me from scrutiny, yet that is the last thing I want. "No, absolutely not. I don't care what they say or think. I enjoy spending time with you, and if you're willing to put up with the gossip, then so am I."

A slow smile spreads across Mr. De La Cruz's face, softening his usual stern features. "That's good to hear. I happen to enjoy your company as well, Ms. Stevens."

The giddy warmth of his admission chases away any lingering discomfort from this morning's drama. As long as we have each other, nothing else mattered.

As the day goes on, the gossip is in full swing. Whenever I pass by clusters of coworkers, their voices will drop to whispers and sideways glances follow me down the hall.

I try to ignore it, but their scrutiny wears on me. Did they doubt my abilities now that I am dating the boss?

When I enter the break room, the conversation dies. Several lawyers who used to greet me with friendly hellos now avert their eyes. Only Tom offers a weak smile, though he seems uncomfortable.

With a sigh, I retreat to my desk. The dynamics of the office have shifted overnight, and navigating the change won't be easy. If this tension continues, it might impact my work and relationships here. I didn't want that, but what can I do to ease the situation?

Just then, Mr. De La Cruz emerges from his office and strides over to me. "Are you free for lunch today?"

Though the invitation is tempting, I hesitate. "I don't know if that's a good idea right now. People already seem uncomfortable with us dating, and being seen together during work hours might make things worse."

"You're probably right." He gazes down at me, a crease forming between his brows. "I hate that they're making you feel unwelcome here because of me. If ending our relationship would resolve things, please say the word. Your happiness and comfort are far more important."

I reach up and smooth the crease with my thumb. "Don't be silly. I care about you too much to let a little gossip scare me off." Standing on my tiptoes, I press a soft kiss to his cheek. "We'll get through this."

A slow, heart-melting smile lights his face as he pulls me into an embrace. No matter what challenges we face, we'll face them side by side.

After lunch, I prepare for more stares and whispers. To my surprise, the tension seems to have dissipated. A few colleagues even greet me with friendly smiles.

Has the gossip mill moved on already? I didn't want to get my hopes up, but the change in attitude is refreshing.

When I enter the break room to fill up my coffee to avoid the afternoon slump, Mr. Taft waves me over to join him and a few others at the table. "So, you and Mr. De La Cruz, huh? I have to say, I didn't see that one coming."

My face heats at the mention of my relationship, old anxieties rising to the surface. But Mr. Taft's tone is light and teasing, not judgmental. "We wanted to keep things professional at work," I explained. "I hope it won't be too distracting."

"Not at all," one paralegal, Jenny, insists. "After the initial shock wore off, we realized you two make a great couple. He's been in a better mood lately, and you seem happy. That's all that matters to us."

"Really?" I blink back tears, touched by their support. "Thank you. That means a lot."

"Besides," Mr. Taft adds with a wink, "we've all had office romances at some point. Who are we to judge?"

The others chuckle in agreement. My anxiety fades, replaced by gratitude for my understanding colleagues and excitement at the new stage of my relationship. Mr. De La Cruz and I will continue to face challenges, but with the support of friends and each other, we'll make it work. After all, the best love stories are the ones that overcome every obstacle.

17

The tangy aroma of fresh coffee wafts through my office as I tackled the towering stack of paperwork on my desk with renewed vigor. Things have been going splendidly since Marco and I started dating. My work seems easier, the hours passing in the blink of an eye, and I even whistle while I file.

He strides up to my desk, a devilish grin lighting up his handsome features. "Laura, we've got a fresh case. A big one."

My heart skips a beat. A high-profile case! This is another opportunity.

"The Johnson account?" I breathe, daring to hope.

Marco nods, his dark eyes glinting with triumph. "They requested me. They know how skilled you are. I told you that charm of yours would come in handy someday."

"That's wonderful!" I leap up and throw my arms around him in delight, inhaling the crisp scent of his cologne. Marco stiffens in surprise before relaxing into the embrace, wrapping me in his arms.

"I knew you were ready for this," he murmurs, pride clear in his tone.

I swat his arm playfully, unable to keep the grin from my face. "Oh, stop. I had an excellent teacher."

"That you did." Marco presses a swift kiss to my forehead before stepping back, a hint of color touching his cheeks. "Shall we get started, then? The Johnsons will be here within the hour to discuss the details of their case."

"Definitely!" I chirp, already sorting through the files on my desk for anything relating to the Johnson account. My relationship with Marco makes everything brighter and more vibrant, including my work. I have never been happier.

My enthusiasm dims as the reality of the high-profile Johnson case sinks in. This is unlike anything I have handled before, and try as I might, I can't shake the feeling of being in over my head.

Marco notices my uncharacteristic silence and furrows his brow. "What's wrong, Laura? You've been quiet all morning."

I bite my lip, hating to admit my doubts, but knowing honesty is the best policy. "I'm worried about the Johnson case," I confess. "What if I mess up? It's so important, and I don't have much experience with cases of this magnitude."

"Hey." he tilts my chin up, forcing me to meet his gaze. "You are capable, intelligent, and diligent. I would not have agreed to take on this case if I didn't think you were ready. We're a team, remember? I'm here to guide you every step of the way."

His unwavering faith in my abilities eases my anxiety, and I manage a small smile. "You're right. I know we can do this together."

"That's my girl." He presses a quick kiss to my forehead and steers me toward the door. "Now, let's go over the details of the case again. The more prepared we are, the less room there is for mistakes."

Bolstered by his support, I follow him out the door with renewed determination. We will win this case, of that I am sure. After all, who can possibly stand against us when we are working as a team?

We meet with the Johnsons to go over their testimony and prepare them for cross-examination. Mr. Johnson is amiable enough, but Mrs.

Johnson keeps shooting me suspicious glares, as if she didn't quite trust me to handle their case. I did my best to reassure them, explaining our strategy in detail and emphasizing the extensive research and preparation that has gone into developing the strongest possible defense.

By the end of our meeting, Mrs. Johnson seems mollified. Her doubt has awakened my own fears again, and I second-guess every decision we have made.

As we leave the Johnsons' house, Marco notices my uncharacteristic silence. "What's bothering you?" he asks, sliding an arm around my waist. "You did great in there. The Johnsons would be foolish not to have full confidence in you."

I sigh, leaning into his side. "I know. It's just...what if I make a mistake?"

"You won't," Marco says. "You're the most dedicated, hardworking person I know. You've poured your heart and soul into this case. When the time comes, you'll be completely in your element."

"You have too much faith in me," I say.

"And you have too little faith in yourself," he retorts. "But that's why we're such a good team. I believe in you enough for both of us."

His unshakable confidence is what I need to silence the doubts swirling in my mind. With Marco by my side, I can face any challenge or setback. Together, we are unstoppable.

Two weeks go by, and this case has taken a toll on both of us, but it's the biggest case I have ever been a part of and hope that it goes in our favor. Marco and I have been staying late at the office almost every night, going over theories, rebuttals, and anything that might come up during the trial. Now, we are waiting for the verdict.

The foreman stands up, clearing his throat. A hush falls over the courtroom. "We the jury find in favor of the plaintiff."

For a moment, I can't breathe. Then the meaning of the words sinks in, and I turn to Marco with a radiant smile. We won!

He pulls me into an exuberant hug, spinning me around. The courtroom erupts into cheers and applause. Even the judge is smiling as he bangs his gavel for order.

All my doubts and fears seem to melt away, replaced by a deep satisfaction in a job well done.

The victory attracts significant media attention, raising the profile of the firm. New clients start calling, impressed by the success in such a high-profile case. My coworkers congratulate me, praising my invaluable contributions. I have proven myself beyond doubt, cementing my reputation as one of the firm's rising stars.

Marco and I go out for a fancy celebratory dinner, toasting our success with glasses of champagne. "Here's to the unstoppable duo," Marco says, his eyes shining with warmth and affection.

I smile, raising my glass. "To new adventures and a bright future together." Our victory is only the beginning. Many more challenges lie ahead, but as long as we have each other, there's no limit to what we can achieve.

18

Things seem different today. The office is quiet when I walk in, and everyone is on their second cup of coffee.

"Morning." Marco says, gesturing me into his office.

"I was thinking..." he begins. "Move in with me. I want to wake up with you in my arms every morning."

I stare at him, stunned into silence. Then a slow smile spreads across my face. "Yes. Absolutely yes."

Marco's face lights up as he pulls me into his arms. "Fantastic! I'll have your things moved in this weekend. This is going to be great, sweetheart!"

My heart swells with joy. Who would've thought that the infamous Mr. De La Cruz would turn out to be such a hopeless romantic? I snuggle into his embrace, excited about this new chapter of our lives together.

The rest of the weekend passes in a blur as Marco's men transfer box after box from my apartment to his spacious home. By Sunday evening, the last of my belongings have found their place in our home. Our home. I still can't quite believe it.

Marco slid his arms around my waist as we admired our combined living room. "Happy with how everything turned out?"

I turned in his arms and smiled up at him. "Very happy. Thank you for this."

"The pleasure is all mine," he murmured, dipping his head to capture my lips in a searing kiss.

When we broke apart, breathless, Marco gazed down at me with a warmth and tenderness I'd never seen before. "Welcome home, darling."

"I was thinking we could take a trip to Tuscany this summer," Marco says, feeding me a strawberry. "We could tour the vineyards, stay in a charming little villa…"

"That sounds amazing." I sigh, leaning into his side. "I've always wanted to visit Italy."

"Consider it done, then." He presses a kiss on my temple. "Anything else you've dreamed of?"

I smile, tracing circles on his chest. "Honestly, just building a life with you is more than I could've ever asked for."

Marco's eyes softens. "You are too good to be true, you know that?" He tips my chin up, gazing at me with unveiled adoration. "I love you with all my heart, Laura Stevens. And I want nothing more than to make you happy every day."

Tears prick at my eyes as I pull him in for a heated kiss. "I love you too, Marco De La Cruz. So much."

We spend the day curled up together, talking and laughing as we form dreams for our future. The rest of the week passes in much the same way, a blissful haze of togetherness I never want it to end. Who knew that the notorious Mr. De La Cruz would turn out to be such an expert cuddler?

"So, did Valerie ask Tom out for drinks?" Marco asks.

"Not yet. I think she's still nervous he'll say no."

"That's ridiculous. Tom is clearly smitten with her. If she doesn't make a move soon, I may have to lock them in a closet until they confess their undying love for each other."

I laugh. "Please don't. As entertaining as that would be, I'd rather Valerie work up the courage in her own time."

Marco sighs. "You're too kind, darling. If it were up to me, true love would always prevail in the end."

"Which is why I'm here to provide balance," I tease, leaning in for a kiss.

Our communication has gotten even better since moving in together. Marco is an open book, sharing his hopes, fears, and insecurities without hesitation. It's helped me to do the same, and I know we can work through any challenge together.

Life with Marco is even better than my wildest dreams, and if the way he's looking at me now is any indication, the feeling is mutual. My heart swells with joy at how far we've come, and the adventures are still left ahead.

Marco tucks a stray hair behind my ear, his fingers lingering against my cheek. "Have I told you today how much I love you?"

His words elicited a warm flush of pleasure. "You may have mentioned it once or twice."

"Only once or twice?" He feigned a wounded look. "I'm clearly not expressing my affection enough."

I laugh, wrapping my arms around his neck. "Don't worry, I get the message loud and clear."

"Good." Marco pulls me close, his embrace strong and sure. "Because you're it for me, Laura."

19

"Good morning, darling," Marco mumbles, wrapping an arm around my waist and pulling me close.

"Morning," I say with a smile, curling into his embrace. We have been dating for over a year now, but waking up next to Marco still gave me butterflies.

"Any fun plans for today?" he asks.

I laugh. "You're looking at a free Saturday for the first time in months. I was thinking we could check out that new art exhibit you've been wanting to see?"

Marco kisses the top of my head, his fingers tracing circles on my back. "Perfect."

"Wonderful," I say. We lay there for a few minutes, enjoying each other's company. Marco and I have such an easy chemistry. We can spend hours together talking, or be perfectly content saying nothing at all. He is the yin to my yang, balancing my Type A tendencies with his laid-back approach to life.

Marco sits up with a yawn, stretching his arms above his head. I admire the lean muscles of his torso, a surge of affection washing over me. Here is a man who could have any woman he wanted, yet he spends his Saturday mornings with me.

"I'm going to make some coffee," he says, leaning down to kiss me again. "Want some?"

I grin up at him, reaching up to run a hand through his already messy bedhead. "Please. And maybe some toast too?"

He arches an eyebrow. "Toast too, huh? Aren't we demanding?"

This is bliss. Pure, unadulterated bliss. And I never want it to end.

As he heads downstairs, I notice something strange in the pocket of his discarded jeans—a small velvet box. Could it be?

I shake my head, trying to dispel the thought.

Still, my curiosity gets the better of me. I slide out of bed and creep over to his jeans, slowly reaching into the pocket. My fingers close around a familiar shape. I gingerly lift out the box, flipping it open to reveal a glittering diamond ring.

My breath catches in my throat. This isn't just any ring; it is utterly breathtaking. Marco has impeccable taste, and he must have spared no expense on this.

Which can only mean one thing. He is going to propose.

I slide the ring back into his pocket, my hands trembling. Marriage. To Marco. The thought fills me with equal parts delight and panic. Our relationship is the most fulfilling one I've ever known, but am I ready to commit my life to another person?

I am still standing there, frozen in place, when he comes back upstairs. One look at my face and he knows. His expression turns sheepish as he runs a hand through his hair.

"You found the ring," he says. My heart thuds in my chest as he sinks down on one knee, gazing up at me with eyes full of love and tenderness.

"Laura Stevens, will you marry me?"

I stare at him, overwhelmed with emotion. "Yes," I breathe. "Yes, of course I'll marry you!"

Marco's face lights up with joy. He surges to his feet and

envelopes me in a warm hug, spinning me around. I cling to him, laughing and crying all at once.

When he sets me down, he takes the ring from his pocket and slides it onto my finger. It is a perfect fit.

"I love you so much," he murmurs, cupping my face in his hands. "You're the best thing that's ever happened to me."

"I love you too," I say. "I can't wait to spend the rest of my life with you."

We sit down on the edge of the bed, eager to plan our future together. "A small wedding would be perfect," I say. "Just close friends and family. Nothing too fancy."

He nods. "I agree. A big wedding isn't important to me. All I care about is making you my wife."

I laugh, filled with joy and gratitude at finding a man who understands and supports me. Our future is bright, and I can't wait to embark on the adventure of marriage together.

After going to the exhibit, we drive to the courthouse. It is a brick building that looks about as romantic as a DMV, but I don't care. I am marrying the love of my life, and that is all that matters.

We walk through the heavy wooden doors, his arm wrapped around my waist. The courthouse is dim and stuffy, with ugly green carpeting and fluorescent lights that buzzes faintly overhead. A few people mill around, waiting in various lines.

He wrinkles his nose. "Not exactly the wedding of your dreams, is it?"

I laugh and squeeze his hand. "Every place is magical when I'm with you."

His eyes soften. "You're too good for me, you know that?"

"Nonsense," I say, standing on my tiptoes to kiss him. "We're made for each other."

After waiting in line for what seems like hours, we reach the front. The clerk looked bored as she shuffles through a stack of papers. "Name?" she asks in a monotone voice.

"Laura Stevens and Marco De La Cruz," I say. Nothing can dampen my enthusiasm today.

She stamps a few forms with a rubber stamp and slides them across the counter. "That'll be fifty dollars. Cash or credit?"

He pays the fee and tucks the marriage license into his jacket pocket. I throw my arms around him, overjoyed that tomorrow I'll be Mrs. Laura De La Cruz. Our unconventional wedding suits us perfectly. All that matters is that we are committing our lives to each other, ready to face any challenge that comes our way.

The next morning, Valerie helps me pick out an outfit for the wedding while we chat on the phone.

"Something simple but elegant," she advises. "You don't want to be overdressed for the courthouse, but you still want to look special."

I settle on a knee-length ivory dress, a string of pearls Marco gave me on our first anniversary, and a pair of nude heels. When I emerge from the bedroom, Marco's eyes lit up.

"You look stunning," he says, enveloping me in a hug.

"So do you," I say, admiring how handsome he looks in his gray suit.

We arrive at the courthouse a few minutes before our scheduled appointment, clutching each other's hands to steady our nerves.

The same bored clerk meets us at the counter, barely glancing up from her phone. "You're late. Go on in. The judge is waiting."

My heart races as we enter the courtroom. Judge Collins, an older man with kind eyes and a warm smile, greets us from behind the bench. "Welcome. Whenever you're ready."

Marco and I walk up to stand before him, our hands still clasped together. We wrote our own vows to keep things simple.

I clear my throat, hoping my voice wouldn't shake. "From the moment I met you, I knew you were special. You've brought so much joy and love to my life, and I cherish each day we spend together. I give you my heart, and pledge my love, devotion, faith and honor, as I join my life to yours forever."

He blinks back tears, gazing at me with such tenderness it makes my breath catch. "Laura, you make me want to be a better man, and together, I know there's nothing we can't face. I vow to love you and care for you as long as we both shall live. You are my best friend and now you will be my wife."

Judge Collins dabs at his eyes with a handkerchief. "What beautiful vows. By the power vested in me, I now pronounce you husband and wife. You may kiss the bride!"

Marco sweeps me into his arms and kisses me, eliciting cheers from our witnesses. When we break apart, I see tears glistening in his eyes to match my own.

We sign the marriage license with trembling fingers, the permanence of our union hitting me in a wave of joy and nervousness. We are married. Mr. and Mrs. De La Cruz.

As we walk down the courthouse steps into the sunshine, he squeezes my hand. "What would you like to do to celebrate, Mrs. De La Cruz?"

I smile up at him. "Anything, as long as we're together. But maybe we could do dinner at our favorite Italian place and then go dancing?"

"Perfect." He kisses the top of my head. "Then whatever comes after."

A delicious shiver runs down my spine at the promise in his tone. I have married this complex, passionate man, and I can't wait to see what the future holds for us. "To the future, Mr. De La Cruz."

"To the future, Mrs. De La Cruz."

20

Our honeymoon in Bora Bora feels like a dream, the turquoise waters and swaying palm trees already fading into a hazy memory. But the silver band on my finger is a cold hard reality. I am Mrs. Laura De La Cruz now.

"Morning, wife." Marco's deep, gravelly voice startles me out of my thoughts. He rolls over and pulls me into his arms, peppering my face with kisses. I giggle, swatting him away.

"We have to get up! Our first day back at work, remember?" As much as I want to stay curled up in bed all day, work is calling.

Marco groans, tightening his grip around me. "Do we have to go in today?" His breath is warm against my neck, and my resolve weakens. "I can think of better ways to spend the day than dealing with clients and paperwork."

I sigh, twisting in his arms to face him. His hair is mussed from sleep, eyes heavy-lidded, a lazy smile on his face. My husband. The thought makes my heart skip a beat.

"You're not getting out of it that easily, Mr. De La Cruz." I kiss the tip of his nose, then rolled out of bed before he can protest further. "Now get up. We'll be late for work!"

Marco grumbles under his breath but follows me out of bed, wrapping his arms around my waist for a quick hug before we start our morning routine. Looks like married life at the De La Cruz household is going to be quite the adventure!

We arrive at the office to curious stares and whispers from the other assistants. I can't blame them - it isn't every day your boss married his assistant! Marco's hand rests comfortably on the small of my back, a subtle display of affection that makes me smile. Things feel different now that we are married, more relaxed and playful.

Marco leans down, lips brushing my ear. "Want to grab lunch together later?"

I tilt my head up, eyes sparkling. "It's a date, Mr. De La Cruz."

He chuckles, giving my waist a quick squeeze before heading into his office. I settle into my desk, organizing files and preparing for the day ahead. A few of the assistants sidle up, questions bubbling from their lips.

"How was the honeymoon?" Valerie asks, eyes gleaming with curiosity. "Did Mr. De La Cruz relax at all?"

"It was wonderful," I say. "And yes, he did relax. It was nice to see him unwind for once."

"I'll bet." She smirks. "Must be quite the change, going from boss and assistant to husband and wife."

"It's an adjustment," I admit, "but a good one. We work well together, and that foundation has helped in navigating this new dynamic in our relationship."

"Speaking of work, I have a question about the Smith case if you have a moment." Marco leans against the entrance to his office, brows raised. I excuse myself, following him inside.

The rest of the morning passes in a flurry as Marco and I debate strategies on various cases, our usual professional dynamic now tinged with casual intimacy. A smile here, a light touch there, all the little details that make working together as a married couple not just bearable but downright enjoyable.

During lunch, we head out to our favorite cafe a few blocks from the office. Marco insists on paying, waving away my protests.

"What kind of husband would I be if I didn't provide for my wife?" he asks, eyes gleaming with humor. I roll my eyes but couldn't suppress a smile.

As we eat, he reaches across the table and takes my hand. "Thank you for making me the happiest man in the world," he says. "This past month has been the best of my life, and I look forward to many more years by your side."

My heart swells at his words. "I love you too, Marco. More than I ever thought I could love anyone."

His gaze turns pensive. "Have you thought any more about starting a family?"

I freeze, my sandwich halfway to my mouth. We've discussed kids before, but now, the idea seems far more real and imminent. Did I want children? Am I ready for such a huge step?

Marco gives my hand a gentle squeeze. "There's no rush. I just want you to know that when or if you do feel ready, I'll be there every step of the way."

His reassurance calms my nerves. I sit down my sandwich, taking a deep breath.

"What if I told you, you won't have to wait long at all?" I say. "Marco, I'm pregnant."

Silence. Then his face lights up with a smile. He leaps up, pulling me into his arms.

"A baby!" he exclaims, spinning me around. "We're going to have a baby!"

Laughter and joyous tears spill out of me as he sets me down again. He cups my face in his hands, gazing at me with wonder and amazement.

"You've made me the happiest man in the world," he whispers. "Again."

This new adventure we are embarking on together will be the greatest one yet.

About the Author

Kaci Bell loves to write romance that is sweet and closed door. You can find more about her and her other pen name Ashley Zakrzewski on her website.

www.ashleyzakrzewski.com

Made in the USA
Columbia, SC
21 February 2024